"Ah'm a-gonna kill ya!" McLowery roared.

"Not until I tell you why I'm here," Crazy Joe replied, no trace of fear in his voice, his thumbs still hooked in his sash.

"Huh?" McLowery slowly replied, apparently not understanding an introduction to violence.

"You murdered two old men for no reason," Crazy Joe began. "You about layed open my partner's skull, then you stole his rifle. You're sick, you've got the law afraid of you and everybody in this country afraid of you. McLowery, you're a bully and a pissant, and now you're going to die."

I looked at McLowery. I don't think he knowed how to take Crazy Joe's matter-of-fact attitude.

"Ah'm still gonna kill ya!" he roared.

Crazy Joe shifted his weight forward and cocked his hips. Then he smiled. "Go for it," he murmured.

PALS

Russell Nelson

IVY BOOKS • NEW YORK

Library of Congress Catalog Card Number: 91-91902

ISBN 0-8041-0709-2

Manufactured in the United States of America

First Edition: August 1991

For

Brewer, Smith, Gray, Carruth
and all the others
who came back
but never went home

and for my Mother and the
memory of my Father,

Dale M. Nelson
MoMMl/c, USNR
MTB Ron 24 & 11

PA: You're the one that keeps us goin', Ma. I ain't no good no more an' I know it. Seems like I spend all my time these days thinkin' how it used to be. Thinkin' a home; I ain't never gonna see it no more.

MA: Well, Pa, a woman can change better'n a man. A man lives sorta, well, in jerks—baby's born or somebody else dies, an' that's a jerk—he gets a farm or loses it, an' that's a jerk. With a woman it's all in one flow like a stream, little eddies an' waterfalls, but the river it goes right on.

PA: Well, maybe, but we shore takin' a beatin'.

MA: I know. That's what makes us tough. Rich fellas come up an' they die and their kids ain't no good an' they die out but we keep a-comin'. We're the people that live. They can't wipe us out, they can't lick us. We'll go on forever, Pa, 'cause we're the people.

Nunnally Johnson, *The Grapes of Wrath* (the film)

Acknowledgments

Thanks are due to: Seymour Feig, who believed in this story from its inception as an idea and never doubted; to Jim Easterbrook and Fred Lewis for being more enthusiastic than myself; to William T. Craig, who grabbed me by the stacking swivel when I was ready to quit; and to Owen Lock for his willingness to take a risk and whose recommendations substantially improved the text. James T. King and Don Rickey critiqued and were supportive of early efforts, and I would like to express my gratitude to them as well.

R.N.

PHILO HARRIS AND me started running around together when we were in the navy. That part of my past I long ago buried and refuse to resurrect even for the purpose of this book. It doesn't have much bearing on this story, in the first place. It ain't very interesting, in the second. And finally, it's nobody's business.

By the time we teamed up on the outside, we were in our mid-twenties and purt near set in our ways. Unlike most folk who dream of chucking it all and getting back to the land, when we got out of the navy, that was exactly what we done. Philo had been a cowboy in his native Oklahoma prior to his service; I had been a trapper and logger in that rolling and green part of western Iowa where I was raised. The skills we possessed were not in high demand in a world turning ever more technologi-cated.

We was different. Throwbacks. Happy in the saddle, barely comfortable in a pickup truck. Neither of us liked machines a whole lot. We figured we belonged to the time of Bridger and Fitzpatrick and the Bents. Or at least in the time of Crazy Horse and Geronimo and Tom Horn. The time of few railroads and little barbed wire; the time of buffalo herds pounding across the Great Plains, the earth shuddering beneath their black hoofs. The time of Cheyenne and Arapaho and Apache, fierce and yelling on war ponies. The time of few white men, and youth in the mountains, and knee-high bluestem grass on the prairies, a big-caliber rifle, and a horse with bottom a man's best friend.

1

Some joke of fate put us in the here and now, instead of in the there and then. There was no point grousing about it. We just made the best of what was left.

This past March found Philo and me trapping our way south through the Salt River Mountains. They lie naked and strong in that stretch of land between Bear River and Green River. When tourists and hunters head for Wyoming they tend to visit the well-knowed spots: Jackson Hole, the Wind River Mountains, and the Bighorns. Over the years there was few streams in those ranges we hadn't traipsed, but there was a couple good reasons we wasn't deep in the high country. First, there had been a near-record snow pack that winter. Going was rough at seven thousand feet; the ten-thousand-foot-high Winds would have been impassable to man or beast, and the avalanche danger would have been too great.

We cherished the aloneness of the Salt River Range. It was good to be away from the well-meaning farmers and ranchers in the more populated areas of Wyoming. Because fur prices were still running low and because we was deep in a near-wilderness area, we had the corner on the local fur-taking.

Our camp was located at the point where Ham's Fork tumbles out of the mountains narrow and fast to meet the high plains. Our plan was to trap our way back north to a little ranch where we'd left our aging pickups and trailers. It was late afternoon, and I was fleshing the two beaver I'd caught that day. The only prime fur that late in the season was short-haired: beaver and muskrat. We'd trapped and shot our share of coyote and fox and coon that winter, and had some money tucked away as a result.

"Ah ain't seed an ugly woman in a month," Philo announced as he joined me by the fire. "We got a serious problem heah."

"Are Ruth's rear quarters in danger of being molestated?" I inquired as I carefully cut little bits of fat and flesh away from a pelt. Ruth was Philo's jenny mule. He used her for packing, preferring to ride his huge if somewhat slow-witted quarter horse.

"She-hit," he grumped as he poured a cup of coffee. "This is been a hellacious winter. Good fer trappin', lousy fer gettin' laid. We gotta go bust some fuzz afore long."

"Was thinking on that myself." I lit my pipe with a hot coal from the fire, and as I blew a cloud of smoke skyward I noticed for the thousandth time how low the clean, white clouds passed overhead. ''Maybe we oughta take a side trip to that cathouse in Rock Springs, once we get back to the outfits. Whaddya think?''

''Sounds lak a winnah. Ah gotta find a woman somewhares what'll put up with all a this.''

''Well, seems we could take our pick of Shoshone or Arapaho off the Wind River Reservation. If, that is, we didn't get our hair lifted in the process. They'd eat regular, they'd only get lodge-poled if they needed it, and they'd know where their husbands was at night.''

''Yeah.'' Philo grinned. ''Jumpin' thar bones twixt the buffler robes.'' He topped off his tin coffee cup and sat down on a vacant canvas packsaddle cover. ''Okay, we gotta plan this out.''

''This child's listenin','' I replied. My big bay gelding let out a whinny from twenty yards away where he stood picketed, pawing through the wet snow for grass.

''The boys are poorly.''

''Like they say, better to have bones than tracks, pard.'' I was still kindly absorbed in fleshing the beaver pelt.

''Ah know thet. All ah'm sayin' is afore we head foah Gunnerson, we'd bettah grain 'em an' git some alfalfa in 'em. Fer a week, anyway. Thet's the icebox a the middle Rockies an' thar'll be snow ass deep yit.'' Our plan was to head south to the Gunnison Valley, ride up as high as we could, and trap down. Beaver in that part of the mountains stay prime till early June. Trouble was, even if we got up there in a week or two, the snow was apt to be up to our necks. We still had some time to kill. Our animals stood in need of solid groceries, as Philo had pointed out.

''So where d'ya want to fatten 'em up 'fore we head south?''

''Wal, seein' as how you ast, thar's a nice l'il clearin' outside Lander. On National Forest land, ah do believe. We might could jest run inta town, git some feed, an' park the outfits right thar. Dry furs an' clean gear an' such.''

''And be right close to Wind River.''

''Nice river.'' Philo grinned.

''Nice reservation,'' I added for him. ''Good plan, amigo. I figure ten days to trap our way up Smith's Fork. We'll be in Lander by the middle of the month.''

''Doan' wait up foah me thet night. Ah'll be tipi-creepin'.''

The next day we headed north up Smith's Fork, trapping as we went. By mid-March the aspen branches beaver put up in their feed beds for winter food have soured with age. That's the time of year when the furry amphibious rodents let their bellies get the best of their judgment. In our ten-day ride we did pretty good: We caught thirty-one beaver, half a dozen muskrats, and one mink. The beaver pelts ran to the pale side, which was good: European furriers have craved pale Rocky Mountain beaver since 1823 when Ashley and Henry's mountaineers, whom the late Jim Clyman likened to Falstaff's Battalion, successfully breached the mountains and began a steady flow of beaver pelts to St. Louis.

On the twentieth of the month we made our outfits. The following day we chugged up the slow grade known as South Pass, which, due to the gentleness of the grade and the fact that it's a sixty-mile-wide gap in the mountains, many people wouldn't take for a pass. A couple hours later we pulled into Philo's chosen meadow and set up camp. We was about ten miles from Lander on a fork of the Popo Agie, and it felt good to be alive and free and have yet another month of good trapping to look forward to.

"Sorry ya lost the draw, Sam," Philo said sincerely. In our initial enthusiasm we'd forgotten that somebody would have to stay with the outfits and the *caballada*. Philo and I had drawed straws; mine had come up short.

"Don't worry about it, old hoss. I'll get my chance in a day or two. You go have a good time. Just watch your hair—I hear the Shoshone are fond of carrot-topped scalps. Just don't forget to bring the grain and alfalfa in all the excitement."

"Whaddya mean, Sam?" he innocently asked through tooth-paste foam.

"You've got that same look I've seen on and off for over ten years. Your face is pale, and you're breathing short and hard." I smiled at him and lit my pipe.

"Meanin'?" he wiped his face with a dirty towel.

"Meaning all the blood has drained from your head to your dick. You're like a stud horse sniffing for a mare in heat."

Without further provocation Philo let out a whinny, dropped to all fours, and started bucking and snorting like a raging stud mustang.

"Them Indian gals are in for it tonight!" I whooped, slapping my knee.

Philo interrupted his stallion impression and grinned. "Wait'll they fin' out ah'm half horse!" He neighed for emphasis.

"Which half?" I innocently inquired. He just grinned, shook his head, and whinnied from head to tail.

I figured come morning there would be one happy but tired Indian lady. A blind man could see that.

The next morning Philo returned with a hundred and fifty pounds of rolled oats and six bales of alfalfa hay. When our animals saw his battered Chevrolet drive up, hay piled high in the pickup bed, they began whinnying and running around their picket pins out of sheer joy.

"Groceries are comin', boys and girls!" I yelled. Philo jumped up into the bed and started handing me bales of hay and feed sacks.

"So how was the big city?"

"Okay," he replied, handing me a feed sack.

"Have a nice evenin'?"

"Yeah," he answered, working fast. "Sam, ya mind watchin' the critters another day? This heah l'il ol' filly kinda wants me t' stop back agin."

"Reckon I could." I smiled. "Just as long as I get my turn. When you supposed to meet her?"

"Coupla hours. Thanks!" He beamed as he handed me the last feed sack. "Ah've got t' git cleaned up an' git back."

"I'll feed Buck and Ruth for you," I volunteered. "We'll start 'em slow on the oats and give them each a few flakes of hay. Won't founder 'em that way, okay?"

"Yeah, sounds fine." Philo Harris could move with the speed of greased lightning when he wanted to. In fifteen minutes he'd shaved, washed, and was again headed down the rutted trail, his old pickup belching little puffs of blue smoke in his wake.

Six days after Philo's initial visit to the Wind River Reservation, the horses not exactly fattened up but with fewer ribs showing, we pulled into Gunnison. I was refreshed, and Philo was pretty much exhausted. We stopped for gas at a station outside of town, and I headed for the pay phone.

"Woof-woof! What's happenin', Dusty?" I said into the mouthpiece.

"This wouldn't be Sam Hawkins, would it?" Dusty inquired.

"You're in luck today, you old coon. Philo don't know it, but he's buying you dinner." I asked Dusty to meet us at the Rusty Spur Diner. He said he'd bring along our mail and whatever beaver tags he had left. Dusty was one of the local game wardens; he always took care of Philo and me. Once a week he'd clean out our post office box in Gunnison and hold on to the mail until we made our reappearance. Dusty was a decent human being and a rare sort of game warden.

"So how'd you fellas do this season?" Dusty asked when he joined us at the café table. "Hell, I haven't seen you guys in a coon's age."

"About eight grand apiece," I answered. "The Uinta's worked out pretty good, but that's some cold freaking country, and we damn near got snowed in at ten thousand. Personally, I'd like to go to Arizona next winter and chase señoritas."

Dusty smiled. "Yeah, it's a lot warmer. I haven't seen you guys since when—early November?"

"Meanin' no offense, Dusty," Philo said over his coffee, "but foah as much as ah lak the Gunnerson Valley, hit's miserable colt. Hit's worse'n the Uinta's or the Wasatch or the Absaroka. Hit's the deep freeze a the Rockies."

The conversation eventually drifted from the varying climates in the West, and I separated the mail as we talked and ate. There was a string of letters from my sister, a few long overdue bills, and a bushel basket full of junk mail.

"I almost forgot, Sam." Dusty smiled as he reached into a shirt pocket and pulled out a folded white envelope. "This came a few days ago for you in care of me."

I looked at the blue lettering on the envelope. "Western Union," I said with a sinking feeling. Telegrams rarely contain good news. I reckoned somebody had died. Then I ripped it open.

"Bad news?" queried Philo.

"Probably." I sighed in relief. "It's from Crazy Joe." Then I read it out loud:

'HEY GUYS, WHAT'S HAPPENING? I'M BEING THROWN OUT OF THE NAVY. DISCHARGE DATE 6 APRIL. TWELVE YEARS OUT THE BILGE PUMPS. OH WELL, WHAT THE HELL. IS THE OFFER TO

JOIN YOU FELLAS STILL GOOD? THANKS, I KNEW IT WOULD
BE. NEED A RIDE TO YOUR AO—DROVE MY TRUCK INTO THE
DRINK. YOU KNOW HOW IT IS. HAVE HORSE AND TRAILER. SEE
YOU THE 6TH OR BEFORE. PIER 5. SAM, AMOR SAYS I LUB YOU
NO CHIT BUY ME DRINK. BOO-HOO-HOO-HAW-HAW-HAW.

CRAZY JOE'

"That crazy son of a bitch," I muttered. I handed the telegram to Philo.

"Who's Amor, Sam?" Dusty asked with a grin. I ignored
him. Philo looked up from the telegram and grinned from ear
to ear.

"Shut up, Philo," I said almost good-naturedly.

"Ah didn't say nothin'!" he innocently complained.

"A girl I knew a long time ago, Dusty," I replied. "In a
place called Subic Bay. Like Crazy Joe says, 'You know how it
is.' "

Dusty smiled over his raised coffee cup. "Was it a 'relationship,' like they say?"

"Only of the sexual kind. And that ended when I returned to
her after a long absence and found out she'd made deck department of the *Oriskany* very happy indeed."

"She broke your heart," Dusty sympathetically offered.

"No. She gave me the clap."

After the guffaws subsided Philo and I drawed straws to see
who would make the dreaded trip to San Diego to pick up Crazy
Joe. I got the short straw, so when I protested we went two out
of three on a coin toss. When Philo won again I threw up my
hands in disgust. Dusty handed Philo the remaining twenty
beaver tags he had for his district, and after finishing our meal
and shooting the breeze a little more, we departed the town of
Gunnison.

Later that afternoon, the snow still deep on the shadowed
sides of the mountains, Philo and I pulled our outfits to a stop
near a stand of lodgepole pine on the far north end of Union
Park. Union Park is a three-mile-wide hole in the mountains;
the always-snow-capped Collegiate Peaks lie thirty miles to the
east; to the south and west the jagged tops of Fossil Ridge and
Park Cone tower directly over it. We entered the park from the
north end on a rutted Forest Service road that parallels the roar-

ing Taylor River. Had we not had four-wheel-drive trucks, we
never would have made it, for the frost was just starting to come
out of the ground. I wasn't worried about getting out; I'd be
leaving minus my trailer and two horses and headed downhill
all the way.

I unloaded Molly and Jack, picketed them, and throwed them
some hay. They would have to paw for whatever grass they could
find under the melting snow.

"Where you gonna be trappin', then?" I asked Philo as I
shoveled the horse apples out of my trailer.

"Gunsight Pass, an' the creeks 'long Fossil Ridge. Ah'm
thankin' thar'll be a heap a snow up thar yit, but thet nevah
stopped me."

"Well, take care of my cavyard," I said. Then I chocked the
trailer wheels and began to crank the trailer off the ball hitch.

"Ah ain't worried 'bout them, ah'm worried 'bout you," he
informed me as I worked the handle round and round.

"Well, all I'm gonna say is that Crazy Joe had better not be
crazy anymore, 'cause if he is I'm gonna leave him standing on
Thirty-second Street with his seabag in one hand and his other
hand up his ass, for all I care." I hadn't seen Crazy Joe Flanigan
in years, and already I was pissed at him. Deep in my heart I
knowed he was still nuts.

Philo grinned at me then, flashing his white ivories in his pet
raccoon grin. "Naw ya won't. We ain't got enough friends we
kin affort t' discard any."

"Sure," I shot back as I jumped in the cab of my truck. "I
just wish you weren't so damned right all the time."

"Haf a nice trip." He smiled.

I cranked my truck over and slowly let out the clutch. "See
you around, hoss." Then I eased back down through the clear,
nippy high country, hit U.S. 50, and headed west.

IT SEEMED LIKE a lifetime since I'd last seen San Diego. The once familiar city had turned hazy in memory, and when I arrived early on the afternoon of April fifth I swung my outfit up Broadway just to see if any of it was recognizable. I wasn't surprised to see that whole streets of old stores, and probably old whores, had disappeared. The old El Cortez Hotel, a once-ritzy place where fighter pilots lounged around, looked abandoned. I doubted I knowed anybody in or about San Diego any longer, so I carefully eased back down to Harbor Drive and made my way to National City. On my way there I avoided two separate collisions and eventually pulled my truck to a stop in front of a cheap motel on National Avenue.

I checked in under my own name, and since I didn't plan on seeing Crazy Joe till later on—he would be off the ship anyway, outprocessing—I walked down to one of my old haunts in another time, the P & L Saloon. In the old days Philo, Crazy Joe, and me had frequented the P & L because it was the only cowboy bar within walking distance of the ship. There had always been a fight coming in the front door and one going out the back, and the place well suited our wild instincts at the time. Now, on a sultry spring afternoon a bunch of years later, it was deserted except for a few off-duty—or Unauthorized Absence—sailors and the barmaid. I recognized her at once.

"Howdy, Becky." I smiled, pulling up a barstool. Becky had aged considerable in the ten years since I'd last seen her. Her

9

teeth was mostly gone, and those left were on the blackened side. Fat hung in folds from her face and neck and arms, and the deep-grained lines around her eyes told me of some hard living since I'd last seen her.

"Do I know you, cowboy?" she asked, cocking her head so to look me over while she wiped the bar in front of me with a dirty rag.

"Long time ago," I replied. "Name's Sam Hawkins. I used to steam with Philo Harris and Crazy Joe Flanigan. We spent a lot of time in here. And a lot of money."

"Sure!" she cried. "Sam Hawkins! I remember ya! Ya got a lot more hair now, but ya look damn good!" Then, faster than a person Becky's size should move according to some law of physics, she grabbed me with her hamlike hands, dragged me across the bar, and gave me a sloppy kiss on the mouth.

"Aw shucks, Becky," I groaned, purely mortified. "I didn't know you cared after all this time." I was sure glad Philo and Crazy Joe wasn't along: they would have doubled over laughing their insides out.

"What'll it be?" Becky beamed. "The first one's on me. Naw, don't tell me. Lemme see—Coors, right?"

"You remembered." I smiled. Well, she should have remembered: in my drinking heyday I'd put down a wagonload of beer in that joint. "Do you still sell them huge dill pickles?"

"Sure do, honey." She smiled as she drawed a tap beer for me. She set the glass down in front of me.

"Could I have one of them pickles, then? And a steak sandwich?"

"Anything fer an old friend." She beamed like I was some kind of lost sweetheart returned from the grave. She casually tossed a sandwich in the microwave oven, stabbed a pickle from the hugesome jar, and handed it to me on a napkin. "So whatcha been up to, Sam, after all these years?"

"Well, I got out—Lord, nine, almost ten years ago. Been living in the Southwest for the most part," I replied, taking a bite out of the pickle.

"What part of the Southwest? We're in the Southwest here, ain't we?"

"Mostly Colorado. Kind of base myself out of there."

"Boy!" She gasped. "Colorado! I always wanted to go there.

Whaddya do, Sam? Are you a real cowboy, huh? Horses and cows and all that stuff, huh, Sam?''

Now, I don't like to lie, but I also don't volunteer information when I don't have to. When I have, it's seemed to come back to haunt me sooner or later. But I also like to make people feel good. If I had told Becky I wasn't no five-hundred-buck-a-month cowhand, why, that would have been akin to telling a small kid there ain't no Santa Claus. I have pulled some desperate stunts in my day, but nobody ever accused me of being small. So if Becky wanted me to be a cowboy, a cowboy I was.

"For the most part," I evenly replied as I sipped my beer.

"Oh boy, a real cowboy! What's it like, Sam? Ridin' the range and all that? And where's that other fella what used to run around with you? You just said his name."

"Philo?"

"Yeah, him!"

"Well, to answer your first question, cowboying is mainly long hours, dirty work, and low pay. And as for Philo, he's still running with me. I see a lot of him."

"Aw, that's just great, Sam." She smiled. Something in the back of the saloon caught her eye. "Just a minute. Gotta go help a customer. Don't run off," she ordered as she waddled toward the far end of the bar. A young fellow I took for a sailor, in spite of the Stetson and blue jeans, had left his table in the back corner and ordered a beer from Becky. She drawed him a tap, and they exchanged a few words. As Becky headed back my direction I saw the kid give me a hard look from his table. I returned the stare.

"Sam, you know that guy?" Becky asked, her voice guarded.

"Nope. Should I?"

"Well, he was asking about you and Crazy Joe Flanigan."

I wanted to run right there. Instead I said, "Give me another beer. In a bottle. To go."

"Sure, hon." She smiled through the holes in her mouth. I looked at the kid then and returned the cold stare I felt boring through my noggin. Becky put the bottled beer on the bar as the sailor got up and headed my direction. He never took his eyes off mine. I slowly turned his way, slid about halfway off the barstool, and put the beer I was drinking in my left hand.

The sailor stopped a foot from me. He was three or four

inches taller than me, so as I stood I stretched myself to my full height and kept my right hand on the bar. "What can I do for you, partner?" I pleasantly asked.

"My name's Barrington. Do you know Bosun's Mate Second Class Flanigan?" he demanded. "Crazy Joe Flanigan?" He had been drinking hard; his breath reeked.

"I might. And if I do, it might not even be the same one you know." Now the odds of there existing two Crazy Joes in the United States Navy was almighty slim, but I was trying to accomplish two things: Protect myself, first and foremost; and then, if I could, save Crazy Joe from this sailor who obviously had a huge case of the ass against him. In my own mind I was sure Crazy Joe was guilty of some form of atrocity against the kid, but he was my friend.

"Crazy Joe Flanigan?" he again demanded, his voice rising. "You know him or not?"

"Look, I'm not really very good on names," I steadily replied. "What if I do?"

"Well, I'm gonna kill him!" he growled, barring his teeth. "He got me busted for smoking dope. Now I'm a four-year seaman with a wife and a kid. It's all his fault, and I'm gonna kill him!"

In the absence of Crazy Joe hisownself, the young sailor was obviously thinking I would do for the time being.

"I'm sure he's terrified."

"What ship's he on?" the kid demanded.

"I don't want any trouble in here, pal," Becky warned the sailor. "You cool down, y'hear?"

"Or maybe I'll just kill you instead," he hissed to yours truly. Then he set his beer on the bar, puffed out his chest, and stepped back.

That sailor had seen too many old movies, for as he stepped back to lay a haymaker on me, with my left hand I tossed the contents of the beer glass in his face. I got him in the eyes, and he instinctively brought his hands up to cover them. By that time I'd grabbed the loaded Coors bottle by the neck with my right hand and swiftly brought it down over his covered head. He hanged there a second or two wobbling, and as I pondered whether or not to bop him again, his eyes rolled back in their sockets like a slot machine coming up apples and oranges, his knees buckled, and he impacted face-forward on the dirty floor.

"Sam, are you okay?" Becky excitedly asked even as the squid hit the hard deck. Her voice was full of concern.

"As well as can be expected," I answered. "I think he'll be okay. That felt softened the bottle, and if not, he's got free medical. Now if I can just have my sandwich, I'll be taking my leave."

"You don't have to go, Sam."

"You mean you ain't gonna call the cops?" I asked in wonderment.

"Hell no, pal!" she exclaimed, a hurt look on her face. "Hey, this is old Becky you're talkin' to. I run my own joint here, see? That asshole had it comin'!" Then she turned her huge bulk and faced the other two customers in the back. "Hey! You swabs saw this creep on the deck assault this nice man, didn't ya!" she commanded in a voice that could have passed for a cow bellering. They nodded their heads in agreement. One cried back, "Anything you say, Becky!"

She grinned at me through the black holes in her mouth. "See?"

"That's okay, Becky," I said, "but I've still gotta be going." Before I could remove myself from the bar she again grabbed me and hauled me over the scarred Formica, giving me another vicious kiss.

"So long, darlin'," she sighed. "When I git to Colorado I'll look ya up." The sailor on the floor moaned. I grabbed my sandwich and stepped over him.

I stopped at the door, turned, and tipped my hat.

"Aw, Sam, you was always such a gentleman."

A faint smile creased my lips. "And, Becky, you was always such a lady, yourownself. See you around." Then I stepped out on to the sidewalk on National Avenue, took a deep breath, and hurried to my motel room, roundly cursing Crazy Joe Flanigan every step of the way.

After a failed attempt at an afternoon nap I sauntered down to Pier 5 at the U.S. Navy 32nd Street Naval Station and quickly located the amphibious transport dock Crazy Joe called home. The petty officer of the watch blasted Crazy Joe's name and rank over the 1MC with an order to report to the quarterdeck to receive a visitor.

Crazy Joe Flanigan hadn't changed a lick. A little over thirty, he still had a full head of black hair. Tiny crow's-feet had appeared at the corners of his eyes, which were located under droopy eyelids that made him look like Robert Mitchum more than ever. His brown eyes still twinkled with that wild, untamed glint which had always foretold of impending disaster or merriment in the old days. He brought me supper, courtesy of the U.S. Navy.

"When I'm dead, Sam," he said as he mopped up gravy with a slice of bread, "just remember to have me buried facedown so all these bastards can kiss my ass."

"At the present rate, that day will not be long in coming," I replied without humor.

"My last meal in this haze-gray canoe club and it stinks," he grumbled with conviction. Then the 1MC blared: *"Restricted men. Now muster all restricted men with the duty master at arms outside the chief master at arms shack."*

"I think that's your cue. I'm about ready to leave anyhow. All this haze-gray paint has a way of making me lose my appetite."

"Hold on for a minute; I've just got to sign in," he said as he jumped up. In a couple minutes he returned to his seat. "All right. Two more musters and I'm done with this crap. They can't restrict a civilian."

"So why'd you throw the seaman deuce down the ladder?" I inquired. Crazy Joe had rapidly descended from bosun's mate second class to seaman in a breathtakingly short time due to that caper. Along with the two-grade bust went the conditional Honorable Discharge he was about to receive, and for which he was not thankful.

"He disobeyed a lawful order during general quarters. About the hundredth direct order I'd given him," he replied, steaming up. "I got tired of writing report chits on the little bastard. The limp-dick division officer just tore 'em up."

"What kind of lieutenant wouldn't support his petty officers?"

"One that's afraid of EO complaints fuckin' up his career. The little shit seaman is black; he filed one against me, along with the assault charges."

"I ain't hearin' this."

"Unfortunately that little faggot chaplain's yeoman saw me dropkick the seaman. Then when I was standing in front of the Old Man with my heels locked he asked me, 'Boats, are you prejudiced?' " I told him, 'Hell, sir, I hate practically everybody: gooks, flips, japs, croakers, limeys, dagos—but I hate 'em all equally.' I figured, 'Oh well, what the hell.' "

"And then?"

"He failed to see the humor in that," Crazy Joe replied seriously. "He said, 'Your attitude is not commensurate with further service in the United States Navy,' and so forth and bullshit."

"Oh fuck a duck!"

"I'm just tired of this shit, Sam. By my standards these kids coming in today are wimps—they're eighteen goin' on twelve. They would have lasted about two seconds on a Mike boat in the fucking Mekong Delta with Charlie launching rounds at 'em."

"That was a long time ago, Joe."

"When I got out the first time I should have stayed the hell out. I went back to goddamned Rhode Island. What a goddamned mistake! I can't even remember those three years," he quietly said.

"You know what they say about going home again." He ignored, or didn't hear, my comment.

"Sam, you can't make these kids go over the side if they don't want to, or go aloft to paint. They sleep on watch and get away with it. They smoke dope all over the goddamned place. I'm just sick and tired of it. The navy doesn't want leaders, they want goddamned Sunday-school teachers, of which I ain't one!"

"I can buy that," I agreed with a smile. "I thought it was getting screwed up when I got out. So anyway, what happened to your truck?" I inquired, changing the subject to an earlier disaster.

"You know the wharves this side of the Coronado Bridge?"

"Sure."

"Well, to make a long story short, this motorcycle gang wanted to kill me. They chased me halfway across San Diego County and, you know how it is, I got lost downtown and drove off the wharf. Boo-hoo-hoo-haw-haw-haw!" Crazy Joe had a way of being modest and self-effacing when it came to relating his wild escapades.

"How's come ya didn't drown?"

"Well, the gang was about a hundred yards behind me. When I saw the water, it was too late to stop so I jumped before the truck went in. Cracked my elbow when I landed." Anybody else would have busted open their head like a throwed watermelon. Crazy Joe always did have the luck of the Irish. "Then, after the truck went in, I jumped in the bay after it. I swam under a pier and held on to a piling till the gang was gone."

"Sounds very incredible. And the truck?"

"I reported it stolen to cover my ass. They'll find it when they dredge the harbor—in about ten fathoms of water." He grinned.

"Might I ask why those guys wanted to kill you?"

"Sure. Eight or ten of 'em beat me up in a bar in Encinitas. Then they threw me out the back door. So when I left I drove over their Harleys with my truck, boo-hoo-hoo-haw-haw-haw!" Then he turned serious. "Unfortunately I didn't get all of 'em. The ones that still had working wheels chased me, and that's how I wound up in the drink."

"You know, nobody would ever believe all this. I do, I reckon, but it sounds like something out of a movie. Who were those guys, anyway? Hell's Angels?"

"Naw, they weren't that high class. Some dirtball gang called the Death Riders. As far as I know, they're still looking for me."

"That's just dandy, but I don't think you'll have anything to worry about in the Rocky Mountains. So what time do they open the cell door tomorrow morning?"

"I'll be a civilian by zero eight hundred. I mean, eight o'clock." He grinned. "Guess I've got to get used to civilian time all over again."

"Yeah. Okay, I'll meet you on the pier. Then we'll clean out your storage space, pick up the horse and trailer and say 'Adios' to San Diego forever."

"Sure thing. I've got just one small thing to do before I leave town."

"What's that?" I asked, an alarm going off inside me.

He waved a hand as if to say, "Don't worry 'bout it." Then he said, "Don't worry 'bout it. It's nothing big."

"It'd better not be," I replied. "By the way, if I ain't here tomorrow you'll know I ran into your friend Barrington again. I may not get the drop on him next time."

"He's all hot air, Sam," Crazy Joe cheerfully informed me.

"Yeah, maybe. But the SOB's bigger than I am. See you in the morning." Having some years experience on ships myself, I found my own way to the quarterdeck, signed out in the guest log, and departed the ship.

The next morning at eight o'clock I was waiting at the foot of the ship's accommodation ladder. Four bells went dinging over the 1MC and a command voice announced, *"Seaman, United States Navy, departing."* Seconds later ex-Seaman Crazy Joe Flanigan, a seabag in each hand, stopped at the top of the ladder. He dropped both bags on the flight deck and gave a ragged salute to the officer of the deck. He then executed a smart right face and snapped a by-the-book salute to the colors on the stern.

"How's it feel?" I asked him when he reached the pier.

"Like I've done all this once before." He grinned. "Let's get the hell outta here."

I grabbed one of his seabags and even before we reached my pickup he began tearing off his crackerjack uniform. When he'd changed into faded Levi's and a flannel shirt he gathered up his dress blues and pitched them into the nearest dumpster. Then he took a few steps back and sailed in his white hat, just like a Frisbee.

"I take it you don't plan on going back in anytime soon."

"No way, Sam. They had their chance at me for twelve years. What's left of my life is mine. Let's go," he ordered as he climbed into the cab.

We spent the rest of the morning running errands. I ran him around town as he cleaned out his bank account and safe-deposit box, and paid several outstanding bills. We stopped at a gunshop on University Avenue where he picked up a Colt Peacemaker he'd left with the gunsmith for a trigger job. It was late in the morning before we were ready to clean out his storage space in Chula Vista.

"So why do you keep your horse in El Centro?" I asked after he'd enlightened me of Geronimo's whereabouts. "That's a good hundred and twenty miles from here."

"I get out there twice a month or so. When we're not under way, that is. He gets good care, Sam. A retired first class I knew on my last ship has a little farm there. I could have boarded him at Camp Pendleton, but on weekends I just like to get the hell away from the military. Know what I mean?"

"Yeah," I answered, recalling those days myself.

"Turn left here," he ordered. "The storage place is just up the road."

Crazy Joe hit the numbers on the cypher lock; as the gate slowly opened I drove through. I pulled to a stop in front of his storage space, which was about the size of a large closet, and when he opened it I was amazed at what it held. A buffalo robe, heavy English point blankets, traps, and an early Denver saddle gave the storage area a distinctly nineteenth-century decor. An ancient-appearing frock coat, style about 1870, hanged on a nail above the artifacts.

"If you're planning on joining Jedediah Smith you're too late," I informed him. "If I remember correct he passed this way in 1826 and isn't scheduled to return anytime soon."

Crazy Joe grinned back. "Hey, I've been planning on joining you guys for a long time. Ever since I more or less decided to get out a couple years ago. The Old Man just kind of hurried up things a bit for me." We started loading the tack, guns, and assorted mountaineering gear in the bed of my truck. After Crazy Joe handed me the initial few boxes of junk, he opened a battered briefcase and tossed me a recent copy of a gun magazine.

"Page seventy-one." He grinned. "Go on, take a look." In a lengthy article on the Wild West reenactment group of which Crazy Joe was a member was plastered a large black-and-white photograph of him—identified as *"C. Joseph Flanigan"*—wearing the outlandish frock coat, high-topped boots, and a low-crowned wide-brimmed hat. A pair of ivory-handled Colt six-shooters was stuck butt-forward into a broad red sash that girthed his waist.

"What are you, insane?" I shot out as I looked up from the story.

"Who, me?"

I let out a sigh. "Joe, if you're gonna run with me, you'd better learn how to be low-key."

"Sure thing, Sam," he said without conviction. I hopped up

on the tailgate and was trying to pack the stacked boxes with some form of order when Crazy Joe stopped piling up gear. He was occupied taking apart a cardboard C-ration case.

"What's in there?" I asked from all fours. By way of an answer he flipped open the box.

"Boo-hoo-hoo!" he cried.

I swung down out of the truck bed and glared at him, my arms folded across my chest. "I am not blind, Joe. That is an Uzi submachine gun. Why do we have Uzi submachine guns, Crazy Joe? We do not use these instruments of mayhem to hunt deer in the Rocky Mountains."

"You're right, Sam," he glowed as he fondled the weapon. "We use them to hunt hoods in big cities." My gut reaction from the moment I'd received the telegram had been right all along: Crazy Joe was still as nuts as a bedbug.

"I will not be a party to murder," I coldly informed him.

"Hey, Sam, I wouldn't drag you in on murder or anything like that. Crazy Joe can take care of himself, and neither does he send his friends up to the big house."

"I am just goddamned gratified to hear that."

"I just need you to drive while I mess up this guy's week," he added matter-of-factly.

"It's one of them bikers, ain't it, you maniac!" I accused.

"Boo-hoo-hoo!" he cried, gaily letting the bolt slam forward.

"You're not using me and my own truck as parties to whatever felonious assault it is you've got planned!"

"Sam," he said with a sigh and a shake of his head, "I can't ask you to do this."

"Goddamned right you can't!"

"But I will." He smiled innocently.

"Forget it, you maniac!" I yelled in his face. Then he let his arms sag, and cradled the weapon like a kid would hold a busted toy. He hung his head; he was hurt, or acting like he was hurt. But I would be damned if I would be a party to one of his vendettas, even if there was supposed to be no bloodshed involved.

"All right," he quietly said, his head lowered. "I'll forget it."

"Look, Crazy Joe," I patiently explained, "this ain't the old days. We're not kids anymore, looking for crazy times and trouble. We're at the age where we look for ways to stay out of trouble, not court it. Times have changed, Joe; the clock's running.''

"You're right, Sam."

"What's the deal, anyway?" I suddenly asked. I don't know why I asked.

"Oh, nothing. No biggie. Really." He pulled the magazine out of the weapon and put it back in the C-ration case.

"Let's hear it, hoss," I said, interested in what could possibly motivate him to plan to use a submachine gun on somebody or something.

"Oh, I only just about got killed. That's all."

"You no doubt had it coming."

"Maybe. I was hosing this stripper, see? But what I didn't know was that she was also hosing this jerk from the Death Riders."

"Your friends from the Encinitas-slant-sinking-pickup incident. You certainly have a way of winning friends and influencing people. You oughta read that book sometime."

"Yeah," he agreed with a nod of his head. "Anyway, a couple months ago I was in this strip joint where she works and this biker I didn't know comes in. So when he asked me if I wanted to play a game of pool, I said, 'Sure.' So I flipped him for the break and lost, and as I was racking the balls the son of a bitch comes up from behind me and cracks me over the head with a pool cue."

"I taught you better than that," I reminded him, steamed that he had forgotten the lesson. For those who've led a sheltered life, the lesson is this: Never play pool with a stranger, and never turn your back to no one.

"Yeah. So a day later I wake up in Balboa with a knot on my head the size of a grapefruit. It was a very severe concussion, Sam. I coulda died," he said without emotion.

"Well, you shoulda had a hat on," I responded without sympathy. It was plain dumb luck Crazy Joe had not been killed. Possibly he owed his life to the thick skull bestowed upon him by his equally-thick-headed Irish ancestors.

"So now all I want to do is even up the score. A cop I shoot with said I could do anything I wanted to him, just so I didn't kill him or put any holes in him. The cops don't have much use for these assholes; they control most of the dope and hooking out here, y'know."

"They have for years." Then I pulled the Uzi from the C-rat case and looked it over. "Fires from a closed bolt, huh?"

He cleared his throat. "I've got a little adapter that makes it rock and roll."

I shook my head. "Not that I'm interested, but just what did you have in mind for this thug?"

Crazy Joe smiled then. "I'd just like to put a magazine into his chopped Harley and ride off into the sunset. That's all, Sam."

"Promise?"

"Sure." He wildly grinned.

"This is against my better judgment," I heard myself saying, "which I've incidentally exercised a lot of these past years, but . . . I'll drive and you pump out rounds." Yessir, I said it.

Crazy Joe punched me lightly on the shoulder. "Sam, I knew you'd be with me," he enthused. "It'll be just like the old days!"

I slapped a magazine home. "I certainly hope not," I answered, already mad at myself.

We finished loading my truck and pulled out for the victim's house. Crazy Joe gave directions as I drove. "So how'd you find out where this gunsel lives?" I asked as I turned off Highway 94 into the poorer section of east San Diego. Abandoned cars lined the street, and the naked and peeling crackerbox houses reminded me of a scene out of that old Henry Fonda movie about the Depression. Well, I thought, they probably have a couple dozen murders a day in this neck of the woods.

"Easy," he replied. "This cop friend of mine gave me the address. I scouted out the place a while back."

"And you're sure he's there now?" I asked, hitting third as I took a corner.

"That was the phone call I made a while back. Support your local sheriff and he'll support you!" Crazy Joe's particular brand of justice was of the stripe practiced by the Earps. I am not here referring to the famous gunfight at the OK Corral where they took out three gunnies: I am referring to the little-known fact that the year after the OK Corral, Wyatt Earp and Doc Holliday returned to Arizona and blasted to ribbons everybody they had missed in that earlier shootout, including but not limited to Frank Stilwell, Curly Bill Brocius, Wes Fuller, and Johnny Ringo.

"Just so you get the right guy's motorscooter," I said with a sigh. Then I had to add, "Joe, it appears you've got a truly marvelous intelligence system. You should be commended. And if we live through this, you oughta consider hiring on with the Charlie India Alpha."

"Turn here," he ordered. I turned, and at the end of the dilapidated street was the shack Crazy Joe identified as Spiderman's. There was three chopped Harley Davidsons parked in front of the ramshackle house. I pulled a sharp U-turn so that Crazy Joe would be on Spiderman's side of the street and have clear fields of fire. Then he rolled down the window and leaned out.

"Spiderman! Kiss my ass, you communist bastard!" he hollered at the top of his lungs.

The screen door of the ancient and battered house flew open and three greasy, bearded bikers came hustling out. Well, I assumed they was bikers, although they could have been executives from General Motors in disguise.

"Well, Flanigan," sneered the first biker, whom I figured for Spiderman, "I thought I'd killed you. But now I'm gonna finish the job." He was standing across the street by his motorcycle and I was wondering how he was going to effect Crazy Joe's termination, unless of course he had an Uzi hisownself. I wasn't too worried; I was idling my truck with the clutch in for a quick getaway. And just in case things went totally to hell, I'd stuck my short-barreled Colt Peacemaker in my belt.

Crazy Joe grinned at him. Then he swiftly grabbed the Uzi off the floor and with a practiced motion dropped the shoulder stock and brought the weapon up to his shoulder.

"Get ready to die, you yellow son of a bitch!" he happily yelled as he let go with a ripping burst from the implement of carnage. The first burst was poorly aimed; it only tore apart the front tire of Spiderman's deluxe custom bike. As the bikers watched in horror, Crazy Joe poured four-to-five-round bursts of hot nine-millimeter bullets into Spiderman's beloved Harley. On the third burst he holed the engine; I heard a ricochet go zinging over my cab.

The inside of that truck was like being trapped in a goddamned dumpster with a dozen maniacs banging in the sides with sledgehammers. With each crashing burst I was going deafer and deafer. Hot brass was flying and rebounding all over the cab, and halfway through the fusilade a hot case went down my shirtfront and proceeded to simmer in the general area of my belly button.

But even as I sat there, going deaf and swatting hot brass away from my face like so many mosquitoes, I'll have to admit I was caught up in the situation: there is something truly overwhelming about watching a man who loves his work.

On the fifth burst Crazy Joe cut the frame in half. Spiderman's two pals had fled when the fireworks began, presumably to call the cops they despised. On the sixth and final burst, hot brass singing gaily around our ears, he tore the rear wheel apart. The bolt suddenly locked back to the rear. Crazy Joe brought the Uzi down from his shoulder then, the smell of cordite bitter in the air.

"Ah hah!" cried Spiderman. "You're out of bullets!" He pulled a large Bowie from its sheath and headed our way.

"But I'm not out of guns!" Crazy Joe cried in joy, pulling his Colt from a shoulder rig and cocking the hammer with an easy motion of his thumb.

"Ohh," groaned Spiderman. He stopped dead in his tracks and turned kind of pale.

"Hold that toadsticker up, you piss-drinkin' bastard!" Crazy Joe commanded. Spiderman raised the blade skyward as instructed. The single .45 Long Colt bullet broke the blade in two at the hilt, and I believe the blast from the revolver took out my eardrums as well. Spiderman grabbed his hand and shrieked in pain.

"You son of a bitch!" he cried.

" 'When you call me that, *smile*,' " Crazy Joe commanded, quoting Gary Cooper's famous line and again cocking his Colt to emphasize it. Then he aimed the partridge sight square with Spiderman's forehead. Spiderman must have finally realized he was up against a man who lived by his own code, a man who truly was a crazy son of a bitch. He smiled then, albeit weakly.

"That's better," Crazy Joe merrily said. "Well, we'd really like to stay and visit, but we've gotta go. You know how it is. See you around, *asshole*!" Needing no further cue to exit, I let out the clutch and sped down the dingy street leaving a patch of rubber behind me. Having little faith in verbal deals with the establishment I figured the cops would be looking for us, but I wasn't sure how hard.

3

I WAS ALL for holing up in the Cleveland National Forest, even though it's more a bunch of rock-strewn foothills than a forest. Heading for Mexico crossed my mind. And if I could have driven my outfit straight on the deck of a freighter headed for New Zealand as they cast off the lines, that would have been fine, too.

"Don't worry 'bout it," Crazy Joe casually commented as I headed east on I-8. As he crawled all over the floor of my cab, searching for expended brass under the floormats and seat, he appeared to have not a care in the world. As he found each empty case he'd fling it out the open window.

"This is the last goddamned time, Crazy Joe. The very last time," I said, more to myself than to him. As I headed up the long Pine Valley grade the sun hit my eyes and I reached up to pull down the visor. A spent nine-millimeter case rolled out, hit my hat brim, and landed by the gas pedal. "You missed one, Machine Gun."

"Boo-hoo-hoo!" he laughed, reaching down by my foot for the case. He casually tossed it out the window. "Well, that's the last one, Sam." He grinned as he slouched back in the seat. He pulled a bag of Bull Durham and papers from his shirt pocket and began rolling a smoke. "I've got thirty-one accounted for. One musta went out the window."

"It went down my shirtfront," I replied with a shake of my

head. Then I had to laugh. "You might have brought some ear-plugs, you jerk. I still can't hear a damn thing."

"What?" he yelled, holding a hand up to his ear. "Sam, ya gotta talk louder! I'm a bit deef!"

"I said the next time you set up a machine gun in my truck, bring some damned earplugs!" I hollered.

He struck a kitchen match on the sole of his boot and once again laughed the famous Crazy Joe laugh. Then he smiled dis-armingly and I was reminded of a kid who'd just flushed a cherry bomb down the school toilet and was proud of blowing up the water main.

"You crazy bastard," I softly muttered.

The miles rolled on without incident and we stopped outside of El Centro to pick up Crazy Joe's bay quarter horse and dinged-up Stidham trailer. His pal, the retired first class, wasn't around, so while Crazy Joe paid the missus the last month's rent and made his good-byes I hooked up the horse trailer. It dropped easily on my two-inch ball, but when I grabbed the taillight plug, then compared it to the female outlet on my truck, I spit in disgust. I was standing there holding the male plug when Crazy Joe nonchalantly walked up leading his gelding.

"Screwed again!" I hotly informed him. "What's this god-damned plug fit, a freaking jeepney?" He tied his horse off at the trailer and took the plug from me.

"It doesn't fit," he casually observed.

"No shit, Tonto."

"Well, I guess we'll have to stop in Yuma and get it fixed. We've still got a couple hours of daylight. Don't worry 'bout it."

"We were gonna make Flag tonight," I reminded him. Then I stuck my head around the trailer and looked at the house. The lady wasn't in sight. "How do you know every cop between here and El Paso ain't lookin' for us?"

"There you go again, Sam, sweating the small stuff," he replied with his usual oh-well-what-the-hell attitude. "We've seen four Chippies between San Diego and here. Nobody's stopped us yet, and nobody's going to stop us."

"Unless I get pulled over for no brake lights, taillights, or turn signals," I informed him. Well, somebody in that outfit had to deal with reality. Crazy Joe did have a point, however:

we did have enough daylight left to make Yuma, and indeed no cops had pulled us over so far.

"All right, let's load up Seabiscuit and get the hell outta here."

"Geronimo," Crazy Joe corrected. I walked over to Geronimo and untied his lead rope. As I reached for the bottom of his halter, he let out a massive roar and reared back.

Fifteen feet later, after Crazy Joe caught the lead rope, the horse quit dragging me. I slowly got up and dusted myself off.

"Are you okay, Sam?"

I didn't answer at first. I slowly hobbled over to get a good look at the cayuse's head. I looked him dead in the eye and it was just as I had suspected.

"*That* is a wild-eyed, crazy son of a bitch!"

"I know." Crazy Joe grinned. "Kinda appropriate, don't ya think, Sam?"

We made Yuma in a little better than an hour, got the taillights hooked up, and grabbed some greasy hamburgers for supper. Then we drove and drove, and slowly the miles began to pile up.

I figured we was home free when we hit the Coconino National Forest north of Phoenix on I-17. I had been more than a little unnerved driving the desert from Yuma to Phoenix. While Crazy Joe slumped in the seat and sawed logs, I'd studied the shadows. The thousands of one- and two-armed saguaro cactus stood like so many shadowy deputies, silhouetted against the black yet starlit sky. Drifting tumbleweeds, propelled by a strong north wind, bounced crazily across the concrete, coming from nowhere and headed the same place.

And, I thought, The Desert at Night.

A damned eerie place to be.

Ever since I was a kid I've felt at home in the dark. Maybe it's part of my wild streak, but I always felt better knowing I could see folks and they couldn't see me. Or knowing I could slip away unseen, in a hurry if I had to. The dark never scared me. Except in the desert.

I was damned happy to pull into that self-service gas station on the outskirts of Phoenix. Crazy Joe woke up as I stopped at the gas pumps, looked around through heavy eyelids, and promptly went back to sleep. He was beat; I figured all that shooting had taken a lot out of him.

As I drove north, getting closer to home and freedom all the time, I felt beat out but good. Real soon the three of us would be back together for the first time in many years.

Mounted on good horseflesh, riding what was left of the wide-open spaces.

Being free, and more or less young. And still as wild as double-cinched rodeo broncs.

And then, as we went higher and higher in elevation, the pine air sharp in my nostrils, I pulled off on a county road forty miles south of Flagstaff. The sky was just lighting up to the east when I parked in a forest clearing, unloaded and watered Geronimo, then rolled up in a buffalo robe.

I never woke Crazy Joe from his cramped position in the front seat. The poor boy was plumb tuckered out.

That same afternoon we made Santa Fe. Crazy Joe removed the little gizmo from his Uzi that made it go full automatic and promptly traded it off. He swapped for a 1894 Winchester carbine and scabbard, a half-dozen Newhouse traps, and a few other odds and ends. It appeared he was getting practical in his old age.

That evening we stayed with an old mountaineer acquaintance of mine outside of Abiquiu. Crazy Joe needed an animal to pack so he bought a nice grade gelding from Tom Farnham, broke to ride or pack. The next morning we headed up the San Luis Valley, crossed the divide at North Pass, and reached Gunnison around noon. We met up with Philo at the same spot I'd left him only five days earlier. He and the stock was okay, and he had eight or ten beaver pelts to show for five days' work. We all had knowed each other too long and too well to get involved in tearful reunions, so as Philo and Crazy Joe shook hands for the first time in something like ten years it went like this:

"Hi-ya, Joe," Philo said as he extended his paw. "Been a while, ah'm thankin'."

"Nice to see ya, Philo." Crazy Joe grinned wildly.

That was about it.

We spent the rest of April lining out Crazy Joe in that triangle of up and down land bordered by Taylor River to the north, Tomichi Creek to the south, and the Continental Divide to the east. He was rusty—well, in all honesty he was green—but he learned fast.

Crazy Joe's horsemanship was passable, but old Geronimo wasn't. Coming from sea level to eight-thousand-feet elevation has an effect on man and beast alike. In my opinion Geronimo was more than half nuts in the first place. He may have been in good shape in California, but he wore down quick in the mountains. He spooked at damn near everything, including blowed-down trees, boulders, creeks a yard wide, and Herefords. Under Philo's and my patient direction Crazy Joe rode hell out of that critter. In ten days Geronimo was lightly stepping over deadfalls instead of jumping them in a mad frenzy and bucking off the owner/operator. He crossed creeks in a civilized fashion, and learned how to stand picketed and hobbled. Geronimo was on his way to becoming a mountain horse, in spite of himself.

The horse Crazy Joe had bought from Tom Farnham in New Mexico was already mountain broke and we had little trouble lining him out. Crazy Joe thought it would be different to have both horses named after famous Indian chiefs, so the second nag was dubbed Cochise.

Between horsemanship classes Philo and I put Crazy Joe through additional lessons in the Rocky Mountain College. He'd never learned how to strike a fire with flint and steel, so I spent several hours coaching him in tinder preparation and char cloth making. Even sulfur kitchen matches get soggy and fall apart, and a man who can't make fire in the mountains is a gone beaver. When I was a porkeater I almost went under from hypothermia—and that was in summer—so I speak from cold, hard experience. Next Crazy Joe used the half-dozen beaver tags Dusty Rhodes scrounged in addition to the ones he'd given us earlier, but he didn't fill the first tag till he'd educated half the beaver in the Gunnison River drainage. After he caught the first one, its thick spring guard-hair downy and extra soft, the rest followed in short order.

Philo and I taught Crazy Joe tanning and packing, and had him tie diamond hitches till he could do them in his sleep. We showed him how to trim and shoe a hoof so he could take care of his own crazy cayuses, forming the cold shoes to fit by placing them on a boulder and banging away with a shoeing hammer. We was always pretty well provisioned but we never carried an anvil and a lot of farrier's tools.

Crazy Joe learned how to make a stew without burning it all

to hell, and, most important of all, he learned how to make a decent pot of boiled coffee. By the end of a month he had a good start at making a mountaineer.

In between Crazy Joe's lessons in mountaincraft we got him into town a time or two. He got a Colorado driver's license and trapping, fishing, and hunting licenses. He also bought an old International three-quarter-ton truck so he could haul his own horses. One evening in early May when we was in town on such errands, I introduced him to Dusty Rhodes.

"I've heard a lot about Crazy Joe," Dusty said with a grin as they shook hands.

"It's all true, Dusty." Crazy Joe grinned back. I didn't see any point in expanding on Dusty's good impression of Joe, so I didn't volunteer, "Hey, did you hear the one about Crazy Joe and the machine gun?"

"Dusty," I offered, "did I ever tell you how Crazy Joe got his name?"

"No, you didn't. But I'll bet it's good."

Crazy Joe nonchalantly sipped his beer. "Rumors concerning my alleged insanity have been greatly exaggerated."

"Well, we was in Hong Kong on liberty a long time ago—" I began.

"Singapore, I thought," interrupted Crazy Joe.

"Anyway, we was in this bar—"

"Whorehouse."

"All right! You tell the damned story!"

"Okay," he said, "I will. It's like this, Dusty. Sam and me were in this bar in Wunchai; that's the red-light and bar district of Hong Kong. We'd been drinkin' all day and we were fallin'-down, persoginated *drunk*! Anyway, these two Russian sailors came in wearin' their uniforms and Donald Duck caps—I re-member now, it was the San Francisco Club—and sat down acrost from us at the horseshoe bar."

"So anyway, Sam and me are all messed up and these two Russians are lookin' us over, and whispering to each other, and grinning like they're peasants just off the farm in Upper Slobovia. And finally one of 'em waves real meekly and smiles and says, 'Hi, buddy.' "

I started to laugh then in the remembering of it all.

"And I waved my arms back and yelled, 'Comrade!' " Crazy

Joe nearly hollered. "Well, they didn't know what to make of that, so in a little while the same Russian waves again and says, 'Buddy, what you doing here?' "

Crazy Joe was waving his arms and imitating the Russian, animated in the telling of the old tale. Besides Dusty we had a couple cowboys for an audience, and they seemed amused, too.

"So I hollers back," he joyfully announced to the bar, " 'We've come here to kill cornholing Russian bastards!' Well, I don't think they knew much English, but some words are universal, know what I mean? Then they talked to each other for a minute, then they looked at me and Sam and jumped over that bar."

"They certainly did," I agreed, recalling the battle that had followed.

"So they comes over the bar and I takes one and Sam takes one—why, we damn near started World War Three—and then the shore patrol showed up and broke it up, and while they held the commies, Sam and I escaped and ran down to the Star Ferry and took a little vacation in Kowloon."

"To The Waltzing Matilda," I added. "Aussie, not, Russian clientele."

Dusty nodded his head. "So how'd you get named Crazy Joe?"

I answered for him. "Easy." Crazy Joe smiled and let out a couple boo-hoo-hoos. "When we got outta that one in one piece I told him, 'Joe, you are truly one crazy son of a bitch. From now on I'm gonna call you Crazy Joe.' "

"So what other crazy things have you done, Crazy Joe?" Dusty was fishing.

"We gotta be going," I quickly answered. One story per visit was enough.

"Well, it's been nice meeting you, Joe. I'm sure you'll obey all the game laws. I tend to take it personally when fellows don't."

"I'm not a poacher," Crazy Joe informed him.

"That's good," Dusty agreed with a nod of his head.

"I like my eggs over medium or hardboiled! Boo-hoo-hoo-haw-haw-haw!"

As we walked out the door Dusty smiled and shook his head.

* * *

Toward the latter part of May we decided to pull stakes and head for new adventures. It had been an exceptionally warmish spring and the beaver pelts were already running to the thin side. In another week or so, there wouldn't be much point in trapping them; it would be better to leave them for the next season. Late one evening we sat around the fire trying to decide where exactly we'd head, the roar of Lottus Creek a dozen yards behind us.

"Hell, ah doan' care jest so's long as hit ain't Oklahoma," Philo drawled. Philo was a year or two older than me and had enlisted in the army to get out of Oklahoma and into the war. A few months after he completed his combat tour in the First Cavalry Division he got bored with civilian life and joined the navy. He was usually genial if impatient, and his blue eyes wouldn't always tell one what he was thinking. At nearly six foot tall he was as rawboned as a range mustang and would fight like a wolverine if provoked.

"I've got it!" Crazy Joe shouted. "We'll go take the refresher course at ABC School! Boo-hoo-hoo-haw-haw-haw!"

"Would you consider kissing my ass?" I quietly queried. ABC School stands for Assault Boat Coxswain School, Naval Amphibious Base, Coronado. That was where Crazy Joe and I met: He was driving a LCM-6 and I was driving a LCM-8. I had the bigger boat and Joe lost; the instructors was not impressed. After that we wound up in Assault Craft Unit One, where Philo had already been sent as a deck seaman. When the government decided to pull the plug on the Vietnam mission most tick, we bribed a personnelman with a case of Scotch I'd taken the liberty of stealing from the officers club and got orders cut to the same amphibious transport dock.

"Do ya ever miss hit, Sam?" Philo asked from across the fire.

"Miss what?"

"The nav."

"You have got to be seriously shitting me, hoss."

"Sam misses Amor," Crazy Joe chimed in. "She still loves him no shit. She told me so on my last WESTPAC."

"Give me a bloody break. In the past fifteen years she's screwed the Seventh Fleet three times over, and you're trying to tell me she remembers *me*? Just let it die, Joe."

"Wal, thar's parts a hit ah miss," Philo announced, more to

the flames than us. "Sometimes ah thank ah'd lak t' see the Southern Cross agin, but we're in the wrong hemisphere t' see hit. Ah thank 'bout the guys in the cav that didn't make hit, an' wonder what happened to them that did. Ah wonder 'bout a lotta things."

"You know," Crazy Joe began thoughtfully, chin on his hand, "I miss the roar of those Detroit Diesels under my feet, and jockeying my Mike boat through the waves. I also miss that hooker in Vung Tau, but I can't for the life of me remember her name."

"Would you guys knock it off? Holy roaring shit! You guys are carrying on like you're at a VFW meeting or something! Look, we're thirty-four, thirty-five, and thirty-two years old, respectively. The bulk of our lives are ahead of us, not behind us. All I'm gonna say is that I miss the navy and the events that surrounded it like I miss a sucking chest wound. Period."

"Yore shore teechy t'night," Philo lamented.

"I'm tired. Not meanin' to change the subject, but what the hell are we going to do next? I'm open for suggestions."

"Ah'd lak t' try out thet new sluice box ah picked up," Philo said as he loaded his mouth with a hugesome chew of Skoal. "Spring runoff's been purty heavy; thet shoulda washed a lotta placer gold downstream."

"That sounds like a blast!" Crazy Joe enthused. "We gonna retire after sluicing for gold?"

"Joe, Joe," I said as I poured a fresh cup of coffee, "we *may* make enough to cover expenses. We *could* hit a little pocket and make a few grand apiece, but don't hold your breath. It ain't all that common."

"Sam, 'member thet spot on Horsefly Creek whar we hit color but nevah got t' pan 'count a thet blizzard?"

"I sure do, Philo. Yeah, we oughta go back and investigate that creek. All right, come tomorrow mornin' we roll out for South Park. Okay with you?"

"Yup."

"Don't I get to vote?" Crazy Joe asked.

"Nope," I responded quickly. "You ain't been with us long enough; you're still a greenhorn."

"Well, thanks for nothin'!"

I grabbed my blankets and started making up my bed. "We've

got a rough idea of where we're goin'; just follow me." With that I hit the blankets and left Philo and Crazy Joe to discuss modern life in the Rocky Mountains.

Early the next morning we loaded up and pulled for South Park. A hundred and fifty years ago the trappers who placed name to the landmarks in the West named the meadowlike openings in the mountains "parks" or sometimes "holes." There are four prominent parks in Colorado: North Park, Middle Park, South Park, and the San Luis Valley. They run north to south, and South Park is a beautiful forty-mile-wide hole in the mountains where deer and elk freely range alongside beeves and domesticated buffalo. The only disadvantage to it is that it sits uncomfortably close to Denver and Colorado Springs. On the positive side, the little creeks that charge down the mountains to fill the Arkansas and South Platte rivers are loaded with gold. It's just a matter of finding it.

We left our outfits in a little clearing, packed everything up including Philo's "portable" five-foot-long sluice box, which ended up sitting kittywumpus on his packsaddle, and headed high. We followed the Forest Service trail that paralleled Horsefly Creek nearly to the timberline. After two miles of steady upward climbing, the air getting thinner and the timberline getting closer, we stopped and made camp in an aspen grove near the recollected placer deposit. We staked our critters in the nearby meadow to fatten up on the lush foliage, put up our lean-to, and started a pot of beans. Then we fetched our hip boots and gold pans and proceeded to look for color until our fingers was numb.

Five days and two visits from the game warden later, we was two ounces richer in placer gold. We worked ten hours a day hauling black sand and gravel to Philo's sluice, the stream water flushing the light material out, the flake gold settling in the riffles. It was Saturday morning and we was just finishing up a breakfast of bannock—pan-fried bread—and trout when I tossed my plate aside and grabbed the coffeepot.

I started to pour but received only a shot of coffee and half a cup of grounds. "Well, that's it for this pot," I said as I held the cup to my lips and strained the last drops of coffee through my teeth. "Whose turn is it to make the next pot?" I knowed it wasn't mine.

"Hit's Joe's," Philo answered from his cross-legged position on the ground.

"All right, it's mine," sighed Crazy Joe as he mopped his plate with a piece of bread. "Where's the coffee, Sam?"

"I used the last of the old can this morning. Where's the three pounds you bought when you went into town the other day?"

"Oh-oh."

"You forgot!" I accused.

"Oh shit!" gasped Philo.

"Oh dear!" I chimed in.

"Geez, I got everything else, guys. It just kind of slipped my mind, I guess."

"I could shoot you down like a dog," I grumbled.

His face tortured, Philo slowly stood up and picked up the coffeepot. He opened the lid, stared at the grounds, then closed his eyes and smelled the contents. "Ahh," he groaned, like he would never see his best friend again.

"Thanks, Crazy Joe. Now we are truly screwed. It's fifteen miles to town and Philo and I will be dead from coffee withdrawal by supper time."

"Somebody's got t' go inta town fer coffee, Sam," Philo grimly drawled, panic in his eyes. "We cain't go on much longa lak this."

"I'll go again," Crazy Joe cheerfully offered.

"Would you piss off!" I nearly hollered at him. Then in a calmer voice I added, "Philo and I will flip for it."

"Let's hurry up an' flip then, Sam." He pulled out his lucky silver dollar and I won with two heads in a row.

"Ah-hah!" I announced with glee. "And while I'm in town, I'm gonna make the best of this desperate situation and visit that stacked waitress at the Double Eagle Hotel. Don't look for me till later on. Much later on."

"Haf a nice trip," Philo grinned.

"But first I gotta wash up and put on some clean duds," I added as I grabbed my saddlebags.

"Sam, is this gonna be an enriching and rewarding relationship?" Crazy Joe queried as I headed for the creek.

"Cheap and meaningless," I shot back. "Only cheap and meaningless."

I shaved and washed up, put on the one pair of for-good Levi's

I'd throwed in my panniers, and took my dress shield-front shirt out of its protective plastic sack. Then I saddled up Molly and left my partners at the sluice.

It was a beautiful mountain morning. The low white clouds touched the rocky tops of the surrounding mountains, and the deep blue patches of sky peeking through the clouds offset the bits of snow still clinging to the sheltered and shadowed parts of the high country. Between the singing larks and the scenery, I was glad to be alive.

I was following the swiftly meandering creek, half dreaming in the saddle as my Winchester rifle lightly bumped against a fender. I broke around a bend and spied a small nylon tent in a little clearing fifty yards ahead. Now, it's poor manners to ride through a camp, so I reined Molly toward the scrub growth off to the east. Molly was walking slow through the undergrowth about thirty yards from the tent when I like to come out of the saddle.

"Hey!" a female voice hollered. "Stop!" Molly pulled up short in surprise before I could rein her in, and tossed her head from side to side muttering "Ho-ho-ho-ho."

"Easy, hoss," I quietly told her, patting her neck. Then from some brush not a dozen feet away a woman stood up and eyed me hard.

She had fear written on her face for only a moment or two, then wonderment, and finally, amusement. I recovered from the surprise and finally tipped my hat.

"Howdy, ma'am. I wasn't tryin' to run you over. Was tryin' to avoid riding through your camp," I said, jabbing my thumb at her tent.

"You gave me quite a start, mister." From a dozen feet away I could see her eyes was brown. For a second they seemed to sparkle, and I couldn't for the life of me figure out why.

"Sorry," I replied sincerely.

We looked at each other hard, for a second or maybe ten.

And I knew I had to get to know this female better.

So I just sat there dumbly staring till I finally said, "I'm headed to town to get some coffee. Me and my partners ran out." Well, it was something to say.

She took a step or two toward Molly and me, and gave myself

and my gear a hard once-over. "Are you John Wayne or some-body?" she asked, half smiling, maybe half wondering.

"Well, no. As a matter of fact I'm Sam Hawkins." She had seen the Colt Peacemaker far back on my hip and the Winchester in its scabbard. No doubt she hadn't seen many shield-front shirts or Santa Fe Trail–styled hats in real life.

"I am curious as to why you are so heavily armed," she stated without fear but with the trace of an accent I took for back-east Yankee.

"Well, in summer these mountains are full of all kinds of lunatics, ma'am," I explained as I shifted uneasily in the saddle. "Fall and winter they pretty much leave, but a man can never be too careful, ma'am."

"And you're not one of them?" she quickly responded, her eyes sparkling.

"A lunatic?"

"Yes," she replied. She said that word funny, like in two parts. It came out "ya-aas," or something like that. I don't know, I failed vowels in grade school, but it was definitely a foreign accent.

"No, ma'am. I'm just a man that wants to be left alone."

"You don't have to call me 'ma'am,' Mr. Hawkins," she suddenly said with a half smile. I smiled back.

"My name is Janet Provost," she said firmly. Again I noted the strange accent.

"Sure thing, Janet. You can make the handle 'Sam.' "

"Sam," she repeated, more relaxed.

"Well, I gotta get into Fairplay and get the coffee." I made no effort to move Molly out.

Out of nowhere she offered, "Would you like to have a cup of tea with me, Sam? If indeed you're not one of the lunatics you claim inhabit these parts." She smiled then. Doggone it, she knowed I wasn't no lunatic.

"Sure enough, Janet," I answered with a smile. "Let me tie off old Molly girl here." Then I climbed off Molly, tied her lead rope to some branches, and gave her three or four foot of rope so she could lightly graze but not roll. Janet walked ahead of me to her campsite, and when I saw what she had in her hand I was plumb embarrassed.

It was a roll of toilet paper.
And I was plumb mortified.

I had never drank tea before, but I was learning how fast.

Janet was the most captivating woman I had ever met. She was near as tall as all five eight of myself, and her faded blue jeans and old gray sweater, set off by her short-cropped dark hair, gave her a tomboyish if not mischievous look. I was right about her eyes from the first: they was brown, but there was a shot of hazel in 'em I hadn't seen at a distance, and maybe something else but I couldn't figure what. Whatever it was, it made her eyes sparkle.

She had a prominent dimple on one side of her mouth, and to the other side a smaller one. Her eyes was set apart just the right distance, and her nose wasn't upturned—or lumpy like my own, which come from it being busted one too many times—or too big or too small, but just right. Her teeth was so white she could have been in a toothpaste commercial, and as we talked I became conscious of my own, stained toward the brown side after too many years of tobacco use.

We was making small talk. I have never been worth a shit at making small talk.

"Janet's a nice name," I offered during a lull in the conversation. "That's what Al Sieber called his jenny mule. Janet." Now I will have to admit that was a fairly stupid thing to say.

She wrinkled her brow and gave me a funny look. "I didn't realize I looked like a jenny mule," she said, not without humor.

I winced. "I didn't mean you looked like a mule! You, uh—I mean—well, you're attractive and jugheads are ugly. Personally I can't stand 'em. But I didn't mean to call you that; it's just that Janet's a nice name."

"Is this Al Sieber a friend of yours?" She refilled my cup with tea.

"Well, not exactly. He was chief of scouts for General Crook. He chased Geronimo and Nana and Victorio and all them wild 'Paches from hell to Holbrook. He was quite a guy; I've just read some about him."

Janet then wanted to know all about Al Sieber and the Apache wars of a hundred years ago, so I related to her what little I knowed of them days and people. She listened intently and I thought that was interesting: most people could care less about things that happened a century ago.

Eventually the conversation drifted to our own lives. I let slip that I'd been in the service.

"So what did you do in the navy, Sam?" she asked as she leaned back on the ground and propped herself up with her elbows.

"Oh, I was a boat coxswain. LCMs, mostly." I took my cup of steaming tea and blew on it to cool it.

"What's an LCM?"

"Landing craft, mechanized. Hauled supplies and other stuff."

"Where were you?"

"Seventh Fleet, mostly. South China Sea. That part of the world."

"Vietnam?"

"For a while. Then I went to a ship. Say, how do you like living in Colorado Springs?" I asked, changing the subject. Janet had mentioned she lived there.

"It's a nice enough city," she answered as she sipped her tea. "However, I don't really care for the army."

"My gosh, I didn't think you was in the army!"

"Yes. Sometimes it's not so bad, but mainly I can't stand it. I'm getting out in less than two months, and boy, will I be glad!"

"What are you, a sergeant?" She seemed like the take-charge type.

"Why no, Sam," she replied with a grin. "I'm a captain."

"A captain!" I was startled. "You're a captain?"

"Why yes! Is that so strange?"

"Well, no, it ain't. I mean, women have been officers for a long time." Then I added, more to myself, "An Army captain is just like a Marine Corps captain, or a Navy full lieutenant." I was impressed.

"Yes, it is," she said.

Then I thought, "I'll bet she *is* hard enough to be a captain." I barely knowed Janet, but I reckoned she could be a tough customer when she had to be. I admired that.

"I never had much use for officers," I offered cheerfully, putting my foot in my mouth and chewing on it. I guess I was looking for a reaction.

"Why was that, Sam?"

"From what I saw, they cared only about their careers, for the most part. The mustangs were the best—the guys that came up through the ranks. A lot of others built careers by walking over their people, from what I could tell. The best ones either got killed in Vietnam or got out. Of course, I could be all wet."

"I think I know what you're talking about, Sam, but I've always tried to be honest and fair with my personnel. Unfortunately, sometimes they have to be punished." How well I remembered, but Janet was so sincere when she said that, I could tell it must have troubled her to drag people up to captain's mast, or whatever they call it in the army. I reckoned she was too sensitive a human being to be real successful in the service.

"I know. That's the way it goes," I replied as I sipped my tea.

"So, do you still have no use for officers?" she suddenly asked.

"Don't know any no more."

"You know me. Do you loathe me, Sam?" I think she really wondered.

"I dunno. I ain't made up my mind yet."

This probably sounds insane, but before an hour had passed I was in love with that woman. No, to be honest about it, I was in love with Janet from the first time our eyes met.

It wasn't her looks, which was attractive enough.

And it wasn't her personality, which was pleasant enough.

It was all of her, and I can't explain it no further than that.

4

"SO AFTER COLLEGE I was commissioned and they sent me to Fort Carson. I've been there ever since."

It was turning out that Janet and me didn't have one hell of a lot in common by way of background. She had graduated number one in her high school class; I had gone over the hill during my junior year. Janet had been in ROTC at some college back east, and the nearest I'd ever come to a college was the college library at Western State in Gunnison. Once I was killing time waiting for Philo to show up, so I went to the library but got throwed out for smoking my pipe over a book.

"Ain't too many people go out camping alone. You can't be too careful no more. Remember, an Injun will just scalp you but a white man'll skin you alive."

"That's good!" she exclaimed. "And how true!" Janet Provost was filled with life and glowed with spirit. I couldn't figure out why I was so happy just sitting there talking to her.

"And what about your background, Sam? What else have you done besides the service?" I filled in some of the blanks and told her about growing up in western Iowa. Paper routes and farm work. Fishing with my dad, and hunting with my uncle Dutch.

"Do you get back to visit your parents much?" she queried.

"Don't need to. They got killed in a car wreck three years ago. A drunk hit 'em. Wasn't much sense in it, really."

"I'm so sorry," she quietly murmured.

41

"That's the way it goes." I sighed, putting a match to my pipe. "I do have a younger sister, though. Laura is her name. She lives in Lincoln with her dilbert husband."

" 'Dilbert?' " she questioned with a laugh. "What's a dilbert?"

It would't have been polite to say "dumb shit," so I responded. "Oh, I don't know. A cross between a schlemiel and a schlock."

"A schlemiel?" she chortled. "I haven't heard that word in years."

"Neither have I," I smiled. "I learned it from a Jewish yeoman in the navy. He had all sorts of neat words I'd never heared." Then I caught myself and corrected my mistake. "Words I'd never heard, I mean."

"And what about this Uncle Dutch of yours?"

"Oh, he's almost ninety years old now and ain't very good. Got a letter from my sister a few weeks ago and she said he's goin' downhill fast. But I stayed with him some when I was a kid, especially after the grandfolks passed on. Well, one time I was there for the weekend, and my second cousins was there, too; half a dozen of 'em, anyway. Uncle Dutch wanted to take us fishing that Sunday morning, but Aunt Margaret insisted we go to Sunday school. They had a hell of a good row and he lost, so we all went to Sunday school to learn about Moses in the bullrushers or whatever. And right as the teacher finished the opening prayer that door flyed open and there stood Uncle Dutch in his hip boots and old fishing hat. He told us, 'C'mon, boys, we're goin' fishing!' and we did. He won that one after all," I concluded with a smile.

"My, that's great! He must be some kind of character."

"Most of the Hawkinses got that streak in 'em."

"Is his real name Dutch?"

"Naw. His ma gave it to him when he was three or so. Ever seen pictures taken of kids back around the turn of the century? You know, with them funny outfits and the boys with long flowing locks like General Custer?"

"Yes," she replied slowly. "We've got photographs like that in my grandmother's album."

"Well, they dressed Dutch up like that, for his picture anyhow. And his ma—my great-grandmother—said, 'He looks like a fat little Dutchman!' I guess it stuck; for these eighty-plus years, anyhow.''

"What did he do for a living?"

"He was a rural mail carrier. Him and my grandpa both. They started on the mail route right after World War One. My grandpa died first, but Uncle Dutch carried mail for fifty years.''

The conversation tapered off at that point, so I leaned back and refilled my pipe. As I took out a match and struck it, Janet said, "You seem to fit in so well out here. You appear so comfortable.''

"I generally sit cross-legged on the ground.''

"No, I don't mean that. I mean, you appear so comfortable with life—with the life you have chosen. Am I right?'' She cocked her head a little to one side.

"I reckon. It's about all I know anymore. I always intended to go back and finish—and start college and use my G.I. Bill, but Philo and me started runnin' around together when we got out of the service and it became too much fun.''

"It's not too late for education, Sam.''

"Maybe it ain't,'' I agreed as my brain slowly went to work. But before I went any further I had to ask a question I'd thus far avoided. I thought, "Here goes nothing.''

"I see that ring there,'' I said, cool as could be. "Are you married or anything?''

Janet looked me in the eye for a long second, maybe half squinting. Then she held her left hand up and studied her finger. "I'm engaged, Sam,'' she replied without emotion, studying the ring.

"When's the wedding?''

"The last week in August.''

"Who's the lucky fella?'' I wasn't being smart.

"Another officer. He's a captain, too. He's in Korea now and will return shortly before the wedding.''

Right there I was ready to say, *"Buenas tardes, señorita,"* jump on my mare, and ride off, never again to see Janet. Furthermore, in all my years of hell-raising I had never, to the best of my knowledge, messed around with a married or even an engaged woman. I have some standards, and even though they may be as antiquated as a Civil War musket they are standards all the same. At that point I could have left and had only a single,

pleasant memory of Janet Provost. And just as I was in fact
ready to do that, she said, "I must confess I am having second
thoughts about marrying a career army officer."

You could have blowed me over with a feather. I know I
gulped.

"You are?" I asked, trying to keep my voice from rising.

"Yes," she quietly replied.

Now, nobody ever accused me of having an overabundance
of brains, but it seemed to me that Janet was really saying she
was having doubts about the guy to whom she was engaged. I
always figured if two people loved each other a whole lot, it
didn't matter much how one or the other made a living. I probably read too much into what she said.

"Is that a fact?" I calmly remarked, more to myself than her.
I relit my pipe and gazed into Janet's small campfire. Inside,
howsomever, I was building up pressure like a twelve-hundred-
pound Babcock & Wilcox boiler.

I had seen a green light.

And I didn't have to be told twice. I lifted my gaze to the
mountains that surrounded us.

"Looks like rain, I'm thinkin'," I said to the blue sky. I had
to stop myself from adding out loud, "I'm going to marry you,
Janet." But I thought it.

The shadows on the mountainsides began to lengthen, and
Janet said she had to roll out. She had to be back in town the
next day for something or another.

I jumped up on Molly and smiled. "Well, I've had a nice time
visiting with you. Take care of yourself, Janet."

"Good-bye, Sam, and watch out for those mules!" She
grinned. I reined Molly around and threw back over my shoulder, *"Hasta luego."* That means "See you later." I had no
intention of saying "Good-bye." That has always sounded like
it's for keeps.

About an hour later I rode back into camp. My compadres
was pleasant until they learned I didn't have the coffee.

"Whaddya mean, 'Ah didn't git the coffee'!" Philo hollered
in my ear.

"So I got sidetracked! Shoot me!" I hollered back. I dropped
down on my knees and began rolling up my bedroll.

"Whar ya goin'? Whaddya doin'? Wot in hell's goin' on

aroun' heah? Sam, ya been gone all day. Ya come back lookin' lak ya been hit over the head with a two-by-foah, talkin' 'bout havin' stimulatin' conversation with an olt' friend. Ya fergit coffee an' now yer rollin' yer gear lak yer goin' somewheres. Wot in hell's goin' on heah?''

"How about giving me my share of the gold?" I asked as I tied up a buffalo robe.

"What *is* going on, Sam?" Crazy Joe asked in puzzlement.

"I'm going to Colorado Springs for a while. Where's my shaving gear?"

"Huh?" asked Philo.

"I said, 'Where's my shaving gear?' "

Philo waved the question away with a motion of his hand. "Wot's in Colorada Springs 'sides a lot a' concrete an' GIs? Who in hell'd ya meet t'day?"

"Who are you, my mother?"

"Who is she and where's she from?" Crazy Joe asked. I'd found my shaving kit and was busy packing my saddlebags.

"Okay, guys, it's like this," I said in resignation. "Her name is Janet Provost. She's twenty-six or so. She lives in Colorado Springs, she's an army officer and a New England Yankee. There, now you know as much about her as me."

"Where'd she go to college?" Crazy Joe asked distractedly as he rolled a Bull Durham.

"That was funny," I answered as I cinched up the buckles on my saddlebags. "She said, 'I went to Colgate,' and I said, 'Oh, you studied toothpaste!' Heh-heh-heh."

"A very first-rate school," Crazy Joe remarked as he lit his cigarette. "I think it's in the Ivy League."

"Ivory League?"

"The Ivy League," he repeated. "Only the most intelligent people go there."

"Hah! I coulda told you that," I snorted as I stalked off to pack up Jack.

In twenty minutes I was ready to roll. "I'll see you guys in a couple weeks," I told them when I reined in by the fire.

"Whar ya gonna stay?" Philo quizzed. "An' ya bettah wait; hit's gittin' dark." Philo could be a regular den mother at times.

"I ain't afraid of the dark, old hoss. And Luke Harrington will put me up. I bought Molly from him, and he said if I ever needed a bunk he'd put me up. Besides, he can always use an extra hand working with the stock. See you around, guys.'' I clucked to Molly, jerked Jack's lead rope, and started for my outfit.

"Whaddya gonna do?'' Philo hollered after me.

I turned in the saddle and barely made out the bewildered look on my partners' faces.

"I'm goin' a-courtin'!'' I yelled over my shoulder. Then I put Molly in her fast walk. It was a long way to Colorado Springs, and I was in a hellacious hurry to get there.

LUKE HARRINGTON'S TATTERED ranch would never be pictured on a calendar cover, but I was quick to call it home for a while.

It was near midnight when I pulled up in front of the ranch house, and by the light of the moon I could make out the huge Smith & Wesson Luke held in his hand. When he recognized me and my outfit, he quickly stuck the six-shooter in his waistband.

"Howdy, Sam! Whar ya been? Runnin' from the law? Need a place t' steah?" He grabbed my hand with his bearlike paw and about crushed it. Old Luke was all heart and curiosity, offering me a bunk on one hand and hoping to hear I'd just had a shootout with the Texas Rangers on the other.

"Can you put me up for a week or two, Luke?" I asked as I broke the death grip. I made a fist several times trying to get the circulation back in my fingers.

"Shore, shore," he said, beaming, in that southern Missouri drawl he'd never got shut of. "Glad t' have ya with me an' the boys!"

We went in the old ranch house to make palaver and have a drink. All I wanted was a bed for myself and pasture for Molly and Jack. In exchange I figured I'd help Luke around the place. I wanted to be free to come and go as I pleased, for I had come to Colorado Springs to court Janet, not practice bronc riding.

47

"Ya take anything in yer whiskey, Sam?" Luke asked as he cracked open a virgin fifth of Old Overholt.

"Just ice." Luke handed me the glass and took himself a chair. From the ancient record player came a scratchy version of Bob Wills singing about his little Cherokee maiden.

"So what brings ya t' this neck a the woods, Sam?" Luke asked as he sipped his whiskey.

"Well, I hate to disappoint you, but I ain't on the dodge or anything. My partners and me are doing okay. I just need a place for my critters and myself for a week or three. Got some personal business to conduct." Luke would probably meet Janet in short order anyhow. I would be damned if he'd get more of an explanation than that for the time being.

Luke shifted his huge bulk in the easy chair and throwed one leg over the other. Then he looked me dead in the eye and grinned. "Hit's a woman, Sam," he volunteered matter-of-factly.

"What makes you think that?"

"Hit's simple." He smiled knowingly. "Yer an old batchler, Sam. Cain't think a anything else that'd blow ya outta them mountains."

We struck a deal without me having to add more to what Luke had concluded. He agreed to let my horses run with his pastured stock, and I could move into the old sixteen-foot trailer that was missing its wheels and windows. To earn my keep I would help water and feed Luke's critters, fix up broken-down fences as required, and ride out gentle-broke horses. I wasn't expected to hang around the place, or spend any long hours in the saddle.

Which suited me just fine. I reckoned I'd need all the time I could get for planning and courting.

The next morning Luke's hired hand Jack Riley and me commenced to fixing up stalls. When we ran out of scrap lumber we drove into town and charged some rough-cut basswood to Luke's account at the local lumberyard.

"So who's this heah girl, Sam?" Jack snooped as I drove. "Luke tolt me all about her."

"Is that a fact?" I answered, slowing down and pulling to the center of the county road to give a couple horsemen some room. "Since you know all about her, I reckon I don't have to say anything else."

"Okay, Sam." He winced as he stuck a Pall Mall between wrinkled lips. "Ah won't ast no more questions."

"Fine."

"Let's stop hit The Cactus Rose an' have a whiskey!" he shot out as the old joint came into sight.

"Forget it, Jack. Luke told me one of my jobs is to keep you from falling off the wagon. I aim to stick to my end of the bargain."

"You shore has got serious since ah seed ya last," he quietly grumped, apparently offended.

"Things have gotten serious, Jack," I quickly replied.

That same evening I called Janet from a phone booth in town. I didn't call from Luke's because I didn't see any need to have a cheering section.

"Howdy, Janet," I said into the mouthpiece. "Sam Hawkins here. How you doin'?"

"Well, Sam! I never planned on hearing from you again! Where are you?" She sounded genuinely happy to hear my voice. I reckoned that was something.

"I'm at a phone booth in Fountain. I'm helping an old boy with some horses for a few days." I didn't see no point in elaborating.

"Oh. I see." You bet she saw. Janet was one of the smartest people I ever knowed. She didn't have to be told much; she knowed why I was there.

"Look, it's early yet and I haven't had supper. How about meeting me for coffee and a sandwich somewhere?" I asked with my fingers crossed. Here I'll impart some advice to any young men who may someday find themselves in a similar situation: If you barely know a lady, and want to get to know her better, don't tell her "I'll pick you up." Give her the option to drive herself. That gives her the chance to escape, and that's important to anybody, especially a woman.

"I guess I could do that," she replied after a few seconds.

See how neat it worked?

"Okay, pick a place and I'll meet you there." Janet gave me the name and location of a restaurant on the north end of town and we agreed to meet there in an hour.

I beat Janet to the restaurant, and when she arrived I greeted her with a light handshake. We grabbed a table in the corner,

ordered, and proceeded to make small talk. I had been practicing small talk in my head all afternoon.

"So, are you an outlaw, Sam?" Janet grinned as she carefully
poured her tea. "Or is that just the impression I receive?"

"Only when I have to be to survive." Then I stopped in
horror. I had piled chili high on a soda cracker and caught myself lifting the conglomeration to my wide-open mouth. Old
habits may die hard, but that was no excuse. I had been a bach-
elor too many years, with too much time spent in the hills, but
that didn't cut it neither. My social graces was about on par with
them of Mike Fink.

"Go ahead, Sam." She smiled. "I know how it is." Now
there was a good-hearted woman for you, with a heap of common sense throwed in. I stuck the whole mess in my mouth and
washed it down with a slug of coffee.

"So tell me more about New England," I asked, being careful not to talk with my mouth full. I wasn't about to commit no
more social foopaws.

"Well, we lived in the country in western Massachusetts. We
lived in an old colonial period house; the Berkshire Hills were
about fifteen miles to the west, and the Connecticut River was
only about ten miles to the east."

"Things are sure scrunched up close together out there."

"Yes," she laughed, "they are. We had a huge yard and in
the summer we'd put in a garden. Since I was the oldest I was
generally the supervisor."

"I don't care much for hoeing. As I recall, it took away from
fishing time." Janet smiled prettily and continued.

"Then when I was—young—my mother started to work.
When I'd come home from school she would have chicken or
hamburger thawing, with instructions taped to the refrigerator.
I would start dinner, then take care of my brother and sister until
my parents got home from work."

I thought, "Responsibility early. Hmmm." That was good. I
always avoided responsibility myself, but I sure admired it in
Janet.

"In the spring we'd go maple-sugaring on my grandfather's
farm. My, what work!" She smiled, and shook her head at the
memory. "We would haul the sap to a huge washtub, then boil

it down and make syrup and candy. We sure had fun," she added wistfully.

"I never got around to that but it sounds like fun," I offered as I murdered my coffee with sugar. "Say, you ever seen one of them covered bridges? I've seen pictures of 'em on calendars." I wanted to make it clear I knowed something of New England myownself.

"Yes." She smiled, her eyes dancing. "I've been over many of them. There is one not far from where we used to live. A covered bridge belongs to the present and future as well as to the past."

That lady had a way with words.

"Yeah, that's the trouble with today. Don't hardly nobody recall the past. That's what made us, I reckon."

"That is an interesting observation, Sam. I happen to believe the past—all of our past—is extremely important. Take history, for example. History isn't just elections and wars and movements; it's people, and they are oh so vital, even though they may be long departed. They have left us a legacy."

"Like Al Sicber." I smiled.

"And Janet, his jenny mule!" We had a good chuckle over that one and the conversation drifted a little from there.

"Were you and your grandparents close?" Janet asked after a bit.

"Oh yeah, I reckon we were, but they're all dead now. How about yours?"

"Well, I still visit my father's parents; they're the ones with the farm. My grandparents on my mother's side . . . well, my parents were divorced nine years ago and that has a way of fragmenting families."

"Yeah, I reckon it does. As far as mine go, I spent a heap of time with them when I was a kid; they and my uncle Dutch and aunt Margaret. They all tried to show me the decent example and I've tried to live by it."

"They must have had a great deal of influence on you."

"I never thought about it much till now, but I reckon they did. If I learned anything from 'em, it was to always keep the family name honorable. I reckon that's why Uncle Dutch has always been so hot on ancestors: his old man was a stinker." I wished at once I hadn't said that.

"Was he an outlaw, too?" she smiled.

"No," I slowly drawled, trying to find a way out. After a bit I couldn't and said, "He was a bum; he gambled away a fortune. If you're going to be a gambler, you've got to be smart enough not to plan on filling inside straights. Doc Holliday could have told him that. Well, my grandpa and Uncle Dutch and the other kids didn't have enough to eat; oatmeal, mostly. There wasn't no game but some birds and fowl in them days: the deer and elk and bear disappeared when they settled and logged off the trees and tore up the prairie in that part of the country. So my grandpa and Dutch started working early, but there was six kids and they was hungry a lot. My great-grandmother died when she was forty-one. They called it consumption but I think it was malnutrition. I don't know why I'm telling you this," I added hastily. And I didn't know. It still bothers hell out of me to ponder on it. It's a dark Hawkins family secret. Well, it was.

"They must have had an awful youth." Janet offered.

"Yeah. You know, Grandpa and Uncle Dutch always told how they liked basic training in World War One so much. They'd never seen so much food before in their lives." Then Janet did a peculiar thing: her hand quickly and lightly touched mine and squeezed it. As she started to withdraw it, something caught her attention and she turned my hand over and gently studied it for a second or two.

"Sam, the top layer of skin is peeling off part of your hand. Do you have psoriasis?"

"Not exactly. I've had it for years. A little souvenir of Southeast Asia."

"What is the condition called?"

"The corpsmen called it a form of jungle rot. I forget the exact name." She quickly withdrew her hand. "Don't worry." I laughed. "It ain't contagious. It only flares up when the humidity gets bad."

"Oh dear," she said. But she said it with genuine concern.

"That's the way it goes," I replied, taking a sip of coffee. "Anyway, to finish up on the grandparents, my grandpa and Uncle Dutch did everything they could to restore the good family name. They always had that dark cloud from their old man hangin' over 'em: they felt they had to live better lives."

"And you feel that way, too, don't you?"

"Well, there again, that's one of those things I never thought about much till a couple minutes ago. But I'll never disgrace the family name, if that makes any sense."

"I don't think I've ever heard that sentiment expressed before," Janet remarked, almost as if in puzzlement.

"I think when you boil it all down, things are pretty simple: about all a man has is his good name and his self-respect. That's all I aim to get out of the world with."

"You certainly are different," she said softly.

"I always thought I was certainly Sam." I smiled.

"You're outrageous!"

After a bit Janet brought the subject around to the late 1960s and early 1970s.

"I never had much use for the hippies," I replied in answer to her question. "They was against everything and for nothing."

"I think you may have more in common with them than you know, Sam. You do your own individual thing, and live by your own rules. You're an independent thinker and don't seem to care what other people think. In many ways, you probably have more in common with the hippies than you would admit to."

"Well, they're all gone now—victims of the system and the changing times, I reckon—and I don't pretend to know. I don't analyze life or myself a whole lot. Besides, them years was a long time ago; a lot of water under the covered bridge, as they say."

Then I changed the subject. Plan Alpha was in the execute stage and I thought, "Well, here goes nothing."

"You know, I've still got a year to use my GI Bill. I've been thinking on using some of it," I offered, nonchalant as could be. I pretended to concentrate on filling my pipe. Actually I'd purt near forgotten about my GI Bill until that day. All of a sudden it seemed like a hell of a good idea.

"Oh, I really think you should, Sam! That's too marvelous an opportunity to waste. What would you study?"

"Oh, I kinda thought I'd take up professional horseshoeing or saddlemaking. Something where I could work for myself." Well, there wasn't no point in lying to her and saying, "Actually I believe I'll study computers at an Ivory League college, myownself."

"That would be so nice, Sam." She smiled, showing them

pretty white teeth, and nodded her head. She was thinking
something but I couldn't quite tell what.

"See, I've got some land, Janet. Forty acres by the Spanish
Peaks, not far from Walsenburg. I've always planned on building an adobe place on it someday, and living there when . . ."
When what? The truth was, I'd never planned on living there,
not while I could still fork a saddle and set a trap. And even in
the event I did settle there, the only dwelling I'd planned on
putting up was a tipi. But I was amending my plans plenty hard
and fast.

". . . I decided to stay put. That's a pretty part of the country.
And a decent little town, too. You've got some elevation there,
so the summers ain't quite so bad."

"I've always wanted to build my own log house in the mountains," Janet said quietly after a bit.

Them words was a symphony to my tone-deaf ears.

"No kiddin'?" I replied, trying not to gulp. "Logs are all
right, I guess."

I never tired talking to Janet. She was intelligent, compas-
sionate, and, I suspected, strong. She was also very much a
lady. I can't define what a lady is, but I know one when I meet
her. Somehow she turned the conversation around to books. You
may have gathered I ain't the guy to discuss literature with, but
I did my best to keep up with her.

"Do you read much, Sam?" Janet asked as she delicately
dunked her tea bag in the little stainless-steel container of hot
water.

"Oh yeah. Quite a bit. Or as time permits."

"Mostly westerns, I'll bet."

"Sure. A lot of westerns. But I pretty much read whatever
comes along. How about yourself?" I asked, tossing the unfa-
miliar ball in her court.

"Oh, I enjoy history and philosophy, and especially a good
novel. Recently I've been reading some of the French classics I
never got full value out of in college. Have you ever read Sar-
tre?" Janet wasn't making fun of me; she had the idea from
somewheres I had.

"Uh, nope," I replied, wondering who in the hell Starter
was.

"Rousseau?"

"Not him neither," I answered, not being up on my Frog authors. I recognized a French name when I heard one.

"Oh Sam! You must read Rousseau!" she exclaimed. "He lived in the eighteenth century and perceived the American Indian to be living in a state of harmony with nature and his fellow man. I think you would really relate to what he says." Janet had a way of glowing when she talked about books and ideas and such.

I smiled at her then. "Well, for fellers living in a 'state of natural harmony,' they done a heap of scalpin' on each other!"

"Sam!"

"I think," I continued, "that if this old Rousseau feller was right, why, Jim Bridger and John Hatcher and old Tom Fitzpatrick should have given a bunch of his books to the Blackfoot. Maybe they wouldn't have been so quick to rub out the trappers if they knowed they was supposed to be Democrats." I couldn't help it; that educated stuff was always over my own head.

"Honestly!" she exclaimed in mock disgust. "You're such a renegade!"

"Well, Jan, I never figured I was quite Old Bill Williams, hisownself. Y'know, Kit Carson was once asked if he reckoned Old Williams was a cannibal."

"And what did Kit Carson reply?" She smiled, cocking her head a little to one side like she didn't believe what was coming.

He said something like, " 'Ah dunno about thet, but ah nevah rode in front a him t' find out.' "

"Oh, Sam! Stop!" she cried, laughing hard.

"And as for them writers, as far as I'm concerned they're all a bunch of Fro—" I was going to say "a bunch of Frogs" but remembered Jan's French-Canadian ancestry in time. It came out "Frogotten fellers."

She smiled queerly at me. "Yes, I suppose to an extent they are, Sam. But anybody who ever published a book is never totally forgotten."

"I've read some of Bill Nye's stuff," I offered, taking a new tack. "He was a writer and he ain't forgotten. Not by me."

"Bill Nye?" she repeated. "I don't believe I've ever heard of him."

"Yeah. His real name was Edgar Wilson Nye. He was a writer in the last century. Pretty funny, too. He started the Laramie

Boomerang and was a friend of Mark Twain. He wrote about cowboys and miners and stuff, but he died pretty young. That's part of the reason he ain't remembered.''

Janet's eyes narrowed just a tad. "What's the rest of the reason?"

"Oh, if you want my opinion, by the time Bill Nye came along the Old West was going fast. People thought he was funny, sure, but later on I think they got tired of him making fun of stuff. Like cities and dudes and the east. Because, you see, the West wanted to be like that even then.''

"I thought Westerners always prided themselves on being individuals. Adapting certain Eastern institutions, and forming others when the established methods didn't work.''

"I don't know. I don't have many firm thoughts on it. I just figure that save for a few men like Boone and Bridger, why, even the early Americans was just Europeans in buckskin britches.''

"Hmmm," she said, raising a finger to her chin in thought. "I've never thought of us that way. That's a unique opinion, Sam, or at least one I've never heard expressed. You really ought to write your thoughts on that.''

"Shucks, Jan, the last thing I ever wrote was my signature on my DD 214.'' I didn't see no point in expanding on my lack of schooling.

She laughed lightly and changed the subject still again. "Have you seen any plays?'' she asked, getting all excited again.

"One comes to mind," I answered, uncomfortable. That was about it.

"I love theater! Are you familiar with the plays of Ibsen?"

"Uh, no," I answered, wondering if that was another Frog author. "But I read a couple of Bill Shakespeare's plays. I dug a book out of a garbage can once. I read some of it.''

"Whatever were you doing going through a garbage can?"

"As I recall, I was looking for something to eat.''

"Oh.''

"Yeah. I read a couple of them plays. *Julius Caesar*, that reminded me of the Republicans and Democrats going at it, what with all the conniving and back-shooting.'' Janet started laughing.

"Then I read *Richard the Turd*," I added.

"Sam! It was *Richard the Third*!" she cried.

"Well, as I recall, he murdered a couple little fellers; little princes, I think they was, and he slit their throats in their sleep so he could get to be king or something. He was a turd; he should have been dragged through the prickly pear and staked out on an anthill with a strip of wet rawhide tied around his head." I was sure enjoying myself with that lady.

When Janet finally quit laughing she asked, "So what plays have you seen, Bill Nye?"

"Just one. I busted my clutch in Green River once and had to wait for a couple days for parts. So one night, instead of goin' to a honky-tonk, I saw in the paper where they had a high school play on. I went to it and really liked it."

"What play was that?"

"Was called *Our Town*, near as I recall."

"Yes," she slowly began, nodding her head, "I respect the work of Thornton Wilder. His work was so homey and American, and seemed to strike a common chord. But I haven't read *Our Town* since high school."

"Well, I only recall one part of it real well," I admitted. "That's the part where this girl dies and she doesn't go to heaven and she doesn't go to hell. She just sits there in the cemetery with the rest of the dead folks. And you see, she finds out she can go back to life for one day, but one day only. And she's there, dead and in a bind 'cause she don't know what day she should live over, and this feller running the play—no, it was one of the dead folks—says, 'Choose the least important day in your life. It will be important enough.' I guess each day is a heap more important than we know when we're alive."

And then, after a very long pause, Janet looked hard into my own eyes and softly said, "I never quite thought of it that way."

Shortly after that we got up and left. Janet insisted on paying for her half of the check, so I respected her wishes. I went back and left the tip, then walked her out to her little car.

"Well, Sam, I've certainly enjoyed this evening. You are very comfortable to be with."

"And outrageous?"

"Yes." She laughed lightly, squeezing my forearm. "That, too." Janet had a way of smiling that made a man feel good just seeing her. Her bright teeth stretched from ear to ear and her eyes danced and sparkled.

Then I got serious. "I sure like being with you, Jan," I said to the ground. I had wanted to say more, but it was all I could force out.

"And I like being with you," she answered quietly, fingering her car keys, not quite looking at me.

"Is it just that I'm outrageous, or is there something there?" I shot out. I had to know.

She looked me in the eye then. She didn't smile and she didn't frown, but still, she had a look on her face I can only describe as pain, or maybe sorrow. "There's something there," she replied, almost in a whisper.

I didn't imagine it.

She said it.

I damn near whooped for joy, but instead I tipped my hat and held out my hand. She took it and we shook hands, but even as I let go, she gave mine a small squeeze.

"Good night, Sam," she said softly.

"Good night, Jan." I smiled, holding myself back.

I got control of myself in time and held back from grabbing her by those strong shoulders and pulling her tight and kissing her pretty mouth and telling her how much I loved her.

Jan knowed, though. She never told me, but I know she did.

Besides, that would all come soon enough, anyway.

6

JAN AND I met for coffee twice more that week. Friday morning found me whistling through chores as I walked out to Luke's pasture and caught up Molly and Jack. I tried to tell them about Janet, but they quickly ripped apart the flake of alfalfa I'd brought along and preoccupied themselves eating it. Them critters was generally more interested in their own bellies than world events, anyway.

That afternoon, after barging past Jack and ignoring his babbling about how he used to play at the Grand Ole Opry, and there knowed a famous lady country singer after the biblical fashion, I grabbed the phone, looked out the window, and announced, "Jack, the fence is down. Horses are out on the road." He shot out the door and I called Jan at work. She'd mentioned what outfit she was in.

Some private answered the phone just the way you're supposed to do in the service. "Eight hundred thirty-second Supply and Transportation Battalion Headquarters, Lieutenant Colonel Gates commanding, Private Schmaltz speaking, may I help you *sir!*" he hollered in my ear. I moved the receiver away from my ear an inch or two, glad to learn there was some respect left in the all-volunteer service.

"Private Schmaltz," I intoned in my best command voice, "This is Captain Nathan Brittles. I need to speak to Captain Provost."

59

"Captain Brittles?" Jan's voice questioned after a few seconds. She was stumped.

"Tell Sergeant Tyree to take the Paradise River patrol. We're gonna catch those Cheyenne Dog Soldiers," I solemnly informed her. It was my best John Wayne imitation.

"Sam, how are you!" she exclaimed. "And who are Captain Brittles and Sergeant Tyree?" Even over the phone I could tell Jan had a wide grin.

"I'm doin' fine," I answered. "Didn't you ever see *She Wore a Yellow Ribbon*?"

"No," she replied slowly. I wondered how she could have missed it.

"Well, Nathan Brittles was the name of the character John Wayne played in that classic film. Ben Johnson was Sergeant Tyree."

"John Wayne is a hero of yours, isn't he?"

"There will never be another like him. So how's work going?"

"TGIF," she sighed. Janet gave me the lowdown on all her latest projects. Military matters don't interest me much but I tried to sound concerned. What did come through in the conversation was the fact that Janet was a hard worker, and even though she was getting out in a few weeks she was still doing her best. That showed true character as opposed to myself, who, when a short-timer, once disappeared for three days on a thirteen-thousand-ton ship at sea. It was a tough trick, but I done it.

Eventually I directed the conversation to the coming weekend. "Say, I was thinking about headin' up to the Garden of the Gods tomorrow. There's something up there I'd like to show you. Wanna go?"

"What is it?" I could about picture her eyes narrowing with the hint of suspicion. I wasn't sure Janet fully trusted me yet.

"A surprise."

"Oh, a surprise," she echoed. "I love surprises, if they're nice ones."

"Well, this is a nice one." Personally, I hate surprises myself.

After a second or two she replied, "Okay. What time?"

"How about ten in the morning? That way we can get up

there, I'll show you the surprise, and you'll have the rest of the day to do your errands and such.''

Janet agreed and gave me directions to her house. But I've got to admit for the record that I had no intention of running her up to the Garden then speeding her back home. Near as I could figure, I had six weeks to convince her to call off one wedding and give the go-ahead to another. Every minute was precious. My intention was to shanghai Janet for the entire day. I needed all the exposure I could get.

All right, I fibbed.

So shoot me.

The next morning I picked her up a little before ten. We chatted as we drove the fifteen miles from her house to the Garden, and when we got there I pulled to a stop in the first parking lot past the entrance.

''Well, here we are.'' Janet grabbed the door handle, pulled it slightly too hard, and as she did so, it came off in her hand.

''Samuel''—she coyly smiled—''was that planned?''

''Uh, no,'' I replied, embarrassed. ''I ain't been so hot on vehicle maintenance. But I plan on fixing up the outfit this summer. Just, uh, put the handle back on and pull it slow.''

She grinned at me. ''Will the door fall off when I open it?''

''Shucks.'' I smiled back. We disembarked my truck without further calamity and I led the way to Balanced Rock, some fifty yards distant.

''Well, this is it,'' I said, admiring the huge boulder.

''Balanced Rock?''

''Yep. It's all yours, Jan. I'm giving you the world-famous Balanced Rock.'' I took off my hat and wiped my forehead with my bandanna. It was only June, but the heat was stifling. ''Think nothing of it,'' I added.

''Well, thank you, Sam. Nobody ever gave me a boulder before. But is it yours to give away so freely?''

''C'mon, I'll explain,'' I replied, leading the way up to a little knoll a few yards distant. We pulled up seats on a small boulder. Tourist cars quickly passed to and fro beneath us.

''It's like this, Jan. The Garden of the Gods here has always been a sacred place; a place of peace. Back in the old days, why, you had the Cheyenne and Arapaho fighting the Comanches and Kiowa. Then the Utes or Apaches would show up and they'd get into it with everybody. But whenever the Indians met up here, even if they was scalp hunting, they'd call off the shooting. 'Course, when they ran into each other a couple miles away, all bets were off.

"The rock here represents that. Peace, I reckon. Nobody owns it, and nobody holds title to it. So I reckon I really can't give it to you, unless you come up with a flatbed truck and a crane, but I can give you what it represents. Peace and decency and calm." I stopped right there, the knowledge of what I was saying slowly dawning on me. I was getting almighty close to a wedding proposal, and that wasn't in the plan. Just yet.

Jan turned her head and gave me a strange look. "That was quite a speech," she quietly remarked as she looked into my eyes. "Thank you, Sam. It's a lovely rock."

"All right, so it's a little corny," I confessed, tossing a pebble to the pavement below. "It was the best I could do on short notice."

"That's okay," she replied with a smile, poking me in the ribs with a finger. "It's a lovely sentiment as well as a lovely rock." Then she paused, picked up her own handful of pebbles, and began tossing them to the pavement below. She kept her gaze on the ground and quietly said, "You know, you go very deep."

"I do?" I was never on a submarine; I didn't know what she was talking about.

"Yes, you do. Where do you get your ideas?"

"Geez, I dunno. I just think 'em up, for the most part." And I do, except for when I borrow 'em from some fellow. When I do that, I mention the fellow's name because even I know it's against the law to quote somebody or use their ideas without giving them credit. There's a word for that; I can't remember what it is for sure, but it's plague-something.

She lightly pitched another rock. "You're so different," she quietly said, her eyes following the rock to the ground.

"Not wrong, just different?"

She smiled prettily then. "Not wrong, just yourself."

I let out a sigh and tossed the whole handful of pebbles. They clattered lightly to the pavement. A tourist family piled back in their station wagon after the father hurriedly took a picture of his tribe by Balanced Rock. As they drove off, the kids waved at us through the rear window and we waved back.

"Jan, there's something I haven't told you," I offered once I'd mustered up the nerve. It seemed like the appropriate time.

She turned her head and looked me in the eye. Her own were so pretty. "Yes?"

"I never graduated from high school. It was my own fault. I probably could have finished in the navy, but I didn't get around to it." There was a major dark secret out in the open.

"From what you've told me about yourself, I've rather suspected that."

"You did?"

"Yes."

"Shoot. I mean, well, I did make bosun's mate third class in the navy, too. I know you figured I wasn't no officer."

Jan smiled prettily and leaned back on her elbows. "Coming clean, eh?"

"Well, it's just important to me that you know I am who I say I am." And it was.

Jan raised herself from her reclining position and propped her chin in her hands. Her eyes appeared to fix on some distant point far away and she quietly said, more to herself than me, "There are things about me you don't know." Now, with the benefit of hindsight, I can see I should have pursued that statement right then and there. That was mistake number one.

"Well, I ain't concerned." I wasn't. Whatever Janet had done, or felt she'd done, didn't have anything to do with the present. I am the last man qualified to hold the past against somebody. Especially somebody I love.

"Hey, let's go for a walk," I offered at last. "My rear end's going to sleep here."

She laughed lightly. "So's mine."

We took the walking tour of the Garden of the Gods and I mentally kicked myself for wearing my heavy boots. If I had knowed Janet was such a hiker I would have worn my hard-soled Navajo moccasins.

"You don't like to walk much, do you, Sam?" she stated, reading my mind. We was walking side by side opposite of the huge, red rock formation that appears to have an Indian's head carved on it if you look at it just right.

"Oh, I've done a heap of walking and expect to do more. Got to, trapping and working in the mountains and such."

"But I'll bet you never take up hiking as a hobby."

"Not so long as there's one horse left on God's green earth. Guarantee you I'll find him rather than walk."

She answered with a smile, then pointed up a gully. "There's a big rock up at the top. I'll race you to it. You take the low road and I'll take the high road."

"You're on, pal," I replied. Even though I hate walking I rarely back down from a dare.

"Go!" she shouted as she shot off in a sprint. Janet dashed ahead of me, following the narrow path on the right side of the gully. I jogged up the left side and in a minute was running even with her, although eight or ten feet away on the other side of the crevice. I reached the saddle between the rocks where the gully began but Janet had encountered rocks in her path. She stopped about six feet away, barely breathing hard. What we hadn't seen from below was the five-foot gorge that now separated us.

"You're out of trail, old hoss," I grinned.

"I'll make it," she firmly announced as she backed up.

She stepped back about a dozen feet and even as I yelled "Don't!" came dashing toward me hollering "Look out!" She cleared the gorge in a flying leap and landed right in front of me, but even as she landed she lost her balance and started to fall backwards. I grabbed her by the shoulders and pulled her to me.

She grinned as she breathed hard, trying to recover her wind, and I was breathing hard myself, but not from a jump. I just looked into her eyes and smiled and said, "You're nuts. You coulda gotten killed."

Janet looked hard into my own eyes, our faces not a foot apart. She cocked her head a little, like she was examining my whole face, half smiled, and said, "I'm all right, old hoss."

She tilted her head back just a bit and half closed her eyes. From the bottom of my guts I got out, "Oh, Janet." Our lips met then and we kissed each other hard, for a minute or maybe ten. I don't recall.

Well, actually I do. And it's nobody's damn business.

Later on we walked to the little snack bar in the Garden and had lunch. There I offered up an idea.

"It's hotter than the hinges of hell down here," I said over my coffee cup. "Maybe we ought to drive up to nine or ten thousand feet or so and get out of this heat."

"The mountains would be fun . . . but I've got to be getting home, Sam. I've got a lot to do yet today." I thought she said that with a distinct lack of conviction.

"Why, it's only one o'clock," I innocently responded.

"Where would we go?" she suddenly shot out.

"Oh, I dunno. Cripple Creek; Victor, maybe. I've got my old rifle and pistol in the truck; maybe you'd like to try your hand at shootin' them."

"What kind of guns are they?" she asked, interested by the idea.

"A .54 caliber Hawken rifle, caplock. It's a full-stock copied after the one Jim Clyman had when he guided a train over the Oregon Trail in 1844. The pistol matches. I had 'em built for me years ago."

"Sure, why not?"

Half an hour later we topped Ute Pass and I turned north for Pike National Forest. After a few miles I wheeled off the pavement onto a Forest Service road and drove back in among the aspen and second-growth pine. We stopped in a deserted clearing dotted with small to large red boulders and got out of the truck.

"The mountain men certainly had their hands full," Janet commented as I hauled out my gear. I slung my shot bag and powderhorn over one shoulder, stuck the pistol in my belt, and grabbed my cased Hawken with my free hand.

Well, my other hand would have been free except that in it I held Janet's own soft yet strong hand.

"Nobody ever said these muzzle-loaders wasn't an operation," I said as I led off. We set up a couple targets at the far end of the meadow, then walked back near the truck to load. I thought I'd make it interesting for Janet, so I let her load the rifle. I handed her a couple percussion caps and explained each part of the operation to her instead of saying "do this" and "do that."

"Okay, after you've got the oil dried out of the barrel—that's why you fired those two caps, Jan—you put about thirty grains down the barrel and shoot it out. That ensures the charge will fire.'' I measured out thirty grains of FFG black powder, handed the measure to Janet, and she dumped it down the barrel. Then she capped the tube, pulled the hammer back, and fired the blank load with a *whoof!* and a cloud of blue-gray smoke.

I explained as she loaded why I used a stiff charge—125 grains of powder for a one-shot kill—and why I used only bear-greased patches—they don't saturate the powder and cause a misfire—and why it's necessary not to ram the ball with the wiping stick. If you mash the round ball and deform it, which can easily happen to a soft lead bullet, accuracy goes out the window. She was sure interested, and learned how to load almost as fast as I could explain the process. Finally she capped the tube and was ready to fire.

''Okay, hoss, where's the target?'' She cradled the rifle with the familiarity and confidence of a pro.

''Why, that Coors can we set up. The one on the stump,'' I answered, pointing to the can thirty yards away. ''See the black in the middle?'' By way of an answer Janet swiftly throwed the twelve-pound rifle to her shoulder.

''Sure do,'' she answered, pulling the hammer back to full cock.

''Back trigger first,'' I reminded her. She set the trigger with a firm pull.

''That front trigger goes off with one pou—'' The rifle fired with a belch and a cloud of smoke. I was watching Jan and didn't see the beer can leap into the air. We then walked up to it.

''A-hem,'' I said as I picked up the can. She had hit it dead center in the black, and the soft lead ball had nearly tore it in half. She grinned at me like a kid, not finding the need for words.

''That's a .54 Hawken rifle for you,'' I smiled as I held the can high and squinted at her through the gaping hole. ''It'll shoot center with the best of 'em.''

''I thought I had something to do with it.''

''Oh, you may have!'' I laughed. Then we both laughed and laughed, and walked back to the other end of the clearing and plinked at cans all the rest of that afternoon.

And it hit me there, off in the pines that Saturday afternoon as we shot my old guns and talked and kidded, that, why, I had never before had a friend like Janet in my life.

I had never known you could like somebody so much, and love her at the same time, so almighty, powerful hard.

THE NEXT MORNING I picked up Jan at seven-thirty so we could get an early start to Bent's Old Fort before the sun started baking the plains. I guess shooting them old fur-trade-era guns had piqued her interest in that period, and she agreed to go quick enough when I asked her.

"What a lovely morning!" she exclaimed as we headed south on the Old Trappers Trail, now known as I-25.

"Qui-bolle Fontaine," I said as I pointed to Fountain Creek off to our left. Them were about the only French words I knowed. "Maybe one of your ancestors named it. Are you sure you ain't related to old Etienne Provost, Jan? I think you probably shoot near as good as he did."

"You ought to see me with an M-16."

"Well, when you start talking that serious stuff I'll take a .50 Maw Deuce Browning with an unlimited supply of ammo, myownself."

Jan did most of the talking as I drove south to Pueblo, then east on U.S. 50. We both sipped tea I'd brought in my Thermos—all right, so I was learning to drink it for her sake—and Jan talked of many things. How things was when her family was all together and trips when she was young and things of that nature. She suggested I'd really enjoy visiting Fort Ticonderoga, and when I responded that there was too many damn Yankees in that part of the country to suit me, she bubbled over laughing.

"But, Sam, I'm a 'damn Yankee'!"

"Aw, you're different. You're a Westerner by adoption, as far as I'm concerned. You dress like a Westerner; you're a bit of a rebel. Give ya another seventy, eighty years you'll fit right in out here."

"So who adopted me? You, Mr. Hawkins?" she inquired with a wry smile.

"Naw. I've—" I almost said, "I've got other plans," but caught myself in time. "I've just been thinkin' on it some. I'm thinkin' the West has adopted you but maybe you don't know it yet."

"And what has led you to conclude that?"

"You've got the look of distance in your eyes."

Jan gave that four or five miles of silent thought. After a bit, the conversation drifted back to her family. She said she had a sister in college in Arizona and was concerned about her future.

"How so?"

"She's picked a hard road for herself. She's an aspiring thespian," Jan said with concern.

I was shocked. Even from the little Jan had told me about her background, I knowed she came from a good family. Them kids wasn't raised to be peculiar. "I'm really sorry to hear that, Jan," I genuinely offered. "But I reckon it takes all kinds."

Jan grinned, and jabbed me lightly in the ribcage. "Oh, Sam!" she exclaimed. "A thespian is an actress; she wants to be on the stage!"

"Oh," I replied in relief. "I thought that meant something entirely different."

We stopped for breakfast at a little restaurant in Fowler and talked about nothing in particular over our eggs and bacon. I was on my second cup of coffee when Janet got a concerned look on her face.

"Sam?"

"That's me."

"I would really appreciate it if you would take your hat off at the table. Would you mind doing that for me?"

I was startled. "Why I never . . . I mean, I always . . ." My hat was off before you knowed it, and I have never forgotten the lesson in manners.

"Thank you," she said quietly with a smile.

"Sure thing, Jan," I replied, surprised at my own self. If some cowpuncher had told me to take my hat off in a saloon, I would have socked him.

We finished breakfast shortly thereafter and drove the remaining forty miles to Bent's Old Fort. As we crossed the Arkansas River bridge I speeded up and passed a tractor pulling a hay wagon. I winked at Jan and said, "We're almost there, amigo."

"Do that again."

"Do what again?"

"Look at me like you just did."

I creased my brow in puzzlement but attempted to repeat whatever movement it was that had caught Jan's eye.

She pursed her lips in thought. "When you looked at me like that, you reminded me of my father. There's a resemblance."

"Well, shucks." I smiled. "I don't know if I should be flattered or if he should be offended." I didn't think any more of it, and shortly thereafter we passed the house of my friend Al Hempstead. His two boys, Robert and George, were out in the yard playing catch. I honked my horn and waved; they waved back.

"Who were those boys, Sam?"

"Al Hempstead's boys, Robert and George. They're eleven and nine. You'll meet old Al directly; he's the resident mountaineer at the fort." I parked in the near-deserted gravel parking lot and Jan and I headed up the quarter-mile path to the adobe fort. It was only ten o'clock and the daily deluge of Bermuda-short-clad, camera-slinging tourists had not yet begun. I say "camera-slinging tourists" because people who traveled the American West not even a hundred years ago as a rule carried a six-shooter or a Winchester manufactured in Connecticut. Today's prairie travelers pack Yashicas and Minoltas made in Japan. I have always found a degree of irony in that.

"See them two grays next to the huge chestnut Belgians?" I asked Jan as we walked the trail.

"Yes."

"Well, they're Spanish Barbs. That's the horse Cortés and Coronado and all them Spanish fellers brought over in the 1500s. They brought Arabs, too, and they've done pretty good, but the Barbs was almost extinct just a few years ago. They're coming back some now, and the fort has got two or three of 'em."

The Stars and Stripes waved mightily from the fort's lodgepole pine flagpole, and as we neared the adobe castlelike structure Jan began asking questions about its history. I explained to her how in 1829 the mountaineers William and Charles Bent decided there was more money in the Santa Fe trade than there was in wading cold beaver streams, so they went into partnership with another trapper named Céran St. Vrain. The fort was constructed between 1829 and 1833 using Mexican labor from Taos and Santa Fe, and not only resupplied trappers but outfitted Santa Fe freighters as their wagons creaked toward Raton Pass. It also served as the major trading post with the Plains Indians of the Southwest. I explained why William Bent blowed up the original fort in 1849: his three brothers had all died untimely deaths in the trade; cholera brought by the California emigrants wiped out about half of the Cheyenne and Arapaho, and the remaining ones became unfriendly. Finally, the government of the United States wanted the fort for a pittance, and that was about all William Bent was going to take. I mentioned that my great-great-grandfather Hawkins had camped near the ruins during the Civil War when he was a cavalry officer.

"Why was that?" Jan asked.

"There was always good grass and plenty of wood alongside the river," I answered.

As we neared the gate, a man clad in buckskin britches, botas, red flannel shirt, and beaded plains moccasins sauntered out to greet us. He was carrying a full-stock Hawken rifle like my own, and wore a long blond beard that would have rivaled the one sported by old Holy Moses hisownself. On his head was perched a battered hat with the brim tacked up, the crown decorated with rows of beadwork.

"How're ya, hoss, an' whar ya been!" he exploded. "An' I see ya got a white woman in tow. Pale skin don't shine in the mountains fer a fact, but this child's thinkin' ya got yourownself a choice filly from the States."

"Howdy, Al." I grinned as we shook hands. Jan had a look on her face I can only describe as pure wonderment. She apparently had never met anybody like Al Hempstead.

"Janet Provost"—I smiled—"I'd like you to meet an old compañero of mine, Al Hempstead."

"Provost!" he cried, a wide smile decorating his face. "I'll be durned! Yer grandaddy and me led a brigade outta Taos in

'24, and glad I was t' leave 'cause brown skin don't shine no-how and them greasers was out t' decorate their lodges with my own scalp.''

"Are you a real mountain man?" Janet asked in awe.

"Well, b'golly, I ain't made outta fiberglass!" Jan's discomfort melted and we all had a good laugh. We followed Al as he led the way into the fort's plaza.

As we walked through the narrow *zaguan*, Al in the lead, I turned and whispered in Jan's ear, "He's really very civilized." She smiled and knowingly nodded her head.

Al ignored the few regular tourists inside the fort and gave Jan and me the grand tour. "Here's Susan Magoffin's quarters," he droned in a disinterested monotone as we entered a second-story room. "She stayed here for twelve days in July of 1846 and birthed a child what died. Wrote a good account of trail life in them days, and they based part of the restoration 'bout what she wrote on the fort." Under his breath he added, "All Susie did was bitch."

We stopped next in the trapper's quarters. Jan wanted to know all about the old-time saddles and traps decorating the room, so Al and me explained—he going into over-necessary detail—every piece of gear in it. She picked up the deck of Spanish cards laying on a rolled buffalo robe and asked, "What are these?"

"Why, that's a Spanish deck, Janet," Al volunteered before I could open my mouth. He took the deck from her and pulled out a few cards. "See, you've got four suits: clubs, coins, chalices, and swords. It's the deck we use t' play Spanish monte."

"Monte?" she questioned.

"Yup," he replied. "Sam and me will show ya. Siddown, hoss." Al and me took cross-legged seats on an open buffalo robe and began to play, him dealing. Janet pulled up a stool so she could look over my shoulder and watched intently as I bet and Al flipped down the cards.

He had two clubs to his side; a coin and chalice showed to mine. "Over here," I said, pointing at my cards. He flipped a card down. It was a sword.

"You lose, hoss." He grinned as he started to shuffle the deck. "And you still owe me that horse from two years ago."

"A horse, Sam!" Janet cried in mock horror.

"We was just playing for fun, Jan," I replied irately. I gave Al a hard look.

"Why, no, we wasn't!" he insisted. "Y'see Jan," he continued between draws on his clay pipe, "Sam ain't just a lousy card player, he's a horse thief, too."

"A moron can play this game," I grumbled, standing up. "C'mon, Jan, let's go see the rest of the fort."

"But I beat you at it, Sam," Al grinned through his whiskers. Just then a couple Boy Scouts stuck their heads through the open door and squinted at us in the near-dark.

"C'mon in!" Al hollered at them. "This hyar's trapper's quarters. Ya kin visit but ya can't stay." Half a dozen Boy Scouts cautiously entered and Al continued to shuffle the deck. "H'yar they come t' the Rocky Mountains, green as grass and soft as turnips," he quipped with a smile.

When Al was surrounded by little fellers in green he shot out, "Why you pilgrims dressed like that? Whose army you in they don't give ya cloth 'nuff fer long britches? What kinda porkeatin' Ned would wear britches cut off at the knee?"

"We're from Illinois and we're going to Philmont," one of the less intimidated scouts volunteered at last.

"You pilgrims are goin' t' go under," Al sadly informed them as he shook his head. "So what part a' Illiney country ya from?"

"Oak Park," the same scout replied.

"Never heard a it. Heard a Fort Dearborn, though. See, this is 1846 and you're in Bent's Fort . . ." He continued for ten minutes with his first-person rendition of life in the Rocky Mountains, Janet enjoying him thoroughly and the Boy Scouts appearing to be thoroughly confused. Al Hempstead was a for-real nineteenth-century trapper caught in a time warp; he took some getting used to by most folk.

As he wound down his talk, one of the Scouts asked, "Do you have a job?"

Al glared at the lad. Through his teeth he slowly replied, "*This* is my job. Beaver ain't primed up so to trap. Pil-grim," he drawled in a menacing tone.

"What do you do the rest of the year?" the same kid persisted.

Slowly and painfully Al replied through clenched teeth, "I trap beavers in the Rocky Mountains."

"Why?"

"Why?" he incredulously repeated, the frustration building inside him. "Why? Bee-cuzz—

'This child hates an American what hasn't seen Injuns skulped, or don't know a Ute from a Khian mokkerson. Sometimes he thinks a making tracks fer white settlement, but when he gets here to Bent's big lodge on the Arkansas, and sees the booshways and you miserable porkeaters from the States, how they roll thar eyes at an Injun yell—worse than if a village of Comanches was on 'em—and pick up a beaver trap, to ask what it is—just shows whar the niggurs had their brunging up—this child says—a little tabacca, if it's a plew a plug, an' Dupont an' Galena, a Green River or so, and he leaves for the Bayou Salade. Damn the white diggins while thar's meat in the mountains!' "*

Al sprang to his feet. "Whoopee!" he cried to Jan and me. "Are you for Touse?"

"That's a go, hoss," I confirmed with a smile.

"Yes!" cried Janet, enthused by his performance.

Then Al jumped toward the Boy Scouts and they quickly took a step back in fright. "Go on, git outta here. This here is trapper's quarters. You kin visit but ya can't stay. You've visited. So leave."

When the last Scout had exited I turned to Al and said, "I believe you do John Hatcher better than he did it hisownself."

Al smiled and lit his pipe. "I know, but I had to change the words around some." He puffed hard on his pipe as he got it going, and blew a wreath of smoke to the ceiling. "I'll call Rosita and tell her you two will be staying for supper."

We spent the rest of the morning touring the fort. Al carved off two hunks of buffalo meat from the skewer over the open fire and handed them to us. That tender and sweet meat—minus the

*The quote with which Al Hempstead assaulted the Boy Scouts can be found in its unaltered form in *Wah-to-Yah and the Taos Trail* by Lewis H. Garrard. First published in 1850, I used the quote without permission from the University of Oklahoma Press, Norman. They may sue me if they like. S.H.

chemicals found in processed beef—curbed my appetite. "It's better than beef," Janet said in surprise once she'd tasted it.

"Sure enough is," I agreed. "Just ain't no sixty million of 'em left anymore." Al got diverted and had to give a tour to a large group of German tourists, so I led Janet up to the southwest bastion. It was a clear, cloudless day. An old sorrel quarter horse contentedly munched hay in the corral below us while a nanny goat in need of milking stared at us stupidly from her perch atop the manger.

"Blaaat!" she croaked.

"Goats," I said, smiling, with a shake of my head. "The Mexicans can keep 'em." I put my right hand on the small swivel cannon mounted atop the bastion wall; my left hand lightly held Jan's. "So what do you think of Bent's Old Fort?"

"I love it, Sam. Just like I love the West. I never want to leave." She faced me then, and words can't describe the look on her face. It was a look that seemed to combine happiness and torture; her own pain went straight to my heart. Then I recalled what I'd brought her up there for.

I opened my shirt pocket and pulled out the little package I'd wrapped in brown paper. "I'd, uh, like you to have this, if you would," I quietly said as I handed her the square parcel.

Janet quickly unwrapped it and held up a beaded flint-and-steel carrying pouch, commonly known as a strike-a-lite pouch. I'd traded for it at a rendezvous a year or two earlier and had never used it. "It's lovely," she slowly said as she turned it over in her hand. "What's it for?"

"It's called a strike-a-lite pouch. The old mountaineers—and today's buckskinners—use 'em to carry flint and steel in. On the inside . . . there's a sentiment."

.Janet's fingers quickly untied the leather thong holding the flap. She pulled out the piece of paper I'd placed inside only after practicing my handwriting for an hour. She slowly read it out loud. " 'Follow your instincts. They are God's way of talking to you.' " She looked at me and whispered, "Thank you."

"My grandma used to say that." The air between us was charged with emotion; I had to do something to lighten up the atmosphere. I let out the huge breath I'd been holding and pointed off to the southwest. "Can you see the tops of the Spanish Peaks over there?"

"Yes," she replied softly.

"Well, Raton Pass is just forty miles to the south of 'em. The Santa Fe trains, they'd cross the river upstream from the fort, right in what's now downtown La Junta. Then they'd follow the Timpas, cross Raton, and bang! be in Santa Fe in nothing flat. Every time I come to Bent's Fort it's like going back in time a hundred and fifty years."

I rested our joined hands on top of the wall. Hers still held the pouch. "Close your eyes for a minute," I instructed her.

"What?"

"Go on, close 'em." She played along. "Okay, right under us the teamsters and packers are in the corral catching up critters. They got a late start and they're cussing a blue streak. Can you hear 'em?"

"Yes," Janet smiled, her eyes still closed. "Almost."

"To the northeast of us, up t'ward Sand Creek, the Arapaho are huntin'. They've stampeded the herd, Jan! A million buffler poundin' across the plains! Can you hear 'em?"

"Yes, I can!" Her face was a smile.

"And John Hatcher and Louy Simmonds are heading down the Picketwire—*El Rio de Las Animas Perdidas en Purgatorio*, Jan, the River of Lost Souls in Purgatory—and there Hatch is going to meet the old gentleman—that's the devil hisownself—and then him and Louy will shoot some meat and trap pelts and raise Cain in Taos. You want to go?"

Then she opened her eyes and her face glowed radiant-like. "Oh yes, Sam! Let's go!" We kissed then, just briefly. I remembered where I was in time.

Had Al Hempstead seen us he would have needled me to death. I wouldn't have cared, though.

By early afternoon the sun was baking the adobe walls of the fort and it was getting intolerable hot. We decided to take a casual walk down to the Arkansas River some two hundred yards distant. We found a shady, grassy spot under an ancient cottonwood where we could watch the river flow, and sat down. We made some more of that small talk—which I think I was getting better at—then Janet got serious.

"Can I ask you something, Sam?"

"Fire away," I replied as I fiddled with my pipe.

"Don't take this as an insult, but I'd like to know why you do what you do. Your friend Al Hempstead is a lot like you. You are both very intelligent; you could have careers in rewarding fields. You're living a dream by your trapping and mining—and obviously making it work—but you could do so much more. I'm just curious, I guess.''

''Well, hell, I've never thought much about it,'' I replied in surprise. I hadn't. ''It all just seemed to come natural. It ain't that I don't have any ambition, for the way I live a fella's got to be ambitious or go under. I guess, in a strange kind of way, it's important.''

''Important? How?''

''Maybe because we're keeping a little bit of the Old West alive. I guess that's why Bent's Old Fort is important, too. A hundred and fifty years ago this was a desolate and raw part of the world. It was inhabited mainly by rattlers and buffler and Indians. The man who came out here to trap beaver or freight goods to New Mexico was a breed apart from the average American at the time.

''Sure, a lot of 'em came out here with the profit motive in mind, just like some came out for the adventure, but the West cast its spell on them and changed them, and they in turn changed the West. They left their mark on it, all of 'em. I guess, maybe in a way, by doing what we're doing today we're honoring them, and keeping alive traditions and ways of living that shouldn't be lost.

''Jedediah Smith discovered South Pass and led the first group of Americans overland to California, yet his bones lie unburied and bleaching a hundred and fifty miles east of here. There's no marker over his grave 'cause it's never been found, and he had no direct descendants to keep him alive in memory. Few Americans have ever heard of him, and part of the reason is that there's no genial . . . genially . . .''

''Genealogical?''

''Yeah, genealogical—that's the word. There's no genealogical link between most people living today and the Rocky Mountain fur trade. Practically everybody had a great-grandfather in the Civil War; between 1822 and 1843 there was only a thousand mountaineers, and most of 'em died alone and hard. One of my ancestors supposedly come out with Nathaniel Wyeth in '32, and I've met a few of Kit Carson's and William Bent's descendants, but few Americans today got a biological link to that era. I think that's significant because a person's interest in history tends to be directly proportional to the way his ancestors participated in it. What I'm saying is that that period has either been forgotten or undiscovered by the masses, and it's a damned crying shame.

"Jim Beckwourth and Tom Fitzpatrick and Milton Sublette and John Hatcher—the list goes on and on, Jan. Brave men and fun-loving men; the men who found the passes so emigrants and later the railroads could bring their forms of progress to the West. The men who found water where there wasn't none, and put name to stream and waterhole so the cattlemen could drive their rangy stock north and the cavalry could round up the Indians without dying from thirst.

"If you want to get down to who was here first, it was the Indian. After him—in this part of the country, anyway—it was the Spaniards. But if you get down to the nuts and bolts of it, the Anglo who was here first—equipped only with the basic tools that were a product of the Industrial Revolution, and which gave him only a small amount of dependence on it—was the Rocky Mountain trapper."

Janet let out a deep breath. "That was quite a speech," she said with a smile. "I think I see now."

"I ain't done yet. You got me worked up. In a lot of ways, our society is like a ship without an anchor, or at least with an anchor that's dragging bad on the bottom. We've lost our grip on the past, and if you're going to know where you're going, you've got to know where you came from. Al Hempstead—he works at the fort interpreting the fur trade and the Santa Fe trade six months a year and traps the other six. Another friend of mine—lives in New Mexico—he's engaged in the Mexican trade and once a year goes to Chihuahua where he routinely gets threatened and shot at so he can bring back saddles and bits and spurs. Talk about the 1840s being alive? Oh, there's plenty of adventure out there. And there's another friend of mine, a full-time mountaineer. Everything he owns he carries on two pack-horses, and he rides the width and length of the West trapping and hunting and showing people what a mountaineer was and is. Is he rich? Naw, he ain't that. But he does give to folks an understanding of the era of the Rocky Mountain fur trade, and thereby maybe makes somebody's life today a little richer. Oh yes indeed, that he does, and when he crosses over *all the trumpets will sound*, at least if Bridger and Fitzpatrick have anything to say about it. I never thought about it much till right now, but all of a sudden what he does seems damned important.

"So maybe we're what they call 'living historians,' Jan. Maybe some would call us living anchorisms, I don't know. I can get along in society, or I can get along in the mountains and on the plains. I wouldn't call me a misfit, 'cause I can fit in when I want to, just like I wouldn't call Philo or Al or Jeff or Charlie a misfit, because we can fall into place when we choose. But we're all good at what we do, we enjoy doing it, and maybe someplace along the line we're keeping a little bit of Americana alive, and *that* seems damned important."

Janet looked solemnly into my eyes. "You're a very intense man. And a very eloquent man when you choose to be."

I put my hands on her shoulders. "And you're a very intelligent and lovely lady. I care about you so much I could bust." Then we kissed and held each other in the shadow of a crooked cottonwood tree and listened to the Arkansas River flow down. I managed to keep myself from getting carried away in full public view, and soon it was time for Al to get off work and us to head to his place for supper.

Jan and Rosita Hempstead was thick as thieves five minutes after they met. Jan went into the kitchen and helped Rosita with supper while Al and me shot the breeze. Robert and George sat cross-legged on the floor while Martha, Al's six-year-old daughter, played with a doll on the couch.

"So anyhow," Al continued, "last March during winter quarters we had this city feller who wanted to learn how to trap beavers."

From the kitchen Rosita yelled, "Al, are you telling that story *again*?"

"So *any*how," he continued with a grin, ignoring the comment, "I took him down to the river and showed him how to make a good scented set. You know, drive the pole down in the mud, and set the trap just so in six inches of water with the scent stick over it."

"Yep," I agreed. "I've done that a time or two myself."

"So I let him make the set." Al smiled. He paused and got

his pipe going. "Well now, winter quarters is what they call 'high visibility' over at the fort, so I had to make sure he caught one. So that night I took a beaver I'd froze solid for such occasion out of the freezer and headed down to the river. Stuck a front leg in that trap, then came home and went to bed." Jan and Rosita had come into the living room and were listening, Jan intently, Rosita shaking her head in mock disgust.

"So *any*how," he continued, smiling at his wife, "that next morning I woke up this city feller and we walked down to the river. Well, sir, he saw that dead beaver in the trap and jumped in clothes and all, up to his knees in that freezing cold water. 'I caught a beaver!' he hollered, 'I caught a beaver!'

"Then he held that critter up, and doggone if I didn't like to fall over. 'Look!' he cried, 'his back legs are wired together!' See, I'd done that to make him easier to carry, and forgot to take the wire off. He said, 'What do you suppose happened to him?'

"Well, sir, I just scratched my beard and said, 'Well, b'golly, it looks like a gangland execution to me!' "

After I quit guffawing—Jan laughed politely—we sat down to supper. Jan sat next to me and Martha sat to her other side. Jan mothered over her and made sure she had enough beans and vermicelli and chicken. She sure looked comfortable with that little girl.

Al and me talked mostly about his mules—he had two—and fall trapping and hunting. Later, when the cantaloupe was gone and the dishes done, we adjourned to the living room. Al occupied his reclining chair and puffed on his pipe while Robert and George played checkers at his feet.

"Y'know, Sam," he began in his low, slow voice, "sometimes I get plumb tired of the fort. Like today with them Boy Scouts. It ain't the dumb questions the tourists ask—you can't blame 'em for that. It's their attitude, or some of 'em, anyway. Everything from 'Hey, Buffalo Bill, how many Injuns you kill today?' to 'How could anybody live like this?' and 'My thirty-ot six is better than that thing.' Seems to this coon the people in this country are preoccupied with violence, but durned few have ever seen any of it. Others are comfort-driven, and know-it-alls to boot. I don't know much 'bout anything 'cept critters

and the fur trade and the Santa Fe trade, but at least *I* admit it.''
He slowly shook his head and got his pipe going again.

"I don't know if I could pull off that routine the way you do,''
I commented as I lit my own pipe. Jan and Rosita were still in
the kitchen talking about who knowed what. From her little table
in the corner where she was coloring, little Martha looked up at
me and smiled. I winked back at her.

"So, the fort wants us to do first-person interpretive history.
Replicate the past through the gear and clothes and speech,
b'golly. Durned if some of the tourists couldn't care . . .'' His
voice trailed off and the trace of a smile creased his weathered
face.

"Madre! Por favor venir aquí! he cried as he jumped out of
his chair. "I've got an idea, b'golly.'' He grinned as he puffed
furiously on his pipe.

The ladies appeared in the living room with puzzled looks on
their faces.

"Que?'' asked Rosita.

"What we'll do is this—'' He grinned. "Living history, heh-
heh. We'll hire a dozen outta-work Comanche fellers, then fix
up the maintenance shed for 'em.'' The maintenance shed was
out near the main road, five hundred yards from the fort. "Then
we'll hook up an alarm system running from the fort to the
shed.'' Rosita and Jan were amused if not confused.

"Well, sir, say it's been a bad day and this tourist family has
been giving us a hard time. You know, the wife is saying''—he
threw his voice in what he considered an imitation of a nagging
wife—'Lester, let's go to our motel and have a martini,' and the
young girl says, 'I wanna go to Disneyland' and the teenage
boy, b'golly, he says, 'Dad, I wanna go get high.' Well, sir,
what I do then is walk over to the wall and press the hidden
buzzer.''

"Well, them Comanche fellers are sitting around the maintenance shed playing cards and drinking sodas when the alarm
goes off. Then, b'golly, they run out, jump on their war ponies,
and take off with hoofs a-flyin' for the gate!

"Hi-yi-yi-yi!'' he yipped, waving his arms. He was no longer
Al Hempstead, he was a Comanche warrior dashing across the
plains. Rosita just shook her head but Jan was watching him in
wide-eyed amazement.

"And as they ride up—*Hi-yi-yi-yi*—the old man gets an arrer in the throat! *Thunk!*" Al became the tourist father, and fell to his knees clutching the pretended arrow, all the while making gurgling sounds.

He jumped up. "Then the teenage boy says, 'This is all fake,' and a Comanche rides up, impales him on a lance, and pitches him over the wall! *Hi-yi-yi-yi!*" Al was now the Comanche, and gestured heaving the skewered kid over the wall.

"And then, b'golly," he roared, hisownself animated, "a brave jumps down off his pony, scalps the old man, waves the bloody scalp at the old lady—*Hi-yi-yi-yi!*—and throws it in her face!" He was getting out of breath and the boys were rolling on the floor laughing. I wasn't far behind them, but Rosita just succeeded in looking disgusted while Jan was thoroughly amused.

"And then, by golly," he slowly said, accenting each word, "when that tourist family goes back to Cleveland, Ohio, and the neighbors ask, 'What happened to Lester and Billy?' the old lady can say, 'Well, b'golly, they participated in living history at Bent's Old Fort!'"

I fell off the davenport laughing, and weakly beat the floor with my fists. When Robert could finally talk, tears rolling down his face, he cried, "Aw, Dad, you're kidding!" Jan smiled and looked pretty, and the expression on her face told me she'd never before heard a yarn like that.

As we recovered Al calmly raised a kitchen match to his pipe and took his chair. Rosita half smiled and lightly tapped a spatula in the palm of her hand. "Al, keep this up and I'm going to take you to the Pueblo booby hatch," she warned with a smile.

"Oh shucks, oh dear," he replied good-naturedly.

After a few more stories—not quite as dynamic—it was time for Jan and me to leave. The Hempstead family escorted us out to my truck.

"So, are you folks going to be down for the rendezvous?" Al asked me.

"I dunno, Al. I guess it depends on Jan's schedule. When is it?"

"Second week in September," he answered. I thought, "This is just grand. Jan is supposed to be married by then."

She surprised me. "Oh, let's go!" she exclaimed. "That would be so much fun!" I about fell over in amazement but managed not to let it show in my face. I think in all the excitement Jan had actually forgotten about the wedding, one, or planned on calling it off. Things was looking good for the home team.

"Yeah, come on down," Rosita chimed in.

Then Jan pursed her lips in thought. "But I don't have anything to wear from that period."

"Oh, that's all right," Rosita smiled as she took her arm. "The next time you and Sam come down I'll get out my frontier dress patterns and we'll make you a costume in an afternoon."

"That would be so much fun." Jan looked at me steadily, her eyes aglow.

"Sure 'nuff," Al added. "You can stay in the lodge with us. There's plenty of room, and if there ain't, why, we'll just throw Sam in the river!"

"Al!" Rosita exclaimed. Then she turned to Jan. "Honest to Pete. Men!" She shook her head.

Then Jan's hand found mine and she smiled into my eyes. "They certainly are," she agreed.

On the way home Jan wanted to know all about the Hempstead family. "It doesn't appear they have much," she concluded.

"Well, shucks," I replied as I hit third, slowing for the only stoplight in Rocky Ford, "that depends on what you call much. They've always got enough to eat and good clothes for the kids. Al works hard at trapping when he's not in the fort. A man does what he has to, to stay in the Rocky Mountains."

"Does he trap with you and your friends?" she asked.

"Nope. He's a family man and likes to stay closer to home. But he sure brings in the pelts."

Jan was getting quiet on me; she wasn't the same bubbly gal she'd been ten minutes before. After a bit she said, "Martha is so sweet."

"They're all good kids, Jan," I replied. Then I smiled at her. "Martha was born in a tipi."

"No!"

"Sure thing. They was living in a tipi lodge up in South Park.

That was before Al had the job at the fort. Martha seems to have survived it good enough.''

''My goodness.''

''I told you Rosita was quite a gal. She has true grit, you know.'' I smiled, and was going to add, ''Just like somebody else I know,'' but she didn't meet my gaze and quickly looked out the window at a passing cornfield.

I couldn't figure out why she suddenly looked so sad.

8

IT WAS SEVEN miles before Jan spoke again. I know—I was watching the odometer.

"We haven't talked about Donald," she said in a monotone as she stared straight ahead. Donald was the son of a bitch—I mean the young gentleman—to whom she was engaged. Donald may have been a number-one dude in the eyes of the world, but he was the enemy to me.

"Well, what's there to say about him?" I asked, trying not to sound sarcastic. It was hard for me to act like I cared about the man whose throat I would happily cut if that meant Janet and I could be together.

"He's about an inch taller than you are," she quietly droned, still looking ahead. "He's not as open as you are, yet he cares about me in his own way."

"What does that mean?"

"He's just different from you. But my—parents—and the rest of my family—approve of him."

"Yeah," I said with a forced smile, "they might not trip the light fantastic if you dragged me home."

"Oh, I don't know." She smiled. There was a long pause.

"So do you?"

"What?"

"Approve of him."

"I'm engaged to him, Sam."

"You're evadin' the question."

85

She didn't answer, and we both looked straight ahead as I drove on in silence. I could just about picture it: Donald had a nice income and security. He would make major in five or six years, and, since he commanded a desk and a platoon of filing cabinets in the Adjutant Generals Corps, he would never know the glory of getting rocketed, mortared, shelled, or shot at. Even if the balloon went up, he'd have a cushy rear-area job; as usual, the grunts would do the dying. Every evening, prior to heading to the club to see what shapes, sizes, and colors of poontang were available, he'd sit down and write Janet a letter and tell her how much he loved her and be sure not to let the car insurance premium go unpaid. If Donald had been an infantryman or artilleryman I would have had some respect for him, but a REMF? Forget it. You can't bullshit me—I've been there.

There didn't seem to be a hell of a lot for either of us to say, so to break the silence I put on a tape. As I punched it in, the rapid, frenzied beat of another time came blasting over my truck speakers. After a four-bar organ lead-in, the famous singer began "Light My Fire" in his high, sweet voice.

After Jim Morrison finished the second refrain I turned the volume down for the rest of the uncut, seven-minute version. Janet lightly tapped her foot to the beat and, when the classic song was over, finally spoke.

"What group was that?"

"*What!*" I gasped. "That's Jim Morrison and the Doors. "Light My Fire" is one of the rock classics of all time. It was the number-three hit in 1967."

"Oh. I was only nine then."

I thought, "Oh, shitfire—I was in high school!"

"Oh," I said.

"My parents, especially my father, felt it was the work of the devil. They rarely let me listen to it." I didn't bother telling her that her parents, especially her father, were full of it.

"Well, I know that's what some people say about it today; I don't know, I don't listen to the modern stuff. But sixteen, seventeen years ago it reflected the times, which in fact were most hairy."

"Are the Doors still going?"

"I think they packed it in when Jim Morrison died."

"He's dead?"

"He died of a drug overdose in 1971. He was a casualty."

"A casualty? Of drugs?"

"I guess. That's what they say killed him, anyway. But the 1960s sealed a lot of people's fate." For the first time, I realized there was a hell of a generation gap between Janet and myself, yet we was only separated by eight years. How would she ever learn of the hundreds of people and places, and the thousands of incidents, that had shaped my life? I couldn't consciously dredge it all up from memory if I wanted to, and it suddenly occurred to me that even if we married and stayed together always, the first thirty-odd years of my life would be pretty much a blank to her. No, I wouldn't deliberately hide anything; that wouldn't be fair. I just had a lot of years and a lot of miles behind me, and there was no way she would ever know the half of it.

Silence again took over in the cab of my truck. Then out of nowhere Janet half smiled and said, "I'd like to have goats, just like Rosita Hempstead."

"Them smelly, yakkin' old things?" I replied in surprise. Then the significance of what Janet had said occurred to me: was she saying what I thought she was saying? I didn't know how to respond.

"Well, we'll have to get down to the Wah-to-Yah someday soon," I told her, pointing toward the distant Spanish Peaks. "I'd like to show you my land."

"I would enjoy that, Sam."

Another period of disturbing calm set over my outfit. I stuck a Marty Robbins tape in the deck to break the silence.

"You like all kinds of music, don't you, Sam?"

"Pretty much; yeah." I decided to try a different tack. I pointed to the mountains due west of us. Sunset was coming and they had that look to 'em. "Alpenglow," I said.

"What?"

"The reddish haze cast on the mountains at sunset time. It's called alpenglow. Ain't it some?" I asked in hope.

"Yes, they're so pretty."

So much for purple mountains' majesty. Jan didn't say another word until I was almost to her place. I didn't neither. I was trying to figure out what was going on, myownself.

When I was almost to Janet's apartment house she shot out,

"Oh, Sam, this weekend has been so wonderful I wish it could last another day!"

"Me too," I replied. For some reason I can't explain, that sounded like a peculiar thing for her to say. Maybe it was the way she said it. At another time it would have fit, and it should have been music to my ears. It just didn't sound right at the time.

I pulled to a stop in the paved lot behind Jan's apartment house and switched off the key.

"You don't have to see me to the door," she said as she swiftly exited my truck.

"I sure do," I shot back, getting out. I tried to make small talk on the way to her door, but Jan was intent on getting inside that apartment and had no thought for me.

When we reached the door she had the key out. As she unlocked the door she half turned and said, "It's been wonderful, Sam. Good night." She swiftly opened the door, ducked in, and shut it in my face without another word.

I stood dumbly on the landing, trying to figure out what had happened. Then I slowly walked down the steps.

I reached the bottom of the stairs, took one more step, and stopped dead in my tracks. A horrible feeling ran through my entire body. I knowed right there and then that Jan was never going to see me again. I could just tell. It's now or never, I thought. The knowledge of what I had to do petrified me; it scared me as nothing before in my life.

I looked up to the clouds and said, "Help."

Then I pulled my hat down low, like I always wear it, turned around, and ran back up the stairs taking them two at a time.

I knocked once, then opened the door. Jan was hanging up her light summer jacket in the hall closet, and when she turned and looked at me she had the most terrified look on her face I'd ever seen on a woman. I shut the door behind me, locked my hands in my rear pants pockets, and began.

"Look, Jan, I can't take this much longer and I don't think you can, either." She just clenched that jacket in her hands, her knuckles turning white, and stared at me. She knowed what was coming.

"Jan, I love you. I want to marry you," I said in a firm voice that surprised even me. She stayed frozen, her hands clutching the light jacket, her eyes riveted on mine.

"Look, Jan," I continued, "you and me—why, I knowed I loved you the first time I saw you. I don't know how; I just did. I felt like I'd known you from before, or all my life. We may be different some, but we're oh so much alike."

"But why?" she asked, her voice a whisper.

"Aw geez, you mean you don't know why I love you?" I asked, not believing she couldn't have known. She slowly shook her head.

"Why, Jan, you're the finest person I ever met. And I like you so. You can't love somebody without liking 'em, and we, why, we're like old friends. And you're smart as a whip and common as an old shoe and—why, you're just you."

"But I don't love you," she softly said.

"Aw, don't worry about it—that'll come. You'll learn to love me, and even if you don't, that's okay, too. Shoot, Jan, we're both smart in our own ways and hard workers, and you're almost as full of the dickens as I am. And don't worry about money. I've got a little nest egg tucked away, and my land's all paid for, and we'll put up an adobe house—or a log house! Then I'll use my GI Bill and go to horseshoeing school and . . ."

I was running out of things to say. There I was, fighting for my future with the woman I loved—and the woman I knowed loved me—and I was stumped. Then I remembered what I'd forgotten. "And we'll have kids—a bunch of 'em, seven or eight, anyhow! Or just as few as you want. And don't worry about furniture. I got all my grandfolks' furniture stored at my sister's place. Well, it is some sixty years old, but it's good furniture all the same. And there will always be food on the table and I will never abuse you. I promise that, Jan."

Her eyes was filling with tears.

Then something else hit me. "You mean nobody ever told you why you're so special?" I asked, not believing nobody ever hadn't.

"No," she whispered, blinking her eyes and slowly shaking her head.

"Why," I drawled, purely outraged, "them miserable SOBs." Then tears overwhelmed Janet's eyes and she let go with

a sob that I felt work its way up from her middle to her throat.
I pulled her tight to me.

"Oh, it's okay, honey," I softly said in her ear as I patted her
back. Her body shook and shook with violent sobs, and I talked
real soft and gentle in her ear, just as I would to Molly when
she'd been bad spooked.

"There, there, honey," I quietly whispered. "Let it all come
out. You've got a friend here, you do for a fact." Janet cried
violently, and I didn't feel so great myself.

After five minutes—it could have been ten, I don't know—
she slowed down the sobbing. She backed away from me a few
inches and looked me in the eyes, her own deep brown eyes red
and heavy with tears. "You're a wonderful man," she softly
said with a smile.

"Aw shucks," I replied, purely flattered. I've been called a
heap of things in my day; nobody had ever accused me of that
before. "Well, what say we get hitched? I'm ready, right now."
I smiled, and held her lightly by the waist.

"Give me a couple of days to think it over," she softly replied.

"Sure thing." I smiled. Then I pulled out my faded blue
bandanna and wiped away her tears. I carefully dabbed her eyes,
then wiped her nose. After that night I put that bandanna away
in a plastic bag and placed it in the bottom of a saddlebag. I
reckoned that way I would always have a remembrance of the
night I asked the woman I loved to marry me. That old bandanna
stayed in its honored place until a day not too long ago when an
emergency I never would have thought possible in my wildest
dreams come up and I ruined it. But that evening, as Janet and
I looked hard into each other's eyes, there was no foretelling the
future, except with her. I know I felt right good about myself
that night. It ain't too often a man gets to be a hero in his own
eyes, but that evening I was. I had done the noblest thing ever
in my life and was right proud of myself.

Then I took my hat off—which I'd forgotten to remove when
I'd proposed—and kissed her long and hard. She kissed me back
passionate-like and we pressed our bodies close together.

"I'd better be leaving now," I said. I pulled her closer to me
and made no effort to depart.

She put her hands on my shoulders and pushed me back a

couple inches. I couldn't quite read the look in her eyes. "You don't have to go, Sam," she said softly.

"You sure?"

"Yes."

I kissed her again deep and hard. Even as I kissed her I removed the jacket from her hand and tossed it in the closet. Then I picked her up and carried her to the bedroom.

I gently set Janet down on the bed and started to undress. She did likewise, but before she got her blouse off she said, "Sam, the lights. Please turn them off."

"Why? I kinda like seeing what I'm doing." I smiled.

"Please?"

"Oh well, have it your way," I sighed as I killed the lights. Then we wrapped ourselves in each other's arms and gave our bodies one to the other.

That night I learned one of the most important lessons in my life. I learned the difference between having sex and making love, and for the first time ever I felt honestly needed and loved.

Because of Janet Provost I discovered romantic love and became a whole man.

I would not let her go without one hell of a fight.

THE NEXT DAY was Monday. Bright and early that morning, Jack Riley and me jumped in Luke's old Ford pickup and headed for the grain elevator to get a load of feed.

"Whar was you all weekend?" Jack asked through his gums even as I pulled out of the driveway.

"Just 'out,' Jack. Where we goin', Calhan feed mill?"

"Uh-huh," he replied as he stuck a Pall Mall between shriveled lips. He lit up and said, "You an' thet girl must be serious." When I didn't answer he gave me a hard look; I ignored the stare and concentrated on the deserted road.

"Luke was lookin' fer ya yestiday." He squinted at me through blue cigarette smoke.

"That's too bad. I was gone."

"Ah knowed," he agreed with a nod. "Thet's what ah tolt Luke." He peered around the truck as though he expected to find somebody looking in on us, reached under the seat, and pulled out a half-full pint of whiskey. Before I could say anything he unscrewed the cap and took several mighty swallows. He licked his chops, then offered me the bottle.

"Ker fer a snort?"

"Sure, Jack," I replied. I grabbed the bottle, unscrewed the cap, rolled down my window, and pitched the firewater in the ditch.

"Sam! What fer ya do thet?" he cried in dismay. "Thet was breakfast!"

"I told you before: Luke said I was to keep you on the wagon. I ain't going to contribute to the delinquency of no senior citizen."

"Ah won't fergit this, Sam," he warned. He tried to effect a sneer.

"Sure, Jack." I laughed. Jack Riley was a likable enough old boy, drunk or sober, and I wasn't worried about him getting even. Besides, in a day the incident would be ancient history. I doubted Jack could recollect what he'd had for supper the night before, if, that is, he'd eaten any supper.

By the time we got back from the grain elevator and shoveled out the four-way horse feed, it was lunchtime. I was sitting on the steps of my shack eating a balogna sandwich and beans when I heard Luke's booming voice getting near. A few seconds later he walked into view. He was escorting a guy dressed in army fatigues.

"Howdy, General," I pleasantly remarked to Luke as the pair strolled past. Luke stopped dead in his tracks, as did the army feller, and stared at me hard. The army feller had a silver oak leaf on his cap, and that told me he was a light colonel.

"Sam, why d'ya hurt me lak that?" Luke pleaded.

"Like how?"

"You know ah was only a sar'ent first class. Why d'ya make fun a the service, an' me helpin' this fine officer find a horse for his boys at thet?"

I let out a sigh. "I reckon I just can't control myself, Luke. Besides, I never found a hell of a lot to laugh at there. Guess I'm just making up for lost time." The light colonel was a squat guy with spit-shined boots and a whitewall haircut. His collar insignia showed he was a transportation officer. The name tape over his right pocket announced his handle in inch-high embroidered letters as GATES. All of that should have struck a chord with me, but it didn't. His penetrating blue eyes would have bored a hole through a bulkhead.

"Sam heah's goin' with a girl from Fort Carson," Luke offered by way of revenge. "Hit's pretty serious."

"That a fact, bubba?" the sawed off, crew-cut lifer fired.

"Yeah. That's a fact. And my name ain't 'bubba,' Field Marshal." The colonel turned about six shades of purple and his eyes got as big as saucers. His eyes was easy to read: he loathed me. Well, that was fine with me; I'd taken my last ration of shit off of military officers several years earlier.

"Maybe she's in yer battalion, pardner." Luke smiled as he grabbed the colonel's arm. I leaned back against my shack and stirred my can of beans, but when I glanced up and read the colonel's name tape I about choked on a mouthful. I then recalled the name from conversations I'd had with Jan. The Napoléan standing in front of me *was* Jan's battalion commander.

"Maybe," the colonel sneered.

"I doubt it," I steadily replied. I tried to act disinterested as I stirred the beans.

"I am just curious. Who are you that you can't respect the uniform?"

"Oh, I respect the uniform good enough. It's just some of the SOBs with brass on their collars who don't think they put on their britches one leg at a time."

"What qualifies you to have that opinion?" he shot back like he was addressing one of his privates.

"Getting shot at."

Luke gave the colonel's arm a hard tug. "We'd bettah git goin' an' look at horses, sir." The colonel didn't budge. He wanted more, and I picked up on the cue.

"It was all lies," I continued. "The colonels lied to the generals and the generals lied to Johnson and Nixon. 'Course, I doubt you was a colonel at that time."

"No," he seethed. Then he said through his teeth, "Give me an example, young man." He was sure a glutton for punishment.

"Okay. The Vietnamization program, or whatever the hell they called it. The 'namese was going to fight their own war and us ease out of it; they was winning. I read that in *Stars & Stripes* one morning, where Nixon said how swell it was working. Well, somebody should have informed old Charlie and Luke of that, 'cause the same day, a good pal of mine—a boat coxswain like myself—had half a dozen palettes of ammo on board and ate a RPG for lunch. Out of nowhere. Blowed one hell of a hole in the water."

"We couldn't round up every individual rocket in that country," the colonel informed me like I was stupid or something.

"Sure. I probably took it too personal." Both Luke and the

colonel just glared at me, so I added, "Eventually I figured out the Vietnamization program was a total flop."

"When was that?" the colonel quickly asked. Military people have always talked too fast for my money.

"April thirtieth, '75."

"What happened thet day?" Luke asked as though he should remember.

"Saigon fell."

They looked at each other, then looked at me. After the longest pause Luke said, "C'mon, pard. Ah've got a four-year-olt buckskin yer boys will really like." I stood there stirring my beans, and watched them walk off.

The next day was Tuesday. Jan's two days was up. I didn't call; I waited till she'd be home from work and went over.

"Howdy." I smiled as she opened the door.

"Hello, Sam." She didn't greet me with her pretty full-face smile; it was what I'd have to describe as a near smile, or maybe a wistful smile.

I turned down her offer of coffee and we both sat down on the davenport. I took her hand in mine and gave it a small squeeze. "Everything okay?"

"It's a complicated life, Sam."

"Aw, no, it ain't, Jan. It's the good guys against the bad guys. I been aiming to get a white hat, myself."

"Or the tourists versus the 'Comanche fellers'?" We both had a good laugh and I used the opportunity to put my arm around her strong shoulders and pull her close.

"I love you, Jan."

She turned her head and looked me in the eye. "I don't love you yet, Sam," she softly said.

Yet. A key word. I knowed I was winning right there and then. I suppressed a smile.

"That's okay, pal," I casually replied.

Then Jan changed the subject on me. "My roommate is coming back in a week." Jan had mentioned earlier that she had a female roommate who was on temporary duty someplace else in the States.

"Well, what'll that change?"

"She knows Donald."

"Have you told him about us?"

"No."

"Is she a stool pigeon?"

"She wouldn't say anything." A long pause. "I don't think."

I thought, "Oh, hell's bells!" I said, "Well, I hope not. It's none of her business nohow."

Janet pulled away from me, half turned on the cushion, and faced me nose-to-nose. "If we got married, would Philo and Joe live with us?" she shot out. I wondered where in the hell that question had come from. I hadn't even pondered my partners' fate.

"Geez, I dunno. I mean, we've been together a lot of years and I hate to see us split up. They're going to help us build our house, you know." Actually, I hadn't asked them yet, but I reckoned they would. Then something else hit me and I added, "They don't got anybody but me."

"They don't *have* anybody but me," she corrected.

"Yeah. I dunno, Jan," I replied, genuinely puzzled.

"Perhaps they could build their own house on your land," she suggested.

"They could?" I was surprised.

"That would be all right with me," she said with a slow nod of her head.

"Geez, that's . . . great," I said with a sigh. Janet Provost was proving to be some kind of woman. I was so proud of her for being so decent and kind I could have busted right there.

Then she fired from a different direction. "Would you want me to work?" I hadn't thought about that, either. This marriage stuff was turning out to be a hell of a lot more complicated than I'd suspected.

"Well, I . . . I dunno," I stalled, thinking fast. "I mean, my ma always worked. My grandma worked." Jan would have to work for a while; that was the long and short of it. I was trying to figure out a way to tell her that. The Hawkins women always pitched in when times was hard, and to be honest about it, they was never that good. "My great-grandma ran a restaurant in a little town on the Missouri River. Then in 1910 a Texican cow-puncher came up with a trainload of steers and got drunk and shot daylight through the sheriff. He was an old Civil War vet-eran and tried to shoot back, but his old cap-and-ball six-gun misfired. They hauled him into my great-grandma's restaurant and tried to dig the bullets out of him, but he died." I was stalling; I didn't know if Jan wanted to work or not.

"What happened to the Texan?" she inquired, only mildly interested.

"Oh. As I understand it, the people waited till he was out of cartridges and his shootin' spree come to an end. Then a mob formed up and took him to the livery stable and hanged him from a rafter. You might say he joined his dead confederates shortly thereafter in the hereafter, heh-heh."

Jan almost smiled, then said in an even voice, "Well, do you want me to work or not?"

"I don't have enough money to build the house, and we'd have to go against my grain and borrow some, so how 'bout until the house is paid off, which should only be a few years?" I shot it out in one breath, hoping mightily.

"That would be all right with me," she answered. "Besides, I don't think I could stand sitting around a house all day." Without letting up she attacked again. "Do you want me to have children right away?"

"Well, I—"

"Donald wants to have children right away. I told him I don't want children immediately." She cocked an eyebrow and gave me a look I can only describe as pained. "I don't know if I want them at all, Sam."

"Why, you'd want to have them with me."

"Why?"

" 'Cause I love you. And you love me, but you won't admit it or don't know it yet. They'd be great kids, Jan. And I'll blow my own horn here by adding I'd make a damn good father. I've got some experience at leadership myself, you know." She almost smiled, but turned her head away from mine and fixed her gaze at an imaginary point on the far wall.

At length she said, "I don't know about any of this, Sam."

"Well, look, how about— Look, Jan, you don't have to make up your mind right now. I figured you'd have an answer tonight . . . but . . . how about we just say 'no more deadlines.' I mean, think it over for a while, then you can tell me." I didn't know what else to say. Then I put my arm around her and pulled her tight. A small smile creased her lips and she slowly nodded her head. "All right, I will."

"Marry me?" I shot out, hoping hard.

She grinned then and poked me in the ribs. "I said I'll think it over some more, wise guy. You stinker." The smile quickly faded from her face as an apparently disturbing thought occurred to her. She turned her head away and gazed at that same damned point on the wall she'd studied earlier.

"About the other night, Sam . . ." Her voice trailed off.

"Well, what about it?" I put my hand on her chin and turned her face to mine. "You ain't feeling guilty or something?"

"I feel—I don't know what I feel," she softly answered. "I am engaged," she added in a low voice that was almost a groan.

Now if I had been undiplomatic, which I ain't, I would have told Janet that at that very moment good old Donald was probably shacked up with some honeysan. I would have also told her that once she and Donald got married, as soon as he was out of the AO he would unzip his pants and stick his dick in anything female. Out of all the sailors and marines I'd served with, maybe one out of fifty was faithful to his wife. I wasn't a monk either, but it wasn't like I had anyone keeping the home fires burning. Had there been a woman waiting for me ten thousand miles away, I would have remained true; I think I have enough self-control to do that. I could be all wet: maybe I just happened to serve with the largest collection of sex maniacs ever assembled in the armed forces of the United States, but I highly doubt it.

"Look, Jan, you want out of this engagement, right?"

No answer. A poker-faced stare, and not a blink of the eye.

"I love Donald," she said woodenly. I didn't believe her; her eyes lied. I had the fleeting thought that she was being railroaded into this marriage, but I quickly disregarded it.

"And you love me?"

"I am very attracted to you. I . . ." She gulped and looked down at her lap. "I wouldn't expect the man I married to remain faithful to me."

"Well, that's one hell of a goddamned thing to say!" I exploded before I could edit the swearwords in my mind. "What we did the other night has nothing to do with being married, 'cause you ain't. You made a tentative deal and now you want out of it bad, and I'm trying to help you out of it."

That last statement of Jan's was a major clue—although I didn't see it at the time—and I should have knowed right there that something was radically wrong.

"Why are you so irate?" she asked calmly.

" 'Cause I expect the woman *I* marry to stay faithful to me! Are you saying you expect a full license to screw around?"

"No. I didn't say that. I wouldn't be unfaithful."

"This conversation isn't making one hell of a lot of sense to me." I wanted to change the subject, but mostly I wanted to get out of there.

I had an idea. "If we leave now, we can catch the old movie playing at the Bijou." The Bijou was a theater in town that showed mostly old classics.

"What's the show?" she inquired, only mildly interested.

"*The Man Who Shot Liberty Valence*. I haven't seen it for twenty years. Ever see it?"

"No. Who's in it and what's it about?"

"Well, Liberty Valance—that's Lee Marvin—he's a bad hombre and the second toughest man south of the Purgatory. They call it the Picketwire in the movie, and I've heard it both ways: Purgatory and Picketwire. Anyway, John Wayne is Tom Doniphan and he *is* the toughest man south of the Purgatory, but he don't shoot Valance straight off. That'd ruin the story. Then Jimmy Stewart shows up as a lawyer named Stoddard and he screws up everything."

"How does he do that?"

"You'll see." Then I gently pulled Janet's head within inches of mine. "Did I ever tell you your teeth are so white they bring to mind snow-capped mountain peaks?"

"No." She smiled. Then I pulled her to me and kissed that pretty mouth. And her cheeks. And her neck. Then Janet sprang up from that davenport like she was spring-loaded. "Let's go to the movie, Romeo."

I let out a long sigh. "Oh shucks, oh dear."

We arrived and took our seats just as the main titles were running, and as the story began to unwind I sat through it petrified. To my mind there was too many parallels that could be drawn between that story and my own situation. It was too close to my own life for comfort. I gently took Jan's hand as we walked out of the theater into the cool June air and strolled down Tejon Street.

"Well, what did you think of the movie?" I hoped she wasn't going to refer to the romantic disaster that befell Tom Doniphan in the story.

"I think the theme is simple," she stated, looking down at the sidewalk. "The West outgrew men like Tom Doniphan. And when Hallie married Rans Stoddard, Doniphan gave up on life. It was quite sad, really. What do you think?"

"Well, in the first place you're wrong, Janet."

"I am?"

"Yeah. The West will never outgrow men like Tom Doniphan, not so long as decency and guts and honor count for something. In the second place, I think the wrong man got all the credit and the ensuing glory for shooting Valance. He also got the girl. But I don't think Tom Doniphan gave up on life."

"You don't?"

"Nope. I think he was just wore out. Let's have a spot of tea," I said as I guided Janet by the arm to a nearby cafe door.

She stopped me in the doorway. "What else do you think about the film?"

"I think John Ford had people and life pegged. And I also think I'm hungry; let's have something to eat."

Instead of taking Jan straight home I detoured by way of Garden of the Gods. I parked by Balanced Rock and we perched ourselves on the same little knoll we'd sat on a couple weeks earlier. Only an occasional car passed beneath us. The clear night air carried to us the voices of a man and woman giggling and carrying on. It sounded like they had found a secluded spot a couple of hundred yards away and was in the process of enjoying life's greatest pleasure. I leaned back and rested my head in my hands.

Janet layed down next to me and put her head on my arm. "Sam, can I ask you something?"

I had no inkling of what was coming. Between our earlier conversation and the movie I was tuckered out. "Ask away, pard," I replied, looking up at the stars.

"What if I told you some things?"

"What kind of things?"

"Just . . . things."

"Well, I wouldn't run out and blab 'em around, I reckon." In my own defense, I did not anticipate at that time I would ever put this story to paper. If somebody had told me that then, I would have laughed.

"Did I ever tell you I took a year off between high school and college?" She perked up her voice when she said that; she said it real cheery-like.

"Oh. That's interestin'," I said, not too interested. Lots of people do that. "You work or something for that year?"

"Yes. I did that. Sam . . ."

"Yes, my dear?" That phrase always sounded corny to me before, but with Janet it came out so natural, I didn't think nothing about it. I pulled her close and kissed her on the forehead.

"Sam," she began again, "you have never talked much about your past. Do you have anything to hide?"

I saw no point in discussing barroom fights, whores knowed and forgotten, or the wild female I got tangled up with in Sydney. As far as I was concerned, the past—hers and mine—just didn't have no bearing on our future together.

"Well, I don't use dope, I didn't leave no kids halfway across the world, and I ain't wanted by the law, if that's what you're wondering." I didn't know what in the hell she was getting at.

"Sometimes things happen we have no control over."

"That's true," I agreed, not without sympathy.

"I am not perfect," she added softly.

"We both know what happened to the only perfect man," I replied casually.

"Sam, I—I want you to know that no man ever cared for me or respected me like this." She gently caressed my chin with her soft hand. Her face was inches away from my own.

"I love you so powerful hard it hurts, Jan."

"Shhh," she whispered, gently touching my lips with a finger. "Don't tell me that, Sam. I want to be able to tell you that."

"Then I have a chance. Still?"

"Still."

Then I wrapped my arms around her and pulled her tight to me. For some reason I can't explain, I about felt like crying.

We layed there talking until two in the morning, Jan resting her head on my shoulder, her body warm against mine.

"I've got to get up in three and a half hours. You are a kidnapper, Sam," she chided while she gazed up at the stars.

"You ain't been complaining so far. Hey, look at that shootin' star!" I said, tracing the star's path across the heavens with my finger. "Ain't it pretty, Jan?"

"It's actually a meteor, Sam. We're only seeing burning gases from behind it. It's quickly burning itself out."

"You're kidding." I was surprised, but Janet ought to have knowed. She was the one with the Ivory League education.

"No, I'm not."

"Well, I don't believe it."

"Calling me a liar, eh?" She smiled and turned her face to mine.

"Nope. But if we're just seeing it here now, well, then somebody on another planet is going to see it in a few thousand years, light traveling the way it does, right?"

"That is possible," she replied.

"Well, then, it ain't burnin' out. It's gonna last for a while."

Janet propped herself up and looked at me hard, her face an inch above my own. "You are so very strange," she whispered.

"I love you so very much."

There was a long pause. I couldn't quite read her eyes. "You'd better take me home now, Sam," she said after some time.

"Okay, pal." Then I pulled her to me and kissed her again and again.

10

THE REST OF that week flew by as though in a dream. I ignored the nosy inquiries of Jack and Luke as to the status of my love life. On Thursday Luke informed me that he and Jack was leaving for a big horse sale in Dodge City; I would have to watch the place through Saturday. That was fine with me; Jan and me would be able to go horseback riding in relative privacy.

Late Friday morning I had visitors. I was filling up a stock tank when two familiar old trucks with horse trailers in tow squealed to a stop in front of the weathered ranch house. I whistled at my friends and waved.

"Howdy, boys." I grinned as they walked up. "What brings you guys to the flatlands?"

Philo spit mightily as we shook hands. "We come t' meet the perspective Mrs. Hawkins," he informed me with his pet coon grin.

"Where is she?" asked Crazy Joe. He looked around as if he expected to see Jan pitching bales of hay.

"At work. Do I need your approval or something?" I shot back as I shut off the spigot.

"Aw, c'mon, Sam," Crazy Joe replied, hurt.

"Doan' be so teechy," added Philo.

"All right. It's just—hey, how's the placer-mining business?"

"Wal," Philo began, taking time to spit again, "if'n ya kin spare a cup a coffee we'll jaw on hit."

"Sure thing, guys." Luke probably wouldn't have been happy

103

with my decision to let Philo's and Crazy Joe's horses run in his pasture, but he was long gone by way of U.S. 50 and he'd made me the commanding officer of his ranch. It was therefore a command decision. Besides, I could hardly allow my compadres' critters to stand tied to their trailers for a day. When the horses was unloaded and turned out to run, we adjourned to my shack.

Philo and Crazy Joe pulled up makeshift stools while I made coffee. As we drank coffee and smoked and chewed, they excitedly told me how they'd dragged in eight ounces of gold in the past few weeks, and all about the fur sign they'd seen in and around South Park. Finally, the coffeepot near empty, Philo asked the question I had knowed was coming.

"What ya gonna do if'n she marries ya, Sam?" He squinted as he opened a fresh can of snuff with a thumbnail.

"Would you guys help Jan and me put a house up on my land?" I was avoiding the question.

Crazy Joe looked up from his coffee cup and grinned. "Sure, Sam. I know a lot about building houses. My uncle owns a construction company."

"Ah expect so," Philo sighed.

I slowly lit my pipe with a kitchen match. "Well, we're going to have to build two of 'em, I'm afraid."

"Two houses!" gasped Philo.

"What?" Crazy Joe exclaimed.

"Yeah. Jan wanted to know all about you characters, and I told her how we've been together so long. I spared her the details, Joe." He grinned wildly at me. "She said it'd be fine with her if you guys put up a place of your own near ours. Then I reckon we'll need a small barn, too."

Philo Harris rarely let his emotions light up his face, but they got the best of him and a huge grin split his wide face in half. "Wal ah'll be go t' hell!"

Crazy Joe just whistled low and slow. "Must be some kinda woman, Sam."

"Kinda been thinkin' that myself," I replied.

We made palaver the rest of the afternoon, and early in the evening I picked up Jan and we headed back down to the ranch. She wanted to know everything there was to know about my partners, and seemed excited she was finally going to meet them.

Without getting overly personal I filled her in on their backgrounds and told her what she should avoid bringing up.

"Well, Philo's wife left him when he was in the First Cavalry in 'Nam. Don't ask if he's ever been married; he never talks about it. Then his family went bust back in the Thirties. They went out to California like the folks in that movie with Hank Fonda and had a rough time of it. He doesn't much care for California on their account."

"*The Grapes of Wrath.*" She nodded.

"That was the one. Joe is just Joe. He's from your part of the country originally, but had a falling out with his family—which is loaded—some time ago. You can talk to him about pretty much anything."

Needless to remark, Jan did not get briefed on certain hairbreadth escapes, former female acquaintances of various virtues, or one particular shootout which was best forgotten. She didn't have a need to know. I figured I'd tell her all at an appropriate time—like our fiftieth wedding anniversary.

As I pulled in the driveway, I saw my partners waiting for us by Joe's International. As we got closer I saw Philo straightening Joe's string tie like a father would for a son he was about to send off to Sunday school. I had to smile.

They was dressed in their Sunday go-to-meeting best. Philo had put on the only pair of britches he owned that wasn't buckskin or Levi's, a real nice pair of gray wool slacks. He wore a snazzy western dress shirt that matched, the Nacona boots he kept stored in their box in his truck, and his fancy Stetson. Crazy Joe sported his ancient-style frock coat he'd had tailor-made in the Far East, and his pressed pants was tucked inside of recently shined boots. A low-crowned, wide-brimmed Resistol was perched on his head at a cocky angle. As we got out and walked up to them, Janet had an "I don't quite believe this" look on her face.

"Janet Provost, I'd like you to meet Philo Harris and Joe Flanigan," I said with a smile.

Crazy Joe removed his hat, delicately took Janet's hand, and bowed deeply from the waist. "How truly delighted I am to make your acquaintance." He smiled like Errol Flynn hisownself. I think my mouth hanged about half open.

"Why, I am too," she replied sincerely with that pretty smile.

"Glad t' meet ya," Philo enthused as he grabbed her soft hand with his meaty bearpaw. "Sam's sait a lot about ya."

"It's very nice to meet you, Philo." Janet smiled back. Just as I was about to disengage Philo's death grip on Jan's hand, he quickly dropped it and turned around. He reached in the bed of Joe's truck and brought out a potted cactus plant.

"Fer you, miss." He grinned as he handed it to her.

"A barrel cactus, although a small one," Crazy Joe offered. "It will certainly bloom in the spring."

"Hit's store-bought!" Philo enthused.

"Why, I am simply touched, gentlemen," Janet smiled genuinely as she admired the plant. Then she addressed me. "Samuel," she scolded, "you never told me you had such lovely friends!"

I smiled back at Janet, who was pretending to be mad. Then I looked at my partners, slicked up to the nines, showing off manners I didn't know they had with grins decorating both their faces. "I never knowed they was," I replied honestly.

Eventually Janet and I broke away from my friends, and we went out to supper at a nice place on the north end of town. After our meal, we headed downtown to a country-and-western nightclub. Janet was becoming more relaxed with me all the time, and as a result was becoming better company. After I'd told her to take as much time as she needed to make up her mind, the tension seemed to slacken. Even though Janet had but a month left in the army—and in Colorado, for all I knowed—I wasn't worried. I knowed I was winning, and was almighty tickled with myself.

We located an empty corner table in the nightclub, and as I guided her to it I took off my hat. I held her chair while she took her seat, and placed my hat on a vacant chair at our table. A cowboy at the next table, whom I imagined was of the drugstore variety, sneered. I smiled back. When the waitress arrived, Janet ordered a lady's drink and I ordered my usual two beers, one bottled.

"Going to be a hard night of drinking?" Janet asked above the din of the band.

"Well, no. I just like to keep an extra beer bottle handy. One never knows."

She glanced down at the table, then looked up. "Sam, I wish

you wouldn't be on guard all the time. Why are you always expecting trouble?''

"Because there's so much of it around,'' I replied.

Then Jan's hand darted across the table and lightly squeezed my own. "I care, Sam. I want you to know that.''

"I care a lot, myownself.'' I smiled back. Then the drinks arrived, we took a couple sips, and commenced to dance.

I never knowed folks from New England could dance so well to country-and-western music. Janet gracefully and lightly followed my lead on the two-steps, and when a slow dance came we held each other close, but at a respectable distance. Janet was, first and foremost, a lady; I was not going to squash her in a public place—the Rexall Ranger cowboys could do that with the barflies. Janet deserved far more respect than that, and, as long as there was life in me, would always receive it.

Just as we were taking our seats, the bandleader announced in his faked Western accent, ''Y'all git on out heah, boys an' girls, fer we're gonna blow off the roof with the Cotton Eyed Joe!''

"Oh, Sam, let's go!'' Janet exclaimed.

"You're kidding,'' I replied, hoping she was.

"No, c'mon,'' she ordered, grabbing my arm and leading me out to the dance floor. I never could do that damned dance, and never did conclude if it was invented by drunk Indians or white men. But Janet gaily led me through it, doing all the swirls and kicks at just the right time. I was about a half a beat behind her. I barely survived that dance, and by the time it was over I was sweaty and out of breath.

"That was sure fun,'' she said as we sat down.

"Oh, it was a riot, Jan,'' I replied. "Really.'' I gave her chair a gentle push as she took her seat. From that point we talked and talked, taking in only an occasional dance. After a bit I excused myself and went to the men's room. On my way back I caught the bandleader in between songs and asked him to play one in particular. To ensure he done it, I filled his hand with a sawbuck.

"Sure, partner.'' He grinned. "We'll do it.'' Then I returned to our table.

"They're going to be playing a song for us shortly,'' I informed Jan with a smile.

"They are?"

"Yep." I looked toward the stage and the bandleader gave me the high sign. "Let's go, amigo." I got up and took her arm. "We're leading."

Then the steel guitar started out with a single note that began low and whined its way up, and the lead singer crooned "Everywhichway But Loose" as the band accompanied.

"You are such a romantic," Janet softly said in my ear as we held each other and danced slow through the tune.

"Only because I love you so," I answered. Then she lightly kissed me on the cheek. "This'll always be our song, Jan. It'll belong to us."

"All right, Sam," she whispered back. Then I opened my eyes and looked up at the bandleader. He gave me a wide grin and the thumbs-up, as if to say, "That oughta do it."

I winked back at him and pulled Jan just a little closer than was respectable. Just like in the song, she turned me everywhichway but loose.

I guess I was barely in control of myself with that woman.

It was well past midnight before we got out of that nightclub. Jan's roommate had returned from temporary duty the day before, so when I took her home I parked behind her apartment house, and we sat in my darkened truck and talked about this and that.

"Philo and Joe are talking about getting lined out for fall trapping," I told her. "They're maybe gonna head up to Wyoming next month and have a look around."

Jan brought her head off my shoulder and studied me in the dark of the cab. "Are you going with them?"

"I dunno." I smiled. "It's all kind of up in the air, if you know what I mean."

"Would you like to live in Wyoming?" she suddenly asked.

"Oh, I could, I guess," I answered, pulling her closer. She snuggled her head on my shoulder and I turned my head an inch or two and smelled her clean hair. "I don't think you'd care for Wyoming, Jan," I added.

"Why not?"

"Oh, I don't know. There ain't much up there, civilization-wise. Nothing but wind and lots of range and mountains. I think you need people more than I do."

"I do, huh?"

"Think so. By the way, I met your CO the other day."

I felt her body stiffen. "No!" she exclaimed. I described the light colonel and told her the name I'd read above his pocket. "That was him," she slowly affirmed with a nod of her head.

"Luke was showing him around. Appeared he was looking for a horse for his kids. Does he know about you and me?"

She turned her head, looked me in the eye, and gave me a look I can't describe. That woman should have played draw poker: half the time, if that, could I read her expression. That particular night it was too dark to see what her eyes were saying. "I don't see how he'd know, Sam. He does treat me like the daughter he never had, but . . ."

"But he don't know about me?"

"No."

"Then nobody where you work knows about us?"

"No."

"You told Donald?"

The same poker face. "No."

"Oh." I don't know why I was feeling so uneasy. That had been the best night out in my life, but some part of me was driving me on asking them hard questions.

We sat there holding each other, neither one of us talking for the longest time. At length Jan spoke up low and slow. "Donald called me from Korea this afternoon. He will be back in two weeks."

"Oh," I groaned.

"He wants to finish planning the wedding. It's been set for the last week in July."

"What!" I hollered in her ear. "Judas H. Priest! Next month? Jan, you said August—I know you did!"

It didn't occur to me at the time, but now I know that miserable son of a bitch Donald had somehow gotten wind of yours truly and moved the wedding date up so to mess up my plans. He was running scared, as well he should have.

"Our families wanted us to have the wedding before school starts," she said in a small voice.

I calmed myself down and cleared my throat. "Sorry I hollered."

"That's all right."

"Where'd you say the wedding was supposed to be?"

She gave me a queer look. "I hadn't thought I mentioned it." Then she let out a long sigh. "Outside of a little town in Illinois named Marble City. The church is a little country church called the Deer Valley Community Church. Why?"

"Just bein' nosy," I replied as if I didn't care. I was, however, making furious mental notes.

After a bit she asked, "So, are you going up to Wyoming with Philo and Joe next month?"

"I was kinda hoping to get hitched next month," I honestly replied.

Jan lifted her head and studied my face in the dark. "I don't know yet, Sam."

"I know. But then there's the rendezvous at Bent's Fort coming up soon. Al and Rosita will be disappointed if you ain't there. Among others."

Jan looked ahead, and laughed low and bitterly. "And I'll disappoint a lot of people if I'm not at my own wedding."

I stared ahead and let out a sigh. To myself more than her I said, "This is gonna be a photo finish."

There was no more words to say, so I gently turned Jan's head and we kissed each other long and hard and—

This here is personal, after all.

11

WE HAD AGREED to go riding the next morning after Janet had finished some chores. As I drove up I-25 to Janet's place I was doing some hard thinking.

I was thinking Janet's Old Man—her commanding officer, not her father—knowed all about us, and hadn't come out to Luke's to buy a horse at all. He was out there to inspect Sam Hawkins, and I knowed I flunked the inspection. I also figured Donald had found out about Jan and I one way or another, and was coming back early to dog the hatches and start the bilge pumps so to keep his ship from sinking.

I hadn't even met Jan's roommate and I didn't like her. I smelt a rat there, too.

All of this was still playing on my mind when I rang the doorbell. I got the notion Jan's roommate, Harriet Fletcher, didn't approve of me when she answered the door. I had figured Janet herself would answer the door, so I'd pulled my bandanna up outlaw-style over my face and made a six-shooter out of my index finger and thumb.

"Stick 'em up," I ordered as the door flew open. I was greeted by the hard glare of a female I'd not met, but felt I knowed from someplace. Her dark brown hair was matted, like she'd just crawled out of bed, and she looked down a prominent Roman nose at me with true distaste. As we made eye contact I decided she had the unkindest eyes I'd ever seen; had she been a mare I would have shipped her, taken the going killer price for horse-meat, and counted my blessings. She was a shrew, make no mistake.

"You are Samuel Hawkins," she announced coldly.

"The accused standing in front of you," I agreed, pulling down the bandanna. "Is Jan around?"

"If you want to see Janet," she haughtily informed me, "you go down the steps and up the sidewalk. Take the sidewalk around the building and go up the steps. That is where you will find Janet. Doing her laundry." Now it was a good thing I didn't have my foot in the door or Fletcher would have succeeded where frostbite had failed, namely in lopping off a few toes. The door slammed powerful hard.

"Thank you!" I said to the door. I headed down the steps to find the laundry room, although I wasn't looking forward to shooting the breeze with Jan while she folded her underwear. I also pondered the difference between a man and a woman, or one of 'em anyway. A man at least will have to be wronged, or have some kind of half-assed excuse, before he hates another man. I was pretty sure all Fletcher had heard about me was from Jan, and also was fairly certain it was good. Yet Fletcher hated me, make no mistake, and she didn't know me from Adam's pet fox. I recall thinking, "There's another miserable bitch trying to pass for a human being," when I ran into Jan as we rounded a corner from opposite directions. She was carrying a laundry basket piled right up to her chin and had a couple fatigue uniforms draped over her shoulder.

"Howdy." I smiled, tipping my hat. "I'll take the basket."

"Okay. Pfew! Have I been busy this morning!" She beamed as I took the laundry. "I took my car to the garage at eight and had the oil changed. Then I had to run to the printer's with the change-of-command program, and after that I went to the post office and mailed some bills. I had a three-hundred-dollar phone bill this month and it's been one thing after another."

"Three hundred bucks! Do you know people on Mars or something?"

"Well, there were some calls to Donald, and then I called my father once or twice."

I was about to follow that up when the sun broke out from under a cloud. It was then I saw in those doelike eyes something I've never beheld before or since in another human being. There was flecks of gold in her eyes, like real fine flour gold, not flake. So that was why they sparkled so: flecks of gold.

"Well, I slept in this morning myself," I said as we walked. "I sacked in till eight. It was great."

"Why was it great, Sam? Ben Franklin said, 'Do not squander time; that is the stuff life is made of.' Don't you believe that?"

"I believe there's a time to accomplish stuff, and a time to knock out some zzz's. I also believe Ben Franklin never spent eight months a year working in the Rocky Mountains. When you sit at a desk eight or ten hours a day, you've got a different version of hard work than I do, I reckon." Jan smiled, and opened the door to her apartment as we walked in. Fletcher had absented herself from the kitchen and living-room area.

"You are such a heretic!" Janet exclaimed in mock sorrow as she took the laundry basket from me. "I'll put this away and we can go. Help yourself to a cup of coffee," she added as she headed for her room. I poured a cup of coffee, which Jan must have made for me, 'cause she drank only tea, and sat down at the kitchen table. As I was reading the comics I heard voices; I recognized Fletcher's as doing most of the talking. The voices was low, but not so low that I didn't hear Fletcher say "derelict." I continued to sip my coffee and was studying the want ads when I heard Jan say real loud, "Harriet, shut up!" I thought, "So Janet is sticking up for me—that's over half the battle right there." Then she walked in.

"Ready to go?"

"Yes," she replied, trying not to show how steamed she was. She did a good job covering up the fact she was mad as hell. "Do I need to bring anything?" Just then the phone rang and she grabbed it off the wall hook.

"Hello. Oh, hi, Dad!" she exclaimed. I thought, "Oh shit, oh dear," and went back to reading the newspaper. I winced for the next twenty minutes as Janet and her father discussed the impending wedding. They didn't miss much: the announcements, photographer, and the cake; where Janet's mother and new husband should sit—her father wasn't remarried—and what tune the organ player should blast out prior to the ceremony.

I felt like a Grade A home-wrecker. I also felt like throwing up all over the place. Finally she hung up the phone.

"Do I need to bring anything else?" Janet repeated, as if the conversation I had heard half of had not even happened. Well, hell, it was pretty hard to miss any of it: I was sitting only ten feet away.

"Gloves, if you want 'em. You aren't going to wear those tennis shoes, are you, Jan? I'd hate to see you put a foot through a stirrup."

"Oh. I hadn't thought of that," she replied. She pursed her lips in thought.

"You got army boondockers? They've got a fair heel on 'em; they'll do. Oh shucks, you can ride my Hope saddle; got wood stirrups the size of redwood trees on it. You don't need to worry about putting a foot through one." I would do the honorable thing and ride my old fifty-dollar Textan roper. "Levy leche, levy leche!"

"What?" she asked in puzzlement.

"Means 'let's go' in mountaineer."

Janet didn't have a word to say in the truck, so as I pulled out on I-25 I started the conversation. "It appears Harriet don't approve of me."

It took a few seconds for her to answer. "I don't know," she replied at length, looking ahead. "We haven't discussed you." There was another unnervingly long pause. It was there that certain parts of my plan began to worry me. What if Jan and Fletcher did discuss me, and what if Fletcher had convinced her she was stupid for going out with me when she was already spoken for, and by a REMF lifer officer to boot? What if I was in deep, dark kimchi and didn't know it? I reckoned all I could do was what I'd been doing, and hope my best would be good enough. It was also about then that it occurred to me Janet seemed to be fighting something that was in the natural scheme of things, namely her and I being together. I recollect being a little irritated when that thought occurred to me, but I didn't say nothing about it.

"Say, I saw in the paper where they're going to show some of Charlie Russell's paintings here in town next week at some art gallery. You want to go?" I was trying to break the dead calm that had settled over my truck, and wrangle a date at the same time.

"That would be interesting," she answered, noncommittal-like.

"Do you like art?" I pulled into the left lane to pass a one-ton.

"Yes, I do. I took art history as an elective in college. I prefer the painters of the post-Renaissance period. I love the wistfulness of Fragonard, the earthiness of Corot. Hogarth is so brutal," she replied quietly.

"So did they hang him or something?"

"Who?"

"Hogarth. You said he was brutal. I think of Tojo or Ho Chi Minh when I hear that word."

"Oh, Sam!" she exclaimed in mock disgust, "you are just impossible. Hogarth was an Englishman who lived in the mid-to-late eighteenth century. His work illustrated all classes of English society. The detail in the situations he portrayed is simply excruciating. It is very lifelike. I think you might enjoy his work."

"Thanks," I answered as I pulled back into the right lane, "but I think I'll stick with Charlie Russell."

"Yes," she slowly said, her index finger on her chin in thought. "Russell and many of the early American artists were unique in their own way. But I think an underlying theme of the American painters of the nineteenth century was one of unapologetic ethnocentrism."

"You shouldn't accuse Charles M. Russell of that. His parents was married." Well, hell, I didn't know what that word meant.

"Ethnocentrism, Sam, is the belief that your culture and values—and mores and folkways—are superior to those found anyplace else. It is a simplistic belief that you are right and all or most all other people are wrong. That's all ethnocentrism is."

"Well, I'll be," I replied, pulling off on the Fountain exit ramp.

"You'll be what?"

"I reckon I'll be one of those fellers."

"An ethnocentric?" she quizzed.

"Sure thing."

"Why is that, Sam?"

"Why, at the bottom, things are pretty simple, like the way I choose to live, for instance. There's right and there's wrong, and a person ain't allowed to mess up somebody's life other than their own for selfish purposes. Lying don't make a bad thing good, nor a wrong thing right.'' We was almost to Luke's place, and I slowed down a little so I'd have time to better explain myself.

"There's a lot of gray area out there," Jan slowly said, looking straight ahead.

"I reckon I don't see much of it, 'cept on cloudy days. It's like this: Take the Southern Cheyenne, Black Kettle's band. Custer went ahead and pretty much rubbed 'em out on the Washita in '68, and the press and politicians claimed it was a big victory in the war against the heathen redskins. 'Course they ignored the fact that a good many killed was women and children. But eight years later, at the Little Bighorn, Sittin' Bull and the Ogalalla Sioux and some of the same Cheyenne that survived the Washita done in Lieutenant Colonel George Armstrong Custer and the greater part of the U.S. Seventh Cavalry. Now, to my way of thinking, Custer personally deserved to get the chop for what he'd done back on the Washita. It was just too damned bad he took two hundred and some soldiers with him.''

"But weren't the Indians supposed to be on the reservation?''

"Yeah,'' I admitted. "They had skipped; they was guilty of trying to find buffalo so to feed their families.''

"Oh. But Custer was only following orders.''

"From what I've read, he disobeyed more than he ever followed. His men was following *his* orders. He was the Charlie Oscar. If he'd got into that camp on the Little Bighorn, he'd have ordered every man, woman, and child killed. And all the lodges burned and the horses shot, just like on the Washita. I don't know much about philosophy, but it seems the nasty things Custer did come back to haunt him that day as he rode up Medicine Bow Coulee.''

Janet shifted in the seat so to get a better look at me.

"But in Vietnam, and in particular the My Lai incident, our soldiers killed women and children, didn't they?'' I pulled to a stop in Luke's driveway.

"I wasn't there. But I once knowed a guy in the Americal Division that was in the same battalion as Calley. That village was in a free-fire zone. Unlike the mamasans there, the Sioux women and kids didn't have AK-47s. Or no reasonable facsimile thereof."

We got out without another word and walked up to the pasture fence in silence. I whistled up my two critters herded together with Luke's cavyard, and as they headed toward me I cut a small apple in half, handed one half to Jan, and eased through the fence.

"They recognize you!" Jan said in amazement.

I whistled again and they both fell into a trot side by side. "They should. I'm their grocery store, their cobbler, and their doctor." Molly got to me first and I rewarded her with half an apple. She was half Arab and half quarter horse, a bright sorrel in color with ears almost as big as a mule's. She had a full rump, that small Arab head, and a white blaze with three white socks. As I fed her the apple, I slipped my old leather halter over her head. I patted her on the neck and talked to her.

"How you been, old hoss? How's old Jack, and how're the kids? C'mon over," I told Jan. She stood next to me and held out her half of the apple, which Molly whoofed in a bite. "Okay, now let her get your scent, Jan. It's important she gets your scent so she gets to know you. Put your hand next to her nose." She did so, and Molly took a sniff. Molly looked hard at me, then looked at Jan, who was starting to pet her nose. She wanted to know who was this other female, two-legged variety, who'd suddenly become part of the picture. By way of introduction I told Jan to blow up her nostrils.

"What?" she replied in surprise.

"Just real easy," I quietly said. "Keep talking to her. She needs to get the manscent. In your case, the womanscent. A horse never forgets a man's own smell. She's got to know you ain't going to hurt her." Jan blew up her nostrils real slow and careful. Molly stood there calmly, taking it all in.

"Good," I said. "Now ease around and rub her all over."

Jan did as instructed. She rubbed Molly's nose and ears, then asked, "Will she bite?"

"Naw," I answered, reminded of a story. "Y'know, used to be when folks asked me if I had a girlfriend, I'd tell 'em a story something like this: 'Sure do. Her shoulders come up to about here, and she's got reddish-brown hair that shines. Her mouth is near perfect, but her nose is a little long. That don't detract

from her, though, 'cause she's got a wonderful personality.' "
Jan was grinning, still rubbing Molly.

I continued. " 'Well, the other day I was, uh, you know,
playing with her feet and darned if she didn't swivel around and
bite me in the ass! So then I popped her on the nose and told
her, "Molly, you ever do that again, I'm gonna turn you into
dogfood!" ' "

Jan laughed from her guts up and lightly hit me on the arm.
"You're so outrageous!" she cried.

"Yeah," I agreed. "That's what my old great-aunt said last
time I saw her, except I think she said 'insanely outrageous!' "
I grinned. Then I tied Molly to the nearby fencepost and caught
old Jack. I gave Jan a brush and showed her how to use it, then
went to my shack and carried back my saddles, pads, and bridles.

"I haven't been around horses much," Jan said as I walked
up with the ancient Textan roping saddle in one hand and my
light Hope in the other. I'd strung the bridles and reins around
my neck and had a couple saddle blankets tucked under an arm.

"Hey, don't worry about it, amigo. You're going to be a natural; I can tell. Besides, Molly's taken to you already. She sets
great store by you."

"How can you tell?" Jan inquired, still currying the mare.

I replied with a grin, "She ain't kicked you yet."

Next I showed Jan how to saddle and bridle a horse, walking
her slowly through each step. "Always let the bit drop out
of her mouth; don't let it drag over her teeth," I said as I showed
her how to remove it. In a few minutes Jan had got down the
process of bridling Molly. Then I showed her how to place the
saddle blanket and cinch up the girth.

"Knee her a little," I said as Molly blowed out her gut. As I
helped Jan cinch up Molly, I noticed the latigo on my Hope was
about shot; I guess it had been like that since I'd traded for it at
a rendezvous some years back. "Don't worry about the frayed
leather at the O-ring," I told Jan as I tugged at the offside latigo.
"It's seen better days, but it'll last awhile longer. Remind me to
replace it sometime, will ya?"

"It won't break today, will it?"

"Naw. It's got a couple dozen mountain passes in it yet. Besides"—I smiled—"even if it does bust, you've got full medi-

cal.'' Then I saddled Jack with the old Textan, got Jan onboard Molly, and had her stand in the stirrups so I could adjust the length. Well, what if her legs was a little longer than mine? I still stood a good half an inch taller than her. Then I swung up on Jack and we headed out the gate for Fountain Creek, my old quarter horse cutting a string of farts in Molly's face as we rode.

We found a huge pasture to ride through, and while we clomped along I couldn't find anything to say. I was pondering taking Jan straight to the airport that day, flying to Las Vegas, and getting married. That would have saved her the embarrassment and family heat from calling off the scheduled wedding. It also would have been a quick yet lawful solution, and I would have shot down like a dog any man that challenged it. Jan interrupted my thoughts.

''Sam, you've done a lot of talking these past few weeks, but . . . is there anything you care to talk about? Is something bothering you?''

''Yeah. You're holding the reins too tight; that's why Molly's tossing her head from time to time.'' Jan let a little slack out of the reins. ''There, like that. Well, I dunno. I'm kinda wondering if we're going to be married or not.''

''I still need time,'' she said with a sigh.

''Well, for the other,'' I began, resigned, ''I thought I've done a pretty good job of laying my guts open as I went.''

''Yes,'' she slowly drawled in that New England Yankee accent, ''you have. And I sincerely appreciate it.''

''Well, I don't know what I can add, then.''

''You haven't said hardly anything about your time in the navy.''

''I hated it,'' I quickly replied. Then I added, ''I made the best friends in my life there. Except for you, Jan. You're my best friend now. But other than that, it stinked.''

''Stinked?''

''Whatever. It's just hard for me to separate the good times from the bad times, in my own mind. I guess a lot of people can do that. It never worked for me, so I don't think about any of it.''

''Are you bitter?'' she softly asked.

''No. No point in it. That just hurts yourself, in the long run. But now that I think about it, when those folks got turned loose

by them maniacs in Iran and got a hero's welcome, I about
heaved. When I was in, there wasn't a hell of a lot of patriotism
going around. I just did my time and did my job like a few
million other people, and learned to expect little in return. Jan,
put your feet forward a little more. And keep your weight farther
back in the saddle. There you go. That way, should Molly pitch,
you grab the horn and throw your feet out and you can ride her
out. Just like on the Wyoming license plates.''

She smiled back, but neither one of us said a word for the
longest time. I am not a first-rate talker anyway; Jan just had a
way of bringing it out of me. Then, after a bit, she said, "I think
you are.''

"What? Bitter? I don't have much right to be, Jan. I slept in
a cot or in a rack, and had hot chow most of the time. There
was a couple million guys had it a whole lot rougher than me,
the ground pounders and marines, namely. I got no room to
gripe.'' I was wishing to hell she would change the subject.

There was another long spell of neither of us talking. Molly
was behaving like a real lady, and we rode through the huge
acreage without incident, except for Jan shooing away a wasp
that kept hovering around her pretty head.

Finally, out of nowhere, she said, "Sam, sometimes you look
so sad.''

"Just tired, I reckon.''

"I'm sorry,'' she said, real quiet. I looked at her then; the
way her mouth was drawed up, and the expression in her eyes,
told me she was.

"Don't be,'' I answered. "I'm sorry, too, but not for myself.
The ones who died, and the ones who got maimed, or who
freaked out, they're the ones I'm sorry for. And for all the kids
who'll never know their dads, who will know only the picture
on the piano of some twenty-year-old PFC or gunner's mate—
they're the ones I'm sorry for. And for the mas and dads.''

"You think about it often, don't you?''

"Just one day a year,'' I assured her. "That's more than
enough.''

"What day is that?''

"Memorial Day.''

We topped a small rise then, and the distant Spanish Peaks
came into full view. "They're pretty, ain't they?'' I asked as I

pointed to the distant twin peaks to the south of us. "The Indians and mountaineers called 'em Wah-to-Yah; I don't know if I mentioned that or not."

"Yes, you did," she replied. "Who named them?" she asked, gently rocking from side to side in the saddle. "And what does Wah-to-Yah mean?" Jan had that gleam in her eye; she suspected what was coming and was up to mischief.

"Oh, probably some lonely redskin named 'em. Maybe the Spaniards applied an Indian name to 'em," I replied in answer to the first question. "Wah-to-Yah means, translated, uh . . . terrain features." I pulled that phrase from the distant past.

She cocked her head a little to one side and grinned. "Terrain features?" she shot back, showing them perfect white teeth.

"Yeah, terrain features," I repeated, getting embarrassed. "Prominent ones. Like a . . . a woman's . . ."

"Boobs, Sam?" She laughed. "Really, Sam, are they?" She glowed, enjoying my discomfort. Her eyes sparkled so when she was happy.

Then I had to laugh at myself. I recall thinking at the time, "I've never been this happy in my life." Then we put the horses in a slow trot, me coaching Jan as we rode.

"You got enough confidence to go a little faster?"

"Sure thing, hoss," she said, grinning, drawing out the "hoss." There wasn't a fence in sight as we rode at a rocking-chair trot across the prairie. Molly was being very patient with her new rider; she was keeping an even gait and just behaving all around. Jack was being his usual ungrateful self, from time to time tossing his head in an attempt to drop the bit and get it between his teeth. Jack and I spent many years together on the trail, and in all that time I rode him no more than ten percent of the time. He usually wound up carrying the packsaddle and the dead weight associated with it for the simple reason he was generally on punishment detail for some stupid stunt. I never quite figured out how his mind worked; the nearest I can come is to say that in many ways he was like a rebellious seaman who, determined to show everybody how tough he was, succeeded only in getting throwed in the brig.

"Okay, Jan, we're going to lope real slow. Remember, keep your feet out." Jan throwed them out even farther. "Now give her just a little more rein, keep your heels down, and stay back

in the saddle.'' She did that, too. ''I'll be with you. Okay, Jan,
now tell her L-O-P-E.''

''Lope, Molly,'' Jan ordered. And she did.

For about two seconds.

Then Molly took off at a dead run, her hoofs a-flying like a
pack of horse-eating Indians was on her tail.

''Saam!'' Jan yelled. ''Help!''

My first reaction was panic.

So was my second.

And my third was, This Is A Golden Opportunity.

I recalled something. When asked why the Western film was
an everlasting art form, John Ford had gruffly replied, ''Because
there's something magnificent about a man on a horse.'' And
then I done something I'm not very proud of, but I'm going to
confess it anyway.

I let that horse run away with Jan.

And in a few seconds, when Molly and Jan was fifty yards or
so ahead of me and burning ground like there was no tomorrow,
I put heel to Jack's flank and told him to move out, pronto.

Molly was tearing up and down the little rises in the pasture,
clods of dirt flying high in her wake. She jumped a little brook
in a flying leap and Jan came half out of the saddle, but had a
death grip on the horn and got back her seat. She was learning
fast and I was gaining fast.

''Saam!'' Jan yelled. I was only a dozen yards behind her and
catching up. As Molly broke the crest of a knoll, Jack came
even with her, him blowing hard, his own sweat stinging my
face. I reached out, got my hand on Molly's bridle, and gave it
a violent tug, at the same time reining in Jack and yelling,
''Whoa! you sons of bitches!'' Both horses stopped after a few
more jerky steps.

''Are you okay, Jan?''

Her face said, ''I'm damned happy to be alive!'' She took a
couple deep breaths.

''I'm okay. Pfew! What a ride! Sam, you were really great!''
she said as she caught her breath. She didn't have to say any
more. Her eyes was saying, ''my hero.''

''You did pretty good yourself, pard.''

Like I said, that was a dirty trick, not stopping Molly as soon
as she bolted. Thinking back on it now, it may even be that

Molly knowed what she was doing and was trying to help me out. Sounds crazy, I guess, but that mare always knowed the score. And she really liked Jan.

Well, anyway, I'm not real proud of what I did. Or what I didn't do right away.

But a runaway Concord stagecoach, pursued by bloodthirsty Apaches, would have been much better.

As usual, I done the best I could with what I had available at the time.

John Ford knew a lot.

12

THE NEXT FEW days after that horseback ride have taken on a pleasant, dreamlike quality in my mind. Jan and I were together each evening; she was learning to love me for who I was, and I was learning to love her more.

Needless to remark, Fletcher and I was learning to despise each other. I hadn't done nothing to her, but she didn't seem to need a reason.

I just don't think she wanted to see Jan happy, seeing as how she was such a miserable bitch herownself. Jealousy tends to be a sickness, and some so-called friends don't always want what's good for one.

So that Wednesday evening Fletcher had the loathsome chore of making small talk with yours truly while Janet got cleaned up. She had got home from work late and was in the bathroom when I rang the doorbell.

"Come in," Fletcher intoned haughtily, "and have a seat. Janet has been waiting for you."

"Whar's she?" I asked as I brushed past her.

"In the bathroom." She glared.

"Well, then, she ain't ready, is she?" I smiled nice as could be.

"You may sit down," she droned like an English butler. I took a seat at the kitchen table. She pulled up a chair at the opposite end and glared at me like a district attorney studying a

124

knowed-guilty defendant and pondering if he should argue for the electric chair, hanging, casteration, or all three.

"I understand you were in the navy some years ago," she said. I heard the shower fire up in the bathroom and thought, "This is going to be a long, unpleasant wait."

"Yep," I replied as I fiddled with my pipe. "I understand you're in the army now. No pun intended."

"Indeed," she droned, her mouth drawed down in a frown. "Why did you get out? If I may ask, of course."

"I got out because it sucked. Of course." I smiled. I can be a genuine, four-ply smart-ass when I want. I began to fill my pipe.

"I do not understand," she glared, her eyes boring through me like she was talking to a Grade A moron.

I lit my pipe and let out a sigh. "It's like this: Up was down, right was wrong, and port was starboard."

She cleared her throat. "I fail to see the significance of your metaphor."

I took a long pull on my pipe. "Read *Catch-22*; it's all in there. Only the war has been changed." Then an afterthought struck me. "I also got out because I hated officers," I cheerfully added.

"Janet is an officer."

"Yep."

"And so am I."

"Well, pardon me all to hell, Harriet."

"Do you hate me?" she suddenly shot out. She couldn't have cared less if I did or not.

I couldn't resist the opportunity to let her have it, so I expelled a cloud of smoke toward her, curled my upper lip in a sneer, and said, " 'Well, if I gave you any thought, I probably would.' " She snorted like a horse then—I've already mentioned she bore no small resemblance to the same—shoved her chair back, and got up. She stalked over to the sink and started washing dishes.

Meanwhile, back in the bathroom, the shower was still running. Now there was a woman that set great store by cleanliness. And that was only one of her good qualities.

At length Harriet looked up from the dishes and addressed me. "My father is a general."

"My father was a farmer," I replied evenly. "He is currently deceased." She merely continued to look disgusted.

She stayed on the same tack, but I was ready for her. "My father was a hero in Vietnam," she stated with authority, like he was MacArthur hisownself.

"And mine was a hero in the Solomon Islands."

Harriet set a dish down and looked at me with pure bewilderment. "When did we fight a war with the Solomon Islands?" she asked in puzzlement.

I wanted to laugh, then I remembered my dad's stories about Savo Island and Ironbottom Bay and the Tokyo Express, and couldn't. I answered with a question of my own. "You say you've been to college?"

"Of course!"

"Of course!" I echoed. She just confirmed my notion that the colleges was turning out technologicated imbeciles these days.

Janet being a happy exception to that rule.

Of course. The first thing I noticed about Jan that evening was that the engagement ring was missing from the fourth finger of her left hand.

I had to do a double take to make sure of it.

And then a grin about split my face in half.

"Levy leche, amigo." I smiled.

"What?" Fletcher scowled from the sink. I took Jan's hand and barely restrained myself from kissing her. Then I opened the door.

As Janet pulled the door shut behind her, she threw back over her shoulder, "It means 'let's go' in mountaineer."

Jan's mood was light and carefree that evening and I wasn't far behind. She was all enthused about going to eat at some coffeehouse place out of the sixties, so that was where we took supper. "Am I going to have to eat wheat germ and putrified asparagus?" I asked as I held the door open.

"Oh, Sam!" she exclaimed in mock sorrow as I held the door open for her, "you are so structured. But we can go somewhere else if you'd like," she offered genuinely.

"That's okay, pal," I replied as we walked in. As we found a corner table I looked around at all the bearded long-hairs and the pasty-skinned, stringy-haired females. Somebody should have told them they was in the wrong decade. As I held Jan's chair I softly said in her ear, "Well, I suppose this means a bloody steak is out of the question."

"You are impossible!" she chided as I sat down next to her.

"I just like to keep you entertained, Jan." I grabbed the menu and softly whistled the first few bars of "That's Entertainment."

"Sam, would you stop it? Honestly!" Her mouth was a wide grin.

"Okay, I'll stop it." I smiled, studying the menu. Then I got a serious look on my face and said, "Outta all the boiled eggplant joints, outta all the college towns, in all the world, we walk into this one. Where's Sam's piano, and where's Sam, for that matter?"

"Sam's piano is sitting in Casablanca, and Sam is sitting with me and has lost his mind."

"Oh, just feeling good, I reckon." As it turned out, the place wasn't half bad. Besides the health-nut food, they also served Mexican chow, so I wolfed down a couple cheese enchiladas and some rice. I trusted the hot peppers to kill any peculiar radical orgasms that may have taken refuse therein. Jan had a plate of rice and gruel that to me looked repulsive, but she seemed to enjoy it.

"That rice reminds me of a story," I began, pointing at her plate.

"Let's hear it."

"Well, once upon a time when Crazy Joe got back from overseas—"

"Crazy Joe?"

"I mean Joe, that crazy guy. Well, anyway, his family invited him over for Thanksgiving dinner. He hadn't been home in quite a spell and was in the process of getting off the . . . list. So his ma—maybe it was the maid—carried in the turkey on a platter. Maybe it was a goose, I disremember. And his ma said, 'Joe, I've made this stuffing just for you.' And he asked, 'What is it?' 'Rice,' she said. Then Cra— then Joe jumped up from his chair, grabbed that bird by the legs, and shook it till all the stuffing fell out, hollering, 'I hate goddamned rice!' "

Janet guffawed hard, and gasped, "Honestly! Is that true?"

"I guess so, Jan. With Joe, fact is always stranger than fiction."

After supper we strolled down Tejon Street in the cool evening air, Jan stopping every so often to look inside a storefront window. We walked in a bookstore that kept evening hours, and I gave her the slip while she was engrossed in the history and philosophy section. I ducked next door to a flower shop and returned in five minutes with a potted plant that filled both hands.

"They're lovely, Sam," she said softly, taking the flowers from me. Darn tooting they was lovely. I would be damned if my partners would one-up me in the gift-giving department. All that courting stuff was new to me, but I was catching on fast.

"They're cyleniums," I said slowly, so to pronounce the word right.

"I know."

Jan said she had to get up early, so I took her home shortly after that. Fletcher had happily vacated the apartment for the evening, so we went inside and sat down on the couch. Eventually the conversation got around to the serious stuff.

"Donald called last night," she said quietly as she gazed off into space, my arm around her.

"Yeah?"

"He is coming home early. Probably next week." She said it without emotion and I thought, "That son of a bitch comes home earlier every time he calls!" I was surprised he wasn't waiting on the steps when Jan and I got home that evening.

"Oh," I said. "So what are you going to tell him?" I kept thinking it had to be her decision.

She turned her head and gave me a hard look. I thought I saw a smile appear then quickly disappear. "I'm still thinking, Sam."

"How am I doing?"

She did smile then. "You're not out of the running yet." I studied her eyes. As far as I could tell she was telling the truth.

"I see the ring is off," I remarked, nonchalant as could be.

"Yes. I've got a lot on my mind, Sam. Perhaps the absence of it will help me decide."

I didn't say nothing in return but I sat there panicking in my own mind. I had since learned from Jan that Fletcher and Donald had been stationed together at Fort Carson; that was how Jan had met him. Say, for the sake of argument, Donald had called before—like when Jan was out with me—and Fletcher had spilled her guts to him concerning Jan and yours truly. She certainly wouldn't have told Jan, "By the way, I gave Donald the lowdown on you and Sam," but she would have done about the same amount of damage to my chances with Jan as that Jap five-hundred-pounder did to the *Arizona*.

I wished to hell Jan would call off the deal over the phone, tell Donald "adios," and mail the ring back postage due. That night it didn't look like she was going to do that; she probably felt she owed the lifer a face-to-face powwow. And if I was right about Fletcher snitching to him—and if he was a silver-tongued devil, which I most certainly am not—I figured there was a good chance I could be up Shit River without a paddle.

I kissed her then because I felt too miserable to say anything. She kissed me back hard, perhaps for the same reason.

She put her head on my shoulder and I patted her back. It was then something else occurred to me. There was a missing piece to the puzzle of Jan's background; something from a long time ago was bothering her. She had hinted around at it and I had more or less blowed it off, not because I didn't care but because it was a long time ago.

I pushed away from her and looked her in the eye. "Jan, I think maybe you've been trying to tell me something. I'm also thinking that whatever it is has something to do with you and me. You're among friends here; let's hear it, once and for all."

I received not a movement of the mouth, a blink of the eye, or a wrinkle of the eyebrow. She looked right through me.

"Jan?"

"Yes." Yes and nothing more, which meant no.

I let out a little sigh and shook my head. "Look, I don't know whether you've figured it out yet, but I'm about the best friend you've got. If there's a secret in your past you feel can come back and hurt you, say it out loud to somebody you love and trust. It will never hurt you again."

Janet just put her head back on my shoulder and offered not a word. Then we headed for her bedroom where, once again, we undressed and made love in total darkness.

13

I STARTED CALLING the next day as soon as I figured Janet would be home from work. That was five-thirty. The phone rang and rang, and when I called about twenty minutes later I got a busy signal. That damned phone stayed busy until seven o'clock, and when I finally got through Janet answered.

"Hello," she quietly said. I knowed something was wrong; she had been crying. I could tell.

"Jan, it's Sam. What's wrong?"

"Nothing," she replied in a small, mousy voice.

"The hell it ain't. You've been crying. Was that Donald on the phone with you for the past hour?"

Pause.

"Yes."

"Well, what'd he say to set you to crying?" The son of a bitch was supposed to love her, after all.

"Nothing. Sam, he's in San Francisco; he'll be here tonight," she nearly whispered into the phone.

"Sam?"

"I heard ya." I felt like the wind had been kicked out of me. "He wasn't supposed to be here for a week. What're you going to tell him, Jan?"

"I will have an answer for you Sunday."

"Will I see you then, huh, Jan?"

"That is a good possibility," she answered softly.

"Look, if you need me this weekend—if something happens—you've got the number here at Luke's place, right?"

"Yes."

"Well, call me. Understand? Am I right in assuming Donald will be out of the AO by Sunday evening?"

"Yes. He has to report to Fort Benjamin Harrison for a two-week school Monday morning."

"All right," I replied, relieved. Donald couldn't do a hell of a lot of damage in two days. What I didn't add was if that skin-headed REMF lifer so much as layed a hand on Janet I would personally dispatch him to a much higher elevation where he could keep company with the spirits. If he hurt Janet, I would kill him. That seemed eminently fair to me.

I didn't realize it at the time, but the very thought of losing Jan was enough to make me start losing my mind.

"I love you, Jan. Always."

Pause.

"I care very much."

"Take it easy."

" 'Bye."

As I walked back to my shack I still felt right confident. I was looking to the ground as I walked, pondering where I could come up with a suitable murder weapon. A gas-operated .22 repeating rifle—with a large Irish potato for a silencer—was my first choice.

Then something hit me and I stopped dead in my tracks.

Jan knowed I never said "good-bye." I had told her that more than once. But she had said it. " 'Bye," she'd said.

My guts built up pressure instantly and I about doubled over in pain.

Then I went out behind the machinery shed, where nobody would see me, and puked my insides out.

That night I didn't sleep at all.

The next morning, Saturday, I was occupied with chores till noon. I shoveled horse dung with a violent passion, nailed up fallen-down stalls like a madman, and pitched bales of hay off Luke's rickety wagon like there was no tomorrow.

It didn't help a damned bit.

Why, I wondered, hadn't I heard from Jan? It was noontime, and certainly Donald would have blown it by now.

Did they sleep together last night?

No.

Jan had made up her mind not to marry him. I knowed it.

The engagement ring was off.

We was going to build our own house. We were going to the Bent's Fort rendezvous in a little over a month.

I would go to horseshoeing school, and we was going to have kids.

She wanted goats, just like Rosita Hempstead's.

That was fine with me.

So long as she took care of the damned varmints herself.

I cleaned all my guns. Twice. Then I changed the oil in my truck. I was laying underneath the engine, hand-tightening the drain plug, when I noticed Luke's size-thirteens staring at me.

"What's wrong, Sam? Why ain't ya with thet girl t'day?" he boomed over my engine.

"Hand me that crescent wrench, will ya?" I answered. It was by my feet and I could have easily reached it; I just wanted to distract him.

"Shore." He bent over and handed it to me. I began tightening the drain plug.

"I'm losing oil in this old girl. The compression's okay; I think it's the valve guides. What d'ya think, Luke?" I asked, still tightening the plug.

"Could be the valve-covah gasket or the head gasket."

"I replaced 'em all last year. Have I had any phone calls?" I tried to sound as if I didn't care as I pretended to examine a shock absorber.

"Nope. Thet girl supposed t' call?" he asked as I slid out from underneath the old truck. I slowly dragged out the stained plastic washbasin I'd fished out of Luke's junkpile. It held the filter and five quarts of thoroughly used oil.

"Yeah. I kinda figured she might."

"Wal, she might yit," he offered as he lit a cigar. As I stood up, Luke done a strange thing. He softly placed a huge ham of a hand on my shoulder and gave it a squeeze. "Thar are happy endings, Sam. Ah believe in 'em."

"Yeah," I said, depressed. "Like Operation Frequent Wind. That was a real happy ending."

"Huh?"

"April 1975. Task Force 76. We pulled out fifteen or twenty thousand 'Namese as Saigon was falling to the slopes. We left twenty million or so behind. That was a real fucking happy ending."

"Ah wisht ya wasn't so bitter, Sam," Luke said, looking hard into my eyes.

"I wish life didn't suck so hard sometimes, Luke."

The next morning I still hadn't heard nothing. When I got up, the smell of fall was brisk in the air, so after finishing my chores with the stock I boiled my traps in logwood dye, and waxed them. Jan would understand that the fall hunt was approaching: with good weather and some luck I could clear four to five thousand. We'd get married, we'd have money in the bank, and as soon as the frost was out of the ground in April we'd start building our house.

But why hadn't she called?

I caught Molly and saddled and bridled her, thinking a ride would do me good. Then, as I was about to climb on, I jerked the latigo free, dropped the saddle and bridle, and led her back to the pasture.

Around four that afternoon I still hadn't heard nothing. Jan had made it clear Donald would be vacating the area that afternoon.

He must be gone by now, I thought.

I was climbing in my pickup when Jack Riley caught me by the arm. "Sam?"

"What?"

"Whar ya goin' to? Luke wants ya t' ride out thet buckskin he traded fer yestiday. Ah'll snub fer ya."

"I'm going into town. Later, all right?"

"He'll be mad," Jack warned. Before I could reply he added, "Hit's 'bout thet girl, hain't hit? What's wrong, Sam, she give ya the slip?"

I quickly pulled out my wallet and fished out a ten. "Here you go, Jack," I said as I shoved the bill at him. "Buy yourself a bottle of grain alcohol. Die happy." Then I slammed the door in his face and backed out of the driveway with gravel flying.

As I drove away I looked in the rearview mirror and saw Jack gaping at me, the ten-spot waving in his hand, his mouth wide open in amazement.

I jerked to a stop at the first phone booth I came to in Fountain. Jan answered the phone on the second ring.

"Jan, what happened?" I shot out.

"Donald and I are getting married."

"No!"

"Yes."

"Look, Jan," I quietly said, trying to regain my composure, "you don't have to do this."

"Yes, I do," she replied in a whisper.

"There's a way out," I quickly offered, thinking fast.

"There is?" Her voice raised half an octave; she was interested.

"Yes! We'll—we'll leave! We'll get on a train and go wherever you want. I'll sell everything and we'll have enough money to start over! The West Coast—Canada—Australia! We'll leave and never look back. We'll start over together."

At length she replied, "It wouldn't work."

"Why not?" I croaked.

Pause.

"I am marrying Donald. In three weeks. I love him," she said without an overage of emotion.

"Oh, and he loves you?"

"Yes."

"Well, he's got one hell of a goddamned way of showing it!"

"Good-bye, my wonderful cowboy," Janet said softly.

"Not yet it ain't!" I fired. Then I hanged up the phone with a bang. After I hung up the receiver it dawned on me what she'd said. "And I ain't a goddamned cowboy!" I hollered at the phone.

I made the drive to Jan's place in a record twenty minutes.

"Open the door, Jan!" I yelled as I hammered on the door. She was home and wasn't about to answer. "I know you're in there, so open up!"

Nothing.

"You can either open this goddamned door or I'll blow it open with my Winchester!" I yelled.

A moment later the door swung open. "Well, I never expected to see you again," she said in mock surprise, like I was a lost Good Humor man.

"Why in the hell not?" I barked as I stalked in.

"Would you care to sit down?" she asked evenly, controlling her anger.

"Yeah. That'd be lovely." I grabbed her by the arm and jerked her to the davenport with me. I tossed my hat on her coffee table and turned to her. "You're fixing to ruin your life," I told her through my teeth. I looked her square in the eye; she avoided my gaze.

"You can't say that, Sam," she said to the far wall.

"The hell I can't! I just did!" Then I pulled her to me and put my hand on her face.

"Don't, Sam," she pleaded weakly. By way of an answer I pulled her head to me. Our lips met and we kissed each other deeply and violently. After a minute she pulled away from me.

"Stop this, Sam," she panted.

"Marry me, goddamn it!" I was holding her tight and not altogether against her will.

"No."

"Why the hell not?" I nearly hollered in her ear.

"I can't."

"What d'ya mean, 'I can't.' This is the United States of America—you can do anything you want! You don't want to marry Donald, you want to marry me!"

"How do you know?"

"Because he's a stinker. I've figured that out from things you've let drop."

"Donald shows his affection for me in different ways than you do, Sam." Not being the most affectionate man in the world, I couldn't for the life of me figure that one out.

"Look, I know I ain't too good at loving, but I've tried awful hard. I've worked harder at it than anything I ever done, learning how to care for you. I'll work at it even harder, Jan. I promise."

"It's not that," she replied softly, meeting my gaze for once.

"Well, what in the hell is it, then?" I cried in exasperation.

"I can't tell you."

"Money? Security?" I shot out. "Look, I admit I don't have 'em now, but I will. For you. I just never cared for things for myself, but for you, why—"

"Stop, Sam," she quietly pleaded. "Please."

"Whatever it is you done, or think you done, Jan—it ain't important to me."

No answer, over.

"You've got to go now, Sam." By way of a response I grabbed her head—no, I did not 'lightly place my hands on it,' I grabbed it—and pulled her face to within inches of my own.

"Look me in the eye and tell me you don't love me."

"I don't love you," she replied, blinking.

My response was in anger. It was also slow and measured. "You are a goddamned liar, Janet." I stood up and jammed my hat on; she followed me to the door. As I opened it, I swiftly turned and caught her off guard.

"Oh!" she cried, startled, as I grabbed her by the shoulders and shook her a couple times to get her attention.

"Listen, kid," I began through my teeth, "you remember this and remember it till the day you die. I love you and always will. Always know that you've made me happier than anything. You are getting set to wreck your life. Well, you can always come back to me. If you remember nothing else, always remember that I loved you for who you were, yourself. Not because you're pretty and smart, or because of your education, but because you were you. That is enough for me."

Then I pulled her close and we kissed again. She pulled back and said through tears, "You've got to go *now*, Sam!"

I moved back a foot and looked her over hard, memorizing everything about her as though I would never see her again. Well, I would.

"I love you, Janet."

"Good-bye," she sobbed, giving me a shove out the door and shutting it fast.

I turned around and faced the door.

"See you around."

14

I ABRUPTLY WOKE up the next morning to the sound of some-
one hammering in my door. The pounding stopped for a few
seconds and as I closed my eyes it started again. My eardrums
were a-shivering like kettledrums, so I just rolled over on my
side and groaned.

"Halloooo!" a soft, young female voice sang to my shack.
"Is anybody home?" I woke up with a start. It was Jan; I knowed
it. She had seen the light and come home. To me.

I wobbled to my feet and pulled the door open. Instead of Jan
I was greeted by the shining face of a girl I'd never seen before.
She was nineteen or twenty and had what I can only describe as
a radiant look about her. I had slept in my clothes—it would be
more accurate to say I had stupored in my clothes—so I was
dressed decent, but I reckon I looked like death warmed over.

"Good morning," she said as she took a step back in fright.
I look like hell when I get up stone cold sober; I can only imagine what a sight I presented as I crawled out from under the
blankets dead drunk.

"How," I croaked, my throat as dry as a popcorn fart. I
propped myself against the doorjamb for support. "What can I
do for you?"

"Have you been saved?" she blurted out. The look on her
face indicated she was pretty sure I hadn't been lately.

"I've been drunk." It was not merely the truth; anybody save
a nose-impaired blind man could have seen it.

137

"The Lord wants you to be happy. It saddens Him to see you like this."

"Yeah. Well, when Mr. Overholt sees his profits this month he's gonna be right happy. So it wasn't a total loss, I reckon."

"The Lord does not approve of levity," she warned pleasantly.

"Yeah, well, I'm thinkin' of giving all this up anyhow. Selling my truck and gear and going to live with the cannibals in New Guinea."

She brightened at once. "To teach them the Word?"

"No. To teach 'em how to cook missionaries."

When I finally got up late in the afternoon, my head still felt like it had been in a vise. I got cleaned up and proceeded to fritter away what was left of the day. I made a halfhearted attempt to clean the stalls. When I filled the stock tanks, the sound of the water shooting out of the hose and hitting the galvanized metal was akin to being trapped under Niagara Falls.

I walked out to the pasture and whistled up Molly and Jack. When Jack saw I didn't have a treat for his always-empty paunch, he wheeled as though on a dime and charged for the far end of the pasture, no doubt fearing he was about to be put to work. Molly let me walk up to her and pet her, and as I babbled she just stared back out of huge, protuberant eyes. It was pretty much a one-sided conversation, but for some reason I felt better afterward.

Later that evening, not being able to sleep, I walked over to Luke's house and knocked. Nobody was home so I eased inside and headed for the phone.

It had been only a day since I'd last seen and held Janet, but when she answered the phone and said, "Hello," I couldn't for the life of me tell if it was her or Fletcher.

"Is Janet there?" I said into the mouthpiece.

"Speak-ing!"

"Hello, Jan. Lord, I've missed you."

There was a longish pause. At length she said, "Hello, Sam."

"I've got to see you again. Let's don't let this die, Jan."

"I can't."

"Let's go out."

"No." I suppose a smarter man would have conceded final defeat there and then, but I drove right along. I was, by any stretch of the imagination, not in control of my emotions with that woman.

"I love you," I offered after a long silence.

Nothing back, over.

"Don't hurt me like this, Jan," I quietly pleaded. "Don't hurt yourself like this." She was going to hurt herself, and in a big way; I could feel it. I was getting frantic. The thought of never again seeing Janet, for as long as I lived, was too horrible to contemplate.

"Jan, it's all so damned important."

She was mildly interested. "What?"

"Life!" I hollered into the phone. "Life is so damned important! You can't know it when you're alive, but it is! Dying people, when they know they're dying, try to tell you. They've tried to tell me, and I never figured out what it was they was trying to say till just the other day. They all tried to tell me something and I didn't understand then, but now I do! Jan, it's just like that guy said in the play!"

"Thornton Wilder," she said quietly.

"Yeah, him! He knowed, Jan, he really did! Please don't waste your life. Don't hurt yourself like this."

"I love Donald."

"And he loves you?"

"Yes."

"Well, that bastard don't know how to show it!"

Surprisingly, she didn't hang up. Then I stupidly said "Well, go on—tell me again you don't love me."

"I don't love you."

"Horseshit!"

"Samuel, you don't work at a relationship for over a year then throw it all away." She said it like she was talking to a moron, the only time Janet ever talked to me that way.

"When you know it ain't gonna work, why the hell not?" Then, not waiting for an answer, I continued. "Look, Jan, that's the beauty of you and me. We only had six weeks together but we didn't have to work at a damned thing. We fit together just perfect 'cause we're supposed to be together."

"I have to experience life."

"Whaat?" I was dumbfounded.

"Yes. I have to experience life. And grow."

I was outraged. I exploded at once. "Who put *that* cocka-mamie horseshit in your head? Experience life, my ass! And you figure you can't do that with me, huh? Let me tell you about 'experiencing life and growing.' Those are catchwords for all the goddamned ugly things that happen to us in our lives, most of which we do to ourselves. Experiencing life and growing is getting rocketed and shot at by people you've got nothing against. It's going to places you don't want to go and doing things you don't want to do, and putting up with the dumb, insensitive sons of bitches who happen to make up the majority of the human race. It's eating out of garbage cans, and sometimes freezing and other times sweltering. It's being so goddamned alone you feel like you yourself wrote the book on it. It's watching people you care about go crazy and kill themselves, and watching other people rot from the inside out from hardening of the arteries or cancer or just from being goddamned tired. It's doing things you don't want to do only to keep some dumb son of a bitch off your case. It's being poor and being miserable, and having money and still being miserable. It's making up lies because people are too goddamned hypocritical and vain to accept the truth. It's doing all the goddamned nasty things you've got to do because this society says so, and being miserable in the process."

"For myself, I don't want any more to do with experiencing life and growing: those are just words for self-inflicted wounds. Don't you see, Jan, that's just a phrase some sage wise-ass cooked up to justify all the crap we're supposed to do with a smile on our faces? All I want to do, Jan, is to marry you and build our house and have kids, and shoe horses and make love about eighty-seven times a week. I don't want to experience another goddamned thing, unless it's with you, and even then I'll avoid all the pain I can. I don't know who 'they' are, but, Jan, you're playing right into 'their' hands. I know that at the bottom you want the same thing I do, and that is to be left the hell alone."

I was beat after that speech. I didn't know if Jan was still there or not, but as I caught up my wind she said, "You're a very intense man."

"That's funny. I always thought I was kind of lazy and laid back, myownself."

Another long pause followed before she spoke again. "Do

you think there is just one person you can marry and be happy with?'' I didn't know where the hell that question came from.

''Hell, I don't know,'' I answered, beat out. ''Maybe there's half a dozen or thirty, or a hundred and seventy-five. But the odds of ever running into that person are slim. I met you after thirty-some years and it happened because it was supposed to happen. Don't you reckon there's some purpose, some master plan that meant for us to meet? Hell's bells, Janet! I ain't even religious and *I* believe *that*. I'll believe that till the day I die.''

''You're an easy man for a woman to love,'' she said softly.

''I'll bet I'd be a hell of a lot easier to love if I was a lifer army officer!''

''I don't have to take this from you!''

''You love me, Jan. Your voice lies as bad as your eyes. You should have learned how as a kid.''

Nothing more.

''Look, I've got to know. At the very least I've got to know. So, why? I mean, you went out with me for a month after I asked you to marry me. Then you took the ring off and I thought—well, why?''

''A ring is a symbol,'' she patiently explained, ''and symbols sometimes stand in the way of rational thought process.'' She tossed a couple jokers in that hand; I was plumb lost.

''Oh, I get it,'' I answered, only half understanding. ''You mean you're like a kid who wanted to learn how to ride and rope, and then after his dad bought him a ranch decided he didn't like horses in the first place.''

''Nothing like that at all, Samuel,'' she said, her anger seeping through the phone. Then she added, ''You gave me my space and I appreciate that.''

''Sure,'' I replied, about exhausted. Prior to meeting Janet I'd always thought space was where they shot satellites. ''Anytime. But the way you talked—about being around this fall, and the house—I got to thinking you was going to be here. You can see how I figured that, can't you?'' I was more confused than ever.

''I was daydreaming out loud,'' she coolly informed me. ''Nothing more.''

''Horseshit!'' I exploded. ''You might as well say you was lying out loud! What did that guy do to you, Jan? You was going to tell him the deal was off and it got all turned around. What the hell happened?''

It seemed to take forever for her reply. "I can't tell you. It's too deep." Deep. There was *that* goddamned word again. I had always thought "going deep" was what submariners did when the diving klaxon sounded.

"It ain't supposed to end like this," I said quietly. "I love you so." How many times had I told her that, and to what effect? Was everything in life distorted and unreal? Didn't kindness and honor count for anything? At that point I seriously doubted it.

As I was about to hang up the phone she asked, "Are you going to chase me when I'm married?"

"Well, Jan," I replied in surprise, "I ain't never before made an ass outta myself chasing a married woman, but—you want an honest answer?"

"Yes."

"Well, then, to be honest about it, in your case I'd have to think it over."

Her reply startled me. "I don't know when I'll be back," she quietly said. I thought I heard teardrops hit the phone.

"Aw, Jan! that's great! I mean, you're coming back, then, aren't you! Hey, that's swell! But listen, since you're coming back anyway, just don't marry him in the first place!" Well, hell, I had the ball and was going for broke.

"I have to," she quietly replied. She certainly wasn't pregnant or anything. At that point I had no idea why she had to.

"Don't do it, Jan," I warned her. "Look, if you marry him, you'll ruin all three of our lives. But if you marry me, he'll get over it soon enough."

There was what the writers call a "discernible pause" on the phone. After a few seconds of unnerving calm she said, "I don't want to have to make you hate me. I saw my father do that to my mother, and I don't want to have to do it with you, but I will."

There was anger and fear and maybe— I don't know what I heard in her voice. I didn't know what else to do but hit her with the truth, so at length I replied, "Aw, Jan, you couldn't do that. There ain't an unkind bone in your body." Then, near as I could tell, she started crying. I thought I heard her choke, and it seemed she removed the phone from her ear.

She didn't say nothing.

It had all been said. Janet was going to live out the duke's command and do what she had to do, or what she thought she had to do. In a crazy way I admired that, being of the headstrong variety myself. But she was fixing to mess up things mighty sorry.

"Well, I reckon there's nothing else to say," I said softly. "Except good-night. And, Jan, I love you."

Then I hanged up the phone, not waiting for a response.

And then I went back to my shack and once again got blind drunk.

15

JACK RILEY WOKE me up the next morning. Had there been a Town Drunk Competition that week, I could have given old Jack a run for his money, and he a shoo-in for first place at that.

"Sam, git up," Jack ordered as he shook my leg. "Luke says ya hain't done nothin' fer two days. He sait t' tell ya—"

"Tell Luke I am fucking leaving. No, I'll tell him," I groaned. I was smack in the middle of one of them crisises that happens to a man every now and again. The choices was roll over and crawl in a bottle and give up like Jack had done years before, or go on. And there was one word never used in the Hawkins family:

Surrender.

So I crawled out of them blankets and went out behind my shack and heaved. I boiled a pot of coffee, using two handfuls instead of the usual one, and after I'd drank the pot I felt better still.

I stuck my head under a spigot, and after that made a half-hearted attempt to shave. As I wiped my face a lark gaily called from the nearby pasture. I glanced to the west and saw Pikes Peak towering and bare-tipped, like it had been before man himself, and then I was glad to be alive, in spite of myself.

At that point in my life I had not been licked by hurricanes, incoming rounds, blizzards, flash floods, spooked horses or wild-eyed mules, rolled trucks, ghetto punks, or starving times.

I decided I would be goddamned if Janet Provost would succeed where everything else had failed. I'd always at least broken even with all other forms of hardship, and I was still alive.

But I still loved her powerful hard. And you've got to admit she had a funny way of saying good-bye.

I packed my gear in the bed of my old truck; I didn't bother to ask for any help trailering my horses. A couple hours after starting to pack I was ready to roll.

I tossed a couple flakes of alfalfa through the trailer feed door and said to my horses, "Well, guys, back to the Bayou Salade. Good grass up there yet." Then Luke and Jack walked out of the house and headed toward me.

As they neared I shot first. "I ain't been a very good hand, Luke."

"Thet's all right, Sam. Ya done right good. Till a coupla days ago when ya started on the sauce." He said it without malice, then throwed Jack a hard look. "Hit must be catchin'. Sorry things didn't work out 'tween thet girl an' you."

"I don't recall telling you," I replied as I extended my hand.

"We figgered hit out!" Jack enthused.

I had to smile. "Yeah. Jack—about that ten and what I said. I—"

"Fergit hit, Sam." He smiled full-mouthed and showed me his gums even as he extended his hand. "We kin still be frans."

"Sure," I answered, unable to say more because of the lump in my throat. All I could figure was that it had something to do with hitting thirty and corresponding old age.

"Well . . ." I mumbled. Luke had been especially kind and Jack had just been Jack. They would forever be linked in my mind with Janet and the happiest days of my life.

I opened my truck door, then stopped and turned around. "Luke, I can't explain, but Janet might come looking for me someday. You're about the only way she could find me. If she shows up, Dusty Rhodes— the game warden in Gunnison— he generally knows where I am within a state or two. I'd be obliged . . ."

The huge man stepped forward, grabbed my arm, and about cut off the circulation. "Ah'll treat her lak mah very owned daughter. Thet's a promise, Sam," he affirmed, nodding his head.

"Thanks," I replied, my throat tight. Then I jumped in my

truck and turned the key. Even as I started to let out the clutch Luke stuck his face in my open window.

"Ah hope ya kin be happy someday."

"Yeah. Y'know, it's funny. I always thought I was, before. See you around."

I pulled out of the driveway and turned onto the old county road. I was hoping Philo and Crazy Joe was still in the bayou where I'd left them six weeks earlier. If they'd left I hoped they'd thought to leave word so I could locate them.

As I drove I hoped it would be just like the old days.

But somehow that didn't seem possible no more.

Two and a half hours later I rolled to a stop in the same little clearing we'd parked in almost two months earlier. To my relief Crazy Joe's aging International and trailer was still there. I figured he'd be near the old campsite a few miles upstream.

Molly and Jack unloaded fast and grateful as always, and then I saddled up my mare. I followed the rocky banks of the meandering creek, and every dozen seconds gave a tug on the lead rope as always-hungry Jack stopped for a mouthful of grass.

"I ain't gonna stop here," I told myself as I neared what had been Janet's campsite. Then, before I knowed what I'd done, I was tying off my critters to small aspens, and walked over to it anyway.

I took a cross-legged seat on the exact spot I'd had tea with Janet, and looked skyward to the same mountain peaks, unchanged and concerned with their own eternal problems. Her small campfire ring was still intact, unused since the day she had left.

Then I bent over that old fire ring and pulled out a handful of ashes. I carefully examined them, as though Janet might have left part of herself behind in them. Then I jumped to my feet and flinged them ashes, white and flourlike, as high as I could and yelled an obscenity to nobody in particular. A man can go crazy in the remembering of it all, and I sat there for the longest time thinking of everything, yet thinking of nothing.

I was absorbed in thought when a voice about ten yards in back of me announced, "Don't move! I've got the drop on you!"

I let out a sigh. "That's really not very funny, Crazy Joe." I didn't bother to turn around.

He walked up then, his face a wild grin, and I turned around to see his horses tied fifty yards behind me. "Where's Jan?" he grinned.

I thought, "Oh, shit." I proceeded to give him the condensed version as I fiddled with my pipe. In fact, that was about all him and Philo ever got; the bare outline. I've run it all through my mind to write down here, and now am going to try to forget it, myownself.

Once I'd finished the story I asked, "So where's Philo?"

"He took off for the Wind River Mountains this morning. I tried calling Luke's from Fairplay a couple days ago and nobody answered. I was going to head down there today and see what was happening. Say, Sam, why don't I just bust a cap on that piss-drinkin' lifer dog?"

"Why'd you want to shoot Philo?" I replied, not giving thought to what he'd said.

"No, Sam—Donald! Then your problems would be over!" I think he was half-serious.

"Oh, shitfire! That'd be just great," I said with a groan. " 'Well, Jan, we can get married now! Crazy Joe just blasted Donald into eternity.' Use your bloody head, would you, Joe?"

"Just tryin' to help."

"Sure. What part of the Winds is Philo headed for?"

"He said the Little Sandy River. He gave me directions. He was going to leave his outfit with some rancher; I wrote it all down."

"That would be Reed Gibson."

"That's the guy," he agreed.

"Say, how much gold you guys wind up with?"

"Fourteen ounces, since you left," he announced, rightly proud. I whistled low, thinking of my own depleted money supply. Somehow, between working on my truck and running around with Jan, I'd run through two grand in as many months. I still had my savings account in Gunnison, but I hated to touch that money.

"Not bad, Joe. Well, let's get your gear loaded and get outta here; it's only one o'clock. We can make the Wyoming line tonight and I know a good place to camp on the Little Snake. Plenty of wood and water and grass."

"You want to get outta here bad, don't ya, Sam?" He flipped a Bull Durham butt into the long-dead campfire ashes.

"Yeah. And remind me never to come back. Still, there's way more to this whole Janet business than meets the eye. I suppose I can live with losing, but it flat pisses me off to have to live not knowing."

"Let me know if I can help."

I stood up and knocked out my pipe on the heel of my hand. "Yeah. But for the meantime, this child's thinkin' white diggin's don't shine nohow ya cut 'em. In other words, let's vamoose."

WE RODE THE west slope of the Wind River Mountains that July, scouting for fur sign and taking what small game we needed to get by. As July 28 approached I became more edgy: Jan was, I thought, a free-spirited woman who loved me more than she knowed. In four days she would be a proper married woman—properly married all right, to the wrong man. Late on the afternoon of July 24 we was camped along the northern stretches of the Little Sandy River, about as far from anywhere as our present civilization measures anywhere. The horses was picketed out, and I was laying propped against my saddle, the bottoms of my feet close enough to the small campfire to toast the soles of my moccasins.

"I think I'll be leaving tomorrow," I said to nobody in particular. Crazy Joe looked up from the horseshoe he was shaping and his expression told me nothing. Philo glanced up from the hunk of meat he was roasting on a stick; I'd seen that glance probably a dozen times in the ten years. It meant "Yore gettin' set t' mess things up purty bad, but ah'm with ya." I knocked the heel out of my pipe and refilled it.

"Beaver won't be primed up for two months. Deer season don't open for six weeks," I said for lack of anything better to offer.

"Ah see yore plannin' on attendin' a weddin'," Philo casually remarked.

"All right! What if I am!" I shouted. "Jan is supposed to

marry that miserable son of a bitch in four days! She don't want to do it, not for herself! Goddamnit t' hell, she's doin' it 'cause it's been set up for months, and for her folks, and probably 'cause of all the crazy stuff that women think, like 'What'll the neighbors say?' Shit!'' I had no business going off on my part- ners like that, and they few in number to boot, but I was very much in love with that woman and not in my right mind.

"Ah do not believe you was invited,'' Philo remarked, ig- noring my outburst.

"No, they musta forgotten my name on the guest list!''

"What are ya gonna do, Sam?'' Crazy Joe asked with a grin. "Shoot the groom? Boo-hoo-hoo-haw-haw-haw!''

"Only if he makes me.'' I had no intention of shooting Don- ald—unless it was necessary. I just couldn't let Jan marry him and ruin her life. I didn't have a plan at the time, but had a thousand-mile drive in which I reckoned I would come up with something original. After all, my intentions at the time was noble; maybe tainted with a bit of insanity, but noble nonethe- less. I know now that you can't save somebody from themself. I probably knowed it then but wouldn't have admitted it. Love, like those still waters, runs pretty deep.

"I figure we're thirty miles from the outfits, more or less. I'm heading out at dawn. Load up the boys, pick up I-80 at Rock Springs, and drive to beat hell.''

"Then what?'' Philo asked as he tore into a chunk of charred meat.

"Well, the wedding's in a little country church, just acrost the Mississippi in Illinois. That's good, 'cause I aim to stake the critters out in a slough—hopefully nobody'll run onto 'em—then head on to the church. Or maybe,'' I continued, thinking out loud, "maybe I'll just leave the outfit and ride to church and Jan and I'll get away on horseback!'' I came up with that plan on the spot and sure liked it. It had my style written all over it.

"Sam, I *am* crazy, but you're nuts,'' Crazy Joe said, wiping his curved Green River skinner on his britches. "You gonna stand up when the preacher comes to the part about anybody objectin' and yell, 'I do, ya sons of bitches!' '' He got up laugh- ing, picked up a couple logs, and placed them on the fire. I didn't say anything further and the conversation dropped at that point. The flames licked the aspen logs and I stared off into space, thinking about nothing in particular but a lot of things in general. After a while Philo got up, wiped his mouth with a greasy sleeve, and tossed his roasting stick into the flames.

"Wal, ah reckon," he said to nobody in particular. I was watching the sun dip over the mountains far to the west; it was a ball of crimson. The sunsets in the West are something, especially in the summer when the air is thick with fresh pine smell and the green on valley and hill more than makes up for the cold camps, cold streams, and ultimate alone. A sunset is also a reminder that tomorrow will come, and there's a promise of itself. A promise of good water and good grass; of fur yet untrapped; of friends waiting and freedom and clear, high passes. There was also the promise—or distant hope—of Janet, and she was in my thoughts when Philo again spoke.

"Wal, ah reckon," he repeated.

"What?"

"Ah reckon ah'm gonna grain the hawses t'night so's ah doan' hafta fuss with 'em come mornin'. Gonna be a long ride to-morrah. Then ah'm gonna turn in."

"Where you goin'?" I asked distractedly as I stirred the dirt with a stick.

"With you."

"Me, too," Crazy Joe chimed in. "I wouldn't miss this for all the pussy in Subic Bay."

"Hell. I appreciate it." I didn't know what else to say. I had hoped my partners would come along, but it wasn't the kind of thing I could ask them to do. We would be going deep into Indian country and far out of our element. If the whole program blowed up in our faces we was apt to be in trouble up to our ears. I should have told them, "Boys, you can't come along," but I didn't.

"Thet's all right, Sam. Ya might need some help. Ah seed this a-comin' anyhow; ah was jest wonderin' when ya was gonna start back." Philo pulled a half-gone plug of tobacco from his shooting bag and bit off a huge chew. He let it soak for a long minute, then spit a long brown stream into the fire. "Jest doan' eveh let hit be sait ah nevah tried t' help the cause a love."

I stood up. "I'll give you a hand with the horses."

"Naw. Joe'n ah'll do hit. C'mon, Joe. Ya bettah work on yore battle plan, Sam, an' make hit a good un. Ya lead us inta an ambush ah'm apt t' be highly pissed.''

Crazy Joe Flanigan and Philo Harris might have been a lot of things, but to me they was friends. That was my hour of need, and they volunteered to help. For all they knowed I was going to crash a church wedding with a Colt six-shooter in each hand, fire a couple rounds for effect, and cause the goddamnedest scene that little church would see till the Second Coming. Philo and Crazy Joe didn't question a damn thing and they didn't ask me to explain; maybe they knowed there was no explaining. They just said they was going, and when those two said they were kicked in, they meant screw the consequences.

They were like that.

Friends.

Anybody who never had one probably wouldn't know what I'm talking about.

We hit the trail at dawn and followed the Little Sandy down out of the high country. When we broke out of the trees the land opened up and we rode three abreast, our pack animals trailing. After three hours we picked up a gravel road and started to make time. I figured we'd be at our outfits by one in the afternoon.

I turned in the saddle and took a long look at the mountains behind us, already getting a little out of focus. "Well, so long to the Winds for a while. Carson or Fremont or somebody called 'em 'the backbone of North America.' I figure 'em for next to home, myself.''

"As close t' home as ha eveh felt,'' Philo commented.

"I don't know about that,'' Crazy Joe happily remarked. "I kind of miss the maid and mansion in Rhode Island, boo-hoo-hoo-haw-haw-haw!'' Philo shook his head and grinned his face-splitting raccoon grin. I smiled back.

"I think it's about time for a story,'' I said as I clucked to Jack to move along smartly. He'd dropped out of his easy rocking-chair trot and the other horses had a habit of picking up on his lead. He was naturally contrary, so among the equine race that made him a natural leader. I nicked him with a heel and he again picked up the slow trot.

"Yeah, Joe,'' Philo drawled, "let's heah 'bout the time ya

screwed the maid when ya was ten." Crazy Joe chuckled and smiled. He was not full of false modesty when it come to women.

"Aw, gee, guys." He grinned. "Okay. Well, it wasn't the maid, it was the cook. And I was thirteen. Anyway . . ."

With the benefit of Crazy Joe's tall tales, the morning ride passed quickly. We made our outfits early in the afternoon. Our rancher friend Reed Gibson was away from his place, and I was busy shaving in my truck mirror, half dressed in my town duds, when Crazy Joe walked up.

"You about ready, Joe? My horses are loaded—are yours?"

His brow was furrowed. "Sam, how much oil pressure are you supposed to have when the engine's running?"

"Thirty to sixty pounds. Why?"

"Did you hear me start my truck?"

"Yeah," I answered, alarm growing inside me.

"Well, I started it, heard this '*clunk*,' and now I don't seem to have any oil pressure. Zero ain't too good, is it?"

I wiped my razor on a dirty towel and let out a sigh. "Oh, fuck a duck," I said with a groan.

Crazy Joe's truck had eaten the valves, rods, pistons, or something that goes up and down or sideways in an engine: I don't know a damn thing about the guts of vehicles: I drive 'em, I don't build 'em.

"Wal, what next, Sam?" Philo drawled as we slammed down the hood of Crazy Joe's International.

"Shit, I dunno. Joe, you still want to go along?"

"Like I said, I wouldn't miss it for all the—"

"All right. You can ride with me. We'll take one horse each and put the others in Reed's pasture; we'll leave a note saying we had a sudden emergency come up, had to leave most tick but will be back in a week to get your outfit and the horses. That's as good as I come up with on the spot."

"Hit's two-thirty, Sam," Philo impatiently informed me. "How fur ya figger on gittin' t'day?"

"I've been thinking we ought to drive straight through. We can make it in twenty-four hours, give or take a couple. And we don't have much time, anyway." The basic insanity underlying my plan was starting to work its way into my thick skull. Win or lose, it depended on Janet playing it game to the end: if she didn't go along with it, I figured we'd meet approximately the same end as the Jameses' and Youngers when they robbed the Northfield bank. As I recall, they was tracked down, shot, and captured in some miserable Minnesota swamp. That idea didn't appeal to me at all, but I'd committed myself.

"Wal, let's git Crazy Joe's critter loaded. Ah'm ready t' roll when y'all are. How fur's hit again?"

"Thousand miles, more or less."

"An' damn Yankees everwhar," he grumbled.

"I ain't worried," Crazy Joe said cheerfully. "I'm bringing my legal representatives with me." As we all were.

Meaning Mssrs. Colt, Winchester & Company.

Around five that afternoon we hit I-80 at Rock Springs and stopped to gas the vehicles and water and feed the animals. Our animals was used to long trailer rides, and while I've always preferred to go no more than five hundred miles a day and unload them for a rest, we didn't have much choice in that situation. We piled six or eight inches of straw on the floor of each trailer so to cushion the ride; I-80 is rougher than a cob, east of Grand Island.

At six the next morning we pulled into the weigh station outside of Council Bluffs. The sign a mile from the exit announced *Weigh Station OPEN* in big neon letters. A little further on, a black-lettered sign had warned *All Trucks with Trailers and Trucks over 6,000 lbs Must Weigh!* An invitation like that is hard to refuse, especially when one knows a state trooper will pinch you half a mile down the road if you don't pull over. They have this habit of chasing fellers that blast past the scales.

I stopped on the scales and to my surprise got a little amber light instead of a green one. The little letters inside the light spelled out *Park, Come Inside*. I pulled my outfit over by an idling eighteen-wheeler, grabbed my manila folder with my licenses and official papers in it, and headed inside.

"Sam, I don't have the paperwork on Geronimo with me. It's in my truck," Crazy Joe said as he walked next to me.

"Don't sweat it. I've got two horses and two sets of health certificates and receipts et cetra. Guarantee you whoever's running this place don't know a roan from a chestnut or sorrel. We'll bullshit our way out."

"Howdy," I said to the fat, pimple-faced almost-smoky as

we walked in. He was filling out a form and didn't bother to look up.

"You got horses in that trailer, cowboy?"

"Yeah. Unless they got out at Gothenburg to take a piss and didn't tell me about it."

He looked up then and stopped writing. "You're not very funny at this early hour. Got papers?"

"All kinds of 'em. What d'ya want to see?"

"Truck registration, trailer registration. Health certificates on the horses," he ordered as he resumed writing. I was pulling out the appropriate forms when Philo walked in.

"Got horses in that trailer?"

"Yup."

"Truck registration, trailer registration. Health certificates on the horses," he repeated.

When I had all my paperwork out, the young cop snatched it out of my hand. He quickly scanned a form. "You live in Montrose, Colorado?"

"Quite a bit of the time." Well, two or three days a year.

He shuffled the papers, examined one health certificate, and then the other. He looked up then, his brow troubled. "One health certificate's from Rawlins, Wyoming; the other's from Cari . . . Carry . . ."

"Carrizozo, New Mexico." I smiled. "I get around a lot."

"That a fact."

"Yep."

He grimaced, tossed my paperwork back at me, and glanced over Philo's. I thought he gave Philo's a pretty cursory look compared to mine. Evidently he didn't see many world travelers and was fascinated by us. More than likely he didn't like my attitude.

"You guys all together?" he inquired as he handed back Philo's paperwork.

"We are traveling together, yes."

"Where you headed with them horses?" he queried, like it was his business to know. I can't stand a nosy anybody, but he was dealing.

"We are horse traders. We are going to a show," I replied. I don't like to lie—except when I have to, to survive—and that was pretty close to the truth. We did trade horses now and then, and I figured the wedding would turn out to be quite a show. The funny part was that the cop, who was a weigh-station attendant and not a real cop at that, smelled something. I thought we looked like any three cowboys you'd spot in Walsenburg or Jackson, yet he figured us for something else, although he apparently wasn't certain what. My medicine was working and it was telling me "don't add nothing."

Almost friendly-like he added, "You ever see *The Long Riders*?"

"Yeah. I did," I replied as Philo stuffed his papers in an old envelope.

"I saw it, too," Crazy Joe remarked as he lit a Bull Durham. "So what?"

"Well, that's who you guys remind me of. The James Gang." That was one hell of a backhanded compliment, but I didn't feel that was the time to get smart-assed. For all I knowed, the cop had a warrant for Crazy Joe's arrest for the murder of Spiderman's motorcycle.

"Thanks a hell of a lot," I grumped as we headed out the door.

"Where'd you guys say you're going?" he added as I let the door swing shut behind me. I stopped in my tracks, opened the door, and stuck my head back inside.

"I didn't say, but it's Northfield, Minnesota." I grinned, baring my teeth.

"You guys stay outta trouble!"

"Sam, whyn't ya keep yore mouth shut?" Philo lamented as we walked to our vehicles.

"He just pissed me off, punk kid anyway," I answered. "There's a truck stop up the road about twenty miles. The last time I was through here they had good apple pie."

"Let's stop," Crazy Joe piped up. "I'm hungry enough to eat hoof parings." He quickly flicked his cigarette off into the weeds.

"Ah jest wisht ya knowed when t' keep yore mouth shut," Philo moaned.

Six hours later we crossed the Mississippi at Davenport. We still had a day and a half till the wedding, and I figured I would have enough time to plan. Enough time to recon the church and plan the operation, but not so much time that we would be noticed. I hoped. The idea was to lay low until our grand entrance. Plenty of people would see us then.

I pulled over at a wayside near Rock Island and Philo followed my lead. Crazy Joe and I grabbed buckets and headed for the hand pump. Molly and Geronimo hadn't been watered for a few hundred miles.

"Ah'm beat," Philo said as he joined us with his own bucket. "How much fartha?"

" 'Bout thirty miles, if I remember the map correctly," I replied. "We'll find a place to camp by the river, and you guys can stay low while I check things out."

"You going to give Jan a chance to back out before D-day?" Crazy Joe asked. I worked the pump handle violently and filled Philo's bucket.

"Not only no, but hell no. I've said all I'm gonna say. Besides, she's probably staying with her potential in-laws: I'd hate to wind up plugging all them people. I'm gonna put her on the spot at the finish line—where in fact we'll have the advantage of surprise—and it'll be 'put up or shut up' time."

Philo shook his head as he walked toward his trailer, water sloshing over the top of his bucket. "Ya mean hit'll be 'shoot 'em up' time," he grumbled to nobody in particular.

As we headed north on the state highway paralleling the river, a thousand thoughts ran through my mind: my sister I hadn't seen for three years, who lived three or four hundred miles away. My uncle Dutch, alone and waiting for death in some miserable rest home a couple hundred miles to the west. I thought of the old times with my family, of fishing with my dad and hunting with Uncle Dutch and . . . and Janet and her impending marriage kept interrupting my thoughts.

I was seeing all of those people and places and times when I glanced in my rearview mirror and saw Philo flashing his headlights. I pulled over on the narrow shoulder and Crazy Joe and I got out.

"Ya say thet church was called the Deer Creek Community Church?"

"Something like that. What's up?"

"We jest drove past hit."

"Oh. Okay."

* * *

We camped alongside a slough just over the Burlington Northern tracks and a mile from the church. We staked our horses out
in a meadow and let them graze on the rich swamp grass. The
next morning Philo and Crazy Joe drove into town and filled
the minnow bucket at a bait shop. If anybody asked, that was
the story: We was up north to sell horses and stopped to take a
rest and do some fishing. We set up a lean-to, kept the guns out
of sight, and made sure the fishing poles was in sight. As long
as nobody asked too many probing questions—and Janet didn't
happen by—we would be in good shape.

" 'Bout time I went to church," I announced to my partners
after we'd set up. "I'm going to drop the trailer, drive on over,
and have a look at the lay of the place. With any luck at all it
won't fall in on me."

"Take mah truck, Sam," Philo offered with a smile. "Jan
prob'ly won't reconnize hit if she come by."

"Good idea. I'll take it, then. Hey, Philo, they wouldn't be
rehearsing today, would they?"

"Naw," he drawled as he carefully hooked a minnow through
the back. "They do all thet crap a few days befoah. Not the day
befoah." Philo was the only one of us who had ever been
hitched, so in matters matrimonial I took his word pretty much
without question. He knowed the logistics of the doings.

I drove Philo's old truck slowly past the church. There was
no cars in sight, and the nearest house was half a mile down the
road. I pulled up in front and got out.

It was a regular Little Brown Church in the Vale and could
have come out of a Currier & Ives print. It belonged to the
America of horse-drawn buggies and muddy roads; the America
of enameled coffeepots and wood cookstoves, and Mississippi
sternwheelers and steam locomotives. It was about as out of
place in the latter quarter of the twentieth century as I was.

I tried the front door; it opened and I walked in. The hard
maple floor squeaked beneath my steps and the oldness of the
place filled the air. Right there and then I felt real bad about
what I was going to have to do the next day in this quaint little
church. Then I recalled Janet had brought all this on in the first
place, for had she married me I wouldn't have been there, a
nineteenth-century man in a nineteenth-century church plotting
how to bust open a twentieth-century wedding.

I snooped around the back and found the side entrance that came in behind the organ, separated from the main part of the church by a partition. From that side door a man could walk unseen to the big blue curtains which covered most of the front wall. I found the drawstring and pulled. Sure enough, they opened swiftly. I had my plan.

That evening around a small fire, catfish skewered on sticks, we rehearsed. After dark I drove my compañeros over to the locked church and we walked through the operation as best we could. In the moonlight Philo noticed what I'd overlooked. The back lawn of the church ran straight into a huge pasture; in the distance I saw patches of white and black that belonged to the hides of holstein cows. The pasture gate wasn't locked, and swung open with a creak.

"Less'n ah miss mah guess, this heah pasture runs over thet l'il knoll clear t' the railroad tracks," Philo observed as he took a fresh chew.

"You thinkin' what I'm thinkin'?" I asked with a smile.

"Horses," said Crazy Joe, grinning. "We *can* ride in and ride out." Then we layed out a couple two-by-fours I'd brought along in the unmowed grass next to the church door.

And the next morning that was exactly what we done.

Rode in and rode out.

So maybe we was Long Riders after all.

The sign by the pulpit—the one that gives last week's contributions and the number in attendance—said *Wedding 10:00* A.M. *Saturday*. I took it at its word. By nine o'clock we had loaded our gear and positioned the outfits so to expedite a quick escape. I figured once I'd saved Jan, why, I'd swing her up behind me, wedding dress and all, and we'd ride off pretty as you please. I will not further comment on my state of mind at the time other than to add that desperate men can be driven to desperate undertakings by believing something which in fact may not be true.

We saddled up shortly before nine-thirty. Had anybody seen us up close they would have taken us for a sight. It took some convincing but I persuaded Crazy Joe not to wear his outlandish 1870s period dress coat; I also talked him into carrying only one Colt. He tucked his pants into his high-topped boots and at my

request wore a cheap flannel shirt. I plain didn't want him advertising his presence with his trademark.

Philo had put on a new pair of Levi's and wore his Colt in
plain sight on his hip. He'd brushed down his 5X Stetson, and
like Crazy Joe and myself adorned his neck with a bandanna.
Hanging from the O-rings of his saddle, to the offside of his
horse, was his scabbard-slung Winchester carbine.

I wore my gray wool shield-front shirt, the same one I'd had
on the day fate or Somebody with a hell of a sense of humor
sent Janet into my life. I too had on a clean pair of Levi's; fact
is, I had bought them on sale and since the legs was too long
rolled them up to about a five-inch cuff. I wore my dress boots,
and stuck my short-barreled Colt in my belt, the hammer resting
on an empty chamber. Anybody seeing us up close would take
us for hardcases, definitely out of place in Illinois, or anywhere
in the twentieth century, for that matter. At a distance, however, we would pass for three guys wearing cowboy hats out on
a ride. We was counting on that.

We crossed the Burlington tracks and rode at a slow trot
through a patch of woods thinned out by grazing. Where the
woods met the pasture we opened the gate and quickened the
trot. It was a quarter to ten. Nobody had said a word, and finally
Philo spoke up.

"Sam, did ya put on clean underwar shorts t'day?"

"What if I didn't?"

"But if'n ya git shot, what'll the folks in the hosspiddle
thank?"

"My grandma used to say that, 'cept she applied it to car
accidents."

"My grandma owned the hospital!" Crazy Joe exclaimed.
"Boo-hoo-hoo-haw-haw-haw!"

We quick-release-tied our horses at the gate behind the church.
I peeked around the corner and saw no one out front, just a
collection of automobiles. From inside the church came what I
took for the screechings of the featured soloist. The old red brick
walls seemed to vibrate from the organ and the soprano's bellering; she was singing some song about love eternal-lasting and
birds or something.

I motioned for Philo to take the front door as planned. I

grabbed him by the shoulder and whispered, "Remember, when he comes to 'if anyone here'— that's the cue."

"Got it." He grinned, Winchester in hand. Then he started for the front of the church. I put my ear to the side door. I could hear the minister's voice real plain. When we hit 'We are gathered here together,' I slowly pushed the door open. Crazy Joe and I eased in, neat as you please.

". . . and if there is anybody present who has any objections to this marriage of Donald and Janet, let him speak up now or forever hold his piece," the preacher intoned, like there would be no takers.

At which point Crazy Joe, from his position behind the partition, gave the cord a violent tug and the curtains parted with a *whoosh!* The preacher turned around with a start and I found myself looking straight at him, Janet, Donald, and a couple hundred friends and relatives who all seemed to have the same blank expression on their faces. I throwed my Winchester out by the lever, cocking it, and stepped forward.

"I'm holding my piece, and I object!" I announced through my bandanna. You could have heard a mouse cut wind in that church. Crazy Joe came up from behind the partition and stepped up to the pulpit, confident as some revivalist preacher hisownself. I thought I saw horror written on Janet's face, and I felt bad about that. Make that Horror with a capital *H*. Donald was quite resplendent in his dress army officer's uniform; he was dressed fit to kill, if you'll pardon the line. It was dead quiet in there, and seeing as how I'd stopped the proceedings, I took charge.

"Folks, we've got a slight interruption here. Please don't nobody move." I waved my rifle toward the front door. "My partner, with the Winchester." At that point Philo pivoted in the aisle from behind the inside door. He waved his rifle pleasantly at the congregation and tipped his hat.

"Please keep yore seats, folks," he requested pleasantly, like he was asking them not to stick chewing gum under the pews. If there was general disbelief by that congregation at what was happening, they did know the guns was real enough. They didn't know for sure that we weren't about to shoot anybody—with the possible exception of Donald—but that big question mark would keep them humble. I stepped up to Jan. The preacher, a balding, skinny old fellow that looked like Hank Worden, sat down on the raised steps with his head in his hands. I patted him on the shoulder.

"Take it easy, old-timer. We're peaceable, in spite of our looks." Then I addressed Jan: "May I have a word with you, please?"

Donald was the first of the two to speak, and it took a second or two for his mouth to form the words. "I'll kill you, whoever you are!" he said with a hiss, his face about six shades of purple.

"Pilgrim," I replied patiently, "I am real peaceable and in a real good mood. My friends and me have all the equalizers here, and Jan and I are going to talk. You just stand there at attention like a good soldier and we'll get along fine." I took Jan by the hand and led her off a dozen feet to the side. It wasn't like we needed our privacy at that point; the damage had been done. There was no good way to do it, anyway.

"Jan, I love you. Marry me," I asked quietly.

She had recovered enough to talk. Her large brown eyes were rimmed with tears, and her voice was choked with emotion when she said, "You rotten son of a bitch!" For the record, I don't take that from anybody. I have cold-cocked men for saying things like that. But the circumstances there was unique, and I was very much in love and not in my right mind, so I took it. However, I couldn't for the life of me figure out what to say next. I had envisioned myself as Jan's rescuer, not as a villain.

While I stood there in shock Crazy Joe took over the running of the church. He was leading the gathered in "Cool Water," waving his Colt like a baton and urging the good folk to sing louder:

> "The nights are cool and I'm a fool,
> each star's a pool of water.
> Cool, clear water."

"Louder, folks!" Crazy Joe implored, waving his Colt high in the air. I can't sing alone!"

I started again. "Jan, I've come to take you home. Back to the West, where you belong. I'm ready to settle down and build that adobe house by the Spanish Peaks. And you'll be freer with me than any man on earth. I know you love me, Jan. And I love you so. I truly do.''

''Get out of my life, you bastard!'' she spat. ''You've ruined my wedding day! Can't you see what you've done? You insensitive bastard!'' By golly if she didn't growl all of the above; she didn't snap it out and she didn't holler it; it was a growl, make no mistake. Then she started crying violently. ''I don't love you, Sam,'' she said through tears, ''so get out of here and get out of my life. Forever!''

I never said I was too smart, but I know when I'm dismissed. I still held her hand in mine, and looked dead into those lying eyes. Meanwhile Crazy Joe and the wedding-goers sang on:

> ''Old Dan and I with throats burned dry
> and souls that cry
> for water,
> Cool, clear water.''

''All right,'' I replied. ''I just want you to know that I know you're lying. And I still love you, Jan. In spite of yourself.'' Then I let go her hand and addressed the congregation. ''All right, folks, you can go on with the proceedings. Sorry about the interruption, and please don't anybody try to leave this house of worship for the next hour. My companion with the Winchester will be stationed out front.'' Crazy Joe stepped down from the pulpit, but not before he told the gathered what a swell bunch of singers they was. I signaled to Philo to exit and he shot out the door. He knowed what to do from there.

I stole a final look at Jan over my shoulder. Donald was holding her and she was on a regular crying jag. Well, I thought, so long to love. Then I ducked out the side door and helped Crazy Joe stick the two-by-four through the handles. I was back on familiar territory—I had a crisis to survive—and I started getting my mind in gear for our exit as we ran the thirty yards to the horses.

''You bolt the door?'' I yelled to Philo.

''Ah hope t' shit!'' he hollered back. We reached our horses at the same time, and in a lot less time than it takes to tell about it had saddled up and were putting heel to flank. As we rode at a dead run through the pasture I figured we had a good half hour before anybody got to a phone. First they had to break out of the church, then the wedding would probably go on anyway. I wasn't exactly sure what crimes it was we committed, but I was plenty sure they was heinous.

"Hey! They couldn't sing for shit!" Crazy Joe yelled as we galloped toward our outfits. "I just told 'em that to be polite!" In a couple minutes we hit the woodline and had to slow to a lope to negotiate our way around the trees.

"Meet us at Reed's early next week!" I hollered to Philo. In another minute we broke across the railroad tracks, and a minute after that we were at our outfits. I reined in Molly a dozen feet from the open trailer door. She knowed something was definitely wrong; we had been together long enough for her to sense when we was in trouble. Even as I swung out of the saddle and cleared my rifle from the scabbard, she walked right in the trailer. I slammed the door fast even as Crazy Joe loaded Geronimo, but twenty feet away Philo was vainly tugging at Buck's reins. Crazy Joe and I ran over.

"Git in thar, you son of a bitch!" Philo ordered as he slapped the beast on the rump. He didn't budge. Crazy Joe put the reins through the feed door and was pulling from the front of the trailer. Buck made the mistake of putting his front hoofs on the trailer floor and the adrenaline must have been pumping through Philo and me, for we each grabbed a cheek of Buck's ass and throwed him in that trailer. Well, purt near.

Crazy Joe and I hit my truck at a run and jumped in. As I started moving out I glanced in my rearview mirror and saw Philo pulling out behind me. Philo was going to head down to Oklahoma and visit his kin on the way back, then meet us at Reed's. Crazy Joe and I were heading due West, and hopefully would have the old International running by the time Philo showed up. As I made the main road I was hoping mightily that Jan was lying when she said she didn't love me. Because if she didn't, I didn't see any way she wouldn't identify me. And Philo and Crazy Joe.

In which case we all three would be in very deep shit indeed.

As near as I could judge, about up to our ears.

17

THERE ARE SOME benefits to having served in the military during the late unpleasantness in Southeast Asia. Anybody who was there can tell you a man got used to things blowing up in his face—literally and figuratively. After all, learning to deal with disappointment and pain is learning to deal with life. If nothing else, it prepared me for what I consider one of the great disasters of my life, the same disaster I've documented in excruciating detail these past pages. It still took some getting used to.

By going ahead and marrying Donald, Janet had ruined three lives, as near as I could tell: hers, mine, and Donald's. I figured that if she had married me, Donald would have recovered quick enough. As far as I was concerned he was using her to get ahead, and I doubted he loved her in the first place. On the off chance he did, he had funny ways of showing it.

I didn't see how Jan could be happy with him after knowing me. I later reckoned I may have planted the seeds of destruction in that marriage. If that's what I unintentionally did, I'm not proud of it, I'm not bragging, and I'm certainly not waiting for Janet to come back: I'm calling them as I see them.

I had layed myself open to that woman right down to my spirit. I'm not so sure she didn't take part of it with her when she left. I had been totally honest and caring, and showed her parts of me I didn't know existed. That was part of my education from Janet: I learned a lot about myself. I also know my half of the human race well enough to have determined Janet would probably not run into another original character like myself as long as she lived. I damn well knowed Donald couldn't hold a candle to me when it came to being open and alive and himself. They would play the cute, proprietied games with each other a lot of married folks play, and in a year it would be "Please pass the sugar, dear," and "You'd better buy a new dress for the formal because all the wives are." As far as I could figure, their lives together would be a joke.

Janet had embarked on living a life of lies, doing what she felt she had to do instead of what she wanted to do. It was almost as if she was coerced into marrying Donald, as strange as that sounds. She told me once, as I held her close, "I'm tired of being told what to do! I was told to go to college! I was told to join ROTC! I was told to get married! I'm tired of it! What would you say if I didn't marry anybody?" Then I pulled her tight and turned her head so to look her in the eye, my hand on her soft chin.

"Jan," I'd told her, "I want you to be happy. I don't want to see you hurt. So if that means not marrying anybody, don't." I really meant that then; I reckon it doesn't matter now. But what I didn't add was that it was in her own best interest not to marry Donald, for she and him would be miserable. Maybe I should have, but I never once bad-mouthed that son of a bitch, as much as I yearned to. I was hoping Jan would be smart enough to compare, and then have the guts to make the right decision, which of course was myself. I think she knowed deep down, her and I was right for each other. I told her she would be freer with me than any other man alive. I had meant that, too. I thought that maybe I offered her too much freedom and she didn't know how to take it. As events turned out, that wasn't the answer, either.

I had held out hope right to the bitter end that she would come back; that she would be mine and I would be hers. I'd stopped a Christian wedding at gunpoint, damned near begged her, and gave those neighbors and relatives I reckoned she was so concerned for plenty to talk about. I had fought one hell of a fight for the woman I was supposed to be with. And I lost.

But you have to admit one thing.

I did it with great style.

* * *

I debated long and hard before deciding to commit this part of my life to paper. It's embarrassing for a man to lay open his insides for all the world to inspect. I decided to tell all for the following reasons, all of them good.

A big part of life is people hurting people. They don't do it for any good reason: they generally don't do it with malice aforethought, and for the most part it's unintentional. I think a lot of them do it because they don't know themselves, like Shakespeare or somebody implored. At any event, it happens.

I could be wrong, but I think men are by far the less stable sex when it comes to emotions, and it seems they go crazy more often than women. I don't know why, for sure, but in my own case I was so caught up in love that nothing else mattered in my life but Janet. The past had almost ceased to exist for me; she was the present and the future. Jan herownself, all of her, and she was all that occupied my every waking moment. When I lost her, it was hard to face the cold knowledge that I would have to live my life without her. I never planned on killing myself, but to be honest about it I didn't care much whether I lived or not.

I once knowed a guy who was very much in love with his wife. I remember us anchored out in Subic Bay riding out the tail end of a hurricane that had trashed out part of Luzon but missed us. That white hat and I were standing at the fo'c'sle rail and he was rattling on and on about his wife; corny but sincere stuff, like the way she scolded him when he stuck his finger in the cookie batter, and how she cried when the neighbor's dog ate her tulips. He thought it was just great, and I thought he was nuts.

A couple days later he got a Dear John letter from her. She had left him for another man. The day after that when we were unloading small-arms ammo at Alava pier a grenade disappeared.

He went to a deserted compartment on the third deck and dogged the hatches.

Then he pulled the pin and let the spoon fly.

I thought he was crazy for killing himself. I would never do that myself. But now I understand why he did it. Love can be a very powerful emotion.

And when he told me his wife had left, tears in his eyes, I never even told him I was sorry, or asked if I could help. But I'm sorry now, because I've got a rough idea of what he was going through.

Maybe if I'd told him that then, and tried to care a little, it might have made a difference.

I don't know.

When Janet left my life there was a lot of things about her I hadn't yet figured out. I was pretty hard on her in my mind, yet if I'd known about the dark cloud which had hovered over her for so many years, and done my best to help her work out of it, it may not have worked anyway. If I could tell her one thing today it would be, "I don't believe you hurt me on purpose." Janet may well not have loved me; now that I think about it, I don't believe she ever told me she did. But she wasn't small; she was a casualty.

Too many people become casualties through the course of everyday living, and that is the purpose of this little detour. If what I write here can help prevent one man from hurting a woman, or one woman from hurting a man, it will have been worthwhile. And if it keeps some poor old fellow from doing himself in, it will have been more than worth the effort.

At one point I figured I was the only one who had suffered.

Well, Janet had suffered, too.

There's too much pain in life; more than enough to go around for everyone. On the day that Janet departed my life I was sure I would never know why she married the wrong man. I was positive it would be the great mystery of my life.

Then, I tried to hate her, and I couldn't.

I tried to stop loving her, and I couldn't do that, either.

I don't think it matters anymore, and it won't change anything at this point, so therefore I'll say it:

If she's out there, and happens to read these words, I'd like her to know that the past does not matter . . . and that after all this time, I love her. I could never stop.

In spite of everything.

Still.

18

WE HAULED ASS across the Mississippi and I turned south on the first paved road I came to. By heading west-southwest I made the Missouri border in a couple hours.

"Don't you think we might be a little conspicious on these back roads?" Crazy Joe asked distractedly as he rolled a Bull Durham.

"Memphis, five," I read out loud off an approaching sign. "Maybe we ought and visit Tom Horn; that's his hometown."

"Isn't he dead?"

"Yeah. I doubt most people living there ever heard of him. By way of answering your question, the way I figure it is this: I'm betting Jan didn't talk, but if she did, the state patrol in at least two states is looking for us, and I'm also willing to bet this state ain't one of 'em. Besides, the county mounties out here in the toolies are less apt to get the word, one, or pay any attention to us if they did. I think we'll be okay once we cross the Missouri; we'll pick up the interstate there."

"And if Jan talks?"

"I'm bettin' that ain't goin' to happen."

We passed through Memphis and a couple hours later stopped for something to eat. It was getting on toward late afternoon when we pulled to a stop in front of a little country tavern out in the middle of nowhere.

The locals didn't pay much attention to us as we walked in; we in turn ignored them. We pulled up stools at the end of the

169

bar and close to the television. An old *Leave It to Beaver* episode was playing on the station owned by the mouth of the south, so I knowed the news would not be long in coming.

"Let's stick around and watch the news," I quietly said to Crazy Joe as I chewed on an awful cheeseburger. "It could be interesting."

"Boo-hoo-hoo," he quietly chortled.

I was almost done with my second cheeseburger when the newscaster announced in stentorian tones, "And this afternoon an unusual story from the Mississippi River town of Marble City, Illinois. Three armed men stopped a wedding service at the Deer Creek Community Church a few miles from that town at about ten this morning. One of the armed men knew the bride and apparently did not wish to see her married. Eyewitnesses report the armed trio made a dramatic entrance at the point where the minister asked if anybody objected. We have this firsthand report:

"Why," a little old lady trembled into the camera, "it was simply awful. When Pastor Carter asked if anybody objected, my goodness, the curtains flew apart and there was a man standing with a ten-gallon hat and a machine gun! Then he said, 'I'll kill anybody that moves!' It was horrible! And then another one of the gang made the congregation sing a dirty song—think of it!—waving *his* machine gun from the pulpit. It was awful! And then this same man who was behind the curtains grabbed Janet—she's my niece-in-law, you see—and held her at gunpoint and threatened to kill her! And then they left and locked everybody in the church, and poor Mr. Peabody cut his hand breaking a window to get us out, you know. It was a good thing I had my nitroglycerin pills with me. I have a bad heart, you see."

"What a crock of shit," I said under my breath.

"We have another eyewitness account, this one from Reverend Andrew Carter," the newscaster continued. The minister was the guy that looked like Hank Worden.

"I have ministered for forty-nine years, and this is the first time in six hundred and eighty-seven weddings I've ever seen or heard anything like it . . ." and so on.

A hush had fallen over the little tavern. I could be wrong, but I felt that all eyes were boring through Crazy Joe and yours truly.

"You know what I think, Sam?" Crazy Joe cheerily asked.

"What?" I quietly replied, wishing to hell he'd shut up and finish his cheeseburger.

"I think our wives are going to kill us if we don't get home pretty soon." Crazy Joe Flanigan may have been a lot of things, but he was by no means stupid. I picked up on the cue.

"You're right. We'd better head on out, or be ready to sleep on the davenport the next week."

I caught the tail end of the newscast as we paid our tabs. The upshot was that the wedding had eventually gone on to its conclusion. It took the assembled matrimony-goers only twenty minutes to bust out of that church; we had gotten away in the nick of time. When the law arrived, the bride either refused to identify the culprits, or couldn't. There was a brief camera shot of Janet being grilled by the county sheriff, tears running down her face, answering "I don't know" to all questions. I reckoned she would have some tall explaining to do to Donald, but she was smart. Janet had an Ivory League education, after all. I figured she'd come up with something original.

As Crazy Joe and I walked outside into the stifling heat and humidity I said, "I knowed she'd play it game to the end."

"Yeah. Even though she told you to fuck off, I still kinda like her. And the authorities found several fresh piles of horseshit by the gate behind the church. They're in the process of searching for three armed men dressed as cowboys. On horses. In western Illinois. Boo-hoo-hoo-haw-haw-haw!"

Lacking anything better to do, I imagine they're still searching.

Crazy Joe took the wheel because I was beat; I hadn't slept at all the night before. I woke up a couple hours later when Crazy Joe nudged me.

"Sam."

"What," I groaned as I pulled my hat off my face.

"I think we've got a little problem here. Hear it?" There was a distinct clatter coming from underneath the hood.

"Fuck a duck. How long's this been going on?"

"The last twenty or thirty miles."

"Pull over." He eased over on the narrow shoulder and I got out. I opened the hood. "Okay, give it a little more gas. Shit!"

I cried as I identified the problem. "C'mon out here!" I hollered.

"Lookit that," I said, pointing to the water pump. Steady droplets of green antifreeze were leaking from it, and the old pump was clattering like a washing machine about to blow its guts. I figured the bearings was shot.

"It appears the water pump is kaput," Crazy Joe matter-of-factly commented.

"Yeah. Where the hell are we, anyway? This don't look like Kansas, Dorothy."

"Uh, I've been meaning to talk to you about that," he casually answered as he started to roll a smoke.

I quickly spun around and surveyed the terrain. "Why are there so many hills around here?"

"Well, I turned south 'cause I didn't want to go through Kansas City on I-70. Have you ever heard of Lake of the Ozarks?"

"You miserable son of a bitch."

"Well, I just saw a sign. We're about twenty miles from it. I must have gotten misoriented."

"What's the nearest town, Magellan?"

"A little place called Shady Grove. I saw a sign a few miles back; it's just down the road. Maybe we can get a water pump there."

I slammed down the hood. "It's probably five-thirty or six o'clock on a Saturday. I highly doubt it."

A mile later the needle on my temperature gauge shot up to two hundred and fifty degrees. The water pump had died a quick and violent death. "This freaking engine is going to blow if I go much farther. Look for a place to pull over." The humidity was so high it was almost as if a mist hanged over the Missouri countryside, the woods of which were broken by only an occasional field.

"There ain't shit out here," Crazy Joe calmly observed as he picked at a tooth with the sharpened end of a kitchen match.

"No shit, Jack. I just want to get this pickup, the critters, and us off this road. I ain't looking for the Best Western."

"Old farmhouse on the right!" Crazy Joe suddenly said as he pointed. "Pull in." I slowed for the rutted driveway and turned in the ancient farmyard. The mailbox post was broken off; the mailbox itself had long since disappeared. The old clapboard two-story farmhouse had been barren of paint since maybe as far back as the Roosevelt administration, and the front door hanged askew, broken off the hinges. Weeds grew three foot high everywhere save on the bare spot of gravel where I ground to a stop. As I shut off the engine a geyser of steam shot out from the grill. We got out.

"You appear to have blown the return radiator hose," Crazy Joe offered. I took out my bandanna and quickly pulled off the radiator cap. What was left of the water and antifreeze gurgled over the top of the radiator. "Now we are fucked. What next, Henry Ford?"

"Shit!" I replied in exasperation. I stalked off to inspect the farmhouse; Crazy Joe tagged along behind me. "I'm gonna pull the outfit back here," I told him as I lit my pipe. "It won't hurt it to drive another fifty feet."

"Let's just leave it out front, Sam. Won't hurt anything."

"Sure, except for one thing: We're on private property. As tumbled down as this place is, somebody owns it, and if they see us we'll probably get throwed off. Or worse. At least back here we're in a concealed position."

"Whaddya mean, 'or worse'?"

"We're in Missouri; nothing good ever happened to me in the South."

"We're only sixty miles or so from Kansas City, Sam. Don't get so upset."

"Would you read my lips? Hell's bells, for your information we're in the heart of Dixie. To these people it's still 1865, Lee surrendered at Appomattox Courthouse last week, and they're highly pissed about it. You and me are damned Yankees, pard."

"Yeah, but we're from the West; we live in Colorado."

"The Confederate Army tried to invade Colorado," I informed him. I hustled back to my truck, started it, and drove the hundred feet behind the farmhouse. The engine coughed when I shut it off, but I didn't figure I'd done it any damage. As I killed the engine a truck whizzed by on the county road.

"Just in a nick of time," I said as I slammed the door behind me. We unloaded Molly and Geronimo and led them out to the ruins of an old corral. Meadow grass was standing knee high and they began chomping away like they was starved. Crazy Joe picketed them as I filled water pails from my jerry can. As we waited for the engine to cool down, we nibbled on some jerky I had tucked away.

"Well, what's the plan, Sam?" Crazy Joe asked as we leaned against the grill.

"We've got a couple hours of daylight left. You pull off the water pump; I'll head into Shady Grove. By the way, how big did the map say this burg is?"

"I think it said population nineteen."

I let out a sigh. "There ain't no parts store there." I had to think for a moment. Due to the zigzag nature of the course we had driven that day, we'd only come three hundred miles or so from the scene of the morning's festivities. I was pretty sure the law wasn't looking for us, but we was still far from home.

After a long minute I added, "Maybe I can find a junk car or truck and make a deal for a water pump. There's been millions of three-fifty GM engines made over the years, and if I know anything about small hamlets, this one will have junkers strown all over it."

Once the engine block had cooled down we got out my wrench set and pulled the water pump. The bearings were shot. Next I caught up Molly, tied her off at the trailer, and began to saddle and bridle her. I was cinching up my rifle scabbard when Crazy Joe walked up.

"Taking your Winchester?"

"Obviously." I shortened the scabbard straps a notch. "No law against it, is there?"

"Probably not. Why d'ya need it here?"

Instead of answering I went to my truck and pulled my rifle out from under the seat. I always carry four rounds in the magazine with the hammer resting on an empty chamber. As I walked back to my horse, I dropped the lever and checked the chamber.

"Because I'm a little short on brotherly trust in general, not to mention in this part of the world," I answered as I slid the rifle in the scabbard.

"Taking your Colt?"

"Nope. If I wore that hogleg it'd look like I was looking for trouble. I just want to get out of here in one piece. Period." I rolled up the horsehair mecate I always left attached to Molly's halter, and tied the coil to the left side of my saddle. Then I swung up.

"A water pump for a three-fifty and two gallons of antifreeze, plus a radiator hose. Anything else?"

"Yeah, don't forget the milk and bread." Crazy Joe grinned wildly. "It's seven o'clock; you've got light till nine. I'll be looking for you if you don't show up directly."

"I'll be okay," I answered as I put Molly's head over and gave her heel.

Molly and I trotted the three miles into Shady Grove in half an hour. The few cars and trucks I met on the old county road gave me a wide berth as they slowed to observe the stranger, and as I rounded a wide corner and the little town came into view, I was less than optimistic about my chances of getting a water pump that night.

Shady Grove was nine or ten old houses, an ancient white clapboard church, a filling station, and a general store–tavern. Across the street from the filling station stood what appeared to be an abandoned town schoolhouse. I didn't see no auto-parts store handy.

"Shit," I softly grumbled to Molly as I reined her in by the filling station. A towheaded guy about my age wearing a greasy green work suit sauntered out to greet me.

"Doan' sell no oats heah," he informed me with a laconic backwoods drawl.

"I ain't looking for oats," I replied as I swung out of the saddle. "I'm standing in need of a water pump for a three-fifty General Motors engine. Know where I can get one?"

"Doan' need no hawseshit by mah gas pumps, neither." He eyed me hard, spit a huge stream of tobacco juice over his shoulder, and added, "Yankee." I wordlessly led Molly away from his precious gas pumps.

Evidently made happy by my meek compliance, he walked over to the tree where I was tying my mare and looked us over. "Thet's an olt saddle," he observed, spitting again.

"Texas stock saddle from the 1840s. Called a Hope."

"Hmmm," he said, nodding his head. "Shore, ah knowed thet. Why you carry thet rifle?" he queried.

"Carried it so many years I feel naked without it."

"Hmmm. Nice hawse. Ah always laked quartered hawses."

"They've been good to me," I answered, not bothering to inform him Molly was only half quarter horse.

"Ya broke down near heah or somepin?"

"A few miles out of town. I see you've got some old vehicles in the back."

"Yup. Might haf a pump fer ya out back. C'mon, an' bring yer nag," he instructed with a jerk of his head. He led me to the local auto graveyard behind the filling station. There was a couple dozen junked cars and trucks dating back to the 1940s scattered over a rusting acre. I tied Molly by the mecate to a transmission sitting off by itself and followed the attendant to a wrecked '69 Chevrolet three-quarter-ton.

"The water pump's still in there," I observed in the fading light.

"Shore is. We'll pull hit right offa thar. Ah'll be right back." In a couple minutes the attendant returned with a socket-wrench set and a flashlight. Before he started loosening the nuts he informed me, "Thet'll be forty dollars." He held out his hand to indicate the time of payment was now.

"Forty dollars?" I repeated. That was what I'd expected to pay for a rebuilt water pump from a store, but I had no choice but to hand him two twenties. He jammed the bills inside a greasy pocket and I figured he didn't plan on putting the money in the till: somehow he just didn't look like the owner.

It was just getting dark when we pulled the water pump free. After that, the attendant, whose name was Homer, headed back to the station and left me to take off a radiator hose and a couple radiator hose clamps. I was sticking the whole works in a gunny-sack when Molly let out a whinny from behind me.

I turned around in the fading light and saw one of the fattest, plain ugliest men I'd ever laid eyes on. He wasn't much taller than me, but would have dressed out at two-fifty. His tangled black hair was streaked with gray; the bird's nest atop his head was covered with an oily ball cap. He was two or three days minus a shave, and what appeared to be a dried brown line of tobacco juice ran down one corner of his mouth. At his side stood Homer, fear written on his face. In one hand the fat man held my Winchester.

"This th' Yankee sumbitch what carries a big rifle an' thanks he's mean? This 'im, Homer?'' he asked with a leer, waving my own rifle at me.

"Uh-huh, Mr. McLowery. He's the one," Homer dutifully answered. Now I don't know where that dumb Reb got the idea I was mean; I had come to town looking for a water pump, not a fight.

"I oughta kill ya and yer hawse!" McLowery suddenly snarled.

"I would like my rifle back," I evenly replied, trying to hold my anger in.

"Haw-haw-haw!" he exploded, like I'd just told a rib-busting joke. He enjoyed my remark so much he slammed the butt of the Winchester in Homer's gut.

"Ugh!" he grunted as he doubled over in pain. McLowery laughed all the harder.

"Come an' git yer rifle, Yankee sumbitch," he sneered.

So I did. And as I approached him, I remembered I still held the towsack loaded with the water pump in my right hand. I intended to hit him upside the head with it.

Well, old McLowery might have been fatter than me, but he was quicker, too.

I think I was out for about five minutes. "Where the hell am I?" I asked nobody in particular. I was seeing about eighty-seven different-colored stars, and my head felt like it'd just come out of a vise.

"Yer in back a Honest George's gas station. Ya been knocked out by the meanest man in Crawfish County, Mr. Billy Joe McLowery," Homer informed me.

"With my own rifle."

"Uh-huh."

"Oh fuck a duck," I groaned. I slowly started to my feet, and Homer grabbed an arm and helped me up. As I gained my feet, the old wrecked cars and nearby trees were all blurred and a-swimming in front of me. My sorrel stood a dozen feet away, calmly grazing.

"Good thing ya had thet hat on. Ya okay?"

"Never felt better. Where's my rifle?"

"Mr. McLowery took hit. He said t' tell ya he eveh see ya agin he'll kill ya."

I rubbed my throbbing head. "That miserable son of a bitch has it back end first. Mind if I use your phone?"

"What fer?"

"To call the sheriff," I replied. "I want my rifle back." I slowly started walking toward the gas station, Homer at my side.

"Hit won't do no good," Homer offered as we walked. He seemed almost apologetic.

"Why not?"

" 'Cause the sheriff's forty mile away an' he doan' come t' Shady Grove. Even he's afeared a Mr. McLowery."

"I don't believe that." I walked inside, dialed the sheriff's department, identified myself as John Smith, and had to talk to a dispatcher since there wasn't any deputies around.

After I talked to him a minute, I did believe it. He asked if anybody was dead.

"No."

"Then thar's no need t' come."

"You yellow son of a bitch!" I hollered into the phone.

He hung up on me.

I slammed down the receiver in disgust, stalked over to Molly, and tied the towsack to the saddle horn. It seemed like too much effort to swing up into the saddle, so I walked Molly down to the general store and tavern fifty yards away. I tied Molly off to an ancient, peeling pillar and walked in.

"Help you, stranger?" the old storekeeper asked.

"Yeah. I want a bag of ice." Then the whole store started moving in front of me; I grabbed a nearby chair and sat down. "And a strawberry soda," I added. The two old men seated at the bar ignored me. That was fine; I was in no mood to take any further crap off anybody. The old man pulled a bag of ice out of an upright freezer, wrapped some cubes in a towel, and handed it to me. I gently removed my hat and put the ice pack over the knot on my head.

"Thanks."

"I hear you met Billy Joe McLowery," he offered. News obviously traveled fast in Shady Grove.

"Yeah. Who's the son of a bitch think he is, Adolph Fucking Hitler?" Then without waiting for an answer I added, "He stole my rifle. And your cops around here won't do nothing. They're about as worthless as teats on a boar hog."

The old man eyed me sorrowfully and cleared his throat. "McLowery murdered my brother six months ago," he said quietly. I didn't know how to respond to that, and he turned and walked away; in another minute he was back with the strawberry soda. I took the bottle.

"And he's still walking the streets?"

"Yes. My brother was murdered over a case of beer. He owned this store. Then six months ago McLowery came in and helped himself to a case of beer. When my brother asked him to pay, McLowery beat him to death with a pickaxe handle."

"Jesus, Joseph, and Mary," I muttered softly. "Didn't anybody see it happen? Wouldn't anybody testify against the bastard?"

"Everybody in the county is afraid of him, Mister . . ."

"Smith." I was in no mood to use my real name.

"Mr. Smith. Two years ago McLowery murdered his neighbor. That was over a fence line."

At that moment a couple middle-aged fellas who looked like farmers walked in. I don't know if they knew who I was or not, but one announced to the storekeep, "Thet Yankee better git afore Billy Joe comes back."

I stood up as fast as I could and loudly said, "Fuck Billy Joe McLowery! Somebody give me a six-shooter!" Everybody in that little joint gave me a long, hard, unsympathetic look.

"You'd better leave now, Mr. Smith," the storekeep kindly offered.

"Better git," somebody else chimed in.

"Yup," yet another added, "he'll kill ya."

I set the ice pack and the half-gone soda pop on the counter. I carefully put my hat on, pulled out a dollar, and threw it on the counter. As I reached the door I stopped, turned around, and said, "You're all yellow. You're a disgrace to the god-damned Confederate States of America." Then I painfully climbed on Molly and headed back to my outfit.

It was pitch black when I reined in behind the old farmhouse.

"What happened to your head and where's your rifle?" Crazy Joe quickly asked.

"Gimme a cup of coffee and I'll tell you about it," I sighed. I threw my saddle next to the little palm-sized fire Crazy Joe had built, and recounted the tale while I drank coffee and ate beef jerky.

"But there is a bright side," I concluded. "I got the water pump and the radiator hose."

Crazy Joe slowly shook his head. "I don't fucking believe all this, Sam. I mean, I do, but I don't. Billy Joe McLowery has got to go; yes, yes indeed, he's got to go."

"Oh, just for once let it go!" I pulled a blanket over me and layed my head on the saddle. "We'll get the water pump in come first light and we'll get the hell outta here."

"We're gonna get you to a VA hospital. You could have a bad concussion."

"Fuck hospitals and fuck concussions. I'll be all right once I get back West." That is the last thing I recall saying that night, so I must have dropped off to sleep shortly thereafter.

The next morning when I awakened, Crazy Joe was whistling as he shaved in my truck mirror. The sun was already high; I figured it for about eight o'clock.

"Mornin', Sam," he cheerily greeted me. "The water pump's in and the radiator hose is on. Since you neglected to get the antifreeze"—he grinned when he said that—"I filled the radiator with water from the jerry can."

"Sounds fine to me," I grumbled. It was then I noticed his attire. He had on his dress high-top boots, the legs of fancy pin-striped wool pants tucked inside. He wore a round-collared shirt after the nineteenth-century fashion, and the long frock coat he'd had tailor-made overseas. In the long red sash that belted his waist were stuck his Colt Peacemaker .45s, the loading gates open so the pieces wouldn't fall through the cloth sash.

"What in hell's goin' on here?" I asked as I poured a cup of coffee.

He finished shaving and wiped his face with a towel. "We're going to get your Winchester back," he informed me with that wild grin.

I grabbed his arm. "How?"

He gently removed my hand from his arm. "Easy, Sam," he smiled. "We're just going to be real nice."

In ten minutes we were at the general store in Shady Grove, where the following conversation took place.

"Billy Joe McLowery?" Crazy Joe politely asked into the

phone. "I'd just like you to know that you are a dry-gulching, mother-humping, back-shootin' snake-fuckin' piss-drinkin' son of a whore!"

Even from the barstool ten feet away I heard the screaming coming over the receiver. Crazy Joe moved it back from his ear a few inches and winced in mockery. After a bit he said, "All right, we'll leave our mothers out of this. My name is James Butler and you are just a common cocksucker. I'm at Shady Grove waiting for you." He hanged up the phone with a bang.

"I take it you two did not hit it off," I remarked.

"You'd better get out of town, Mr. Butler," Harold the storekeep informed Crazy Joe. "Mr. McLowery will be here in five minutes. He'll kill you for that, he really will."

By way of reply Crazy Joe yawned mightily and stretched his arms over his head. "That's the general idea, Harold. I don't expect he'd want to visit with me about the crops after that conversation."

A cursory reconnaissance of Shady Grove had shown there to be maybe twenty or thirty people in town that morning, most of them in church. Honest George's filling station was closed, and apart from Harold and two old ladies in the back of the store, the burg was empty.

One of the gray-haired crones walked up to Crazy Joe then and said, "Don't leave now, Mr. Butler. Mr. McLowery is evil. He killed Harold's brother, Walter, and his neighbor Old Man Dyer."

"Now he'll kill everybody," whined the second old lady.

"Oh hush up, Lucille! These young men know what they're doing." I am certainly glad that lady thought so, 'cause this coon was playing it strictly by ear.

The fact was, there was going to be blood shed in Shady Grove within the next few minutes, and the probability was high some of it would be Crazy Joe's and mine. I let out a sigh of resignation as I tossed four bits on the counter to pay for a cold soda.

"Where ya going, hoss?" Crazy Joe asked.

"Out. To dig a foxhole."

"Just a minute; I'll come with you." Then he addressed Harold. "Harold, McLowery rubbed out your brother, right?"

"That is correct, Mr. Butler."

"I assume there is no love lost between you and him then."

"That is also correct, suh."

"Good. Now all I need is your word you'll keep everybody away from that phone all the rest of this morning."

"You have it."

"Outstanding. How many other phones in this ville?"

"Most all of the houses and at Honest George's. If you are alive in five minutes, Mr. Butler, nobody will say a word. Ever. I believe I can speak for all the residents."

Crazy Joe joined me on the porch then, and a dashing figure he cut, straight out of the pages of either history, infamy, or insanity. The ridiculousness of his costume was offset in a deadly way by the two ivory-handled Colts stuck in the red sash. The black mustache he'd grown dropped well below his lip, and he reminded me of a picture I'd seen of somebody from the last century, but I couldn't quite remember who.

As he carefully rolled a cigarette he said, "Sam, to paraphrase Butch Cassidy, 'I hate to sound like a sore loser, but if he wins and I'm dead—kill him.' "

"Do I have a choice?" I shot back. "Look, I'm gonna take my soda and my six-gun and head over to that schoolhouse. It's up to you to draw him your way. I don't quite trust my aim with this banging head, and in the second place, since you called him out, I ain't wild about collecting any bullets intended for your person."

"Okay, old hoss." He grinned. I walked across the street and took a seat on an old bench in front of the abandoned schoolhouse. I took off my hat and let the crown rest over the barrel of my cocked Colt. Then I folded the newspaper I'd appropriated from Harold and held it up in my left hand, pretending to read, while Crazy Joe reclined against the porch rail, smoking his cigarette like he didn't have a care in the world.

It was only a minute or so until a green 1961 Ford pickup came into full view, boring down the road at full tilt. When Crazy Joe saw the approaching truck he casually flicked his cigarette and swung out into the street.

The early morning sun was at his back as he carefully cocked his hat back on his head. I figured Billy Joe McLowery might just dispense with the formalities and run him over, but as he neared Crazy Joe he slowed down. He stopped about twenty yards away from the lone shootist, who cast a long shadow in the morning sun.

Crazy Joe glared at him, his thumbs hooked in the red sash. Crazy Joe Flanigan, I thought. James Butler . . . *Hickok*! So that was why he used the name James Butler! The first two names of the most famous shootist ever, James Butler Wild Bill Hickok, hisownself! I sat on that bench in near shock, petrified by the weirdness of it all.

Billy Joe McLowery flung the door open and got out. He was even more ugly than the previous evening, the stereotype of a local bully who had failed at everything in life except terrorizing people. He wore faded bib overalls and a tee shirt—evidently Crazy Joe had called around hog-slopping time—and his white and gray whiskers still had the line of brown cutting through them. When he got out of the truck, it was not Crazy Joe he addressed but yours truly.

"You Yankee sumbitch!" he sneered, barring his teeth at me.

"Over here, you piss-drinkin' cocksucker!" Crazy Joe happily yelled. McLowery turned his attention to the man at his front.

"Ah'm a-gonna kill ya!" he roared.

"Not until I tell you why I'm here," Crazy Joe replied, no trace of fear in his voice. His thumbs was still hooked in the sash.

"Huh?" McLowery slowly replied, apparently not understanding an introduction to violence.

"You murdered two old men for no reason," Crazy Joe began. "You about layed open my partner's skull, then you stole his rifle. You're sick, you've got the law afraid of you and everybody in this country afraid of you. McLowery, you're a bully and a pissant, and now you're going to die."

I looked at McLowery. I didn't think he knowed how to take Crazy Joe's matter-of-fact attitude. He was breathing powerful hard, opening and closing his hands into fists. From my seat I couldn't get a look at his eyes, but I had the feeling that for the first time in his life Billy Joe McLowery was scared to death. As well he ought to have been. A small white line of drool ran down one corner of his mouth.

"Ah'm still gonna kill ya!" he roared.

Crazy Joe shifted his weight forward and cocked his hips. Then he smiled. "Go for it," he murmured.

McLowery pivoted in a whirl and in two steps was at the open truck door. He reached inside the cab and filled his hands with a cut-down pump-action shotgun.

"Die, you bastard!" he bellowed at Crazy Joe as he snapped off a shot with a fluid motion of the weapon.

I saw it all. I saw the flame leap from the shotgun, and I thought I saw a load of shot cut a hole in the air between Crazy Joe and myself. But even as McLowery swung out with the shotgun and bellered, "Die!" Crazy Joe was moving.

His hands were too fast for my eyes to follow. I remember only seeing and hearing the stacatto burst from Crazy Joe's Colt Peacemaker. McLowery never finished the word "bastard" because six .45 soft lead bullets entered his hugesome bulk and interrupted his voice patterns. Forever.

He lurched back with each bullet Crazy Joe fanned into his body, the shots spaced not a tenth of a second apart. His shotgun had fired even as he died on his feet. The gun fell from his hands and, the surprise of death written on his face, he clutched his hands over his chest, as if trying to stop the leaks. He looked at his hands, and then at Crazy Joe in horror. And then his legs gave way and he fell face forward on the ground. I thought I felt the ground shake when his body connected with the earth.

But even as Crazy Joe had fired his last round, he threw the empty Colt from his right hand high into the air, and deftly grabbed the loaded gun with his left and lightly tossed it to his right. Catching the empty gun in his left hand he spun in a crouch, making a complete circle searching for any more adversaries. I watched it all: McLowery die on his last word and hit the ground. And Crazy Joe do the border shift, quick and neat as the best of the gunfighters had ever done it. I saw the sun glint off his empty Colt as it rotated in midair for what seemed an eternity, and heard the tails of his frock coat slice the humid air as he spun around.

Then, after I came out of shock and tried my feet, I thought to myself, "The crazy son of a bitch *is* Wild Bill Hickok!"

And then I walked over to look at the body and congratulate Crazy Joe on being alive.

19

" '*MAJOR STRASSER HAS* been shot,' " I said as I looked at the body of the recently departed McLowery. A fly buzzed in and out of his open mouth. I glanced up at Crazy Joe. " 'Round up the usual suspects.' " Crazy Joe looked me square in the eye; maybe he half smiled.

I can read eyes well, yet his told me nothing, save maybe that he had accomplished a job. There was no hint of emotion on his face. Then he stuck the loaded Colt in his sash, put the empty revolver on half-cock, and calmly began shaking out the fired brass. As an empty case hit the ground he looked up from the gun and said, "You'd better see if your rifle is in his truck."

A quick look in the cab revealed my rifle butt protruding from under the seat. I was thankful that McLowery was so thoughtful—or forgetful—to bring it along.

Then the three old people came running out of the general store. Well, they wasn't running, actually. They was pretty ancient and came hobbling fast. They reined in next to us and McLowery's still form. They studied the corpse, relief written on their faces. Then the lady who had figured Crazy Joe knowed what he was doing spoke up.

"You have shot Mr. McLowery," she flatly declared. The way she said those words she may just as well have said, "There's a bit of shaving cream under your left ear."

"That is correct, ma'am," Crazy Joe politely replied as he stuffed fresh rounds in his Colt.

"Why?" croaked the second old lady. It was pretty obvious she was more afraid of what would happen to her than she was for Crazy Joe.

"He was a bully and a murderer. He didn't deserve to live," he firmly stated, snapping the loading gate shut and sticking the Colt back in his sash.

At that moment the church doors flew open and the local Baptists came a-pouring out. Well, there was twenty of them or so. The crowd hustled over to us, the kids coming to screeching halts with mouths agape, the adults looking almighty relieved. The preacher, a chubby young fellow, came running after his flock and pulled up at McLowery's still form.

"Praise be to God!" he cried. "It was the Lord's will!" he enthused with a shout.

"It was self-defense," Crazy Joe dryly corrected as he began to roll a cigarette.

"Yes, it was," agreed Harold.

" 'I am the resurrection and the life,' " the preacher began in a false baritone. " 'Whosoever believeth in me, though he be dead, yea shall he live.' "

"I don't think he believed," Crazy Joe said sarcastically. He licked the gummed edge of his cigarette paper and fished in his pocket for a match.

"We have laws to deal with people like him, Mr. Butler," the second old crone cried. She added, "This is just ghastly."

"The law didn't help Harold's brother, or Old Man Dyer, did it?" Crazy Joe turned and addressed the crowd. "Did the law and police protect you people from this animal?" A murmur came up from the group; they agreed plenty hard.

"No!" Harold exclaimed, loud enough for all to hear.

"Well, then, it doesn't work," Crazy Joe said with conviction.

"We were hoping he'd change," sighed the second old lady. "We just wanted to be left alone."

"Death changed him. And now you will be left alone," he nonchalantly said as he lit the cigarette.

"One day you will have to answer to God for this," the second old lady informed him.

"Oh, Lucille! Hush up!" Crazy Joe's elderly female ally scolded.

"I suppose there's that possibility," he politely conceded.

"And what will you tell Him?" she demanded, loud enough for the entire crowd to hear.

Crazy Joe smiled then, and with an easy motion of his hand brought the hat brim down just an inch above his eyes. "Why, I'll tell Him the truth," he replied without rancor. "I'll tell Him a .45 Long Colt bullet will make a bad man good."

"You men need to leave now," the young preacher said. He wasn't just whistling "Dixie."

"Yep," I agreed.

The preacher then turned and faced Harold, the two old ladies, and his congregation. "The Lord works in mysterious ways!" he cried.

"Hallelujah!" a few cried in reply.

"Yarrsuh!" one voice responded.

"These men appeared from out of nowhere. As we all know, this man here was brutalized by the late Billy Joe McLowery." Whom incidentally had taken on the pallor of death. The flies had already discovered his body, and I figured as hot as it was, he would be ripening in the sun by the time we blowed town.

"He was assaulted when he came to this village merely looking for a fuel pump so he could continue his sojourn to . . ." He looked to me for help.

"Tennessee," I supplied. Always send the hounds in the wrong direction if possible.

"To Tennessee. We were in communion with the Lord not five minutes ago when, for reasons unknown, this man"—he aimed his arm at Crazy Joe like a javelin—"and that miserable bastard McLowery fired their weapons at each other unto the death. That this man is still alive," he bellered, still pointing at Crazy Joe, "is testimony to the fact that God's will was done!"

"Amen!" they cried.

"Hallelujah!" some sang.

"Yarrsuh!" a lone voice agreed.

Personally I thought Crazy Joe had won for a variety of reasons, not the least of which was that he had practiced religiously for a dozen years. The considerable sum of money he'd poured into powder, lead, and primers also had something to do with it, but the preacher had the bit in his teeth and was running like a blooded stallion out of control.

"Would this man," he hollered, his finger aimed at Crazy Joe's nose, "and this man"—he aimed his free arm at me—"receive a fair trial in today's socialist courts? Has not Billy Joe McLowery been tried by the Lord, with this man as his instrument? Was not the will of God done?" he demanded in a shriek.

"His will be done!"

"Hallelujah!"

"Amen!"

"Yarrsuh!"

"That's what I thought," he continued, sweat pouring off him in rivers. "You're with me. Are you folks with me?" he implored, his arms lifted high.

You've figured out the general chorus of agreement by now.

"Should we turn these men over to be persecuted by them big-city slickers?" he hollered.

"No!"

"Would they be tried fairly?"

"No!"

"And did McLowery give Old Man Dyer and Walter Landry a fair trial?" he screamed.

"No!"

"Then they must go now, and we must unite and never tell them left-wing big-city folk and that pinko faggot district attorney about these men or this morning's events!" he hollered to the heavens, his arms stretched skyward.

"Yes," and "Hallelujah," et cetera, et cetera.

I was getting almighty unnerved myownself. I appreciated the preacher's support, but somebody was going to have some tall explaining to do when the authorities eventually happened on McLowery's ventilated body. I was ready to leave.

"Then let them go in peace with our profoundest thanks for riddin' us of this genuine, unrepentant, Godless, four-ply son of a bitch!"

"A-men!" the crowed hollered in unison.

"Oh, fuck me to tears," I said under my breath.

The preacher then pulled out a white handkerchief and mopped his sweaty brow. He turned to Crazy Joe and me and quietly said, "You guys better get the hell outta here."

I didn't need to be told twice, but even as Crazy Joe and me turned to leave, the old lady whose name was Martha grabbed Crazy Joe by the sleeve.

"May I have your autograph?" she asked eagerly.

"Sure thing, lady." Crazy Joe grinned, enjoying celebrity status. She pulled an envelope and pen from her purse and handed them to him.

I was getting plumb annoyed, and as Crazy Joe scrawled a signature on the back of the envelope I bent over and picked up the empty .45 Long Colt cases and put them in a pocket. There was no point in advertising any further.

"You remind me a my grandfather," Martha croaked as Crazy Joe handed back the envelope. "He rode with Major Quantrill in the war and you are just like him."

"And how is that, ma'am?" Crazy Joe asked politely.

"Desperate! But I ain't gonna talk." He just smiled at her and tipped his hat.

We then got away without another word or autograph, headed for the back of the general store, jumped in my truck, and departed Shady Grove post haste.

But I saw the envelope Crazy Joe handed to that lady, and read what he'd scrawled on the back. Written in a nineteenth-century flourish, it merely said, "Your Obedient Servent, James Butler Hickok."

20

I STARTED BREATHING again once we crossed the Missouri border and headed into central Kansas. While Crazy Joe drove, I listened intently to the radio, expecting to hear an all-points bulletin for us at any moment. As we rolled west through the rolling woodlands of eastern Kansas I played with the dial and changed radio stations as we got out of range of one and came into range of others. Crazy Joe was his usual unperturbed self. He about drove me nuts.

"The corn is doing quite well this summer," he observed, pointing at a nearby field. "However, if it wasn't for massive infusions of nitrogen fertilizer and sophisticated hybridization, this nation's agricultural base never would have expanded to the heights it's reached today."

Crazy Joe Flanigan. Expatriate rich kid. Coxswain and sailor. Trapper and miner. Shootist. And now, introducing Professor Flanigan, dean of the agricultural school.

"Who are you, an editor for *The Farm Journal*?"

"Oh, I like farms," he happily said. "My family owns eight or ten of them."

"Right," I sighed.

By taking the back roads into Kansas we avoided the scales. Eventually we worked north and hit I-70 just as the woodlands thinned out and were replaced by rolling, seemingly barren plains.

"What time is it?"

Crazy Joe pulled out his timepiece. "Two-thirty."

"I'm gonna sleep. If I ain't awake by the time we hit Goodland, wake me up. We've gotta take the back roads into Colorado to avoid the scales."

"Roger, dodger," he cheerily agreed.

I put my hat over my face, slumped down in the seat, and tried to sleep. The McLowery shooting bothered me and I figured we hadn't heard the last of it. As near as I could figure, Crazy Joe was guilty of some form of manslaughter, and probably second- or third-degree murder. I was an accessory and was probably not far behind; I had in fact agreed to blast daylight through McLowery if he got Crazy Joe, a contingency I hadn't been too worried about, to be honest about it.

More than anything else, I thought of Janet. I was still at the stage where I was feeling powerful sorry for myself, but there was more to it than that. As I've stated earlier, I can stand losing, but it pisses me off not to know. I was beginning to suspect there was way more to Janet Provost's story than I had first reckoned. As I drifted off to sleep that hot and humid Kansas afternoon, I was figuring ways I could get some answers.

That evening I took the wheel and we snaked over the Colorado border. Around eight that night we pulled into a nearly deserted campground on the Republican River.

" 'No horses allowed,' " Crazy Joe read off the sign as we entered.

"Fuck it, we're home," I said as I hit second. "That sign's for nonresidents." As I drove past the few tents and campers, Crazy Joe waved happily to the gawking Bermuda-short-clad tourists and campers. We took a long bath in the tepid Republican and got through the night without incident.

The next morning around seven I made a couple violent turns outside of Limon to avoid the scales at U.S. 24 and I-70, then eased downtown. I parked on a side street and we walked half a block to a greasy spoon.

I dropped two bits in a vending machine and pulled out a copy of that morning's Denver newspaper. As we walked in the cafe I quickly scanned the front page. There was nothing about the shooting in Shady Grove. No news was good news.

Page two was more national and international news.

And smack in the middle of page three, four columns across

and eight inches high, was a photograph of the late Billy Joe McLowery stiffly propped up against the front of his green pickup, his chest full of holes. His front was black with dried blood, and a resident of Shady Grove with a sense of humor had placed the scattergun in his lifeless hands. On his face he wore a gap-toothed smile of death.

"My, my, look at this," I gulped, trying to keep my voice low. I handed the newspaper to Crazy Joe.

"Hmmm. Interesting picture," he commented over his glass of water. "Reminds me of the Dalton gang."

"What a sense of humor them people got," I replied, taking the newspaper from him. I proceeded to read the story under the headline, which read, COUNTY BULLY SHOT TO DEATH IN 'HIGH NOON' GUNFIGHT, then in smaller print, *Witnesses Say Was Like 1870s Shootout*.

It was all good news. The story confirmed McLowery's reputation as a hardcase and murderer. Harold Landry, the old storekeep, and the widow of Old Man Dyer were quoted at length. The story hinted that the county sheriff and district attorney was yellow. Howsomever, the Crawfish County D.A. was highly indignant because some stranger had the gall to visit one of the hamlets in his jurisdiction and hasten the departure of one of its residents to the hereafter. Authorities was searching for a late-model Ford pickup—blue—and the one suspect occupying it.

Thing was, I drove an old-model white Chevrolet pickup and there was two of us. There was likewise no mention made of the horse trailer I had in tow. Furthermore, the law was looking in Missouri and Arkansas, the presumed direction of travel of the suspect.

That fat little preacher and them Missourians had been as good as their word. They wasn't talking much, and when they had to, they peppered the tracks to confuse the hounds. Everything they told the authorities was bass-ackwards for our benefit. They had lacked the gumption to stand up to McLowery, but they did a damn fine job of stuttering and stammering—and lying outright—when it came to protecting Crazy Joe and me.

And even Crazy Joe's greatest fan—the little old lady named Martha—had put a plug in for him. " 'It was the fastest draw I ever seed!' " she told the reporters in glee. " 'He just fanned that six-shooter Bam! Bam! Bam! and sent McLowery to his eternal reward. I think he's Wild Bill Hickok's great-grandson!' ''

By the time I finished the story, my eggs and bacon had arrived, and I set down the newspaper with a sigh of relief.

It made me feel right good about people.

Late the next afternoon we pulled into Reed Gibson's ranch. Philo's outfit was there, but his favorite mount was gone from the corral; I surmised he was out helping Reed work stock.

Crazy Joe and I unloaded our animals, dropped my trailer, and, with the help of thirty feet of chain borrowed from Reed's poleshed, rigged up my truck to pull the old International into town.

"I hope you've got plenty of cash. If you need a rebuilt engine it'll be expensive," I told Crazy Joe as I wrapped chain around my ball hitch and secured it.

"Oh, well, what the hell." Crazy Joe smiled. "It's only money." Just then Philo and Reed rode into view.

We shook hands all around and I introduced Crazy Joe to Reed. Reed Gibson was all sinew and weathered skin that could have passed for deep-tanned saddle leather. He worked the four sections he owned and the adjoining BLM land he leased hard enough for any two men. In his fifties, he had a flat stomach and a perfect smile that showed off his store-bought teeth. He'd inherited the ranch from his father, and as far as I knowed the only break he'd ever had from ranching was the three years he'd spent in the army during the Korean War. A stranger or an Easterner would possibly mistake his unwillingness to talk as a sign of hostility, but in the Western tradition he spoke only when he had something to say, and was in general a good-hearted soul. We made a little small talk about the weather and the prospects for fall trapping. After a few minutes Reed dismissed himself with, "I'm gonna go burn some steaks and beans. C'mon in the house in half an hour if you boys are hungry."

We all quickly agreed to that offer, and when he was out of earshot Philo said, "Whar the hell you guys been? Ah figgered ya'd be here yestiday."

"We took a little detour, Philo. My water pump crapped out

in Missouri. The story gets real interesting from there; I think the proper authority should tell it.''

I leaned against my truck and smoked my pipe as Crazy Joe recounted the tale of McLowery versus Flanigan with apparent glee. Philo was awestruck by the wild story, and I myself winced at several parts of it.

''Lordy, Lordy,'' he softly exclaimed when Crazy Joe finished the story. ''Lordy, Lordy. We're all gonna go t' prison, one, or git kilt ovah this. Ah kin smell hit comin'.''

''Oh, hell's bells, there you go thinkin' negative again!'' I exploded. ''Joe, show him the newspaper.'' Crazy Joe fished the day-old Denver newspaper out of the cab of the truck and handed it to him.

''Jest lak ol' Grat Dalton hisownself!'' Philo enthused when he saw McLowery's photograph.

''That's what I kinda thought,'' I agreed with a sigh. ''But we ought not insult the Daltons like that. Some of them was peace officers, and good ones at that, before they hit the outlaw trail. They wasn't thugs in the sense of the word that McLowery was.''

Crazy Joe grinned up at me from the cigarette he was rolling. His eyes danced. ''But they were desperate,'' he said with a gleam in his eye.

The next day we learned Crazy Joe's International had put a rod through the block. We spent the next week helping Reed mend fence, bail hay, and irrigate while we waited for that odd-ball engine to arrive in Rock Springs. It was well into the second week of August by the time we rolled into Gunnison. Dusty was out on a mounted patrol, so we picked up our mail from his wife and headed north-northwest to Taylor Park, our stomping grounds.

The next week was spent boiling traps, scouting for fur sign, and doing a little placer mining. I imagine I had not been my usual genial self; the whole Janet question weighed heavy on my mind. Philo probably thought he was reading my mind when he spoke up one evening around the fire.

''Ah really didn't thank she'd marry thet old boy,'' he remarked as he oiled his Winchester. ''But, Sam, ya gotta git over this sometime.''

''Get over what?'' I hotly retorted.

"Janet."

"Have I been carpin' and bitchin' to you guys? Huh? God-damnit to hell, I've just been doing some serious thinking, something you two would be well advised to do more of."

"Hey, cool down, Sam," Crazy Joe interjected over a raised coffee cup. "We're on your side, remember?"

"Yeah, sure, Joe." I aimed my next comment at Philo. "And for your information, it ain't over yet 'cause life ain't over yet. I'm figuring how I can get some answers, but I got a gut feeling she'll be back someday."

Philo fired right back. "Ya mean ya'd take 'er back? Afteh what she done t' ya?" Bewilderment was written all over his face.

I was irate. "Yeah, I would, and what the fuck's it to ya?"

"Easy does it, Sam," Crazy Joe suggested.

"For that fucking matter, Philo, world authority that you are on women, you don't know the half of it. There's a lot more to Janet and this whole situation than I ever let you in on, mainly because it's none of your fucking business. There was what they call 'mitigating circumstances' that come between us. And for that matter," I continued, my voice rising, "she didn't do nothing to me—not intentionally, anyhow. She didn't want to hurt me; she wanted to marry me."

"Are you nuts? Sam, do you hear what you're sayin'?" Crazy Joe exploded.

"And you would be well advised to keep your mouth shut!" I yelled at him.

"She drove you nuts!" he continued. "She broke your heart, she married some son of a bitch—whom you say she don't love—and *you'd* take her back. Sam, you're outta your goddamned mind!"

"She loves me, goddamnit!"

"Wal, she's gotta funny way a showin' hit," Philo cracked, his sarcasm splitting the air.

"Gentlemen, leave Janet alone. I am not kidding. This is not a fucking drill."

"Look, Sam," Crazy Joe patiently began, "the only way to get over Jan—or any woman—is to fuck as many as you can! Boo-hoo-hoo-haw-haw-haw!"

"Piss. Off."

"C'mon, Sam," Philo chided. "What ya need t' do is head foah Gunnerson. Fin' a college girl an' screw her lights out. Ya'll fergit 'bout Jan soon enough."

I flung my coffee cup and jumped to my feet. "Listen, you bastards! I have had it with your shit! I appreciate your help at the wedding but I sure as hell don't appreciate you bad-mouthing Janet!" My partners stared at me in hurt and wonder. That was too bad; I was mad as hell. "And there's more, too! Maybe I didn't know her that long, but it's like I knowed her all my life! She's coming back someday, and if on that day I've gotta choose between you scrounges and her, it's her!"

Then I stalked over and retrieved the coffee cup I'd pitched, refilled it, and sat on a nearby stump. I lit my pipe and stared into the campfire flames.

Philo was the first to speak. "All right. Ah won't talk 'bout her no more."

"Good!"

"Me neither, Sam," Crazy Joe added without conviction.

"That's just grand," I grumped, feeling no better. Shortly thereafter I crawled in between my blankets without speaking another word to my partners.

The next day I shoed my horses, cleaned and oiled my leather gear, and minded my own business. Around four in the afternoon I was starting a supper of beans and trout and caught myself talking out loud. The flames of an open fire always make me reflective, and I hadn't seen Philo or Crazy Joe around, so I assumed they was long out of earshot.

"He can do more for her than I could," I said to the flames. "He can take her places; buy her things. All that kind of stuff."

"That's the way it goes!" Crazy Joe piped up from behind me.

"Oh, fuck a duck," I groaned.

"Talking to ourselves, are we?"

"The fire don't smart back," I retorted. "C'mon and eat, goddamnit. Where's Philo?"

"Did ah heah somebody say 'food'?" Philo grinned as he sauntered into camp.

"Yeah. Let's eat."

Supper was going fine until the delegation from Oklahoma saw fit to give me some fatherly advice.

"Thank a hit thisaway, Sam," he began.

"Think of what what way?"

"Wal, lak the olt mountaineer Black Harris. 'Member him an' thet white woman?"

"What of it?" At that time I could not have cared less about the personal life of some trapper who lived a hundred and fifty years ago.

"Wal, ol' Black Harris had a crush on her. Was hit thet preacher's wife?" he asked, his brow furrowed in thought. Before I could answer he went on. "Wal, no 'count; I disremember. But ol' Black had quite a crush on 'er. Y'know, 'Ah've trapped in heaven an' Ah've trapped in hell, an' Ah've even seed a putrified forest.' An' she sait, 'La, Mr. Harris, how you talk.' "

"So. What."

"Wal," he cheerily continued as he attacked his beans, "ol' Black Harris hisownself was a gone beaver on 'er. Lak you on Jan, ah reckon. Yit she married ol' Whitman 'cause he was eddicated an' had money an' position."

"She was already married to Whitman when she met Black Harris," I informed him with a disinterested sigh.

"Eggsactly. An' Jan was engaged when ya met her," he said with a smile.

"I don't want to hear any more of this."

"But," he continued, ignoring me, "she'd a been bettah off with ol' Black Harris hisself. Thin she wouldn't a got her head busted in by a Cayuse hatchet in '48, or whatever year hit was."

"So what in the hell does Narcissa Whitman got to do with Jan?"

"Wal, all ah'm sayin' his thet wimmen doan' always know what's good fer 'em. Jan would be bettah off with ya in the long run, but hit'll prob'ly take a day or two fer her t' figger hit out. If eveh."

"So I've got something in common with old Black Harris," I said as I set down my tin plate. "Big deal." I started fiddling with my pipe. "Well, still I don't blame her."

"She went for the best deal!" Crazy Joe suddenly blurted out.

"Like I said"—slow and calm—"I couldn't do that much for

her. 'Cept feed her and clothe her. And love her. Women need things."

"Things," Crazy Joe quickly repeated, a hostile tone in his voice. "He will buy her more things. I think I understand."

"Yeah. He will," I slowly replied as I steamed up.

"And all she has to do is lay there and spread her legs," he continued with sudden venom.

I quickly stood up, took a couple steps over the fire, and stood in front of him. "Joe, enough." He slowly got to his feet.

"Well, we've got a word for that where I come from. And that's—"

As Crazy Joe started to say "that's," I feinted with my right, dropped my weight to my left side, and sucker-punched him as hard as I could. I heard his teeth click as my fist caught his jawbone and set him a foot up in the air then down on his back with a solid thud. I stood over him, pondering jumping on him and killing him, when Philo's strong hands got a death grip on my biceps.

"Unhand me, Philo, goddamn you! I'm gonna knock some respect into that shithead, right fucking now!"

"Enough's enough!" he hollered in my ear. To Crazy Joe, who was rubbing his face and wiggling his head, he said, "Crazy Joe, you steh right thar! You was outta line. Ya git up offa the ground ah'll rip ya t' shreds!"

Crazy Joe rubbed his jaw and leaned back on an elbow. "Jesus, Sam. I was just trying to tell you the way things were. Shock you back to reality."

Philo sensed the fight was over and let got of my arms.

"Is that a fuckin' fact?" I said. "Well, see if you can get this reality through that thick Mick head: You might think you're a bad-ass, and maybe in your own crazy way you are. But you ever talk about Janet that way again I'm gonna kill ya, and it won't be fair and square like with McLowery. I'll just wait till you ain't lookin' and blow daylight through you, and I'll put a little flat rock under your thick head and everybody will think Tom Horn done it. Whaddya think a that, goddamnit!"

"Sam, shut up! Crazy Joe, come 'ere!" Philo barked. Crazy Joe slowly got up and walked over to us, rubbing his jaw as he moved. He stopped directly in front of me.

"Joe, ya apologize right now. Ah ain't gonna see us break up oveh a woman. Say hit, Joe,'' Philo warned with an edge in his voice.

"I'm sorry, Sam,'' he said, not quite looking me in the eye.

"You mean that?'' I fired back, my voice rising.

"Yeah, I do. I was just mad at her on account of what she did to you.''

"Well, I ain't sorry I hit you! I already told you what I'll do—''

"Sam, shut up!'' Philo interrupted. "Thar ain't enough a us we kin affort t' go fightin' an' killin' each other! Now, both a ya shake hands!'' We shook hands and let it go. Shortly thereafter Crazy Joe walked down the creek to soak his sore jaw in the cold stream water.

And he never mentioned Janet again until the day he died.

An hour after the fight we were all sitting around the fire making use of the remaining light to clean guns. As I stood up to pour a cup of coffee a loudspeaker blasted at us from a stand of aspen to our rear: "DON'T ANYBODY MOVE. YOU ARE SURROUNDED. THIS IS THE POLICE. GIVE YOURSELVES UP!''

"What the hell!'' cried Crazy Joe as he jumped up with a Colt in his hand, minus the cylinder.

I turned and faced the trees. "Hello, Dusty,'' I hollered. Then some branches moved and Dusty Rhodes walked out of the trees, a bullhorn in his hand, a wide grin on his face.

"Hi, fellas.'' Dusty smiled. Through the smile, however, his face looked troubled. "Sam, how'd you know it was me?''

"Doan' ya got nothin' bettah t' do then terrorize the fair taxpayers a this state?'' Philo asked, acting insulted.

"Philo, I know for a fact you guys ain't paid taxes in years.''

"It was just a wild-assed guess it was you, Dusty. Pour yourself a cup of coffee and have a sit.''

"You bet.'' He set down the bullhorn and filled an empty tin cup with coffee.

"Have some trout,'' Crazy Joe offered as he took his seat. "It's legal-caught.''

"No thanks,'' he replied. "I didn't get around to eating my lunch till just a little while ago. My wife packs it every

day. Say, where you fellas been the last few weeks, anyway?''

"Wyomin'," Philo shot out.

"Utah," Crazy Joe answered at the same time.

"We've just been around, Dusty," I replied as calm as I
could. "Here and there. We're just now planning the fall
hunt. How many beaver tags we good for?" I asked as I
tried to change the subject.

"Oh, twenty apiece or so. That's one of the reasons I
stopped. I'd like you guys to check out Otter Creek for me;
I've had a report there's over a hundred beaver lodges on it.
If that's the case, we'll have to thin 'em out quite a bit, and
I don't know any other trappers interested in going in on
horseback.''

"Souns damn good t' me!" Philo grinned. "We'll jest
take the two a-dults outta each colony lak we always do,
Dusty. Let's see, thet's—''

"A hundred beaver, period," Dusty smiled through
pursed lips, trying to conceal his amusement. "But I didn't
say you could take any hundred beaver. What I did say was,
we've got to get an accurate count first.''

"Well, we can head right on up there and play wildlife
conservation manager for you. We'll get a close count," I
assured him.

"I knew I could count on you guys." He smiled over his
coffee. "Then I'll give you the tags. Good." He smiled.
Then he turned the conversation around again. "So, you
fellas haven't been doing any long-distance traveling,
right?''

"Like I said, Dusty, we've just been around," I lied for
all three of us. "You know how it is. Why?''

"Oh, I don't know," he replied as he reached into a shirt
pocket. "I just thought one of you might know something
about this." He handed me a folded newspaper page.

It was a page out of a two-week-old Denver newspaper.
Dusty had circled the story smack in the middle of the page
with a red grease pencil. The story told of three armed men
who had ridden horseback to a church wedding in Illinois
and crashed it. It was believed they had traveled far and had
a secret base of operations in the woodlands of western Il-

linois. The main perpetrator had taken the bride off to one side, and on and on. In the end, though, the bride had not identified the miscreants. The local district attorney had issued a warrant for their arrest, whoever they was.

"A very interesting story, Dusty," I said as I handed him the page. He grinned at me, then handed it to Philo. "That's something like out of a movie," I added, uncomfortable as hell.

"Yeah. That's just what I was thinking," he agreed with a smile. "I forgot to bring the story that ran a couple days later. Some weigh-station attendant in Iowa remembered three strange characters passing through with horses. He said he could identify them if he saw them again." I didn't think Dusty was being vicious; I always counted him as a friend, or as much of a friend as a game warden can be. I didn't think he'd run us in, but he wasn't about to get anything resembling a confession from me.

"Soun's crazy," Philo quietly said when he finished the story. He handed it to Crazy Joe.

Dusty helped himself to another cup of coffee. "That guy who held up the wedding must have loved that girl very much," he said as he looked me straight in the eye. I didn't blink.

"Yeah. He must have. But I don't know much about that shit, hoss." I went back to cleaning my Colt.

"Yep, that was sure something," Crazy Joe agreed when he finished the story. "Wild and crazy guys, I guess." I throwed him a hard look.

"You know, that's exactly what I was thinking." Dusty smiled as he stuffed the page back in his shirt pocket. "I don't see how any law officer could run those guys in. Not with a clear conscience."

"That would be a very white thing not to do," I concurred.

"Wal, ah've gotta go check on the hawses," Philo announced as he hurriedly got to his feet and walked off.

"Joe, what happened to your chin? It looks puffy."

"Oh. I walked into a tree, Dusty. I've got to learn to be more careful."

"Trees can certainly jump right out and attack one," Dusty agreed.

"Well, I've gotta go do the dishes," Crazy Joe suddenly offered. Crazy Joe never volunteered to do the dishes. He quickly grabbed the kettle, frypan, and tin plates and headed for the creek. I was intently rubbing down the cylinder of my Colt. It was slick as a whistle but I always occupy my hands when I'm nervous. Or scared.

When Crazy Joe was out of earshot Dusty spoke up. "Sam, we got anything you care to talk about?" he kindly asked.

"Sure. Huntin' and trappin', same as always. You might tell me where the elk are hiding these days; haven't seen much sign of 'em around here."

Dusty stood up and poured out the grounds from the tin cup. "Anything you care to chew the fat over?"

"Nope." I was studiously examining the frame of my Colt in the fading light.

"Well, I'll be seeing you around."

"Okay."

"Don't forget to get me a count on those beaver lodges."

"Sure thing."

"Okay." Then Dusty grabbed his bullhorn and walked off in the same direction he'd come. I leaned back, layed my head on my saddle, and took a deep breath. I was looking skyward in relief when a few seconds later he was back. Dusty stood straight over me and looked down.

"Sam."

"Yeah," I answered, looking up. I didn't flinch.

"I'm really sorry things didn't work out for you. I mean that."

I raised the Colt cylinder above my eye and squinted at him through one of the chambers. I let out a long sigh. "You figured it out, huh?"

He slowly shook his head. "Not at all. My wife did." That figured: Ann Rhodes was a neat lady and smart to boot. She apparently knowed me better than I'd thought. That came as a surprise to me.

I sat up and started putting my six-gun back together. "Is that offer to talk still open?"

"For you, always."

"Well, let's take a walk, then; I don't like an audience."
I quickly assembled my Colt, loaded it, and stuck it in my
belt. We silently walked up a hillside a couple hundred yards
from camp and pulled up seats on a fallen-down log.

I spilled my guts and told Dusty everything, the same as
I've recounted it in these pages. It was long past dark and
the stars was winking at us by the time I'd finished.

"And what bothers hell out of me, Dusty, are them things
she said. You might not believe this, but I took a notepad
and wrote down everything she ever said, other than 'Pass
the salt.' I've run over it time and again, and I just can't
figure it out."

Dusty pitched the stick he'd been absently whittling on.
"Sam, I never heard a story like that in my life. If it was
anybody else I'd say it was a crock of bullshit. Have you
ever wondered why all this weird shit happens to you?"

"Been pondering that a bit lately," I admitted. "Maybe
I bring it to myself, I don't know."

"Well . . ." Dusty sighed. He didn't continue.

" 'Well,' what?"

"I've got some ideas as to what might have happened.
Not that I know a hell of a lot about women—other than the
one I'm married to. And sometimes I don't know much
about her, either."

"I'm a big boy, old hoss. Let's hear 'em." I knocked the
heel out of my pipe and started refilling it.

"Okay, point blank and straight from the shoulder, Sam,
you were screwed before you even started."

"You've made my day."

Dusty picked up another stick and started shaving it. "The
obvious answer is that you were some kind of diversion for
Janet, you being somewhat, ahem—colorful, shall we say?—
and her probably never having been west of the Hudson River
prior to the army shipping her to C Springs. Then one day
Sam Hawkins rides into her camp: big horse, Colt hogleg,
wearing a greasy hat that's the only known survivor of the
Fetterman Massacre—"

"Leave my hat outta this!"

"—and general style of costume, around, oh, 1880."

"Harumph."

"You fascinated her. It doesn't take a degree in psychology to understand why. You represented a challenge, Sam, something wild that needed taming."

I blew a cloud of smoke skyward. "I don't see myself in need of taming."

"Precisely. But here again, Sam, that's only one possibility. There are others."

"Like?"

"Say she really did love you. Obviously she feels something for you, 'cause she didn't rat you out to the authorities for crashing the wedding. From what I've gathered from this conversation, and everything you've repeated that Janet in fact said, I would say the possibility also exists that she's been programmed."

"Programmed. Like a computer?"

"Exactly. Do you know what 'parent tapes' are?"

I had to think on that one for a bit. "I once saw the movie *The Parent Trap*—am I close?"

Dusty chuckled, and shook his head. "There you go again, being homespun."

"Me'n linsey-woolsey," I countered. I puffed hard to bring the coal in my pipe back to life. "What the hell you mean?"

"Well, all of us are programmed to one extent or another by our parents. By imposing our value system and beliefs on our children, we sometimes go overboard when we're too self-righteous, stern, humorless, or whatever, so that when a child reaches adulthood he or she does not automatically think, when faced with a perplexing situation, 'Is this the correct course of action?' If a person has been overprogrammed as a child, he or she will more likely think, 'What would Mommy and Daddy want me to do?' "

"This bullshit is amazing. Where'd you ever learn this stuff?"

"So all the stuff that kids get fed," Dusty continued, ignoring my remark, "winds up stored in our brain in what are called 'subliminal messages.' "

I solemnly nodded my head. "Uh-huh. Of course. Sublimeable messages. I should have knowed."

Dusty sighed. "So that, when faced in adulthood with a decision, the former programmed child will go ahead and do what he thinks his folks would want him to do rather than what he or she really wants to do.''

''Shitfire.''

''Sam, you were fighting those 'sublimeable' messages. And her family. And New England upbringing and Calvinism and three hundred years of starch-collared-wearing people acting like, well, like Yankees.''

''This bull's a little deep for this coon,'' I grumbled.

''I don't think it is,'' Dusty said sympathetically. ''Sam, how much did you draw on your paycheck last week?''

''Uh, well . . .''

''Have your stocks been doing well? Did you put much into your IRA last year?''

''You know I don't send them Micks any money.''

''Building up any assets other than guns, horses, and traps?''

''My land's paid for, dammit! Paid cash money for it, too— and I own the water rights, that oughta count for something!''

''Yucca, greasewood, and cottonwood,'' Dusty said mockingly. He gently poked me in the side with a skinny finger. ''Sam, a polite word for you is 'vagabond.' ''

''And her family would have translated that inta 'bum,' '' I said in resignation.

''You know I don't think that; I know how hard you guys work. But New England might use the latter adjective.''

''Damn Yankees,'' I grumbled.

''There's a final possibility. And I'll give you my gut reaction to this whole mess: for some reason I think it's the most likely possibility, but don't ask me why.''

''Which is?''

''Somebody had the goods on her; Donald or her family.''

''You mean she was framed?''

''I said I can't explain why, 'cause I don't know. But as screwy as it sounds, I think the woman loved you; I think she really did want to marry you. I think that all I've said notwithstanding, there's more to this than meets the eye.''

I jumped up as though spring-loaded, pulled my Colt, and jabbed it at empty space. ''Then, I'll kill the miserable son of a bitch that screwed this up for me, Dusty! I swear, I'll fill his guts with hot lead and he'll know who done it! He'll die hard, I fucking-A guarantee it.''

"I don't think so," Dusty responded steadily.

"And why the hell not!" I hollered.

"Because there's been too much killing already. Sit down.''

"Huh?''

"And besides," he continued, "you don't want to see Janet hurt any more, do you?''

"Well, no.''

"Well, if you killed whoever it is you're going to kill, you'd go to prison and it'd ruin the rest of Janet's life. It would just create problems and solve nothing. I don't see where you can do more than you've already done.''

"Somebody involved in this cluster-fuck doesn't deserve to live," I said through my teeth.

"Look, Sam, this is the last quarter of the twentieth century. You've got to adapt to the times, at least before the century runs out.''

"Fuck the times!" I shot back. "Nobody railroads a friend of mine! I know what Bill Bonney or Doc Holliday would have done: they would have put several soft lead slugs in the bastard responsible, counted the deed well done, and went off and had a drink! They believed in evening up scores, just like yours truly.''

"And they suffered for it. Doc Holliday died at thirty-six a little way up the road in Glenwood Springs, broke and alone in a hotel room. Billy the Kid was killed by Pat Garrett in Fort Sumner before—''

"Garrett never got him! Ask any old-timer in the Ruidoso Valley! He lived on and had a wife and kids and—''

"Sam!" Dusty ordered, his voice sharp. "Sit down and be quiet! Right now.''

I sat back down and rested my chin on my hands. "Oh, fuck a duck," I groaned.

"Like I said, that stuff about Janet being set up was only my gut reaction. I could be way outta the ball park.''

"It sounds too close," I muttered, my stomach working into knots.

"Sam, there's more." Dusty pitched the whittled-down stick

off at a nearby bush. "I think I know who killed that guy in Missouri a couple weeks ago."

I didn't catch the groan in time, and didn't know how to correct it.

"It's been all over the papers and television. There's been quite a stink raised over that little gunfight."

I turned and looked at him in the dark. "Gunfight? What gunfight?" I asked, trying to play dumb.

"Forget it, Sam. There is only one man I know who's that good with a handgun and crazy enough to do it. When you add up who was in the immediate vicinity, the probability becomes high it was Crazy Joe who busted the caps on that cracker."

"Well, then, go ahead and arrest me right here, goddamn it!" I hotly shot out.

There was a pause that seemed to last an hour. It was probably only about five seconds. "I'm not arresting anybody," Dusty said at length.

"You're not?" I think I let out a sigh of relief.

"No. As a law-enforcement official, I will say that a class-B felony was committed: a good D.A. could probably make an excellent case for second-degree murder. But as a private citizen, and judging from everything I've heard and read, that gunsel got what he deserved. Some of this filth walking the streets has got to be dealt with. But, Sam, that is as a private citizen and strictly off the record."

"Strictly off the record," I agreed.

"I will say this, however: Sam, I like you. The kids just love you and Philo, and Ann thinks a lot of you, too." He didn't continue.

"It's always nice to hear that," I replied to the ground.

"Look, I'm not a preacher or a counselor, but I am your friend. Therefore I'm going to give you some advice, unsolicited though it may be: find some new company or you're going to die bloody."

"Think so?"

"I can feel it coming," he replied softly.

I looked back down at the ground. An owl hooted from up the hill. I've always hated owls; they sound like they're mocking you. That one sounded like he was agreeing with Dusty.

I didn't say anything as I pulled out my pipe, refilled it, and lit it. Dusty gazed up at the blinking stars and shivered a little. Although it was August, there's quite a nip to the mountain air come nightfall at that elevation.

I blew a puff of smoke skyward. "Let me tell you something."

"Okay."

"I'm not so sure I give a roaring fuck if I live or not."

"You're feeling sorry for yourself," he said quietly. "Life is too precious to piss away, you ought to know that, Sam. Didn't you learn anything from 'Nam?"

"Sometimes I've wished I died there."

Dusty bolted to his feet with a start. "Don't you talk to me that way, goddamn it! So you've been hurt, huh?" His finger was aimed two inches from my nose.

"Well—"

"Well, you're not the only one! You know where I was?" he demanded.

"You never said. Dusty, your finger is—"

"Quiet!" he roared. "Ever hear of Khe Sanh? Didn't know I was there in the Corps, did you? Well, I was, and it sucked! Every goddamn inch of that miserable hill bracketed by mortars; they might just as well have had our positions down to eight-digit grid coordinates. And rockets? They came in like roman candles on the Fourth of July! Then the gooks would come through the wire and turn our own claymores around on us! Fuck! We lived like rats—we lived *with* the rats—in fucking tunnels in the mud, and every day I survived that bullshit, I said, 'If I only get out of here, Lord, I will not fuck off another day: I will make the most of my life, and I will certainly *not* blow my brains out when Luke the Gook tried many times and failed!' "

"I didn't know," I replied to the ground, unable to meet his gaze. I couldn't look him in the eye. For some reason I can't explain there was a lump in my throat. I was glad Dusty couldn't see me. "So many of 'em bought it. There and here."

"But we're alive!" he cried. He suddenly grabbed me by my shirt and hauled me to my feet. "Listen, Sam, you've been shot at and I've been shot at. For some reason we'll never know, that bastard the Grim Reaper skipped us that go-around. The guys we knew that didn't make it, they're a memory: their names are carved on a hunk of granite; they got unlucky and we didn't and who knows why. But since we're living, it's up to us to work hard, live decent lives, and honor their memories in the doing of it. We had most of the country against us in those days, Sam, but we didn't quit: we drove on with the mission. We did it because we knew we were better than anybody else, and we did it for our pals. The mission today is to go on with life, Sam: that's your patrol order. Put the bad things behind you, trusting the pain will lessen as weeks turn into months, *and drive on*.''

"I never looked at it that way," I replied, slowly saying the words so as not to choke on them.

Dusty let go of my shoulders then. "I've never given a sermon like that in my life. Then again, I've never known anybody who needed it so bad, either."

I looked at him hard in the dark. A small smile graced his lips.

"Thanks. Dusty, I never had a brother—"

"Stow it, squid!" He grinned.

"But I feel like you're one. I just wanted you to know that. And if you ever tell anybody I said that, I'll sock you."

He punched me lightly in the ribs. "Let's go have a cup of coffee. You're buying."

On the walk back to camp I asked him, "All right, I'm getting on with my life, but I've still got to know about Janet. You got any ideas how I can find out?"

"Depends on whether or not you're going to shoot."

"Probably not."

"Then I wouldn't know, Sam."

I stopped him as we neared the trees bordering our camp. "All right." I sighed. "No shooting. I promise. Any ideas?"

"Yeah. You said she has a sister in Arizona, right?"

"Yeah?"

"Go see her. If you can get your foot in the door without her freaking out and calling the law on you, she might tell you some things. Tell her just what you told me earlier. A lot of men are phony; your honesty just might impress her. It's worth a try."

As we neared camp I saw Philo and Crazy Joe still sitting around the campfire. They was probably wondering what had become of Dusty and me.

"Thanks. I think I'll do it." Then I added in a low voice, "Dusty, about that other thing—"

We were ten yards from the fire then, and Dusty interrupted me and hollered, "Hey, guys, any coffee left?" Under his breath he added, "I don't know what you're talking about."

21

SILENCE HOVERED OVER our camp the next day like a dark cloud.

I spent that morning and most of the afternoon cleaning my gear. I set my Hope saddle on a stump and soaped it, leaving the wind and sun to dry the leather. After I finished with the saddle, I once again applied neatsfoot oil to my bridle, reins, and halters. Later on I molded bullets, patched up a pair of winter moccasins, and paste-wormed Molly and Jack.

Philo and Crazy Joe occupied themselves in similar ways, and in the course of the day we didn't speak more than a handful of words to each other. It was late in the morning when I said to Crazy Joe, "I'll be leaving for a few days. I've got some personal business to conduct."

"You coming back?"

"Reckon so."

That was about it.

Late in the afternoon I was sitting cross-legged by the small fire when Philo walked up. "Mind if'n ah jine ya?"

"It's still a free country," I informed him, not looking up from the butcher knife I was slowly drawing across a whetstone. He poured a cup of coffee and sat down. A few minutes later Crazy Joe showed up and took a seat.

"Crazy Joe an' ah've been talkin'," Philo began. "We figger hit hain't right a woman should come 'twixt us lak this."

"I suppose," I said at length.

"We thought a lot of her, Sam," Crazy Joe quietly offered.

I looked up from the knife and gazed at my partners. "Yeah. But she's gone, ain't she?" They nodded their heads in agreement.

A cup or two of coffee later Crazy Joe suddenly shot out, "Women! They're crazy! Once, just once, I'd like to meet one with some common sense! Or one who was at least honest enough to admit she didn't have any! One honest enough to say, 'Joe, I don't have enough brains to pour piss out of a boot,' or 'Joe, your dick is too short—I'm leaving you for a nigger'!"

I tried to suppress a laugh but couldn't. It started as a low rumble deep in my guts and I couldn't prevent it from working its way up to my throat. Then Philo grinned and exploded.

"Ah'd lak t' meet one with tits lak a Jersey, an' brains t' match!" he enthused. That was Philo: he would have big boobs on his mind till the day he died.

"And I," I tossed in, "I'd like to meet one whose family lived on Mars!"

"I'd like a deaf and dumb nymphomaniac!" Crazy Joe hollered through tears.

"An ah'd settle fer one thet jest laked t' fuck!" Philo cried in joy.

My body was shaking so hard from laughing, I layed belly down and weakly beat the ground with my hands, my ribs about bursting through my lungs. They, whoever they was, was right: Laughter is the best medicine. As I layed there laughing, I tried to say through hiccups and tears, "I'd settle for one who just wouldn't break my heart."

22

THE NEXT DAY I got up at dawn and loaded all my gear and the horses.

"Whar ya goin'?" Philo asked as I tied Molly's lead rope off to the O-ring fastened to the inside wall of my trailer.

"Like I said last night, I got some personal business to conduct. I'll be out of the area for a few days."

"Wal, ya kin leave yer critters an' gear heah," he volunteered. "We'll watch yer stuff fer ya."

"Yeah, but you're settin' to go check on how many beavers are on Otter Creek, ain't you?" I asked as I shut the trailer feed door.

"Yeah," he slowly drawled.

"Well, then, you wouldn't be able to watch my gear, and my horses would just be in the way."

"Guess yer right," he replied as he took a fresh chew of snuff. Crazy Joe had overheard our conversation and walked up.

"Well, Sam, we'll get a good count on the beavers," he said cheerily. "And have a good trip, wherever you're goin'."

"Sure thing," I replied with a nod. "If you guys gotta move camp for any reason, put a note inside an old tin can and bury it in the campfire ashes. If you're west of the Missouri and east of the Sierra Nevada, I'll find ya."

Then I pulled down from the mountain campsite and headed for town. I stopped at the bank and withdrew five hundred dollars from my savings account and headed straight to Dusty's.

He helped me unload my horses; we each led one to his small, fenced ten-acre pasture.

"I sure appreciate you watching the animals and my gear, Dusty," I said as I opened the gate.

"It's no imposition," he answered with a smile. "By the way, we aren't taking any guns, are we?"

"Hell, Dusty," I quickly shot back, "give me some credit. Even *I* know you don't walk through an airport with a six-shooter on. Besides, I've gotta make a good impression with this woman. Hrrrumph," I grumped.

"That's what I thought." He sighed as he dropped Jack's halter. "You're putting it in the bag."

I grinned sheepishly at him. "Geez, I'm a little old to change, don't you think?" After a shower and a change into my best clothes, which included a western-cut sport coat and vest, and a good-luck kiss from Dusty's wife, he dropped me at the little town airport. I made it just in time to catch a nonstop commuter flight for Colorado Springs.

Dusty walked with me down to the little airport's one gate, ignoring the stares of travelers at his green-and-gray conservation warden's uniform. He pulled me to the side before I walked out the gate to the little two-engine propeller aircraft.

"One more bit of advice, Sam."

I quickly opened my sports jacket and growled at him.

"No, not that! Now don't take this wrong, but you catch more flies with honey than you do with vinegar."

"You've been reading *The Farmer's Almanac*." I sighed.

"In other words, don't be an asshole."

"Well, thanks one hell of a lot! I like you, too," I grumbled.

"One other thing," he continued. "Janet's sister—what's her name, Nancy?" I nodded my head.

"Well, Nancy will obviously know who you are once you identify yourself. Given she still may be slightly upset over what happened at the wedding, what are you going to do if she calls the law?"

"I've thought about that," I conceded. "My plan is to get in there quickly, explain myself, and kill her with kindness. By the time I'm done with old Nancy, she'll be convinced her sister married the wrong guy."

"You've got a lot of confidence."

"Well, you don't live the way I do being weak-kneed and afeared of your own shadow. *Hasta luego*, Dusty."

The flight from Colorado Springs to Phoenix lasted a little over an hour. When I arrived at the Phoenix airport, the first thing I did was run to a pay phone; it was a little after four and I knowed business offices tend to close early. As I had suspected, Nancy's name wasn't in the Phoenix phone book so I quickly paged through the dog-eared phone book and dialed the registrar's office at Arizona State University.

"Registrar's office," a pleasant female voice answered.

"Good afternoon. This is Walter Provost. I'm laying over on a trip en route to Fort Worth and am trying to contact my cousin, Nancy Provost. She's a junior majoring in theater and it seems I've misplaced her address; would you mind looking it up for me?"

"Sure, please wait a minute," the lady pleasantly responded. I let out a sigh of relief. "So," I thought, "this is gonna work."

In half a minute she was back on the phone. "Hello?"

"Yes."

"Her address is 386 Carr Street. Would you like her phone number?"

"If I may have it, please," I drawled in that false baritone. She gave me the phone number as well.

"Thank you," I said as I hung up the phone with a click. To myself I said, "Boo-hoo-hoo-haw-haw-haw," and headed to the baggage-claim area to see if my tattered duffel bag had made it or was on its way to Iloilo.

None of the major rental-car businesses in the airport would rent me a car without a credit card so I had to take a cab to Rent-A-Bomb. I got a '79 Pontiac Bonneville with a bad muffler. The needle on the gas gauge was buried on Empty, so I pulled into a filling station a couple blocks from the airport and filled it up. The heat in Phoenix was stifling; it must have been a hundred degrees. I peeled off my sport coat even as I pumped the gas, and tossed it on the front seat. As I paid for the gas I grabbed a map from a nearby rack and told the attendant to figure it in the total.

"Is it always this hot here the first day of September?" I asked the kid.

"It's only ninety-eight today; it's cool," he answered as he handed me my change. Cool, hell! I'll take the high country. I need some elevation in my life to live normal.

I maneuvered my way back on I-17 and found a motel within a mile of Nancy's place. It was still the off-season and I got a good rate on the room. After I dumped my gear and showered, I jumped back in the rented car and headed for Nancy's. I located Carr Street easily enough; it was a small side street six blocks from the white buildings and spreading palm trees of the Tempe campus.

The house at Nancy's address was a small blue duplex. There wasn't any cars parked in front, and I turned around at the end of the block and thought, "Uh-huh. She will in all likelihood have a roommate." I headed back to my motel room to plan further from there.

The next day was Saturday; it was already seven in the evening on Friday. There was no point in barging in on Nancy on Friday night; she'd possibly be out on a date, one, or maybe at work. If I called her from my motel room and explained who I was, requesting a meeting, it could easily blow up in my face. Assuming she wasn't very happy with the stunt I'd pulled at Janet's wedding, it could get downright nasty. If, however, I confronted her face-to-face I could hope to win her over with my personality and sincerity. I would have to get my foot in the door, and that meant doing it physically.

So since I was in Arizona, I decided I would do exactly what one of its most famous residents—Geronimo—would have done under similar circumstances.

The enemy is always groggy early in the morning, especially before he's had his first cup of coffee. That was the main reason the Yawner always attacked at dawn.

Which was exactly what I done.

I rang Nancy's doorbell at exactly zero-six-fifty-five hours the next morning. When I didn't hear any rumblings after a minute or so, I rang the buzzer again, that time more violently.

Then, as the soft footsteps got closer to the door, it occurred to me I had only the vaguest idea of what Nancy Provost looked like. I recall thinking, "This is a fine fucking mess," when the party inside started undoing the chain lock.

"Who's there?" a young female voice sleepily queried from inside. Ah-hah, the Yankee accent! It was Janet's sister.

I cleared my throat and effected my best southern New Mexico accent. "This is yer cousin, Walter Provost, from Tularosa, New Mexico," I drawled out. "I'm just passin' through an' thought we could meet."

There was a deathly long pause from inside the house. Even though Nancy had undone the chain lock, I was sure she still had the door bolted.

"I don't *have* any cousins in New Mexico," she informed me in a firm voice.

It was time to improvise. At that point the truth could have gotten me killed; lies obviously weren't working. I dropped my voice an octave and loudly said in my best John Wayne imitation, "Well, baby sister, if ya don't open the door you'll never find out."

She quickly unbolted the lock and opened the door a crack. "Who the hell are you?" I saw a blue eye and part of a cheek through the crack in the door. It wasn't open quite far enough for me to get my size-ten in.

I smiled. "I'm Ed Bradley. Congratulations, you're on *Sixty Minutes*." She attempted not to but couldn't keep from chortling a bit. In the second she relaxed, I jammed my foot through the door, grabbed the knob, and threw my weight against it. As I flew through the door the edge banged her on the head. She recoiled from the impact and I quickly shut the door behind me.

"You son of a bitch!" she snapped as she rubbed her head. She braced herself against the wall. "Sharon!" she yelled, "Bring the shotgun!"

"Oh, hells bells, lady! I just want to talk!" I grabbed my sport coat by the lapels and jerked it wide open. "Look"—I attempted to smile—"no guns this time!"

"You're . . . *him*!" Her light robe bunched up as she slid sideways along the wall trying to get away from me. I smiled, and removed my hat.

"Buenas dias, señorita," I politely said, bowing a bit. "Sam Hawkins, formerly of Iowa, latterly of the Rocky Mountains, at your exclusive service."

It was then I heard the sharp metallic clanking sound behind me.

I knowed that sound.

It was the sound a pump shotgun makes when somebody jacks a round into the chamber.

From the stairs off to my right a young female voice sternly intoned, "Go ahead, asshole. Make my day." I slowly half turned and looked down the bore of the biggest goddamn cannon I've ever seen in my life. It was probably a twelve-gauge but it might as well have been a sixteen-inch naval gun. An angular, tall blond girl about Nancy's age had it trained on my midsection from ten feet away.

I cleared my throat. "There is no need for violence here. I am peaceable. And unarmed. I mean nobody no harm."

"Nancy, who the hell is this creep? Should I let him have it? We can call the cops and tell them he tried to rape us. What's another stiff in Phoenix, more or less?" Sharon may have been Nancy's roommate, and was therefore probably a decent person, but the sweetheart of Sigma Chi she weren't. Furthermore, her index finger was right on that goddamn trigger. If she'd slipped the safety, as near as I could reckon, I was about six pounds of trigger pull away from death.

I thought I saw the flicker of a smile flash across Nancy's face for a second then disappear. "Sam Hawkins," she softly said.

"Yes, ma'am." I would have offered her my hand, but my own were reaching for the sky.

"Sam Hawkins," she repeated, relaxing a little, "you have got some goddamn nerve! You ruin my sister's wedding! You barge into my house at six in the morning and scare the hell out of my roommate and myself. I suppose next you're going to ask me to cook breakfast for you."

"Well, that'd be right kindly of you, miss"—I smiled—"but right now I'd settle for not getting shot."

She couldn't hide her amusement then. "I should call the police."

"We can still let him have it!" Sharon loudly suggested. Lord, I hate trigger-happy people.

Nancy lightly rubbed her head where the door had bopped her.

"Uh, I didn't mean to hit you with the door. I just need to talk to you real bad."

"About what?" Her light blue eyes narrowed just a tad. Nancy

Provost bore almost no physical resemblance to her sister. Her face was pretty yet considerably more rounded than Janet's. She was probably an inch or two shorter than Janet, and her hair was dishwater blonde whereas Janet's was almost jet black. Still, there was a resemblance.

"Janet. I'm concerned for her."

Nancy let out a sigh. "Put the gun away, Sharon. I'll take care of Jesse James here."

"All right, I'll call the cops!" Sharon said enthusiastically.

I started to lower my hands. "I'd appreciate it if—"

"Get 'em up!" Sharon barked.

"Sharon!" Nancy ordered, "I said I'll handle it. Put the gun away and go back to bed."

I liked Nancy right off. She had a lot of common sense.

When Sharon had tromped back upstairs I lowered my hands.

"Well, Nancy, I'd just—"

"Why in the hell did you ruin my sister's wedding day?" she shot out. "That was the most ill-conceived, arrogant, stupid act I've ever witnessed in my life! Do you have any idea of how bad that hurt Janet? How do you think the families felt?"

"Well, I—"

"Well, this is for Janet!" With that she slapped me full force across the face. It was hard to stand there and take it; that sting hurt my pride worse than anything else.

I slowly rubbed my cheek. "I reckon I had that coming, huh?"

"Yes. Maybe I should still call the cops. I'm sure they'd like to talk to you about July's events in Illinois."

"Well, I'm sorry if I ruined her wedding day. When I pulled that stunt I was thinking of the rest of her life."

"You were, huh?"

"Yeah. And I'll never apologize for loving Janet. I'm prouder of that than anything I've ever done. You can carve them words in stone, miss."

We gazed hard into each other's eyes from two feet away. Nancy had a kind eye, just like her sister. I thought I saw her features soften a little. Once a woman vents her frustrations she generally reverts to her usual self, whatever that may be. She was definitely more at ease once she'd slapped me; that slap was probably for a whole lot of things.

"You are a genuine ballsy character, Mr. Sam Hawkins. What do you want?"

"Like I said, I'd just like some of your time. There's some things about Janet I'd like to discuss, then I'll leave *muy pronto*."

"You will, will you?"

"Sure thing. I appreciate the offer for you to cook me breakfast, but I'm willing to buy if you'll go with me."

She slowly shook her head and laughed lightly. "All right. Have a seat in the living room. I'll go get dressed." As Nancy headed back upstairs, I took a half a dozen steps into the adjoining living room and collapsed in the frayed easy chair. I tried to read the day-old paper laying on the floor, and when I couldn't concentrate long enough to read I just layed my head back and let my heart rate return to normal.

In fifteen minutes Nancy was ready to go. She was dressed in faded blue jeans, sneakers, and a blue ASU sweatshirt. I got up from the chair and opened the front door.

"Your roommate ain't going to call the law, is she?" I asked as we headed outside.

"I talked her out of it. Sharon's a ranch kid from the Tonto Basin area. As I understand it, that's a shoot-first-ask-questions-later part of the country."

"Yeah, the Pleasant Valley War. I've read some about it. Say, we can drive, but I saw a nice little restaurant three blocks from here. How about an early morning walk?"

"Okay."

Nancy had a fast pace, just like her sister. "So what are you studying?" I asked as if I didn't already know.

"Theater; minor in education. What do you do for a living?"

I was surprised—and not a little hurt—that Janet hadn't told her. "Well, I'm self-employed; mostly I trap and mine. I've cowboyed some and logged some. Mostly I do what it takes to survive."

"Sounds like a hard life."

"It's hard everywhere, Nancy," I replied, not without feeling. After a few more words we entered the restaurant and quickly found a vacant booth. We took seats on opposite sides of the table.

The waitress brought us coffee and we ordered at the same

time. I was stirring sugar into my coffee, trying to figure out where to start, when Nancy spoke up.

"All right, Sam Hawkins. What gives?" She eyed me intently as she took a sip of coffee.

"If I understand correct, Janet didn't talk much about me."

"To me, no. Of course on her wedding day you became famous—or infamous, as it were—but she refused to identify you by name or discuss anything about your relationship. Prior to that I had heard of you; not by name, by reputation."

"Reputation?"

"My mother or father mentioned that Janet had met a guy she was fond of; that was about it."

Fond of. That was a Grade-A disappointment.

"Oh. Well, I reckon you deserve to hear the story. Got time?"

"For my sister's sake, yes. This all must be leading to something."

"Okay. Here we go." For the next two hours we sat as I poured out the whole story, the same as I recounted it to Dusty, the same as I've written it here. The plates had long been cleared, and all that remained between us was a lone, half-full coffeepot when I finished.

Nancy blinked her eyes several times and gazed out the window at the passing traffic. "I don't know, Sam," she softly said, "but I'll tell you this: You weren't up against Donald. You were up against my father—among other things."

"I was?"

"Yes."

"Well, you can see why I figured she was going to marry me."

"Yes." Nancy then excused herself and went to the ladies' room. She returned in about ten minutes.

As she took her seat she said, "I suppose you want some answers."

"If you want to give 'em," I replied. "It just don't add up in my mind; it's got me puzzled. I mean, Janet hated the army, and now she might as well be in it. She didn't want to go to Germany, she wanted to work outside, and she wanted to stay in the West. For what it's worth, I don't think she loves that old boy one whole helluva lot."

Nancy let out a sigh and looked up from her coffee cup.

"You're probably right. Sam, there's something you've got to understand: Janet has never had any control over her life for as long as I can remember."

"Uh-huh," I agreed. I eyed her steadily and didn't offer another word. I figured more was coming.

Nancy shifted her gaze to the traffic outside and continued. "I suppose I can tell you this. You . . . were almost family, and it's nothing nobody back home doesn't know about." She turned her eyes to meet mine; I tried to pour her another shot of coffee but she put her hand over the cup. "This is going to take a while," she began. Maybe Nancy was hoping I was going to say "I've got to dash to an appointment," I don't know.

"I've got plenty of time."

"All right. Here's the Nancy Provost version of the family history:

"Sam, Janet was not a wanted child. In fact, my parents were married when my mother was three months' pregnant. They met in college; my father was two years older than my mother and . . . after Janet there were two more of us. Mom had three kids by the time she was twenty-three.

"She went back to college when I was two; I am the youngest, you know."

I nodded my head in agreement.

"Then, when she finished school, she went right to work. My father was rarely around; he was busy with his business and . . . other things. What I am trying to say is this: Janet practically raised me. I'm not so sure I knew who my real mother was until I was six or seven years old.

"Janet got pushed into a role early. I think one of my earliest memories goes back to when I was three and Janet was seven. She'd come straight home from school, the babysitter would go home, and she'd start cleaning the house and cooking supper. I'd follow her around and try to help. I just loved that crazy old vacuum cleaner," she recalled with a smile.

"Well, life went on—this is the 1960s—and we kids grew up. By the time I was eight or nine my parents were fighting constantly. Sam, my mother is a wonderful woman; she's considerate and caring, something my father never was. Now that I think about it, I believe my mother and you would hit it off. At any rate, by the time I was ten, it was fairly obvious even to me that the marriage was in the advanced stages of disintegration.

"Janet was caught in the middle of it. She would have been fourteen when things started turning ugly. And what's funny is that she always seemed to take my father's side. Janet's life consisted of studying and housework; she never got to have much fun. Oh, she had friends, certainly, but I just mean she didn't have much fun. Is this making sense to you?"

It was making way too much sense to me. "Yeah. I'm following, Nancy."

"All right. Where was I? Oh, the divorce . . ." Her voice trailed off and she gazed out the window for a few seconds. After a bit her eyes returned to meet mine. "All right, Sam, the long and the short of it is that as far as I'm concerned, my father is not a nice man. It started out with an affair with his secretary. It's no secret . . . Sam, this is going to sound extremely crude, but he screwed everything he could get his hands on in the western part of the state. My mother just had to take and take it, and she took it all those many years for the sake of us kids."

My blood was coming to a slow boil. I hate to see people hurt; I've seen too much of that. "Did your ma have any brothers?" I quietly interrupted, my voice controlled.

"Well, yes, two. Why?"

"Well, why in the hell didn't they drag that son of a bitch out into the street and horsewhip him!" I shot out.

Nancy wordlessly studied my every feature for a dozen long seconds. I had just called her old man a son of a bitch; I guess that slipped right out, but I wasn't sorry for saying it. I hate to see a woman and kids abused; I just goddamn hate it.

The second before Nancy answered, I thought I saw a slight twinkle in her eye. "I don't know, Sam; I never asked. But it sounds like you're up for it."

"Damn right, lady," I grumbled through my teeth as I murdered my coffee with sugar. "Excuse my Mexican there, please."

"You're excused. *Habla se Español?*"

"*Un poco,*" I replied with a smile. "Or enough to know when some hombre's planning on murdering me." Nancy laughed lightly at that one, and that was when I caught a definite resemblance; it could have been Janet's laugh.

"We'll leave our neighbors to the south out of this. Any-way . . . as things turned out, my parents were divorced—finally—when I was thirteen. I was at the age where I was fully aware, you might say. My brother and I went to live with my mother. Janet had just a year of high school left—we moved, Sam—so she stayed with my father."

"She told me once she was told to go to college," I quietly interrupted. "I assume your father did the telling."

"You've got to understand my father, Sam. He's very old-fashioned"— I was thinking, "Yeah, the hypocritical, misera-ble son of a bitch"—"and he's very domineering. His way is right. Janet was scheduled to go to college on a ROTC schol-arship, at an excellent eastern university, and that was that. When Janet was a junior she wanted to quit ROTC; she just hated it. She called home and asked my father for advice. Do you know what he did?"

"Lord knows," I softly grumbled.

"He browbeat her on the phone. She was in tears, Sam. I know, because she called my mother right after that and she was practically hysterical. I don't know what my father told her, but he didn't need to hurt her like that. At any event, as you well know, Janet stuck it out. She did her four years in the army and paid them back, got out, and a month later got married to it. Doesn't make one hell of a lot of sense, does it?"

"Funny how I was just thinking the same thing," I evenly replied. I was thinking a whole lot of things, none of them pleasant. My first thought was the sheer delight I would take in beating Janet's father within a fraction of his life, one, or just outright plugging him.

"The point is, Janet has never been able to stand up to my father. I was the youngest; my brother and I never had to deal with him too much. Oh, he still has a way of getting his point across. For instance, he didn't want me to come to Arizona to college; he felt I should go to a New England school. I am where I want to be, doing what I want to do, and just last month—and I'm almost a senior—he told me I won't make it. Can you imag-ine that? Do you know how much money he's put out for my education?"

"I wouldn't hazard a guess," I replied. I shoved my empty

coffee cup off to the side. It was only ten in the morning and I was ready for a drink.

"Not a red cent. I've done all this on my own. I've worked two part-time jobs for the last three years. Sure, I've taken out a couple student loans, but mostly I've paid for my education as I've gone. And he had the gall to tell me I wouldn't make it, and here I am, in the home stretch."

By then I was mad for Nancy's sake as well as Janet's. There was something definitely askew here and I felt lost, out of control and desperate.

I reached across the table and gave her hand a squeeze. "You'll make it and you'll win, too. That's the best revenge, Nancy: be a success and you can laugh in everybody's face." I quickly withdrew my hand.

"Are you?" she queried.

"A success?"

"Yes."

"Yeah. In my own way you could say I am. I've lived pretty hard and am still here to talk about it. I'm very, very good at what I do: horses, trapping, mining. I can survive anywhere; that's what I am, a survivor, Nancy. I don't have much money 'cause I never much cared whether I had it. Since I got out of the service I've been too busy trying to live what's left of the frontier to do much else, and you think that ain't a daily challenge, just stayin' alive? Oh, yes indeed.

"Oh, when Janet and I was going out I had this idea I'd go become a saddlemaker or something, you know, kind of settle down. Since she left . . . hell, I don't know. I guess I'll just go on doing what I do."

Nancy looked down and half frowned at the table. An instant later her eyes met mine. "That was half your problem right there," she said in resignation.

"What was half my problem?"

She cleared her throat. "Sam, do you know what my father would say about you?"

"I am dying to find out."

"He would say you're 'shiftless.' Please don't take that as an insult from me; I'm not saying that. The point is, now that I think about it, I believe Janet and my father discussed you. Probably at some length. As usual, he beat her—verbally—into doing what he wanted. When he asked Janet what you did for a living, I'm sure he replied with something like that.'' She made a face and half threw her hands in the air.

"Well, he wouldn't meet me face to face, say that, and walk away.''

"Probably not,'' she agreed with a small smile.

"There's one more thing. Janet told me she took a year off between high school and college. Seems your old man would have wanted her to go right away, her being number one in her class and all. She told me she worked that year. What else happened?''

Nancy looked straight into my eyes and did not move a muscle. "Just what she told you,'' she firmly said. Then she quickly looked the other way.

"Oh. Guess I'm just bein' nosy. Can I ask one more question?''

"Try me.''

"Do you suppose she'll come back?''

Nancy let out a sigh and slowly shook her head. "Sam, I've tried to spell it out for you. Janet well may not have much love for Donald, as you claim, but that isn't the point. I don't know; I only met him once and he seemed all right to me. The point is, Janet has been coerced all of her life. She is going on twenty-seven years old; I wouldn't look for her to change. In a sense, Sam, she's a martyr. I think she will play that role the rest of her life.''

"She never had a chance,'' I softly said to myself.

Nancy nodded her head. "I am grateful I was not in Janet's shoes. Now may I ask you a question?''

"Fire one,'' I said as I banged my pipe out in the ashtray.

"Are you going to keep pursuing this?''

"I reckon not,'' I lied as I ran a cleaner through my pipestem. There was a long pause.

"For some reason I don't think you're going to back off, Sam. But you'd be advised to drop the matter here; there's no more to the story than what I've already told you.''

Which made me think there was indeed way more to the story.

"You know what they say,'' I quipped with a smile. '' 'Show me a good loser and I'll show you a loser.' '' Nancy said nothing, and shifted her gaze to the street outside.

"Look, Nancy, I want to write Janet a letter but I don't know how to get it to her. I mean, with APO mail and all, if Donald got his hands on it, it could go hard on her, and Lord knows I don't want to see her hurt anymore. If I wrote a letter to her— right here and now—would you put it in with a letter of yours and send it to her for me?"

"Life is funny, isn't it, Sam? I mean, I've known you less than five hours, and when you barged into my house and I learned who you were, I was ready to call the cops and see you dragged off in chains. Now, I kind of like you. Of course I'll do it."

With that I got some tablet paper and a pen from the cashier and returned to the table. Nancy sipped on a Coke while I slowly composed the letter, trying to make my horrible handwriting legible. To my best recollection the following is what I wrote:

Dear Jan,

I don't know if this is right or if it's wrong. I only know what I feel. I haven't stopped loving you.

The last time we talked you asked me if I was going to chase you after you were married. Well, you can consider this letter—like my interruption of the wedding—the chase. Don't be mad at Nancy for sending it to you. I didn't know any other way to get you word.

I hope you are well. There hasn't been a hour the past five weeks I haven't thought about you. I hope you don't think too bad of me and the boys for what we did at your wedding. I did it cause I love you and they did it cause they're good sports.

Janet, don't take what comes next as being said out of bitterness, for it ain't. I'm not saying it out of a smug fashion, neither. But I've got a rough idea as to what happened. I've run it over in my mind, and when I finally added it up and subtracted I had the answer. And if not the exact answer I think I'm probably close.

What I'm saying is this: Janet, there ain't nothing you could have done in the past that would effect the love I've got for you. There aren't no catches. Looking back on events now, you was trying to tell me something and I wasn't listening close enough. Well, whatever it was, it don't matter. What is irony here is that I was and am a man you can trust, but I reckon you felt you couldn't. For a while I was pretty hard on you in my own mind. I am sorry for that. And I am damned sorry for the way things turned out, particularly if you ain't happy.

I guess I've said it all, except for this last: Jan, it's never too late. I love you the way you are and there ain't any conditions. Always know that I love you more than any living thing.

                                                                        Sam

I quickly reread the letter and folded up the pages. "There you go, Nancy. I reckon I owe you one for that."

"I've got to be to work at one. Let's go," she said. She stuffed the letter in her pants pocket. I knowed she would send it to Janet: she was that kind of lady, namely, honorable.

Neither one of us spoke more than a few words on the walk back to her house. I pulled up short at my rented Pontiac.

"Nancy," I began. It was the strangest thing, but I couldn't go on. There was a lump in my throat the size of a Rocky Ford melon. I put a hand on her shoulder and tried again.

"Look, thanks for being a pal," I steadily said, not letting my voice betray me. "Consider me in your debt."

"Sincerity counts for a lot with me," she quietly replied, looking me in the eye.

I stuck out my paw so to shake hands with her, but Nancy ignored it. To my surprise she put her hands on my shoulders and gave me a quick, soft kiss on the lips and then a hug.

"I hope everything works out for you, Sam. I only wish everybody would be loved as you have loved my sister," she softly said in my ear.

I think I was blinking back tears by then, and gently pushed her away. "It will," I croaked over that same damned lump in my throat. Then I pulled my hat down low, like I always wear it, and said, "I just have the feeling nobody has won. Everybody has lost."

A look of pain flashed across Nancy's face, and she quickly said, "Good-bye," and headed for the house. I took off my hat and waved. As she opened the door she turned and looked back. *"Via con Dios!"* I added with a forced smile.

23

EARLY THE NEXT afternoon I quickly walked the mile from the Gunnison airport into town. I headed straight to a hardware store where I had done business for years.

"Howdy, Pete," I said to the skinny old owner as I walked past.

"Where you goin' with that bag, Sam?"

I stopped at the glass case that held pistols of various models and calibers and squinted at the ammunition shelved on the far wall. Pete ambled up behind the counter, spread his hands out, and leaned on the cash register.

"What can I do you out of today?"

"I'm looking for .45 Long Colt ammunition; don't see any back there."

"Oh, I've got some," he said, turning around. He walked to the far end of the shelf. "How much you need? A box?"

"How many boxes you got?"

"Four. Winchester-Western."

"I'll take 'em all."

As I paid for the ammo Pete observed, "Gonna be doin' some target-practicin', huh?"

"Yeah."

"You need a sack?"

"Nope. I'll just stick it all in my duffel bag here." I didn't pay any attention when I heard the little brass bell above the

229

outside door ring crazily. I was bent over jamming the ammo in my duffel bag when I heard a familiar voice from behind me.

"Going to do a little target-practicing, are we, Sam?"

I let out a deep breath, stood up, and turned around. "Hello, Dusty."

"You just get in?"

"Yeah."

"It looks like you're leaving again."

"Not right away."

"How was Arizona?"

"Hotter'n the hinges of hell."

"That isn't what I meant. So what's with all the rounds?"

"I heard tell in Arizona that Geronimo skipped the reservation again; he's headed this way," I cracked with a smile.

"That's not very funny," Dusty soberly responded. "C'mon, I'll give you a ride to the house and you can pick up your truck and horses. I happened to be in town today, so Ann is fixing me lunch; there's enough for you if you care to stay."

"Sure thing. Appreciate it," I replied as I heaved the duffel bag up on my shoulder and followed Dusty out to his lime-colored pickup. I was positive a lecture was coming.

"So, how was Nancy?" Dusty inquired as he pulled out on US 50.

"She's a nice girl," I answered, noncommittal-like.

"Learn anything?"

I ignored the question and stared out the window. We was almost to Dusty's house when I said in resignation, "Pull over here. I don't want to say this in front of Ann and the kids." Dusty eased the truck over to the narrow shoulder of the county road, slowed to a stop, and put it in neutral.

"I'm all ears."

"All right. Dusty, Nancy told me a whole lot more than what she knowed. I don't think even she knows what happened to Janet for sure, but she loosened up and talked and talked. The more she talked, the more everything fit into place. I'll tell you, hoss, I about threw up! I just felt sick to my stomach. And as Nancy talked I thought about something you said: You said, 'Sam, do you ever wonder why all this weird shit happens to you?' Remember?"

"Sure."

"Well, shitfire! I ain't the one all the weird shit has happened to! Here I've been, feeling sorry for myself and pouty to boot, and *I'm the one* who's had a normal life. Janet has been so beat down, and like you said has been so 'programmed,' that she'd *never* admit it, 'cause she couldn't figure it out if her life depended on it! Nancy called her a martyr; I ain't sure that's the right word. She's a casualty, Dusty; symbolically talkin' she's an emergency medevac, and all these years she's been laying there with a sucking chest wound and no chopper come to get her." I leaned out the window and spit mightily.

"Man, this is sad, Sam," Dusty slowly said as he shook his head. "I can see why you want to bust a cap on— Who did you say you were going to shoot?"

"Who said I was going to plug anybody?" I retorted.

"What's with all the ammo if you're not?"

"I haven't target-practiced in a long time. That is the truth," I replied honestly.

"Sure. Right. Geronimo's coming; I almost forgot. So are you going to hole him or what?"

"Goddamn it, I ain't going to kill nobody! I told you that the other night. Let's get to your place and eat."

Dusty put the truck in gear and headed down the cracked pavement to his little country home. I had promised him I wasn't going to shoot, and I wasn't.

Unless I had to.

It was early evening by the time I reached our camp in Taylor Park. Philo's and Crazy Joe's outfits was parked in the same spot I'd seen them last, but they and their horses was long gone. I figured they'd headed on up to Otter Creek to check on the beaver population for Dusty. I hurriedly saddled Molly, put a lead rope on Jack, and picked up their trail.

Three hours later I found them camped next to a little spring. Philo was fishing in the beaver pond next to their campsite and greeted me with a loud "Hi-dee!" as I rode in.

"So how was the trip, Sam?" Crazy Joe asked.

"Just fine." I got off Molly and tied her to a small aspen. Crazy Joe took Jack's lead rope and tied him next to my mare.

"So where's your gear? There ain't any packs on Jack—how you gonna camp?"

''Whar's yer gear?'' Philo repeated as he walked up.

''Look, I've got to go back to town and make a phone call; then I'll join you guys.''

''Ya shore is doin' a lotta travelin' ovah—''

''Over what?'' I challenged.

''Nothin', Sam.''

I turned my attention to Crazy Joe. ''You once said you've got a cousin back east that's a private dick. I need to talk to him; what's his name and where's he live?''

''Oh, he's pretty expensive, Sam,'' Crazy Joe replied, shaking his head.

''This is important. How good is he?''

''He's very, very good. That's why he's very expensive.''

''What's his name?''

''Steady Eddie,'' Crazy Joe answered with a grin.

''Steady Eddie,'' I slowly repeated. ''With a name like that it sounds like he carries around a Thompson in a violin case.''

''I don't think he's done any of that kind of work lately,'' Crazy Joe confessed. ''Hold on a minute; I'll write this down for you.'' He fished some paper and a pencil out of a saddlebag and wrote down the name and the town.

I couldn't keep the surprise out of my voice as I read the name out loud. ''Mario Eduardo O'Hara? You have got to be seriously shitting me.''

''Not a bit, Sam. Y'see, my mother's sister married his father; she is really my mother's half sister, who is half Italian by her real father, and Eddie's father is half Italian, so—''

''I get the picture.''

''So that's why he goes by Steady Eddie.''

''I see. Boston, Massachusetts. Hah! Massachusetts, home of the Puritans. That's fuckin' rich.''

''What do you mean?''

''Never mind.''

''Sam, this is Sunday; he won't be in his office today.''

''Is his house listed in the phone book?''

''Think so.''

''Then I'll call him at home.''

It was close to midnight by the time I got back to my truck. Instead of driving back to town that night, I laid down under the open sky and tried to sleep. After three hours of fitfully rolling around in my blankets, I got up and made a pot of coffee. Several cups and a couple bowls of tobacco later I again rolled up in my blankets. I think I finally dropped off to sleep a little before false dawn.

By seven o'clock I was at a pay phone in town. It was already nine o'clock on the east coast, so I called information and got the number for Steady Eddie's office. I had to drop a pile of quarters into the machine for the first three minutes.

"O'Hara Investigative Agency," a reedy, nasal male voice answered.

"Howdy. This is Sam Hawkins calling from Colorado. I'm a friend of your cousin, Joe Flanigan."

"That crazy son of a bitch! You mean he's still alive?" the voice replied in awe.

"He was yesterday. We're partners out here."

"No doubt in some larcenous scheme. What can I do for you, Hawkins?"

"I need some investigating done in your neck of the woods. I need a professional to ferret out some stuff for me; stuff going back quite a number of years."

"What part of my 'neck of the woods'?" He sounded amused.

"Western part of Massachusetts. You interested?"

"Tell me what you want."

I'd dropped ten dollars' worth of quarters into the phone by the time I was done explaining exactly what it was I needed. I didn't tell Eddie any more about Janet and me than I had to, but to make a living in a place like Boston old Steady Eddie had to be pretty smart to begin with.

"So what are you going to do once I get you this information? Assuming I agree to take on the case, that is."

"I'm writing my memoirs. All this is going for the footnotes."

There was a long pause. Finally the party in Boston spoke up. "Hawkins, my business is people. I study them; dissect them, if you will. It takes no genius to figure out you are highly upset with somebody. Assuming that what you are inferring is essentially correct—and you have made a great leap of faith assuming that you are—it sounds like you're not planning on using this information for footnotes."

"You don't want to do it, then?"

"I didn't say that."

"Well, if you don't, I'll just head back there and find it out for myself. It might take me a year or two, but that's all right: I learned patience a long time ago. I know how to find a county courthouse; I think I can figure out how to read old newspapers, too. How much you get a day?"

"Four hundred, plus expenses."

"All right. I'll express a money order to you today for a thousand bucks. That'll get you started. How many days' work you think this'll take?"

"Hawkins," he sighed, "I didn't say I'd take it. And I also didn't say I'd drop everything in the eventuality that I do."

"Fine. The Yellow Pages are loaded with gumshoes."

"But," he continued, "you sound like a man obsessed. And this does sound like an interesting case. Right now I'm working a divorce that has me bored to distraction. You're on."

"Give me your full mailing address." I already had a pen and paper out. When I'd written it down, I said, "The check's in the mail."

"One of the three great lies," Steady Eddie wearily replied. "Call me in a week. I may have something for you by then."

"Hasta luego," I cheerfully said. Then I hanged up the phone.

I spent the next week counting beaver with Philo and Crazy Joe on Otter Creek and all its tributaries. We trapped one super blanket male for food and to inspect the pelt: although it was mid-September and we'd had one killing frost after another, the pelt was still thin, the downy guard hair not quite prime enough. It would be a couple more weeks before beaver had a decent enough fall coat to trap.

"It seems a shame to kill these critters for thirty bucks a plew," I told Philo as he carefully cut little bits of fat away from the leather. Crazy Joe was off roasting the beaver's hindquarters over an unnecessarily large fire. "Even back in 1846 they was worth a buck and a half a pound. If you put that in today's money and figured in inflation, that'd be eighty or ninety bucks a plew."

"Wal, hit's what we do, Sam," Philo replied. "Beaver's bound t' come back. Hit ain't natural fer prime fur t' sell thirty dollars fer a perfect plew. Ya jest watch; beaver'll shine agin!"

I think he really believed that. The odds of beaver ever being worth big money again in this civilization was about on par with them of the Great Plains once again being blackened with buffalo, or the Cheyenne and Arapaho taking to the warpath and driving the white man out of the West. I had knowed all along we was living a dream; I guess I'd just assumed Philo knowed it, too. I wasn't about to tell him there was no point in expecting the impossible to happen.

"Yeah, reckon so," I said without conviction.

"When ya goin' back t' town?"

"Tomorrow."

"Gonna be gone long?"

"Oh, I dunno. Might. Why?"

"Wal, brang some coffee an' sugar back. An' 'bout ten pounds a pintos."

"Sure thing, Philo." I smiled.

The next day I arrived in Gunnison around noon. Steady Eddie's partner answered the phone and told me "just a minute."

"Hawkins?"

"What'd you find out?"

"A veritable encyclopedia of interesting things. I got so wrapped up in your case I overspent your thousand dollars several days ago. I broke my own cardinal rule: I never work on credit."

"So how much do I owe you?"

"One thousand, two hundred and sixteen dollars. We'll forget the three cents."

"I'm good for it."

"Okay. Send me the money and I'll send you the portfolio."

"Portfolio?"

"I told you I've got a lot of information here."

"Just hold on to it. I'll pick it up in person."

"When?"

"Tomorrow. One other thing: I'll need a car once I get to Boston. I'd like you to scrounge me one."

"So rent one."

"Can't. Don't have a credit card."

I thought he sounded irate when he said, "I don't do hot cars, Hawkins."

"Loan me one. I don't expect it for nothing."

"Is this vehicle going to be used in the commission of a felony?"

"No."

"I'll see what I can do."

"Good. I'll call you from the Denver airport once I know what flight I'll be coming in on. If you would, meet me at the Boston airport with the car and the dope."

"The dope?" he quickly said.

"The hot poop. The straight skinny. You know, the portfolio."

"Oh." Pause. "You will have, of course, the gelt."

"The what?"

"The money."

"I said I would, didn't I? See you tomorrow."

I had anticipated Steady Eddie would come through for me, so I had brought my horses and all my gear into town. I really didn't care to confront Dusty, so after making a quick stop at the bank I jumped in my truck, gassed up, and headed straight for Colorado Springs. It took me four hours to make the drive to Luke's crumbled-down ranch.

"Why howdy, Sam!" Luke called as he greeted me at the door. "Ah'm shore glad ya come!"

"Well, it's nice to see you, too, Luke."

"Thet goddamned Jack Riley falled offa the wagon agin, Sam. He run off with some toothless barfly a week ago an' left me a-hangin'. He'll be back when he runs outta money and sobers up, but ah need a hand. Wanna job?"

"Well, that isn't exactly why I'm here, pard. But I'll tell you what: I've got to go east for a few days. I'd like to leave the horses and my trappings here; I know it'll all be safe with you. Then when I get back, if you ain't found nobody and I've got some time to spare, I'll give you a hand."

"Thet's right white a ya, Sam." He smiled. "C'mon in an' let's haf a drank."

I kicked Luke out of bed at five-thirty the next morning so I could catch the commuter flight to Denver and make the first nonstop flight to Boston, or, as Steady Eddie pronounced it, "Baw-sthun."

"Whar ya off t' so fast?" Luke asked sleepily as I drove.

"Got to go to Iowa and see my great-uncle. He's goin' under; this'll be my last chance." As a matter of fact my uncle Dutch had been on my mind for the past couple months and I had every intention of seeing him one last time. It was half the truth.

"Oh. Ah thought mebbe hit was 'bout thet girl."

"That was over quite a while ago, Luke," I answered as I put the gas pedal to the floorboard and blasted a yellow light as it turned red.

"Thet's what ah thought." He yawned.

Six hours after Luke dropped me off, the three-engine Boeing pulled up to the concourse at Boston's Logan International Airport. As I walked out the gate I immediately felt out of place in my boots, Western coat, and hat. Well, that's what I am: a Westerner. I'll be damned if I change my dress just to visit the East.

A dark-haired, dark-complected guy in a natty three-piece suit walked up to me as I was getting my bearings. He was about my age, and smiled. "Invariably, you are Sam Hawkins."

"Howdy, Eddie," I replied as I extended my hand. He shifted a large manila folder from his right to left hand and we shook.

"Normally I don't meet my clients at airport gates. I assumed you would be as interesting as your case. So far I've not been disappointed."

I nodded at the folder. "That it?"

"The complete rundown back to year one."

"Got the car?"

"A '79 Plymouth. It's a spare I keep around for this and that. I just put a new transmission in it."

"I'll be careful. I drive like a regular little old lady. Let's go get my duffel bag and I'll buy you a drink."

"Duffel bag?"

As we walked out into the parking lot, the smell of salt air filled my nostrils. I thought the breeze smelled different than the Pacific air, but maybe it was just my imagination. As we swiftly walked toward the car Eddie spoke up. "Why don't you let me buy you lunch; I know how atrocious airline food can be."

"Was right tasty to me. I don't know why people bitch about food so much; some of them should eat what I've eaten in my life."

"Nonetheless"—he smiled—"I want to talk to you about a

few things. Ethical questions and so forth.'' I walked alongside as we headed down Row G to his blue Plymouth. Twenty-five minutes later we strolled into the lounge of the Copley Plaza Hotel and were escorted to a table.

"This joint's a little outta my league," I mumbled as I removed my hat. There was a white linen cloth on the table and the red napkins were made out of cotton, not paper. "More or less I hang around greasy spoons."

Steady Eddie let out a small laugh from across the table. "I never would have guessed."

As I tore into my cheeseburger—Eddie had some kind of diet salad—he said, "Sam, we may have a problem here."

"What problem? I already paid you, remember?"

"No, not that. You have spent at least twenty-five hundred dollars on this woman in just the past week, and you're not even married to her. I have never been west of Chicago, but I have seen a lot of motion pictures. Would you like to know what I think?"

"You're buying dinner. I suppose I should listen."

"I think you're harboring a grudge of some fashion and would like to get even in the tradition of your violent historical antecedents. Are you by any chance armed?"

"Naw. Don't like guns. I've got a couple, but they're back in Colorado." That was, of course, a first-class lie.

"Good." I thought I heard him let out a sigh of relief. "You'd have a hell of a time buying one in this state."

"Look, I ain't going to rub out anybody. I ain't even going to smack anybody. Maybe I'll just have a talk with one or two people and head home. That's all."

He eyed me evenly. "Could I have your word on that?"

I pitched my half-eaten cheeseburger to the fancy plate. "Goddamn it, I just gave you my word! Sam Hawkins stands by what he says. I don't want to hear any more of this; you're supposed to be a gumshoe, not a district attorney."

"Relax, Sam. Look at it from my standpoint, will you? First, you pay all this money to get essentially dated and worthless information on a woman you will never see again. Then you travel a couple thousand miles at considerable expense to receive it. I realize that love is a powerful emotion, but—"

"So whoever said I loved the dame?"

"But one must let things go when one must let things go."

I picked up my cheeseburger and took a bite. "You sound like Pat O'Brien as Father What's-his-name talking to the Dead End Kids."

"Father Murphy."

"Whatever."

Steady Eddie distractedly stirred his iced tea. "I told you once that I know people and study them; pretty much I know what makes them work. What puzzles me about your case is that if one rules out revenge, there's no motivation. I don't think you—"

"You're right, I'm not," I shot out, reading his mind. Let's get on with it and see what I paid all these big bucks for." With that, I grabbed the folder and flipped it open. I gave at least a passing glance to every bit of information inside; Eddie elaborated on a few of the items for me. In half an hour I was satisfied he'd done his job.

"Here are the keys," Steady Eddie said as he handed them over. "My office is three blocks away. If you leave town during nonbusiness hours, just put the keys on the visor, lock the car, and park in the ramp behind my office; you can't miss it."

"Thanks, Eddie. You by any chance got a map of Boston in the car?"

"In the glovebox. There is one other thing you should be aware of. During the course of the investigation I talked to one of Janet's old boyfriends; you can read the summary later. He was evidently going out with her around the time Donald appeared in her life. One night this young man received a phone call at around two in the morning. The caller merely said, 'Leave her alone or your future is written on the end of a .357.' He seemed to think Donald learned of him and made that call; he didn't have any enemies he knew of."

"I hate people that make threats, Eddie. I just hate a yellow bastard like that." I figured that Donald was behind that call. I hadn't liked him from the start, just from little things Jan had let slip. I loathed him then.

"You don't, do you?"

"What?"

"Make threats."

"No."

He let out a small sigh. "That's what I was afraid of."

"I'll be back tomorrow or the next day. I'm getting the hell outta this place; I'm tired of all these people staring at me like I'm outta some freak show."

With that I headed to the car, fished my pistol and holster out of my duffel bag so to be fully clothed, and wound my way south through the miserable Boston traffic. It was about three times worse than driving in Denver. I cut off the interstate at the Plymouth exit and headed east, figuring that eventually I'd wind up at the Atlantic Ocean. There was something down there I wanted to see.

After making a wrong turn which would have taken me to Cape Cod, I did a one-eighty and eventually found the town of Plymouth. I parked on a side street running down to the ocean, walked in the little Howard Johnson's fronting the ocean, and bought an ice cream cone. Then I hoofed the eighty or hundred yards to Plymouth Rock.

Plymouth Rock lays about ten feet in the ground in a tomblike arrangement. A four-foot-high iron picket fence surrounds the rock, which itself is unimpressive. It's probably twelve foot across and three or four foot high.

As long as I was in the area, I just wanted to see the rock my great-grandfather of ten generations ago and his family supposedly stepped on when they arrived in the New World. One branch of my family did come over on that boat; to me it's never been a big thing. I've got friends in New Mexico whose families have been here a hell of a lot longer. In fact, if my ancestors had been smart, they would have gone to Santa Fe instead, which already was a thriving town by the time the Pilgrims landed in New England in 1620.

According to my uncle Dutch, the family historian, my ancestors departed Plymouth shortly after a disaster befelled them. To my knowledge they had never returned. Till now.

The disaster was, my great-grandfather of ten generations ago took an old smoothbore musket and blowed a hole through a fellow Pilgrim the size of a grapefruit. The name of my great-grandfather of ten generations ago was John Billington. And there is a biography on him in the *Encyclopedia of American Outlaws* right next to the one on Billy the Kid.

He was hung.

And I was wondering powerful hard what was going to happen to me.

I checked into a motel down by the water and kept a low profile in Plymouth the rest of the day. I carefully read every scrap of information Steady Eddie had gathered. A lot of it was public information: weddings, births, divorces; things you can find in newspapers. He had several firsthand interviews in the portfolio; the most interesting was one he'd had with a former college roommate of Janet's. I figured how Steady Eddie got people to talk was his business, but I reckoned he had to pose as some kind of cop or fed to get it. At least one item in the portfolio seemed to be highly sensitive in nature and I wondered if he'd had to pilfer it somewhere; actually, it was a Xerox copy of an original, but even I knowed it took some fancy legwork to get ahold of it.

I kept the "Do Not Disturb" sign on the door that day and alternated between reading the contents of the portfolio and my favorite book, Bernard De Voto's *Across the Wide Missouri*. I cleaned and oiled my pistol, even though it didn't need it, and an hour before dark I jumped in Eddie's Plymouth and went out on a reconnaissance patrol.

I found the house easily enough. It looked like a small two-bedroom affair and was located in an older but nice part of town. Old Lawrence Provost didn't need a lot of room; he hadn't remarried. I drove by slowly, turned the corner, and came back through the alley. I thought, "Uh-huh," and headed back to my motel room.

At eight-thirty it was good and dark. As I exited my motel room and loaded my bag in the car, a wet wind off the Atlantic about drove through me. Then I jumped in the Plymouth and headed for the house.

I parked half a block away from the house on a side street. As I strolled up the walk I saw lights on inside. Being a direct sort of person I rang the doorbell. Nobody answered after four rings, so I headed back down the walk, went around the block, come up the alley. A mangy yellow dog snarled at me as I walked up the flagstone to the back door. I growled back and he cowered.

I tried the doorknob; it was locked. Then I looked around to make sure I wasn't being watched, took from my coat pocket a screwdriver I'd brought along for just that contingency, and jimmied the lock. People really ought to be more careful. They'll buy a fifty- or sixty-thousand-dollar house, then put an outside door lock on that cost five ninety-five at the hardware store.

All kinds of people can bust one of them locks.

Like murderers.

I swiftly shut the kitchen door behind me and looked around. I pulled a quick check of the well-lighted house and observed that when somebody came in the front door they wouldn't be able to tell if a person was waiting for them in the kitchen. I figured I'd wait there.

Janet's old man had conveniently left the coffeepot plugged in, so I helped myself to a cup—it was pretty weak—and took a seat and waited. At a quarter to ten I was rewarded. My intended victim had walked into a trap in his own home. How neat.

He shut the front door hard and bolted it behind him. When I heard him fiddling with his keys, I quietly stood up and leaned against the kitchen counter. That way he would definitely be in the kitchen by the time he saw me.

He strode in the kitchen at a fast walk.

"Buenos noches, pelado." I smiled.

He was taking his light jacket off as he entered the kitchen, and froze in horror. It looked like he was going to run or yell, so I pulled the fastest draw of my life and stuck my Colt Peacemaker within six inches of his nose.

"You let out any sound louder than a whisper, you're gonna die right here, Lawrence," I informed him pleasantly.

"Who are you?" he gasped.

"Take your jacket off." He finished removing the windbreaker from his arms. "Now sit down." He didn't move. His eyes were fixed on mine.

I pulled out a chair, put my free hand on his shoulder, and gave him a shove. "That's better," I cheerily said. Then with my left hand I carefully raised my bandanna above my nose.

"This bring back any memories, Lawrence?" I quickly removed the bandanna and frowned. "You don't look at all happy to see me."

"You madman! You're the one who ruined my daughter's wedding! *You are crazy!*" he declared through the mask of fright on his face. He was concerned for his own safety, and with the memory of the wedding fresh in mind was no doubt convinced I was crazy enough to remove him from planet Earth most tick.

"Sam Hawkins. Not whacko crazy. Maybe crazy like a red fox. Would you like to call the police?"

"Most certainly."

"Well, I'll tell you what, Lawrence: I'll let you do that. Yeah, you can call the cops. But first we're gonna have a little talk." I reached behind me and grabbed the manila folder off the counter.

"Janet is a happily married woman! You have no right to interfere in her life! You have absolutely no right to break in my house and threaten me! You're a filthy, rapacious vagrant!"

I let out a long sigh. "Lawrence, Lawrence," I sadly began. "Do you see this Colt's Patent Revolver I'm casually pointing at your midsection? It fires a two-hundred-and-fifty-five-grain soft lead .45 caliber bullet at approximately eight hundred and fifty feet per second. It will make a hole slightly under half an inch in diameter as it enters your body. As it exits it will take with it bone, tissue, muscle, and any organs it may encounter. It will leave an exit wound approximately the size of your fist. Now I would like you to apologize for calling me a 'filthy, rapacious vagrant.' "

He glared at me, but slowly his eyes turned downward. "I apologize," he said through his teeth.

"That's real white of ya," I cheerfully responded. Then I pulled up a seat on the opposite end of the table. "I am going to sit here and we are going to have a little talk. First off, I need you to put your hands on the table. Palms up."

"You have some kind of gall, buster."

"And if you move fast, I'll blast daylight through you," I continued. "I am going to keep this six-shooter pointed at your chest. Don't think you can move fast enough to grab it; I can cock and shoot in a tenth of a second."

"You arrogant—"

"Ah, ah, ah," I warned. "There is no need for cursing. I don't see your hands yet, Lawrence." He slowly laid his hands out as instructed.

"Good. Now that we've established the ground rules, let's get to work, shall we?"

"I have friends coming over in ten minutes."

"Sure you do," I agreed, unfazed. "Oh, one other thing: I'm gonna talk and you're gonna listen. Do we understand each other?"

"You have the gun, don't you?" he said in a sneer.

"That's what I like. Cooperation."

He next asked in an incredulous whisper, "What is the meaning of all this?"

"Would you please listen? Crap! I hate to be interrupted! All right!" I glanced at the first page of the folder. "Lawrence, you were married when your wife was three months pregnant with Janet. Is that or is that not correct?"

He glared icily at me.

"Okay, it's correct. Michael and Nancy followed in short order. Boom, boom, boom, in fact. Ah, yes, a busy man in bed. But you were busy other places, weren't you?"

No answer. The same icy glare.

"According to my research—which I've accumulated at great time and expense, I will add—you managed to get your secretary pregnant when Janet was about"—I had to flip a couple of pages—"when she was about nine. You know, Lawrence, you may not believe this, but do you know whose name is on the birth certificate as the father of the little boy your secretary bore you?"

"Swine!"

"Ah, ah, ah," I warned with a sad shake of my head. "Yours. As they say, a stiff dick has no conscience, and obviously you don't, either. Your secretary moved to Pennsylvania shortly after the child was born. You never paid her a red cent for child support. Of course, there was other ongoing affairs concurrent with that one."

"Where are you finding this?" he asked in a whisper, his voice strained.

"The public library. Moving right along . . . let's see, let's flip to something interesting here. Ah, the divorce settlement. You got the house and the car. The ex–Mrs. Provost and the children got the shaft."

"I've worked hard for everything I have," he said hotly.

"Ah, that's what I like to hear, the work ethic from one that

ought to know; a real Massachusser. A real pilgrim. What did
John Calvin say? 'Work hard and get to heaven'?''

"How would you know, reprobate?''

"Lawrence," I sighed, "I am getting fucking-A tired of you
calling me names. Keep it up and you might get somewhere in
a hurry, but it won't be heaven.''

"All right," he muttered, his eyes boring through mine.

"After you—dare I say 'trashed out'?—Mrs. Provost, who in
my opinion ought to be nominated for the sainthood for puttin'
up with your bullshit, you continued to fuck everything you
could get your hands on. It was years later"—I flipped through
a couple of pages—"it was a few years later when the divorce
was final that Janet moved in and stayed with you. She wanted
to finish her education in her own high school. That's under-
standable, I reckon.''

"What would you know about education?''

"Damn it to hell! This is wearing me out!" I flipped the
manila folder shut and banged my fist down on it. "All right,
Provost, I've got the facts in here, more than you ever dreamed
possible. Beyond your wildest dreams. Or maybe in your case,
beyond your wildest nightmares.

"We'll cut the history lesson. Now you're going to hear the
facts from me.

"Janet Provost is a lovely, considerate person. But you know
what hit me the very first time I laid eyes on her? I said to myself,
'This is somebody that has been hurt bad.' I don't know how I
knew it; it was just one of those things you know. I thought it
once, then forgot it. Until recently.''

"While we was going out, Janet always talked about you in a
positive way. The one time she discussed your divorce, she almost made it sound like it was your wife's fault. Again, I thought
nothing of it.

"Janet was a busy young lady from the time she was seven
years old. I thought responsibility early was good; I had no idea
how much she shouldered. There never was much money in the
house, was there?''

"I had a family to feed," he grumbled.

"Sure, Provost, but it's hard to feed a family when you're
escorting little honeys all over the state, and taking them out to
eat at nice restaurants. And then, of course, them motel bills do

add up. Mrs. Provost and your children—at least until she started working—ate macaroni and hot dogs way too often. How about daily? You know something? I just hate macaroni and hot dogs. I've got a good mind to shoot you just for that.''

''You—''

''Ah, ah, ah,'' I warned with a shake of the six-shooter and my head.

''But life went on,'' I continued. ''Let's move up to the early seventies. Let's see, I was just starting 'Nam; Janet was just finishing junior high school. You were busy being the important man about town that you were. And, of course, the unexhaustable hoser.'' I paused for effect and stared him down. ''And now, you have the opportunity to speak on your behalf. I am going to ask you a question; you will answer it.''

''Perhaps,'' he sniffed.

''Why do you hate Janet?''

''Hate? Janet?'' he slowly repeated in disbelief.

''Why do you hate Janet?'' I repeated. ''I did not stutter.''

''The nerve of you! I love my daughter! I—''

''Answer's over,'' I informed him. ''Now, Lawrence, you may find this hard to believe, but I never went to college.'' He ''harrumped'' at that one. ''I never went,'' I continued, ''but I've got a pretty good idea of what goes on at one. Besides the academics there's quite the opportunity for a social life. Why, there's women all over the place; yes, yes indeed, a lot of targets of opportunity for a virile fellow like you.

''When you got Janet's mother pregnant you were slightly ahead of your time. Pity, Provost, but you missed the sexual revolution by a few years. But, nah, it didn't matter to you, sexual revolution or not: it appears you were always on a sexual search-and-destroy mission.

''Since this was all a few years before that famed revolution, you did the honorable thing: you married the woman you impregnated. I will give you credit for that. Personally I think you're a Grade A son of a bitch, but at least you married the poor lady so Janet could be born under legitimate circumstances. At least you didn't opt for an abortion.''

''It occurred to me!'' he suddenly shot out.

I slowly nodded my head. ''Did it now? Did it indeed?''

''No, I didn't mean that!'' he quickly corrected. ''Look, I

was young—you've got to understand—I had my whole life ahead of me! I—''

''The point is, Lawrence, that Janet robbed you of your youth. Yes, with marriage and her subsequent arrival you were saddled with a whole raft of responsibilities you didn't want in the first place. You blamed her for it—a harmless baby, imagine that—and vowed to get even one day.''

''I don't know what you're talking about,'' he muttered, his eyes downcast.

''I'm sure you don't,'' I agreed sarcastically.

''But enough of your sordid life, Lawrence. You're commencing to bore the hell out of me. Let's move on to more interesting topics of conversation. Like Janet.''

''Let's not,'' he mumbled.

''You know, you may find this hard to believe, but Janet told me several things that gave you away. Had I thought about it at the time I would have possibily figured it out, but hell, nobody wants to think nasty thoughts like that, right?''

I received a stony glare. I also saw fear in his eyes.

''Among other things, she said there were things about her I didn't know. Well, hell, I blowed that off: everybody has a skeleton or two, right?''

He didn't answer.

''You've got a whole closet full of 'em. Then she said that sometimes things happened that we have no control over. Well, I wasn't quite sure of what she was talking about. I guess in my own case you could say I had no control over the war. It was pretty hard to control them enemy .51 cal machine guns and rockets. That's a joke, Provost.''

He wasn't laughing.

''But you know what really corked it? Oh, this is rich. She once told me I resemble you, and I'll be goddamned if she ain't right! Personally I think you're a little uglier than I am, but—''

''Harrumph.''

''I would have to agree that there's a definite resemblance. Then, moving right along here, it struck me as strange that Janet would take a year off between high school and college. You were, after all, on the school board; a member of the Lions Club and—''

''How do you know all this?'' he asked, his voice amazed.

"The public library." I sighed. "You browbeat her when she wanted to quit ROTC. The poor girl. She hated the military; she just wanted to work with trees and be free. But no, she had to follow Daddy's program for her life, didn't she? She followed your plan almost to the letter, except for one little zigzag off course."

"You!" he snapped.

"Great minds think alike," I agreed with a phony smile. "But nonetheless, she married the army officer as you wanted. Provost, do you know that that son of a bitch isn't even a combat arms officer? Don't you find it highly disgusting that the turkey married to your daughter is going to be a REMF—that's a Rear Echelon Mother Fucker, Provost—and live nice and cushy even in a combat zone and screw a lot of women while the less cagey are out getting their asses shot off?"

"I think it was rather intelligent of her, actually. Any idiot can carry a rifle."

"Oh, Lawrence," I said slowly, "now you're getting awful close to home. The guys who I knowed that bought it were mostly deck rates—gunners, bosuns, quartermasters—but, no, you wouldn't know anything about that, would you? You never had the balls to go in—I mean, you didn't have the honor of serving your country, did you?"

"No," he said with a sneer.

"Okay, then shut the fuck up! Because I knowed some of those 'idiots' who carried rifles that didn't make it; their names are carved on a hunk of black granite in Washington. If you look careful you can sometimes see one of those 'idiots' walking around on stumps. Or go to a VA hospital; yeah, there's a lot of 'em there. You know, when I was in the navy I hated civilians. I'm beginning to recall why."

"You are a self-righteous, arrogant—"

"Well-armed man," I concluded for him. "Just sit tight. We're getting close. Then I'll maybe let you call the cops.

"Oh, there was other things. You may not believe this either, but Janet once told me 'I was told to go to college! I was told to join ROTC! I was told to get married! I'm tired of it!' " I paused for effect. "You don't happen to have any idea of who done the telling, do you?"

"I have no idea."

"Oh, Provost, you insult my intelligence," I said wearily. "You know, I was told just recently by somebody that knows you very, very well that you have always had a lot of control over Janet's life. This person couldn't understand why. But I do."

"Who was that?" he shot out.

"None of your business," I quickly answered. "Okay, let's wrap this up. This is all making me very tired.

"In summary, you don't like your daughter, much less love her. Remember how she took away your youth?"

"Who are you, Freud?"

I affected a stupid grin. "Does he play for the Tigers or the Padres?"

"Harrumph."

"I thought so. The Brewers. At any event, Janet took away your youth, or so you reckoned. All of her life you have dictated to her; that's part of your revenge. You know, now that I think about it, you don't like women at all, do you? You have no respect for yourself; why should you have any respect for them miserable bitches, right?"

A glare full of hate.

"Now, Provost, I could have bought off on you being just a mean, self-centered son of a bitch. I mean, the world's full of nasty people, right? But do you know what I found out? Do you know what all them hidden references of Janet's was hinting at?"

A look of panic had overtaken the old man's face. I took a deep breath and drove on with the hardest thing I ever said in my life.

"She was referring to the fact that you forced sex on her at an early age *and fathered a child by your own daughter*!"

"Liar!" he yelled, jumping to his feet. "Liar! Liar!" His breath came short and fast as sweat poured down his face and onto his neck in rivers.

"Sit down before I shoot you down," I said calmly. He sat down, his face frozen.

"You are the most foul-mouthed, hateful, filthy—"

"Shut the fuck up. Now!" I commanded. I took a couple of breaths and continued. "My turn to stand up." I stood up and twirled my Colt around my index finger a couple of times.

"Provost, the records don't lie. The birth certificate and adoption papers was somewhat illuminating. She had a number of real interesting talks with a psychiatrist when she was in college."

"That's privileged information! You stole it! You—" A look of horror blanketed his face as he realized what he had just said.

"And you just confessed," I softly murmured. I hated him then. I hated him so bad I can't put it into words.

"And this further explains," I continued with a calm I didn't feel, "why Janet always insisted the lights were off the few times we made love. Stretch marks have a way of hanging around, don't they?" He didn't answer; his face was the color of campfire ashes, as white as a sheet. "But you know, the bottom line is, and the thing that makes me want to puke my guts out right here, is that you imposed yourself on Janet. You threatened, cajoled, probably pleaded, until you had your way. Now, I ain't into philosophy, but I do know deep in my guts that there must be some sort of universal law that says we aren't allowed to impose ourselves on the small, the weak, and the helpless. Not to mention the trusting."

"She's a little slut!" he blurted out through clenched teeth.

I let out a long breath. I felt like crying. "I just want to tell you one thing before you go."

"Before I go!" he gasped in horror.

"I never had the papers. Like you say, that's privileged information. I just made an educated guess based on the information I've got here. If you hadn't gotten pissed off and blowed your cool, I never would have knowed for sure."

"Bastard."

"I came back because I had to find out. Now I know."

"You came back because of Janet, didn't you?" he shrieked. "You came here because you envision yourself as some white knight in shining armor! Fool! Yes, you fool! Don't you see, she isn't worth it? And you came back because of her?" He started laughing like a madman then, out of control. I let him laugh.

As his laughing slowly tapered off, I quietly said, "Provost."

He looked up at me then from two feet away. "I hate to tell you this, but I didn't come back for Janet's sake at all."

"You didn't?" he gasped in a whisper.

"No. I love Janet, but I came here for a different reason. I came here because you ruined my fucking life."

He started to laugh again.

But he ceased laughing immediately.

Because I cocked my Colt Peacemaker and aimed it slightly under his right eyeball.

His face was a mask of horror.

Then I gently squeezed the trigger.

24

THE SOUND OF the firing pin smashing against the empty chamber echoed like a blacksmith's hammer hitting a cold anvil.

"Surprise," I muttered through my teeth. "You're still alive."

"You're not going to kill me," he whispered, a blank look of relief on his face. His eyes was fixed on the cylinder of my Colt; the conical projectiles in the five loaded chambers glared back at him ominously.

"Not right now," I conceded. "And you know why? I'll tell you why. You are a miserable goddamn excuse for a human being; I don't see how you can stand to look at yourself in the mirror. But every day, when you get up and shave, I want you to remember that for a few brief seconds in history, Sam Hawkins held your life in the palm of his hand in the form of a Colt six-shooter. I only let you live because I want you to suffer; I want you to remember that I'm out there, somewhere, and I know."

I took a few steps to the side, grabbed the phone off the wall, dialed, and said, "Hello, Operator. Give me the police."

"Is this an emergency?"

"Yes."

"Just a moment, please."

The desk sergeant answered the phone on the second ring. "Police station," he growled.

"Hold on a second, please," I cheerily said. Then I tried to hand the phone to Provost; he waved his hand and shook his head as if to say "don't bother." He covered his eyes with a hand.

"I thought I had a problem here, but I don't, Officer. So long." I hanged up the phone with a bang.

"It's probably a good thing you didn't talk to them, Provost."

"I don't know anymore," he wept, his face in his hands. "I just don't know."

"Because if you had, then I woulda had to take all this highly embarrassin' material along, and don't you suppose a lot of folks in this little hamlet—and your hometown—would be interested in it? Then we could subpoena Janet to testify, and I think somebody would go to the slammer, but it wouldn't be me. Then we'd just have to tell Ann Landers; she'd get just one helluva kick out of this story, I would say."

"Get out of here," he softly sobbed into his cupped hands.

With that I grabbed the manila folder, holstered my Colt, and started for the door. As I was half through I remembered I'd forgotten to tell him something, and turned around. Lawrence Provost's head lay in his folded arms. He was crying hard.

I cleared my throat.

"Provost."

He looked up from the table then, his eyes red with tears. "What?" he croaked with a sob.

"You fucking pig."

Then I slammed the door behind me and walked back to Steady Eddie's car.

On the way out of town I stopped at a convenience store and bought a can of lighter fluid. On my way to the interstate I pulled over to a wayside, ripped the top off a trash can, doused the folder with lighter fluid, and tossed a match on it. I didn't want to be reminded, ever again, of that whole mess.

It was coming on midnight when I parked Steady Eddie's Plymouth in the ramp as he'd instructed. I flagged down a cab and told the driver to make tracks for the airport.

Major airports at midnight are only half alive, if that. I quickly walked to the ticket counter of a major western-states carrier. There was no line; a pretty blond lady about my age was the ticket agent.

"Evenin', miss."

"And how are you tonight?" she inquired with a smile.

"Fine. How soon can I get to Omaha?" She punched a few numbers or letters into the keyboard of her computer.

"The next direct flight leaves at seven-thirty."

"Try Des Moines." She punched more keys on the computer.

"There's a flight leaving from O'Hare at four-thirty; it arrives at five-twenty. I can put you on our connecting flight to Chicago which leaves in an hour and you'll make it in plenty of time."

I paid for the ticket, checked my bag, and eventually located the only bar still open in the terminal. I pulled up a stool near the television and ordered a beer. When the bartender informed me they didn't carry Coors, I ordered a bottle of the local brew and watched the late-night cable newscast from the blaring TV. I had my mouth half-full of pretzels and was sipping a beer that tasted like it'd been pumped straight from the bilges of a LST when a map of Colorado flashed on the screen behind the cute anchor female's desk.

"And now," she chirped, "we have this special report from the remote mountain terrain of the Gunnison National Forest in Colorado." I stopped chewing the pretzels and slowly brought the beer glass to my mouth.

"Earlier today two unemployed woodsmen apparently saved the life of a child as she was being attacked by an angry black bear. Three year-old Samantha Barnes, daughter of Rachel and Wilbur Barnes of Denver, was taking an afternoon nap in her family's tent at their campsite alongside a roaring mountain stream when a black bear allegedly came out of nowhere, ripped the back of the tent apart, and swatted the girl. The parents heard the screams from thirty yards away where they were visiting with two colorful local characters at a neighboring campsite. One of the men, identified as C. Joseph Flanigan, grabbed his nearby rifle and ran to the screams, killing the bear with two shots. We have this special footage from our Denver affiliate."

"That grandstanding son of a bitch," I muttered under my breath.

"Say something?" the bartender inquired.

"No."

"Well, actually, it was quite easy," a smiling Crazy Joe told the reporter. "Philo and me were having coffee with Mr. and Mrs. Barnes when we heard the kid scream. I grabs my rifle—I always keep a gun or two around, you see—and ran to the tent and saw the kid gettin' tore up, so I let the old boar have it twice in the ear. He was dead when he hit the ground, not unlike other shots I've made.''

"Why did you shoot the bear in the ear, Mr. Flanigan? Couldn't you have just scared him off?''

"Look, lady,'' Crazy Joe patiently intoned, "that bear was playing for keeps and so does Cr— and so do I. Anybody but a pork-eater knows the only place to shoot a bear is in the ear or the eye; the front of his head is sloped like armor plating; bullets will just bounce off, and I wasn't taking no chances with that kid's life.''

"But weren't you endangering the child's life by shooting when she was so near the animal?''

"The bear was endangering her life a whole lot worse, 'cause when I shoot I never miss. Fifty-caliber Browning to .22 rimfire, I *always* hit what I'm aiming at. Now in this particular weapon''—Crazy Joe held up his scarred Winchester—"I use a 150-grain copper-jacketed bullet loaded to twenty-two hundred and fifty feet per second muzzle velocity. In spite of what some say, the .30–30 is not an obsolete cartridge, as it develops enough foot pounds of energy—''

"Thank you, Mr. Flanigan.'' The camera zoomed in on the reporter, who continued, "The local conservation officer, Eugene M. Rhodes, has told us that poaching charges will not be filed against C. Joseph Flanigan as this was in fact a legitimate bear attack. Three-year-old Samantha Barnes is being treated for cuts and abrasions at an area hospital, where doctors expect her to make a quick recovery with no permanent, visible scarring. From deep in the wilderness of Gunnison National Forest, this is your cable-live reporter Dorothy Parker with cameraman Darryl F. Mayer.''

I think I was still staring trancelike at the boob tube when the bartender asked me, "Care for another beer, cowboy?''

"Yeah. And a double shot of Old Overholt.''

"Don't sell that stuff here.''

"Then a double shot of any rye whiskey you got.'' I paid up, pitched down the boilermaker, and shuffled off to find my aircraft, all the way muttering foul remarks about Crazy Joe under my breath as I very possibly walked with a slight list to starboard.

* * *

When I arrived in Des Moines half a dozen hours later, my head was remarkably clear and I learned to my relief that my bag hadn't been lost at O'Hare. I took a cab out to an I-80 on-ramp. It was a little after six in the morning and it took me all the rest of the morning and part of the afternoon to hitchhike to the little burg where Uncle Dutch's life was wasting away in an old folks home.

When I got into town I stopped at the local Ford dealer to see if I could rent a car for the rest of the day. I wanted to take my uncle out to supper if he felt up to it. The car dealer was a short, balding guy in his sixties; he looked kind of familiar.

"I can't rent a car to you without a credit card or a local address," he informed me with regret.

"All right." I hoisted my duffel bag up to my shoulder and started to head out of his office.

"Did you used to live around here?" he asked as I was leaving.

I stopped and turned around. "I spent a lot of time around here when I was a kid, yeah. I just come back to see my uncle."

"What's his name?"

"Dutch Hawkins."

"No kidding? I'll be damned. I was his adjutant in the Legion when he was the post commander. How is he, anyway?"

"Ain't seen him yet. I heard he's goin' under; that's why I come back."

The car dealer furrowed his brow. "Sorry to hear that. Just a minute . . ."

"Sam. Sam Hawkins."

"Just a minute, Sam." The man quickly ducked out of the office; in half a minute he was back.

"Here," he said as he handed me a key attached to a yellow plastic tag. "It's the white '75 half-ton Ford out back."

"I appreciate it. I'll be done with it by this evening; how much do you need?"

"Nothing."

"Well, then, uh, what d'ya want? I mean, I should sign something, right?"

"You're Dutch Hawkins's nephew; you'll bring it back."

I cleared my throat. "Well, thanks."

He slapped me on the shoulder. "Just tell him Bob Logan said hello. And tell him my wife and I will be up to see him soon."

"Sure thing," I replied quietly. I can only attribute it to the stress of the previous day and the traveling, but I about felt like crying. I knowed I couldn't trust my voice no more, so I quickly headed outside the garage and found the pickup.

"Howdy, Uncle Dutch," I said to the still form on the hospital bed. When I gently nudged his shoulder he woke up.

"What the hell!" he shot out, his blinking eyes trying to focus on me. I handed him his glasses off the nightstand. When he put them on, he fixed his old blue eyes on me and cried, "Nooo! Sam! I'll be damned!" He stiffly got up and swung his bony legs over the side of the bed. I held out my hand.

"Nice to see ya, you old wildcat," I said with a forced smile. Uncle Dutch looked like hell. His face, always deeply lined, looked as though furrows had been plowed in it. His skin had taken on that pale sickish hue that declared death was not far off. His full head of snow-white hair was tousled and shot out in all directions; it hadn't seen a comb in days. He breathed hard as he looked at me, the emphysema and cancer overworking his diseased, worn-out lungs. Even with death knocking at his door, his pale blue eyes was bright as ever. He was always about the most alert fellow I ever knowed.

"Nice to see you, too, Sam." He smiled as he worked my hand like a pump handle. Uncle Dutch may have been dying, but his grip was rock hard. "What brings you this way?"

"Oh, I've come to see a man about a horse." I smiled. Then I pulled up a chair and filled him in on my activities for the past two years, obviously leaving out the McLowery shooting, Janet, and her father.

"You don't say!" he exclaimed when I told him about the last season's fur catch. "Eight thousand dollars at that!" He paused and lit a cigarette. "I remember when Sam and I were boys—your Grandpa. Had an old dugout boat we made from a log. Trapped the Little Sioux River all fall till it froze up. Then we'd—we had an old double-barrel caplock shotgun—paid a dollar for it, we did—and could only use one barrel 'cause the nipple was rusted off the other one, and"—he paused to gasp for air—"and we'd come home way past dark with rats and coon to skin, and the bottom of that boat filled with mallards and teal. There wasn't any limit in those days. Not till 1912, I do believe."

He was all talked out, and wheezed for breath. As he did so, a fat nurse's aide waddled in. In one hand she carried a little paper cup.

"Well, Mr. Hawkins! I see we have company today." She beamed through puffy cheeks. She handed Uncle Dutch the little cup filled with pills. He promptly set it on the nightstand.

"I'm not taking your pills, Flossie," he snorted as he made a grand gesture of flicking cigarette ash on the floor.

"Now, Mr. Hawkins, is that any way to act in front of your son? What will he think?" she chided in mock disgust, her triple chins waggling as she shook her head.

"I don't care what he thinks. And I sure as hell don't care what you jailers think. And he isn't my son, he's my . . ." His voice dropped off. I'd never knowed my uncle Dutch to have a lapse of memory before.

"Great-nephew, ma'am," I courteously replied.

"Yeah. Great-nephew. My brother's son. No, my brother's grandson. He's come here to help me escape, haven't you, Sam?"

"You bet!"

"Well!" she exclaimed. I almost laughed, because she said that the same way Jack Benny used to. "We'll see about that. Escape indeed! I'll leave your medicine here on the nightstand, Mr. Hawkins. Perhaps your nephew will convince you to take it." She throwed me a hard look.

"I doubt it," I replied cheerfully.

She glared at me then. "What did you say your name was, young man?"

"Sam Hawkins."

"Your uncle may not leave these premises, Mr. Hawkins."

"Why not? I thought I'd take him out for a drive; it's a nice day. Maybe we'll go get something to eat."

"Goddamn right, Sam!"

"Besides, this is a nursing home, not a hospital. Or a prison."

"Your uncle is an extremely ill man," the fat woman steadily intoned.

" 'Extremely ill'!" Uncle Dutch exclaimed. "I'm dying and

you know it and I know it! What are you gonna do, kill me? Yeah, do me a favor, Flossie!''

With that, Flossie puffed out her cheeks two or three times, failed to find words, and departed in an outraged huff.

''You got about as much tact as I do,'' I said good-naturedly.

''Aaagh,'' he snorted as he mashed out his cigarette butt in an ashtray. He slowly found his feet, took the pills from the nightstand, and headed for the bathroom. The next sound I heard was a ceremonious flush. Uncle Dutch slowly walked back to his bed, an ear-to-ear grin showing off his perfect false teeth. After a few seconds, the grin faded and he pursed his lips in thought.

''I'm ready to die now, Sam,'' he said without emotion.

I nodded my head. Uncle Dutch was dealing; I would listen.

''I've had a good life. And a long life. I've seen it all, Sam. We had horses then, when I was young, like you've got now. But everybody had them then. That's the way it always had been, and that's the way we figured it'd always be. I ran the mail route with horses till I got my first car. That was a Model T in 1932, I do believe. Did thirty-five miles a day with the horses before that. Changed teams at Robert's Crossing. Can you imagine mail carriers doing that today?''

I slowly shook my head. I couldn't imagine anybody doing it today. ''I can't either,'' he agreed as he lit another cigarette. ''Then sometime, don't know when, machines took over. They—'' A horrible racking cough exploded from Uncle Dutch's innards then; he spit up the rottenest looking phlem I'd ever seen into an old bandanna.

''Goddamn!'' he cried. I handed him some tissue paper off the nightstand.

I saw that tissue after he coughed into it.

It was red with his own blood, and black with the disease that was killing him.

And then I understood why Uncle Dutch was smoking more than ever.

He was trying to end it as soon as possible.

''Pull in here,'' he ordered as I slowed to turn in the cemetery which lay on a high bluff overlooking the Missouri. It had taken some convincing before the rest-home staff gave Uncle Dutch a three-hour pass; I nearly had to promise in blood that I'd bring him back safe and sound, which of course I had every intention of doing.

We got out of the truck and walked over to the Hawkins family plot. There was a lot of Hawkinses planted in that ground; the earliest one had been a trapper that died during the administration of James K. Polk.

"Goddamn hot out here," he grumped as he pulled out a bandanna to mop his brow. He slowly took a seat on a headstone and pulled out another smoke. He lit up, then blew a cloud of smoke to the heavens, fixing his gaze on a passing low cloud. After a bit he simply said, "I'll miss all this."

"Yeah," I agreed. I didn't know what else to say.

"There's my Grandpa Hawkins." He pointed at an old marble headstone. "I've told you about him.

"He moved here from Illinois after his older brother. In '52, I do believe. Then in '57 his wife died of the cholera. He took it hard. Hawkins men always take it hard when they lose their women. Then he went out to the Pikes Peak gold rush. When the war started he joined the First Colorado Cavalry. Fought the Texicans at Glorietta Pass and scouted the Indians on the Santa Fe Trail."

"Out of Fort Lyon and Fort Larned," I added.

His brow furrowed and his blue eyes gave me a hard, quizzical look. "Funny you should remember that."

"I don't know why not, Dutch."

"Most don't care, Sam," he said in resignation. "But you always cared about the family. Even the dead ones."

I took a seat on a stone opposite him. "Nothing ever dies. All things live forever." I admit it was a funny thing to say.

He gave a strange look. "You think so?"

"I don't see why not."

Then he let go as long a sigh as his diseased lungs would let out. "I'd like to think that. Maybe everything does. I don't know." There was a long pause. When his cigarette had burned down to a stub he said, "I'm going to be buried over there, next to Margaret. There's room there for you, too, Sam. Alongside me someday," he offered. He said it matter-of-factly, like, "No point in you renting a motel room when I've got a spare bed in mine."

"Maybe I'll take you up on that someday."

He changed the subject. "Sam, I was always glad you did your time in service."

"And I'm glad it's over with."

"You can always be proud of that, Sam. My war was seventy years ago," he quietly said to the ground, slowly shaking his head. Then he repeated "seventy years" as if he didn't believe it possible.

He swiftly stood up with a sudden burst of energy and pitched his smoke to the ground. "I have had a good life and a long life! I've raised nine children and saw they all got to college! I took care of my wife the best I knew how, and always saw there was food on the table! I fought for my country in war and lived an honorable life in peace, and I never shamed my family name!"

"No Hawkins man ever ran!" he continued, filled with the old-time spirit I hadn't seen in years. "They might have been scared, a little, but they always stuck it out to the end. They kept their self-respect and their good name. They were never sorry for a goddamned thing! They had nothing to be sorry for, Sam! *They kept their good name to the end!*" Almost under his breath he added, "Some of the bastards didn't. Well, those of us who were left righted things as good we could."

"Did they care about what other folks thought?" I quietly asked.

"Not so long as they knew they were right! No sir! They always did as they saw fit, and let their conscience be their guide. That's what I've always done, the right thing as I saw it. A man can do no more," he added, less passionately. He looked me dead in the eye, his own light blue eyes showing defiance. "I am not sorry for a damned thing, Sam," he firmly stated. He said it like a challenge, as though he was daring me to say he should be sorry for something.

"I hope I can say that someday," I said quietly.

He walked over to me and put his wrinkled, ancient hand on my shoulder. "Sam, I've told you everything I've learned. Eighty-nine years. And you've heard it all." He softly said those words like he was wondering why there wasn't more.

"It's enough," I answered, trying not to choke on the words.

"Well, hell," he said after a bit. "Let's go take a look at the river."

"All right." We slowly walked past the granite and marble headstones to the little wire gate at the back of the cemetery. I opened it and we walked along the grassy hillside until Uncle Dutch plopped down under a huge walnut tree.

"Quite a view," I commented as I filled my pipe. Two hundred feet below us was the turbulent, swirling Missouri River. The water was high for September; I watched an old tree stump as it tumbled end over end downriver.

"Lot of history come up and down this old river," Uncle Dutch said as he lit still another cigarette. "Lewis and Clark in 1804. Ashley and Henry in '22. To the north of us the Missouri Breaks . . ." His voice trailed off.

"Yep. A lot of history." I was wondering what was coming next, when again he spoke.

"Sam, I'm not going back there."

"You're what?"

"You heard me. I said I'm not going back to that goddamn pigsty."

"Oh, bullshit. Listen, Dutch—"

"You listen to me!" he ordered, jabbing a finger at me. "It's a beautiful September day; not too hot, not too cool. I can sit here on the grass and watch the river I grew up on pass below. I can hear a bobwhite quail, and meadowlarks and robins singing. I'm dying, Sam, a 'gone beaver' like the trappers used to say. You can accept that, right?"

I slowly nodded my head.

"Well, then, goddamn it, accept the fact I ain't going back there! I'm not going to wind up laying in a bed, shitting and pissing all over myself, then to have fifteen tubes stuck in me at the end!"

"Dutch, you really—"

"Quiet. Sam, my world is over; it's gone. Gone as though a Canada norther just blowed it to . . . where? Where did it go, Sam? Where is it? It has to be somewhere in time, but where does time disappear to, that all you've got is a faded memory?"

"I don't know," I slowly said in awe.

"Margaret is two years' dead. My children are all moved away to God knows where. Sam, my friends are all dead."

"Aw, you gotta have—"

"They're all dead. I'm the last one. The last World War One man in town. Probably the last man who knows how to harness a team and hook up a buggy. Sam, I belong in a goddamn museum."

"No, you don't. Look, Dutch, them hospital people are going to be rightly pissed if you don't show up."

"Screw them," he muttered, a small smile on his face.

I knew then what I had to do. I recall wondering why there was so many hard decisions come to me as of late; hard, gut-wrenching decisions. I recall thinking there was no answer: it was just the luck of the draw, I reckoned.

"You contrary old wolverine!" I suddenly shot out. I would be damned if I'd get all sentimental and mushy with him. I have seen men die before. "I suppose you're just going to sit here on your ass, smoke another dozen cigarettes, and up and die."

"Something like that," he replied with a nod of his head, his lips pursed.

"Oh, fuck me to tears," I groaned.

"I'd rather not."

"Oh, damn it to hell, Dutch! All right, you want to be ornery and contrary right to the end, fine! *I'll* probably go to prison for murdering you."

"No, you won't. Go on, leave!"

We stared at each other hard, for five seconds or maybe five minutes. I took off my hat and walked over to him. I bent over and whispered something in his ear.

"Bah!" he cried. "Get out of here! Go on, get out!" I held my ground and glared back at him. Then I held out my hand. He took it and we shook.

I quickly turned, but had not gotten ten feet away when again he spoke.

"Sam!"

I turned around. "Yeah?"

"You take care of yourself."

"I will, Uncle Dutch," I softly replied.

He lit another cigarette. "Take it easy," he casually added, like we was going fishing next Saturday.

And that was the bottom line.

No tear-filled embraces.

No elaborate farewells.

Just, "Take it easy."

We was Hawkinses, you see.

I pulled my hat down low then, like I always wear it, and done a strange thing. I saluted him, and right smart at that.

And he sprouted a proud grin a mile wide and saluted right back.

"See you around, Dutch," I said over the knot in my throat. Then I headed back to the truck. A man can't say, or do, much more.

You've got to believe in something, after all.

"You make all things and direct them in their ways, O Grandfather, and now you have decided that the Human Beings will soon have to walk a new road. Thank you for letting us win once before that happened. Even if my people must eventually pass from the face of the earth, they will live on in whatever men are fierce and strong. So that when women see a man who is proud and brave and vengeful, even if he has a white face, they will cry: 'That is a Human Being!' "

—Thomas Berger, *Little Big Man* (the novel)

THE CAR DEALER was closed by the time I got back, so I left
the truck in the back lot as he had instructed. That evening I
hitchhiked out of town heading west-southwest and got as far as
Wahoo, Nebraska. I had enough money for a bus or plane ticket;
I just wanted to take in the sights on the Great Plains again.

Whenever I could, I took the back roads. It was mid-
September and the feel of fall was in the air. The corn was
starting to top out; the smell of fresh-mowed, third-crop alfalfa
was everywhere. I rode into Luke's place in the bed of a farm
pickup loaded with shelled corn. I had left Uncle Dutch exactly
twenty-four hours earlier.

I wondered if he was still alive.

Then I hoped that wherever he was, he was happier.

"Stick 'em up, Luke," I smiled to Luke's backside as I snuck
up on him. He was busy boarding up a busted-down corral gate.

"Wal, thet was a short trip, Sam. How'd it go?"

"Fine. Let me stow my bag here in the shack and I'll give
you a hand. We've still got a couple hours of daylight." I put up
my duffel bag, got into some old clothes, and worked on the old
corrals with Luke till dark.

It was over a supper of beans, potatoes, and old deer meat
too long in the freezer that Luke brought up Crazy Joe's new
celebrity status.

"Say, what's the name a them two fellers ya trap with?"

"Philo Harris and Joe Flanigan. Why?"

266

"Wal, ah was watchin' the news last night an' hit seems yer frand Flanigan is quite a hero. Saved some kid from an attackin' bar. Hit was in the mornin' paper, too."

"Yeah. I saw the story on television last night. Crazy Joe Flanigan is fast becoming a legend in his own mind," I quipped as I stabbed a piece of meat.

"Sounds lak yer mad at him," Luke commented soberly. "Ah thank he done the prime thing by killin' thet bear."

"Course he did, Luke; woulda done the same thing myself, and so would you. He just likes the limelight, that's all. Pass the bread."

"An' you don't?"

"Nope. Besides, I don't like publicity. Pass the ketchup."

"Sam, ya've been actin' teechy all day, and fer a while back at thet. What's wrong?"

I saturated the meat with ketchup. "I feel like things are closing in on me," I said with resignation.

Luke half closed an eye and cocked his head to one side. "You in any kind a trouble?" he asked suspiciously but hopefully.

"Not that I know of," I half-truthfully answered. "I just like to keep a low profile, that's all. Look, I'd like to stay around and help, but I've got to get back to the high country. I'd appreciate it if you'd help me load up the horses in a little bit; they don't like to hop in that trailer at dark."

"Shore ah will," he drawled with a nod of his head. As he raised the coffee cup he asked, "So who'd ya kill?"

"Nobody, damn it! I probably should have, but it's just that—shitfire, I don't know."

I parked my outfit in Taylor Park shortly after dawn the next morning. I quickly saddled Molly, put a lead rope on Jack, and picked up my partners' trail. Thanks to the news footage I had a real good idea of where they were, and around noon I rode into their camp. I tied off my horses and stalked over to them.

"Hi-dee!" Philo grinned. "How was the trip? An' ya brang back the beans an' coffee?"

"Yeah, Sam, where's the coffee and how's old Steady Eddie?" Crazy Joe piped up. "We've had some excitement up here, ourselves!" he beamed.

"Are you guys nuts?"

"Wal, ah sartinly hope not."

"Of course. What's wrong?"

"Crazy Joe, did you know your ugly mug has been blasted all over the United States, thanks to that television station? Huh? You done the right thing by shootin' that bear, but you sure as hell didn't have to advertise it."

"Look, Sam, it's no big thing. Dusty happened to have a TV reporter with him from Boulder or someplace doing a story on the elk herd when I shot that bear in the lights. It was just a matter of being at the right place at the right time."

"Crazy Joe, your ugly mug was seen on twenty or thirty million boob tubes in the country; the story's probably been in four hundred newspapers across the country by now."

"Is that a fact?" He smiled, pleased at the thought.

I shook my head. "Let's play a game. We'll play charades, okay? All right, I'll do a charade and you tell me the word it reminds you of." I quickly drew my right hand and fanned my thumb like a Colt hammer.

"McLowery!" he beamed.

"You're a fucking genius! Has it ever occurred to you that somebody *just* might be looking for us on account of that little caper? Remember it happened only the day after Janet's wedding? Huh? You don't gotta be Sherlock Holmes to conclude that somebody might just figure this all out. Shit!"

Philo furrowed his brow in thought. "Ah hadn't put thet all togetheh in mah own mind, Sam. Whaddya reckon we oughta do?"

"Aw, Sam, you're getting all alarmed over nothing. Hell, we'll just—"

"Would you read my lips? Damn it all to hell, you may as well have murdered that son of a bitch in cold blood! Don't you suppose some cop, *somewhere*, just might put all this together? Remember that pimple-faced kid at the scales in Council Bluffs? I'll fucking-A guarantee you Janet didn't talk, and the other members of her family I know are either allies of mine or scared shitless of me, *but somebody with some brains can put this all together*."

"Sam, ah didn't know ya knowed Janet's kin. How'd ya—"

"I don't. I was just talking figuratively," I shot back.

Crazy Joe cleared his throat. "I suppose, that under the present circumstances, we should clear the premises for a while."

"Australia's lovely this time of year," I agreed.

"Sariously, Sam, whar ya plannin' on headin'?"

"I thought of that on the drive here. Look, Philo, beaver ain't worth squat; thirty dollars for a top pelt. We can go after bobcat—they're bringing upwards of two hundred bucks per—and coyotes—and make a hell of a lot more in a couple months than we'd make trapping beaver till the first of the year. Plus we'll be in an area where nobody would ever think to look for us."

"Which is where?" Crazy Joe asked.

"The country to the north of the Purgatory River. You've got Smith Cañon, Taylor Cañon, Pinon Cañon and Purgatory Cañon; rough country that's loaded with cats, coon, and coyote. To the north is the Comanche National Grasslands; that's all government land that ranchers lease to run stock on. It's all deserted country, and it's the last place *I'd* ever look for anybody."

"Yup," Philo agreed with a nod. "We did right good trappin' the Picketwire three, four years ago. Ah'm fer hit."

"Joe?"

"Might as well go along." He sighed. "But, Sam, I think you're getting all worked up over nothing."

"Well, I sure as hell hope you're right. I've just got a real uneasy feeling in my guts about this whole thing."

My partners had their camp tore down and horses packed in half an hour. By six o'clock in the evening we had loaded the trucks and trailers and were headed down the paved road that parallels Taylor River. Halfway to Gunnison we met Dusty's green pickup; he flashed his headlights at me and we all pulled over.

"Heading out so soon, Sam?" he asked. Philo and Crazy Joe joined me at my truck.

"Yeah. Look, Dusty, we've had a change of plans. We're—"

"Are you in any trouble?"

"Ah—no. Look, we've just decided to get out of the high country. There'll be a blizzard sure as hell any day now."

"Oh c'mon, Sam! It's only September!"

"Wal, ah'll be damned!" Philo beamed. "An' here ah thought hit was Novembah!"

Dusty was smart and he was a friend; he had already told me he wouldn't turn us in for the McLowery doings. I wanted to tell him what was what, but with Philo and Crazy Joe standing there I couldn't very well do that. Dusty Rhodes was, after all, the law.

"Look, we're probably not going to heaven and we sure ain't going to hell. We'll probably be somewhere in between."

Dusty's brow wrinkled for a tenth of a second, then his eyebrows raised in comprehension. He knowed all my stomping grounds. "Oh, okay." He smiled. "You want me to start picking up your mail again?"

"If you would. I'll let you know when we've got a place to forward it to."

"Sure. Well, you guys have a nice trip. I'll see you when I see you."

That night we stopped at the eastern base of Monarch Pass and camped in a little Forest Service picnic ground. We was up at dawn, and by noon rolled into a little general store and filling station combination forty miles north of the New Mexico border.

"Let me talk to the guy inside," I told Crazy Joe. "The last time I was in these parts he had an empty barn he let us park the outfits in. Maybe we can put all three of 'em inside somewheres."

"Hit'll keep the weather offa 'em," Philo said.

I didn't add that it would also keep anybody from seeing them.

"Howdy, Steve," I said as we walked in the quaint general store that smelled of oldness and stale beer. "Remember me?"

The weathered old man gave me a hard look. "Cain't say ah do."

"Sam Hawkins. I trapped the Grasslands and the Purgatory a few years ago with this fella here." I jabbed a thumb at Philo. "We're all three gonna hit it this season."

"Let's haf a beer an' make palaver," Philo suggested as he pulled up a barstool. We all pulled up seats then; Philo bought. It had been downright cool in the high country, but the southern plains was hotter than the hinges of hell. It must have been around ninety.

As we sipped our beers Steve lit up a beat-up briar pipe and commented, "Wal, ya oughta do good trappin' on the Grasslands. Don't plan on goin' too far south of 'em, though."

I grabbed some of Crazy Joe's potato chips. "Why not?"

"You ain't heard 'bout Pinon Cañon?"

"Well, I've ridden up and down it, down there t'ward the Purgatory. Why?"

"What's happened is this: Two, three years ago the army decided t' make all thet country a trainin' area fer thar infantry an' tank divisions. They spent millions a dollars buyin' up all thet ranchland; they bought everythin' from the Picketwire clear t' the Grasslands, quarter of a million acres. All them little ranchers just got drove out."

"You mean they're building a damned fort down here?" I asked in disbelief.

"Naw," Steve said with a shake of his head. "Thar just goin' t' use hit fer maneuvers. They bring in a division fer a month, from Texas or Fort Carson or somewhere, do thar maneuverin', an' leave. They only got ten, fifteen fellas in the garrison thar."

I turned on the stool to face my partners. "This is just fucking great. We can't even get south of the Grasslands now. Tell me, Steve, is any army outfit training there now?"

"Not thet ah know of. Ah heared tell thar's goin' t' be some dogfaces come in sometime next week, but ah dunno fer sure."

"Would we get in trouble if we trapped there?"

"Not if ya didn't git caught."

"How about fences?"

"Ah heared tell they still replacin' em: thar tearin' down all the triple-strand bobbed wire the ranchers had up an' replacin' hit with a eight-foot-high fence. Ah don't thank thar done yit."

"What do they call this fort or whatever it is?" Crazy Joe asked.

"Call hit Pinon Cañon Maneuver Site. You fellas oughta stop down thar an' meet the major in charge. He stopped in the other night; helluva fine guy."

"Thanks, I think I'll pass." Crazy Joe smiled.

"Hell, Sam, won't be no cats t' speak of on th' Grasslands," Philo grumped.

"Not so fast. The army ain't bought everything: We can still trap the Purgatory up to where the army don't own it; we'll get some cats. And you yourself know the Grasslands are full of coyotes. Joe, what are your thoughts concerning this latest mess?"

"Well, since we're here, I say go for it."

Which was what we done. Steve still had the vacant barn and he agreed to store our vehicles for the month or so we'd be in the area. Philo suggested heading to New Mexico after that. I hadn't quite firmed up my plans in my own mind; Dusty's advice from a couple weeks earlier was still fresh in my mind.

For the next five days we rode the Comanche National Grasslands and got reacquainted with the area. "There sure isn't a hell of a lot of trees out here," Crazy Joe complained. "Just some piñon and cedar. And too damn much prickly pear cactus. I think I prefer the high country."

"Well, I do, too," I answered over my evening coffee. "But at this particular time it seemed like a hell of a good idea to get out of there."

We spent the next two days pre-baiting sets so to get the coon, fox, coyote, and cats used to coming to them. It was only the third week of September and the fur wouldn't be getting primed for a few more weeks, but once the animals were worth taking I wanted to make some money and get out. I still hadn't gotten up the nerve to tell my partners I would be splitting. As I crawled into my blankets I figured I'd tell them both come morning. I was going to Australia.

The next morning at dawn, a light dew covering my blankets as the sun began peeking over the plains in a ball of red, Crazy Joe jabbed me in the side.

"Sam. Wake up."

"Leave me alone," I grumbled, a heavy four-point blanket pulled over my head.

"We've got company."

I pulled the blanket from my face and looked up into the twin barrels of a ten- or twelve-gauge hammer shotgun. The man holding the shotgun held a Colt Peacemaker in his left hand, which was casually pointed at Philo's still form, located off to my left side.

"Philo. Rise and shine," I said in a loud voice.

Philo rolled over and pitched his blankets off. As he sat up he looked straight up the barrel of that Peacemaker. "Oh, Lordy, Lordy," he softly muttered.

"Good morning, gentlemen," the stranger pleasantly began. He motioned the shotgun at Crazy Joe. "You are Joseph D. Flanigan, also known as Crazy Joe Flanigan. I am United States

Marshal Ben Lone Eagle of Sedalia, Missouri. You are under arrest for the murder of one Billy Joe McLowery of Shady Grove, Missouri, this July past.''

I took a hard look at the lawman then as I overcame shock. He was one of the biggest men I've ever seen; he was thick all over, but not fat. He had to stand six foot six. He wore two-hundred-dollar lizardskin boots, Levi's, a denim shirt, and leather vest. A shock of unruly coal-black hair peeked out from underneath the brim of his expensive Stetson. He had high cheekbones, black eyes, and a copper complexion.

We had been captured by a goddamned Indian.

"Gentlemen," the marshal slowly but firmly began, "you are known to have more than one trick up your collective sleeves. It is with sincere regret that I must inform you that if anybody moves fast I will shoot."

"Yer an' Injun!" Philo exclaimed.

"I will shoot," the marshal repeated, "and I never miss. Is that understood?"

We all three slowly nodded our heads.

"All right, that being understood, I want you to stand up slowly, one at a time. Flanigan, don't even think about pulling a piece," he warned softly.

Crazy Joe sighed and got to his feet. When he was up, his hands reaching for the clear blue dawning sky, I stood up, then Philo.

"Where's your guns?"

"I sleep with my Colt under my saddle. Obviously I should have slept with it in my hand last night," Crazy Joe replied cheerfully.

"Mine's under my saddle, too," I answered.

"So's mine," added Philo.

The marshal then methodically handcuffed us all together. After he'd manacled us, he read us our rights, then had us sit around our dead campfire circle.

"You don't reckon I could put my boots on?" I asked. "My toes are like to freezin'."

"Later. In the meantime, I'm hungry. I've spent the last two days in the saddle trying to cut your trail. What have we got to eat around here?"

"You've got some gall, copper," Crazy Joe offered.

"Flanigan, hostility will get you nowhere. I'll tell you guys what: You all sit down real nice and get that fire going again, and I'll rustle us up some grub. That's what they say in the westerns, isn't it?" He grinned.

I motioned my head toward my saddle panniers. "There's bacon, eggs, and some tortillas in my panniers. Help yourself."

"Coffee?"

"That too."

"Good," he said with a wide grin and nod of his head. "I've been dying for a cup of coffee."

Once we got the fire going, the marshal moved us a dozen feet away so he could cook. We sat manacled together as he happily fried bacon, occasionally tossing a piece in his mouth, and explained how he'd figured us out. I shivered in the early morning cool and listened. There wasn't much else to do.

"I suppose you guys are wondering how I caught you," he nonchalantly remarked to the frying pan.

"I hate to sound like a nosy son of a bitch, but just how in the hell did you do it?" I asked.

"Well, I've been on a winning streak lately," he confessed with a wide smile that showed off his ivory white teeth. "It's like this: The Crawfish County district attorney is a gelding, and the sheriff isn't much better. I work out of Sedalia; normally I handle transport of prisoners, serving of papers, that type of thing. For some reason the Billy Joe McLowery shooting really fascinated me. Flanigan, you may have a hard time believing this, but mainly I just wanted to meet you." He grinned. Crazy Joe did not reply.

"Oh well," the marshal sighed. "At any rate, the local law opened and shut the case in a couple days. They didn't look too hard. Flanigan, do you know you're a hero in Shady Grove?"

"Have they built me a statue yet?"

"Not yet. However, the whole case compelled me. What struck me about the shooting was this: It wasn't premeditated to the extent that any great amount of planning had gone into it; as I saw it, the case was largely circumstantial in nature. After the sheriff gave up on the case, I decided to take a little trip to Shady Grove myself. I talked to Harold Landry and didn't get anywhere. They covered for you pretty good, Flanigan."

"That was really white of them," Crazy Joe quickly replied. "No pun intended."

The marshal smiled as he stirred the bacon. "No offense taken. Then it so happened—oh, a few weeks later—I was going through some of my old gun magazines looking for an advertisement I'd seen some months earlier. There was an article in that magazine that caught my attention; I guess I'd read it before and forgotten it. It was about a bunch of guys in California who did Wild West stunt shows, and I'll be damned if one of them wasn't dressed like old Wild Bill Hickok, the syphilitic shootist!"

"Oh, fuck a duck," I groaned.

"So anyway," the marshal happily continued as he started to break eggs and dump them in the grease, "I took that magazine to Shady Grove. Call it a guess, or a gut feeling. I had already met Martha Hudson; she'd told me nothing. I said to her, 'Ma'am, in the newspaper it quoted you as saying the man looked like Wild Bill Hickok. Did he look like this?' She looked at the picture and said, 'That's him!' Heh-heh-heh.

"Well, Flanigan, she immediately corrected herself and said that wasn't you, but of course the damage was done: one of your own fan club fingered you.

"After that it was a fairly simple matter to track you down. I went to San Diego and talked to some of your shipmates; they said you'd taken off for the Colorado Rockies with a guy named Hawkins. With information procured from your service record, it was a small matter to run your DL and locate your Gunnison address. And then of course you know what capped it."

"I like my eggs medium," I grumbled.

"Just last week the media was full of reports where—Was it 'C. Joseph Flanigan'? Nice touch, Crazy Joe—where C. Joseph Flanigan had killed a bear and saved some kid's life. Then I looked up your friend, Dusty Rhodes. You know, you guys got quite an ally there."

"I never told him where we were going! Leave him the fuck outta this, Marshal!"

"Easy on the language there, Hawkins," the marshal pleasantly warned. He took a break to fill a tin plate with eggs. Then he stood up.

"You're right: he didn't talk. I had to threaten him with a trip to Denver and a visit to the United States attorney before he'd tell me anything. All he told me was exactly what you'd said, that you didn't go to heaven and didn't go to hell, you'd be somewhere in between.

"Well, gentlemen, you can thank my Catholic upbringing for providing the answer. I said to myself, 'Between heaven and hell? That's purgatory.' Then I recalled the stories my great-grandfather used to tell—he's been dead thirty years—of when our Southern Cheyenne ancestors used to live in what is now Colorado. I said, 'Ah hah, the Purgatory River!' From there it was a simple matter of renting a horse and cutting sign to this pleasant little campsite. Let's eat, men!"

"Ah thought you was Osage," Philo grumbled.

"And what part of Oklahoma do you hail from?" the marshal genially inquired as he wolfed down another piece of bacon.

"Sallisaw. An' you?"

"El Reno."

"Figgers," Philo grumped.

The marshal was courteous enough to wrap up bacon and eggs inside tortillas and give us a couple each. We had a hell of a time eating: as I bit into a burrito with my right hand raised to my mouth, Crazy Joe moved his left hand downward and jerked the burrito from my teeth.

"Watch it, goddamn it!"

"Well, if you were coordinated we wouldn't have a problem," he retorted. And so it went.

After breakfast Marshal Lone Eagle took it upon himself to break down our camp and pack up the animals. We sat in sullen silence as he whistled through the chores.

"Where's our guns?" Crazy Joe whispered in my ear as the Marshal cinched up my packsaddle on Jack.

"Didn't you see him put our six-guns in his saddlebags?" He had also taken the precaution of levering the rounds out of our Winchesters, then returning them empty to their scabbards. He didn't miss much.

"All right, fellas, time to go," he cheerily informed us when we had the horses saddled. "What we're going to do is this: I'm going to handcuff you all with your hands in front. That violates SOP but I'm responsible for your safety now; you can't control a horse with your hands behind your back. However, to preclude your trying anything, I'm going to tie the lead ropes of your horses to the animal in front of you. We don't want anybody running off for, say, Mexico, for instance, do we?''

"I still don't understand why you arrested me and Philo," I bitched as the marshal unlocked my handcuffs only to snap them fast with my hands in front of my body.

"Oh, there's a couple answers for that: in the first place, you're in the company of a suspected felon; that makes you a suspect by association. Then there are all sorts of additional possibilities like conspiracy, interstate flight, accessory before and after—''

"I get the picture.''

We mounted up and began the ten-mile westward trek to Steve Goodnight's little country store. The marshal took the lead, the reins of his rented bay in his left hand, the short double-barreled shotgun cocked lazily over his right shoulder. Crazy Joe was tied off directly behind him, followed by me, then Philo and the pack string. Halfway through the trip I turned around in the saddle and yelled at Philo, "Now I know how Billy the Kid felt when that bastard Garrett snuck up on him at Stinking Springs!''

Marshal Lone Eagle immediately whoa'ed up the string and turned in the saddle. "Hawkins, you shouldn't insult an officer of the law like that. Pat Garrett was a fine peace officer and the man who brought some semblance of law and order to New Mexico Territory.''

"He was a dipshit and a drunk!" I hollered back.

Thus ended the conversation.

That ten miles took forever to cover. Our horses slowly plodded on, heads down as if they knowed something was radically wrong. They probably did. As we rode to Goodnight's store I vowed I would get out of there: Sam Hawkins would not go to jail, especially for crimes he didn't commit.

Four hours after we left our campsite, we arrived at Goodnight's parched and dry. We dismounted in back of the store by an old tin shed and the marshal made us line up with our backs to the building. When he'd tied off our animals to the old hitching rail that had been there since the place was a stagecoach stop, he happily announced, "Let's go inside, fellas, and have a soda. I'm buying.''

"Big-hearted son of a bitch," Philo muttered under his breath.

We pulled up barstools and Steve Goodnight casually took in

the sight of our handcuffed hands. "You boys git catched with a runnin' arn?" he drawled as he brought our sodas. The marshal was making a long-distance call from the pay phone on the wall.

I took a sip of my soda, the handcuffs jingling as I lifted the can to my mouth. "Naw. We wouldn't a got caught if we'd been rustling, Steve. Actually this is a case of mistaken identity."

"Wal, ah sartinly hope so," Steve replied as he expelled a whitish-gray cloud of smoke skyward.

Marshal Lone Eagle finished his phone call and pulled up a seat at a table where he could keep an eye on us. "Okay, just sit tight, fellas. Some of my associates from our Denver office will be here in a couple hours to pick us up."

"I get one phone call, right?" I asked.

"That's right, Hawkins. Want to call somebody?"

"For a fact."

He nodded toward the phone. "Go ahead. Here, wait." He fished in a pocket and handed me a dime.

"Thanks, hoss."

He smiled back. "I'll put it on my expense account."

I quickly dialed the operator and placed a collect call to Dusty's. His eight-year-old daughter Peggy answered on the fourth ring; she accepted the charges with a meek "Yes."

"Peggy, this is Sam. Your dad there?"

"No," she answered in a small voice.

"How about your mom?"

"She's at the hospital with Daddy," she softly said. I thought I heard a small sob catch in her throat. Alarm was building inside me.

"Peggy—what's wrong with your dad?"

She was fighting to hold back tears and keep her composure. "Yesterday some men found him on Ohio Creek. They beat him up, Sam. He has broken ribs and a broken arm and a brain conc— a brain concoct— his face is all cut up. Sam, his face is all cut up," she repeated with a choke.

"A brain concussion," I softly said. "Is he going to be all right, Peggy?"

"The doctors think so." She sobbed quietly.

"Who did this to him?"

"I don't know, Sam," she cried as she broke down. "All Mom said was that they were on motorcycles."

A cold shiver ran up and down my spine three times faster than the speed of light. "Peggy," I firmly began, "now listen to me very carefully. Were the men who did this to your father riding big motorcycles and dressed in black leather jackets?"

"I think so," she cried in the same small voice.

"Do you know what their name was? This is very, very important, Peggy."

"The Death Something," she said between sobs.

I tried to keep the anxiety out of my voice. "Peggy, tell your dad this: Tell him I'm sorry, and tell him he'll always be my friend, no matter what happens. Can you remember to tell him that?"

"Yes," she cried softly.

"And you give your mom a big hug for me and Philo and Crazy Joe, okay, *hovacita*?"

"Yes, Sam. Sam, are you going someplace?"

I didn't choke on the knot in my throat. "I think so, darlin'. *Via con Dios.*" I hanged up the phone with a bang.

Crazy Joe was staring at me like he'd just seen a ghost. Philo's face was the color of alkali.

"What the hell was that all about, Hawkins?" Marshal Lone Eagle shot out.

I quickly headed for the front door. "Don't shoot! I'm just going to see if anybody's coming down the highway!"

"Marshal," Crazy Joe pleasantly began, "have you ever heard of a motorcycle gang called the Death Riders?"

He nodded his head. "Of course. California boys, I believe."

Crazy Joe nodded his head as I turned from the door. "Well, there's something you ought to know," he began. For a change Crazy Joe capsulized the story into a couple minutes. He wasn't even through before the marshal grimly stalked to the phone and placed a call to the Las Animas County Sheriff's Office.

But it was too late.

Because even before he hung up the phone I heard the chainsaw-like roar of highly tuned motorcycle engines outside the store.

And then the sound of gravel flying, and then the sputtering stop. Marshal Lone Eagle quickly ducked in the restroom in the corner of the store.

Our backs were to the bar as three greasy, leather-clad bikers tromped in Goodnight's Saloon & General Store.

The lead one pulled off his goggles.

It was Spiderman.

26

"HELLO, ASSHOLE," CRAZY Joe said cheerfully.

"Flanigan. Oh, Flanigan." Spiderman laughed in mirth. He chortled and shook his head as if he'd just encountered the eighth wonder of the world. "Those handcuffs are a real nice touch. So where's the pig that's onto your little game?"

Marshal Lone Eagle swung into the store from the restroom, the shotgun aimed casually from his midsection. "I'm the pig, dirtbag," he informed him with that smile that never quit.

"Oh wow!" Spiderman cried in phony amusement. "Oh wow, like I don't fuckin' believe this! A real Indian! Oh fuck, man, this is too much!" His two cronies laughed on cue, following the lead of their führer.

"So tell me, what brings you to this naked prairie?" I piped up. Spiderman looked at me hard.

"I remember you," he slowly said.

"Rat-tat-tat-tat," I evenly replied.

"Oh wow! Another one I'm gonna even up a score with!"

"There will be no scores evened here today," the marshal coolly announced, cocking the twin hammers of his shotgun for emphasis.

Spiderman quickly turned his attention to the marshal. "Hey, pig redskin, I think you're threatening me, y'know? I just happened to see on the tube the other day where my good friend Crazy Joe Flanigan was now a big hero and living in Colorado.

Since I was just down the road a ways in New Mexico I thought I'd come up for a visit.''

"You are under arrest for assault and battery against the person of Conservation Officer Eugene M. Rhodes," the marshal firmly informed him.

"Oh, Marshal," Spiderman sighed with a shake of his head. "That is like definitely downbeat. You got my drift?"

"You see this ten-bore Greener? That's my drift, punk."

Spiderman tried a new tack. "Look, Chief, Edgar and Tommy here are with me on a little scouting mission. There's ninety-five of my boys heading down this little highway. You would be advised to be cool and not so hostile, got it?"

"Hoist 'em," the marshal ordered with a smile.

Spiderman let out a sigh of resignation. "All right, boys, hands up." We was still leaning against the bar as Spiderman moved. When his hands was level with his chest, his right hand dove underneath the leather jacket even as his person dived for the floor. It happened in the space of a second.

As Spiderman hit the floor he rolled and came up with an automatic pistol in his hand. He and the marshal fired at the same time, the shotgun blast ripping off the top of the biker's head. Crazy Joe, Philo, and me were splattered with blood and bits of brain matter that looked like finely diced hamburger.

Spiderman had fired the pistol in death, and although his intent was to kill either Crazy Joe or the marshal or both, he drilled me high through the shoulder.

"Get 'em up, you assholes!" Marshal Lone Eagle hoarsely commanded. The remaining two bikers grabbed for the ceiling.

"That fucker shot me," I said in amazement. A warm river of blood seeped through a ragged hole in the fleshy part of my shoulder.

Marshal Lone Eagle quickly removed our handcuffs and used them to join the two bikers around an old wooden pillar set in the middle of the floor.

"You're gonna die," Edgar laughed.

"It looks like a good day for it, dirtbag," the marshal solemnly replied as he clamped the cuffs around their wrists unnecessarily tight.

Philo dashed over the lifeless form of Spiderman and made

for the door. "Hey! Thar's more of 'em a-comin'! Judas H. Priestly, the road's fulla 'em!"

By then the marshal had finished cuffing the bikers to the post. With our own hands free, Crazy Joe and I headed to the door even as he tied a bandanna around my bleeding shoulder.

"I think it was a .22 or a .25," I grumbled. "It don't hurt too bad yet."

Philo had been right. On the southern plains, with a view unobstructed by terrain features, a man can generally see for miles. Three or four miles up the state highway, buzzing down a little grade, was upwards of a hundred black specks headed our way.

We all four stopped in the doorway and looked at each other. "Marshal, I am not a coward, but like they say, 'There comes a time to turn Mother's picture to the wall and get out.' I suggest we depart most tick."

"Was just thinking the same thing myself. Hawkins, what do you know about the local sheriff's department?" he quickly asked.

"Las Animas County is the second largest county in the United States; last I heard they had eight deputies. Two or three on at any given time."

The buzzing was getting louder.

"They're gonna kill you all!" one of the bikers cried in merriment.

"Old man, get out of here!" the marshal ordered Steve. "Just jump in your truck and go!"

"Nobody comes t' mah owned place an' threatens me. Nobody," Steve firmly replied. By way of further emphasis he calmly pulled an ancient Smith & Wesson American from underneath the bar. He broke the pistol open and inspected the contents of the cylinder.

"Have it your way. Boys, to the horses!" the marshal commanded.

We was aboard and had left Steve Goodnight's at a gallop in less time than it takes to write it. We let the packhorses loose in hopes they'd follow.

We cut due south from the store, myself in the lead. "Where the hell we goin', Hawkins?" the marshal yelled as he rode next to me.

"We're three miles north of that deserted army post. Once we get inside there, we'll be on government property. I don't know if that'll help or not, but it's my best idea now!" I yelled back in choppy bursts.

A mile from Steve's we reined in, the horses breathing hard, the sweat pouring off ourselves. As we turned to get a look at the store my worst fears was realized. By then a few of the bikers had started cross-country to catch us; the rest was at the store.

"Goddamn! Here they come!" Crazy Joe exclaimed.

"Let's go!" the marshal ordered. "Hi-yi, giddap!"

We tore off at breakneck speed across the prairie. I didn't have spurs on, and lashed Molly hard with the reins as I jabbed her in the ribs with my heels. The marshal's bay was fresh; he kept up with me while Philo and Crazy Joe dropped a little to the rear.

Half a mile later I took a glance behind me; all of the bikers had left the store and was strung out in a ragged pack behind us. It sounded like we had a hive of angry, buzzing bees to our rear.

"Whoa!" I hollered as I violently reined in Molly. She planted all fours and skidded to a stop inches from a ten-foot-wide arroyo.

"We gotta jump it!" the marshal hoarsely ordered.

"They'll never make it with them bikes!" Crazy Joe happily added.

We quickly turned around and rode back thirty yards. "I'll go first," I said, my arm beginning to ache. "Molly, don't fail me now," I muttered. "Yiii-hi," I yelled as I kicked her in the ribs with my heels and lashed her with my reins.

We sailed over that arroyo, Molly clearing the chasm with feet to spare, and was followed in order by the marshal, Philo, and Crazy Joe.

Half a mile from the arroyo we stopped. Crazy Joe was only half right; the bikers hadn't made it. There. Instead they had ridden west half a mile, and found a little berm that sat perpendicular to the arroyo and was two or three feet higher than it. They was jumping their bikes across one at a time.

"Fuck a duck!" I yelled. "The sons of bitches are still coming!"

"C'mon!" commanded the marshal, whipping his bay into a gallop.

Six or seven hundred yards up ahead I saw the olive-drab army truck and jeep. "Hey!" I yelled to the marshal, "Head for them!" I quickly glanced behind me again; almost all of the bikers had jumped the arroyo and a gaggle of them was unnervingly close upon our rear. Molly was blowing hard as she dodged bayonet cactus and prickly pear. The marshal veered off toward the army vehicles, Philo and Crazy Joe thrashing their own mounts slightly behind me.

We reined up at the army trucks in a lather; they was a jeep and a deuce-and-a-half truck.

"Who's in charge!" Marshal Lone Eagle demanded in a hoarse shout.

A skinny young lieutenant ran the twenty yards from the fencing crew he was supervising to where we'd stopped by the jeep.

"What's going—"

"I am United States Marshal Ben Lone Eagle of Sedalia, Missouri. These men are my prisoners. We're entering your military reservation. You got a radio?"

"Yes, but, Marshal, I'm afraid you don't understand. Civilians are not permitted on the maneuver site. There is currently—"

"You idiot! Tell *them*!" he shouted, pointing to our rear. The young lieutenant quickly looked to our rear; behind us not half a mile was the buzzing bikers.

"Oh Lord," he softly muttered.

"Get on that fucking radio and tell somebody we need help! Now! C'mon, boys, follow me!"

Even as we dashed through the ten-foot hole in the fence I heard the young lieutenant frantically call into the handset of his jeep radio, "Sierra Zero Five, this is Charlie Two Six! Come in!"

Five hundred yards later I looked behind me. The bikers was pouring through the same hole in the fence. "Hey! They're closing the gap!" I hollered. As they passed through the fence they was forming up in a ragged half-moon formation, and while we was going faster, their progress was steady and unnerving.

A couple minutes later some of them had pulled even with our right rear. Then I heard the air sharply part around us and couldn't figure out right away what it was.

"Thar shootin' at us!" Philo cried.

"Goddamn it!" Crazy Joe added.

"Make for that butte!" the marshal hollered over the frenzied hoofbeats of the horses, our own hard breathing, and the wind that was sucking the air from our mouths.

I knowed then that that was the end. We was going to be boxed in. Trapped. Even as we rode, reins in my right hand and my left gripping the horn, I recall thinking, "This is the old ball game." As we neared the butte I could tell it was a lousy defensive position at best. It was nothing more than an outcropping of rocks maybe ten yards across and fifteen feet high.

Behind us, it sounded like every goddamned motorcycle in the world was converging. When we was maybe two hundred yards from the butte, the bikers holding their own by the sound of their machines, I throwed another look behind me. All I could see was dust and the motorcycles.

The marshal reached the butte first and even as he swung out of the saddle dropped the bridle. He pulled a large butcher knife from its sheath, then slashed the latigo free and pulled off the saddle. Philo dismounted, and I reined in next; Crazy Joe came in a slow fourth.

I pulled my empty Winchester from its scabbard even as Marshal Lone Eagle slapped his mount on the rear. He quickly unbuckled the leather straps on his saddlebags and dumped six-shooters and ammunition in a pile on the ground.

I unbridled and unsaddled Molly as fast as I could, my arm and shoulder aching. "Go on, girl, get out of here and run free! Hah!" I hollered as I slapped her on the rump.

"Boys, I'll probably be in deep shit if I live through this, but here's your guns and ammo. We're not going to shoot unless we have to. I'm gonna try to talk our way out of this."

Crazy Joe looked up from his Winchester. He was grimly stuffing rounds through the loading gate. "Fat fuckin' chance, Marshal," he said with a smile.

I had finished loading my rifle and pistol and had taken up a prone position behind some rocks when a lone biker rode up to us. The rest had stopped in a little swale three or four hundred yards away that was a few feet lower than the prairie, and thus concealed themselves. Somebody in that mob knowed something about tactics.

As the biker neared on his fancy motorcycle, his long beard and blond hair gaily blowing in the wind, I thought to myself, "He ain't no coward." Twenty yards away he stopped and killed the engine; it quit with a cough.

"Hey you, Flanigan!" he growled.

"Hey you, greaseball!!" Crazy Joe retorted.

"Flanigan, shut up!" Marshal Lone Eagle commanded from my left as he stood up and walked down the knoll to meet the biker. The big Cheyenne stopped a dozen feet from the man, his shadow towering over man and machine.

"What do you want?"

"We want Flanigan, pig. The rest of you can go."

"Take him, ya gotta take all us!" Philo hollered. The floor recognized the delegation from Oklahoma.

"If that's the way you want it!" he barked.

"Punk, I am United States Marshal Ben Lone Eagle of Sedalia, Missouri," the marshal coolly announced, the Greener ten-gauge resting carelessly in the crook of his arm. "I am ordering you and your gang to surrender to me for the assault on Conservation Warden Eugene M. Rhodes. Have all of your people put their hands in the air and walk forward."

I have seen nerve before. I always thought that I had a good dose of it myself. But I have never, ever seen such a bold and unafraid display of grit as United States Marshal Ben Lone Eagle, of Sedalia, Missouri, displayed that afternoon.

"Oh, like wow!" the biker howled. "This is fuckin' rich! I don't fuckin' believe this! Man, we've got shotguns and submachine guns and rifles, not antiques! You don't have a fuckin' prayer. You must be *stupid*. I'm telling *you* to surrender to *us*!"

"We've got rifles!" Crazy Joe hollered. He didn't add that we had very little ammo.

"If that's the way you assholes want it!" the biker howled. With that, he kicked his machine to life and sped off in a cloud of dust for his wolfpack. Marshal Lone Eagle stood and watched him ride off. He slowly lifted a hand to his hat brim and turned his head to the sun. The wind caught his quietly spoken words and threw them back to me. In a low voice he said, "Thank you." Then he returned to the knoll and took up a prone position next to me.

"Nice try," I told him.

The marshal ignored the remark. "All right, men," he calmly began, "don't anybody shoot until I give the order. They might be bluffing."

"I'm a poker player. I fuckin' doubt it, Marshal," I said over my rifle barrel. Then I remembered my shoulder, quickly leaned my rifle against the rock, and fished in my saddlebags for a blue bandanna I carried in a plastic bag. The blood had long since saturated the first bandanna, and Marshal Lone Eagle quickly wrapped the blue cloth over the first and tied if off hard.

He smiled as he tied the knot. "Like they say in the westerns, it's just a flesh wound."

"Well, it hurts like a son of a bitch," I grunted.

"Here they come!" Crazy Joe yelled.

The Death Riders crested the little swale in a cloud of dust and headed for our position in a ragged half-moon formation. As the bikers headed toward us, slowing for the broken ground, the prairie to our front and the rocks behind us come alive. Little furrows were suddenly plowed up to all sides of us; the large boulder to our rear screamed as bullets impacted and quickly ricocheted off in unnerving whines.

"All right, men!" the marshal loudly commanded. "Shoot the leaders!"

"With pleasure!" Crazy Joe hollered.

All three Winchesters crashed at once. I pulled down on a biker far out in front who was gesturing with a pistol held high in the air. I held a foot high, took careful aim, and let him have it. His arms flew skyward as the impact of the bullet throwed him from the bike.

When they was a hundred yards out, Marshal Lone Eagle opened up with the Greener. As the Death Riders leading the pack fell to our fusillade the rearward ones had to swerve and slow down even more to avoid running over their dead and wounded comrades. As one such biker turned broadside to us, his Harley Davidson exploded and throwed his body a dozen feet in the air.

"Shoot the gas tanks!" Crazy Joe yelled above the belching of our weapons. That was Crazy Joe: he went for dramatics till the bitter end.

Marshal Lone Eagle was out of shotgun shells by then and was quickly firing his long-barreled Colt, cocking with his left hand and snapping off rounds as fast as the weapon locked in battery. There was a lull in firing from our position as Crazy Joe and I reloaded our Winchesters at the same time. Philo covered the gap in the fire, emptying his Winchester of six quick shots, then dropping it and blazing away with his Colt.

"Sam!" Crazy Joe yelled as he levered a fresh round in his Winchester.

"What!"

"Try to get out of here alive! I think Janet's coming back!"

"Thanks for the offer, but I don't think they're gonna let me!"

They say you never hear the one that gets you, and I didn't. I don't think it had my name on it; it was one of them addressed "To Whom It May Concern," and they are the worst because there's no ducking them. It must have been a ricochet from the large boulder behind us. All I recall is that one second I was reloading my Colt—we was out of rifle ammo by then—and the next I was on the ground. The impact of the bullet shredded one of my leg bones; it protruded white and ugly from a ragged hole in my blue jeans. The force of the bullet throwed me backwards and sideways; I remember looking up and seeing clear blue sky, and hearing the air being sliced to shreds all around me.

Marshal Lone Eagle was there in a second. He grabbed me under the arms and began to drag me back to safety as orange flame leaped from Philo's and Crazy Joe's weapons. We was three feet away from the protection of the rocks when I looked up at him. Then, as if in slow motion, the big Cheyenne's teeth set in a death-defying grin, his head exploded like a burst watermelon.

Even as he fell on his side he didn't have time to scream, because half of his head was gone. Crazy Joe saw what happened and came running, a smoking Colt in each hand. He blasted off three or four quick shots as Philo covered him, grabbed me by the arm, and dragged me to the safety of the rocks.

I leaned against the rocks and slowly reloaded my Colt from the cartridges scattered on the ground. I slowly looked over at Philo, who had quit firing. He was merely laying on his rifle. I recall thinking, "This is one hell of a time to take a nap," and I yelled at him, but he didn't answer.

The next thing I recall hearing, faint and from far away, was the light, happy strains of "The Garryowen." I figured at that point I was delirious, or possibly losing my mind.

Then a Death Rider who had flanked our position jumped out of nowhere to the left of Crazy Joe. The burst from his submachine gun brought Crazy Joe to his knees, and I felt another hot iron tear into my body. Crazy Joe screamed as he fell, firing both Colts from the hip as the biker dropped.

And then that goddamned music got louder. It *was* "The Garryowen."

The first olive-drab Huey banked violently above me and let go with a long, ripping burst from the 7.62mm minigun mounted on the side as it made a strafing pass in front of the attackers. The ground in front of the Death Riders exploded as a thousand 7.62mm bullets plowed a ditch and threw dirt high into the air. Then another Huey banked toward the Death Riders from the far left flank and hovered not ten feet over our position. The starboard M-60 gunner poured out long bursts over the heads of the gang, red tracers arcing from the muzzle while expended brass cartridge cases flew from the feed tray in a nearly solid stream of yellow. I pulled myself to the top of the rock then, the air buzzing with the sound of rotors, the sky alive with Hueys, Cobra gunships, and OH-58s. Hueys swooped and dived as the Death Riders' advance halted ten yards from our position, and made passes so low that the remaining mounted bikers bailed off their motorcycles so as not to get impaled by the skids.

With all my strength I yelled, "It's the goddamned cavalry!" I couldn't understand why none of my compadres responded, and I was too weak to crawl over to them to find out why.

An OH-58 landed in front of me then, the wind from the rotor and blade blowing dust and sand high and sucking the air from my lungs. The shooting slowed and finally stopped as those beautiful birds landed. I recall thinking, "I ain't never seen nothing so beautiful in my life."

I think I passed out then. I know when I came to, the music had stopped. I was laying on my back, and looked up into the lined face of a hugesome soldier. A tight crewcut left his bare, bullet-shaped head almost hairless. He was about fifty years old and looked like he could lick his weight in alligators. As my eyes focused on him I saw him withdraw a syringe from my side and with another hand put a battle dressing on my leg wound. He wore sergeant's stripes with three rockers. In the middle was a diamond. The diamond of a first sergeant.

"Hey, Top. What's happening?" I weakly said through the pain. On the left arm of his battle-dress shirt he wore the black-and-green oblong patch of the First Cavalry Division. When he turned his body to work on my leg, I saw he had an identical patch on his right arm, signifying combat service. That was Philo's old outfit: He always called it the First Air Cav.

"Laddie, shot up you are, but not the worst of the lot. You're alive I'm thinkin', an' stayin' that way." He smiled at me. I tried to focus my eyes on the nametape above his pocket. I think it spelled QUINCANNON. I could have sworn he talked with an Irish accent.

"My friends," I asked through the pain that made moving or talking a nearly excruciating, unbearable effort.

"An' bein' taken care of they are," he assured me, his bloody hands working on my leg and middle.

I think I passed out for a bit. When I came to another man was kneeling next to the first sergeant. He wore captain's bars on his collar and was an even larger man than his first sergeant. He was around forty-five and old for a captain; his chest was thick but tapered down to a narrow waist. With his helmet cocked back on his head and the chinstrap unfastened, he gave off a rakish, confident air. His face was rugged and lined. It was a hard face, as though carved from oak, and his blue eyes were penetrating and about bored through me.

"Son, you fellas killed a lot of people here today," he softly said.

"No choice," I replied with a croak.

He slowly nodded his head. "No choice," he repeated.

"My friends."

"The dark-haired fella's been medevaced out. The other two are dead." I think I started to cry. Then I turned my head and saw Philo's still body ten feet away. The captain turned his head to follow my gaze, and when he did so I saw he also wore the First Cavalry Division patch on his right arm. When I tried to talk but couldn't, he put his ear close to my mouth.

"He was First Cav in 'Nam," I said. For some reason it seemed important to tell the captain that.

He jerked a thumb at Philo's body and furrowed his brow. "Him?" I weakly nodded my head and blinked my eyes. He took the cue and again put his ear to my mouth.

"His name's Philo Harris," I whispered as the morphine began to take effect. What happened after that is all dreamlike and fuzzy in my mind. I felt like I was floating and floating, going nowhere.

The captain seemed to study me for a long minute. "Can you tell me what outfit, son?" he asked softly, his face not inches from my own.

I am sure I said, "The Seventh."

He nodded his head in affirmation. "The Seventh Cavalry. George Custer's outfit." It was so strange the way he said that, almost as if he knowed the late general personally. For some reason I figured he did.

Then the captain set down his rifle and pulled the knife from the sheath fastened upside down to his web suspenders. He reached over my body and grabbed at First Sergeant Quincannon's sleeve. He started to make a cut at the thread holding the black-and-green patch.

"An', sir, me beloved combat patch you cannot be takin'!" he cried, his bloody hands too occupied with my shot-up body to further protest.

"Hold still, you big Mick," the captain growled. He made a couple light cuts, then ripped the patch from his first sergeant's right arm. He stood up and looked at me hard, then walked the ten feet to Philo's still body. He unbent the rigid body from the grotesque position it had taken on after the fashion of those who die quickly and violently. He carefully closed Philo's eyes and folded his hands over his chest. Then he wedged the oblong patch in between the stiffening fingers. He removed his helmet.

"Sir," he softly began, "we commend to your keeping the soul of Trooper Harris, formerly of the United States Seventh Cavalry. Please take care of him. Amen."

And this may sound crazy, but the way that captain said the prayer, it was more like an order, or a declaration, as though the Lord should understand that Trooper Harris was to be accepted upon arrival, and that was that. Then the captain was again standing over me, helmet under his arm. In his eyes I thought I saw and recognized what I'd seen only a very few times in my life. They were eyes which had seen much sadness and pain; the eyes of a man who could not prevent the sorrows of the world, but who greatly wished he could. The eyes told me all about the man. The captain could be either tough or tender, depending on the situation.

Then the stretcher team arrived, and with them a young lieutenant. He was a thin, curly-haired blond fellow.

"Sir, the first five birds are off with the emergencies and priorities. Colonel Ford just radioed on the command net; he wants to know what the hell happened here."

"Very well, Lieutenant Carey," the captain tiredly replied. "I'll give him a sitrep." He took a few steps past me then and looked out to the prairie in front of him. "Did our people kill any of them?"

"No, sir. Not that I'm aware of."

"Thank the Lord," he muttered. He stood easily then, his hands resting on his hips. Even from where I lay, then being loaded on the stretcher, I could tell his eyes wasn't seeing what was in front of him: they was looking back across the years, and the thousands of miles.

"Ten minutes earlier and I could have prevented this," he quietly said, as though to himself.

"Sir, there are over twenty dead," the young lieutenant offered. "We've got to tell the colonel and the sheriff something about the dirtballs."

"They are the *dead*, Lieutenant Carey!" the captain impatiently barked. "Do you understand that?"

The lieutenant took a step back in surprise. "Yes, sir!"

"The dead," the captain softly repeated, looking out at the carnage in front of him.

After a long pause the lieutenant asked, "Sir, what are you going to tell them . . . about the dead?"

Just as the troops lifted me off the ground, the captain let out a little sigh, then slightly nodded his head, which seemed to be his habit before he spoke. As they carried me away I heard his reply.

All he said was, "I'll tell 'em they died with their boots on."

CRAZY JOE DIED on the way to the hospital.

But Dusty Rhodes lived and made a full recovery.

I am mending up slow and will probably never dance ballet.

But that's okay, because I'm alive. And where there's life, there's hope.

And I've been cleared of all charges by a grand jury. So there's more good news mixed with the bad.

Last week I got a letter from Nancy. She wished me well, and said I set in motion some important changes in Janet's life. I didn't intend to; I just wanted to find out the Why of things, and that I did.

Nancy said she would discuss all that happened in more detail with me at a later date. So I think I'll stop and visit her on my way to Australia.

Well, that's the whole story, or pretty much all of it. What little I've left out don't bear recollecting, because it didn't figure into the overall scheme of things.

The scheme of things. Now there's an interesting question.

Is there one?

And if there is, how much of it do we mess up by our own little shortsighted and self-serving maneuvers?

I don't know.

In fact, I don't know much at all.

I only know that not an hour passes that I don't think of Philo,

Crazy Joe, and Marshal Lone Eagle. You don't forget the men who saved your life, and died when you lived on.

The doctor has said I'm withdrawn and need to talk it out. But I've never been a talker, so I wrote this book instead.

I expect it was the same with my dad. He was one of the handful of men out of the crew of seven hundred who lived when the Japs sunk the *Juneau* off Guadalcanal. I don't think he ever got over it, but he never talked much about it.

Until one time he came out to see me in Pearl Harbor and we went up to the Punchbowl. And he finally found the names of five of his shipmates, and ran his callused hands over the letters deeply chiseled in the white marble.

Albert, Francis, Madison, Joseph, and George.

The Five Sullivans.

And then, for the first time in my life, I saw my dad cry. Because you expect to lose men in combat. But not a whole family of pals. Not all of them at once.

I guess that's kind of the way I feel. The Sullivans stuck together with their brothers, and I stuck together with friends who were as close as brothers.

I'm only real proud of two things I've done in my own life:

I stuck by my friends in a tight, and I loved a woman the best I knowed how.

I ain't sorry for a damned thing.

And I'd do it all over again. Even though life has a way of breaking your heart.

But only if you let it.

—The End—

About the Author

Russell Nelson was born and grew up in Wisconsin, where he graduated from the state university at River Falls. He served for four years in the navy as a petty officer in the 3d and 7th Fleets. He has lived and worked in the Western states for over ten years, gaining firsthand knowledge of the land and furthering his study of the Rocky Mountain Fur Trade, 1807–1843. His frontiering ancestors include a gold rusher, a scout, and a trapper. Most recently he has co-authored a work on the life of William H. Bonney, as yet unpublished. A member of the army reserve with the rank of major, he is a graduate of OCS Fort Benning and is an airborne-qualified infantryman who has served in both mechanized and light infantry units. He currently resides in Colorado.